11/22

The Shopkeeper's Daughter

Other Victor Books by George MacDonald

A Quiet Neighborhood
The Seaboard Parish
The Vicar's Daughter
The Last Castle
The Prodigal Apprentice

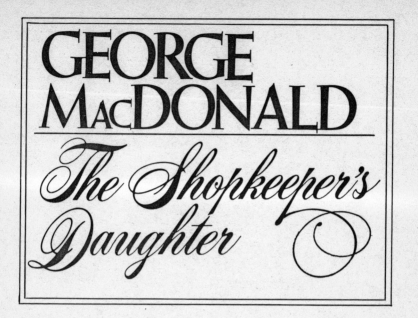

GEORGE MacDONALD
The Shopkeeper's Daughter

edited by ELIZABETH GUIGNARD HAMILTON

VICTOR BOOKS™
A DIVISION OF SCRIPTURE PRESS PUBLICATIONS INC.
USA CANADA ENGLAND

Second printing, 1986

The Shopkeeper's Daughter was first published in 1881 in England, under the title of *Mary Marston.*

Library of Congress Catalog Card Number: 85-62714
ISBN: 0-89693-270-2

VICTOR BOOKS
A division of SP Publications, Inc.
Wheaton, Illinois 60187

Contents

5

Editor's Foreword

The Shopkeeper's Daughter is the fourth George MacDonald novel from Victor Books. The first three, *The Marshmallows Trilogy: A Quiet Neighborhood, The Seaboard Parish,* and *The Vicar's Daughter* were edited by my husband, Dan, and published in March 1985.

Our copy of *Mary Marston,* the original title of *The Shopkeeper's Daughter,* surfaced in an antique china cabinet that had recently been imported from Scotland. It is a very quiet novel, focusing mainly on interpersonal relationships and domestic difficulties.

Although *Mary Marston* is one of MacDonald's least organized novels, and required extensive effort to unravel, the book's many merits began to emerge during my first reading. The more times I read the book, the more I appreciated it.

The heroine Mary's unshakable security comes through strongly, and the source of her security echoes MacDonald's life: her father (in both the earthly and heavenly senses) loved her, and if her father loved her and approved of her actions, what did anyone else's opinion matter? Mary's sense of servanthood is contagious as well; since any good work is worth doing, and doing well, then no good work is beneath anyone's dignity or station in life. MacDonald's view of death is unusually comforting; it is not theoretical or rhetorical, but personal. Prior to writing *Mary Marston,* he lost many family members (three of them his children) to tuberculosis, the disease from which he himself suffered greatly, and which he wryly termed "the family attendant."

Mary Marston was published in 1881, near the peak of MacDonald's popularity. He had already written some twenty-two novels and had completed collections of poetry, translations, and sermons. He had made a successful speaking tour of the United States in 1872-1873. Yet his health was not good and he was spending much of his time in the milder climate of Italy. Compared to his earlier works, *Mary Marston* contains little preaching. MacDonald had been maturing as a writer during the previous twenty-five years of novel-writing, and was now able to develop his lessons more through the *actions* of his characters and less through their *narrations*.

Yet for all his skills and success, even MacDonald enthusiasts will grant that he had limitations as a writer; he was wordy, often awkward, and tended to branch away on unrelated discussions. Such habits were not only acceptable but approved in that era, long before radio and television and the horseless carriage—all inventions that helped broaden one's world, occupy one's time, and shorten one's attention span.

So the point of the editing was to make *Mary Marston* more understandable and pleasurable to a new generation of readers. This involved shortening the book and straightening the story line. The original contained some 200,000 words; this version is closer to 100,000. Whole chapters were transplanted and a handful of sections moved from one chapter to another. The result reads more like a continuous story and less like a series of haphazardly connected episodes.

This edition is not presented as *better* than the original—only shorter and easier to follow. The original manuscript, written in longhand, resides at the Brander Library in Huntly, Scotland, MacDonald's birthplace. Original editions of *Mary Marston* and many other MacDonald books can be seen at the Marion E. Wade Collection, Wheaton College, Wheaton, Illinois.

Because *The Shopkeeper's Daughter* is not my own creation, I do not feel free to make a formal dedication. However, were that freedom mine, it would be for women, young and old, but especially for Carole, my sister in two special ways.

Elizabeth Guignard Hamilton
Indianapolis, Indiana
July 1985

Introduction

George MacDonald (1824-1905), a Scottish preacher, poet, novelist, fantasist, expositor, and public figure, is most known today for his children's books—*At the Back of the North Wind, The Princess and the Goblin, The Princess and Curdie,* and his fantasies *Lilith* and *Phantastes.*

But his fame is based on far more than his fantasies. His lifetime output of more than fifty popular books placed him in the same literary realm as Charles Dickens, Wilkie Collins, William Thackeray, and Thomas Carlyle. He numbered among his friends and acquaintances Lewis Carroll, Mark Twain, Lady Byron, and John Ruskin.

Among his later admirers were G.K. Chesterton, W.H. Auden, and C.S. Lewis. MacDonald's fantasy *Phantastes* was a turning point in Lewis' conversion; Lewis acknowledged MacDonald as his spiritual master, and declared that he had never written a book without quoting from MacDonald.

1.
The Shop

The sun lay low this early May evening. Although spring was busy and summer was at hand, the wind was blowing from the north and the air was chill. The sky was clear except for a few clouds in the west, which were hardly visible in the dazzle of the huge light which lay amongst them like a liquid that had broken its vessel and was pouring over the fragments.

The almost empty street was mottled with the shadows of its uneven paving stones. The street was not a common one, but the main street of an old country town, dwindled by the rise of larger and more prosperous places, but holding and exercising a charm none of them would ever gain. The shadowy fronts of the old houses wore something like a human expression, having the look of both having known and suffered.

Some of the oldest houses, most of them with more than one projecting story, stood about the middle of the street. The central and oldest of these was a draper's shop. The door was wide and very low, the upper half of it glass—old, and bottle-colored, and its threshold was a deep step down into the shop. As a place for purchases it might not to some eyes look promising, but both the ladies and the housekeepers of Testbridge knew that they could rarely do better in London itself than at the shop of Turnbull and Marston.

The moment one's eyes grew accustomed to the gloom inside, the spaciousness of the shop suggested a large home. The low ceiling was used for storage by means of well-contrived slides and

shelves attached to the great beams crossing it in several directions. During the day many articles, light as lace or heavy as
broadcloth, were taken from overhead to lay on the counter. The
shop had a special reputation for all kinds of linen goods, from
cambric handkerchiefs to towels, and from table napkins to sheets.
It had been enlarged at the back, and that portion of it was a little
higher and better lit than at the front. But the whole place still was
dark enough to have awakened the envy of any swindling London
shopkeeper. Its owners, however, had so long enjoyed the confidence of the neighborhood that faith readily took the place of sight
with their customers.

This evening, the shop was on the point of being closed. Behind
the counter stood George Turnbull, a youth of about twenty and
son of the principal partner, leisurely folding and putting aside a
number of things he had shown to a farmer's wife. He was an
ordinary-looking lad, with a high forehead, a self-satisfied expression, and keen hazel eyes that kept wandering from his occupation
to the other side of the shop.

A young woman stood behind the opposite counter showing a
well-dressed youth a pair of driving gloves. His air and carriage
were those of a gentleman who was more than ordinarily desirous
of pleasing the young woman. She answered him politely, and even
with friendliness, but seemed unaware of anything unusual in his
attentions.

"They're splendid," he said, "but don't you think it a great
price for a pair of gloves, Miss Marston?"

"It *is* a good deal of money," she answered, in a quiet voice,
whose very tone suggested simplicity and straightforwardness,
"but they will last a long time. Just look at the work, Mr. Helmer.
See how they are made? It is much more difficult to stitch them
like that, one edge over the other, than to sew the two edges
together as they do with ladies' gloves. But I'll just ask my father
whether he marked them himself."

"He did mark those, I know," said young Turnbull, who had
been listening to all that went on, "for I heard my father say they
ought to be sixpence more."

Mary, being satisfied, laid the gloves on the box before her, from
where Helmer took them, and tried them on.

"They certainly are the best gloves for handling of reins," he
said.

"That is what Mr. Wardour said also," rejoined Miss Marston.

"By the way," Helmer continued, lowering his voice, "when did you last see anybody from Thornwick?"

"Their man was in town yesterday with the cart."

"Nobody with him?"

"Miss Letty. She came in for a few minutes."

"How was she?"

"Very well," answered Miss Marston, with what to Helmer seemed indifference.

"You girls don't see each other with the same eyes as we do," he said with a look of knowingness. "I grant Letty is not very tall, and has not much of a complexion. But did you ever see such eyes?"

"You must excuse me, Mr. Helmer," returned Mary, with a smile, "if I don't choose to discuss Letty's merits with you. She is my friend."

"Where would be the harm? I am not likely to say anything against her. You know perfectly well I admire her beyond any woman in the world. I don't care who knows it."

"Your mother?" ventured Mary.

"Come now, Miss Marston! Don't turn my mother loose on me. I shall be of age in a few months, and then my mother may think as she pleases. I know she would never consent to my marrying Letty—"

"I should think not!" exclaimed Mary. "Who ever thought of such an absurdity? What would your mother say?"

"Let my mother mind her own business!" retorted the youth angrily. "I shall mind mine. She ought to know that by now."

Mary said no more. She knew Mrs. Helmer was not a mother to deserve her son's confidence, for she treated him as if she had made him and was not satisfied with her work.

"When are you going to see Miss Letty?" resumed Helmer, after a brief pause of angry feeling.

"Next Sunday evening, probably."

"Take me with you. I would give my bay mare for a good talk with Letty Lovel," he returned.

Mary's silence spoke for her.

"Why won't you? Where would be the harm?" pleaded the agitated youth.

"One is not bound to do everything in which there is no harm," answered Mary. "Besides, I don't choose to go out walking with you on a Sunday evening."

"Come, come, this is all nonsense. I shall be at the stile just beyond the arched gate all afternoon waiting for you."

"The moment I see you I shall turn back. Do you think," she added with half-amused indignation, "I would put up with having all the gossips of Testbridge talk of my going out on a Sunday evening with a boy like you?"

Tom Helmer's face flushed. He caught up the gloves, threw the price of them down on the counter, and walked from the shop without even a good-night.

George Turnbull vaulted over the counter, and taking the place Helmer had just left opposite Mary asked, "What did you say that for? Mr. Helmer isn't likely to come near us again after a comment like that!"

"He'll be back tomorrow," answered Mary. "He won't be able to bear the thought that he left a bad impression of himself on me. I said nothing that ought to have put him out of temper like that. I only called him a boy, and besides, he did buy the gloves," she added as she dropped the money into the till.

"Mary! You could not have called him a worse name. That is the most offensive word a man could hear from the mouth of a woman," said George loftily.

"A man! Mr. Helmer can't be nineteen yet!"

"How can you say so, when he told you himself that he would be of age in a few months? The fellow is older than I am. Soon you'll be calling *me* a boy."

"What else are you? At least, you are not twenty-one."

"And how old do you say *you* are, *Miss* Marston?"

"Twenty-three."

"A mighty difference, indeed! Now, if it were Mr. Wardour that was spreading his tail for you to see, you would not complain of that peacock."

A vivid rose blossomed instantly in Mary's cheek. Mr. Wardour was not even an acquaintance of hers. He was cousin and friend to Letty Lovel, and she had never spoken to him except in the shop.

"Mr. Wardour is a gentleman," said Mary calmly as she took the glove box and placed it on the shelf behind her.

"So, any man you don't choose to count a gentleman, you look down on. And you call yourself a lady!"

"I do nothing of the kind," interrupted Mary sharply. "I should *like* to be a lady, but I leave it to others to call me this or that. Everything depends on what people are in themselves. Mr. Wardour would be a gentleman even if he were a shopkeeper or a blacksmith."

"And wouldn't I be as good a gentleman as Mr. Wardour if I had inherited a house and a few acres of land?" asked George.

"If it be the house and the land that makes the difference, of course you would," answered Mary in a tone that implied there was a good deal more of a difference between them than that.

"I know you don't think me fit to hold a candle to him," he said, "but I happen to know that although he rides such a good horse, he's not above doing the work of a servant, for he polishes his own stirrup irons."

"I'm very glad to hear it," rejoined Mary. "He must be more of a gentleman than I thought."

"Then why should you count him a better gentleman than me?"

"I'm afraid you would rather go with your stirrup irons rusty than clean them yourself, George. But I will tell you one thing Mr. Wardour would not do if he were a shopkeeper—he would not, like you, talk one way to the rich and another way to the poor. If you go on like that, you'll never come within sight of being a gentleman."

"Thank you, Miss Marston. It's a fine thing to have a *lady* in the shop. I'm blowed if I know how a fellow is to get on with you. It ain't *my* fault if we're not friends." And with that he went back to his own side of the shop, jumped the counter, and with a bang put the cover on a box he had left open.

Mary made no reply. She could not help but understand what George meant, for the great desire of George's father was a match between George and her, for that would secure the Marston money to the business. Mary flushed with honest anger from brow to chin, but her anger had no hate in it.

Everything about Mary suggested the repose of satisfied order, even to the extent of a slight tinge of primness. Her plain black silk dress, with its linen collar and cuffs, rose calm and motionless above the counter where she stood, in spite of her displeasure. Her dark hair was dressed simply, and its natural wave fell across a forehead of sweet and composing proportions. Mary's features were regular, her nose straight and perhaps a little too thin; but the curve of her upper lip was carefully drawn above her well-shaped chin. Her speech and manners were direct and simple, corresponding with her person and dress. Neatness was notable in her rather than grace, but grace was not absent. Good breeding was more evident than delicacy, but delicacy was there, and unity was plain throughout.

George shoved his closed box into its place, shouting as he did so to an invisible shopboy to make haste and put up the shutters. Mary left the shop by a door on the inside of the counter, for she and her father lived in the same building with Beenie the house-keeper. As soon as the shop was closed, George went home to the house his father had built at the edge of town.

2.
Customers

The next day was Saturday, a busy one at the shop. The entire staff of the establishment was called out to wait on the customers who came from the neighboring villages and farms.

Busiest in serving was the senior partner, Mr. Turnbull. He was stout and bald, and his heavy watch chain of the best gold stretched across the wide space between waistcoat buttonhole and pocket. Close-shaved and double-chinned, he had cultivated an ordinary smile to such an extraordinary degree that it reached from ear to ear. By nature he was good-tempered and friendly, but having devoted every physical and mental endowment to the making of money, he had lost much of his natural congeniality. In his own eyes he was a strong churchman, but the only sign of this visible to others was the strength of his contempt for dissenters. Still, he took their money, for he had often remarked that, once in the till, it was as good as the best churchman's.

He was a sight not soon to be forgotten. As John Turnbull drove along in his gig to town and approached his shop, he showed to the chance observer a man who knew himself of importance. As he drew up, threw the reins to the stableboy, and stepped down and into the shop, he looked to be a man in whom son or daughter or friend might feel some honest pride. But the moment he was behind the counter and in front of a customer, he changed to a creature whose appearance was plainly contemptible. He lost the upright bearing of a man and cringed like an ape.

17

As he bent over a piece of goods spread before a customer, one hand resting on the stuff, the other on the yardstick, his chest touched the counter as nearly as the adjacent parts would permit, and his broad smooth face turned up at right angles, his mouth now hiding, now disclosing a gulf of white teeth. No sooner was anything admitted into stock than he bent his soul to the selling of it—doing everything he could, saying everything he could think of short of plain lying as to its quality. To buy well was a care to him, to sell well was a greater; but to make money, and that as speedily as possible, was his greatest care and whole ambition.

It was thus he had gained a portion of his favor with the country folk, many of whom much preferred his ministrations to those of his partner, William Marston. A glance from the one side to the other was enough to reveal which must be the better salesman, and to some eyes, the better man.

Marston and Turnbull had been in business together almost from boyhood, and Marston's greatness had yet a certain repressive power upon those who despised him, so that they never uttered their worst thoughts or revealed their worst baseness in his presence. Marston flattered himself that poor John was gradually improving, coming to see things more and more as he should.

Marston himself stood up tall and straight, lank and lean. His forehead was high and narrow, his face pale and lean, his hair long and thin, his nose aquiline, his eyes large, and his mouth and chin small. He seldom spoke a syllable more than was needful, but his words breathed calm respect to every customer. His conversation was all but over as he laid something for approval or rejection on the counter. He had already taken every pain to learn the precise nature of the necessity or desire, and what he then offered he submitted without comment. If it was not satisfactory, he removed it and brought another. Many did not like this mode of service— they wanted to be helped to buy and welcomed any aid toward it. Therefore they preferred Mr. Turnbull, who gave them every imaginable and unimaginable assistance, groveling before them, while Mr. Marston, the moment the thing he presented was on the counter, stood up straight like a poplar in a sudden calm.

Turnbull and his like-minded son despised Marston. His unbusinesslike habits, as they counted them, were the constantly recurring themes of their scorn. But Mary saw nothing which did not stamp her father the superior of all other men she knew.

For example, he often sold things under the price marked by his partner. Turnbull would be furious, and would usually display his indignation by quoting Scripture like a canting dissenter, reminding his partner of what would become of a house divided against itself. (He did not see that the best thing for some houses must be to fall to pieces.)

"But, Mr. Turnbull, I thought it was marked too high," was the other's invariable answer.

"William, you are a fool," his partner would rejoin for the hundredth time. "Will you never understand that, if we get a little more than the customary profit upon one thing, we get less on another? You must make the thing even, or go to the workhouse."

And, for the hundredth time also, William Marston would reply, "That *might* hold, Mr. Turnbull, if every customer always bought an article of each of the two sorts together. But I can't in good conscience allow one customer to pay too much because I let another pay too little. Besides, I think the general scale of profit is set too high. I fear you and I will have to part, Mr. Turnbull."

But nothing was farther from Turnbull's desire than to part with Marston. He could not keep the business going without the other's money, not to mention that he never doubted Marston would open another shop, and, even if he did not undersell him, take from him all his dissenting customers. Marston was deacon of a small Baptist church in Testbridge, a fact which, although like vinegar to the teeth and smoke to the eyes of John Turnbull in his own house, was invaluable in the eyes of John Turnbull behind the counter.

Well into the morning of this particular Saturday, an open carriage with a pair of showy but ill-matched horses drew up at the door, and a visible wave of interest ran from end to end in the shop. The carriage was well known in Testbridge—it belonged to Lady Margaret Mortimer. She did not like the *Margaret* and signed only her second name, *Alice,* from which her friends derived the name Lady Malice. She did not leave the carriage, but the two ladies who were with her got down. One of them was her daughter, Hesper, who entered the shop like a gleam of sunshine, dusky-golden, and was followed by a glowing shadow, her cousin, Miss Yolland.

Turnbull hurried to meet them, but they turned aside to where Mary stood, and in a few minutes the counter was covered with merchandise.

19

From the moment Mary first looked Miss Hesper Mortimer in the face, she could hardly take her eyes off her. Large and grandly made, Hesper stood tall in her dusky-golden stateliness. Her rich brown hair rolled back from her creamy forehead in a rebellious coronet. Her eyes were large and hazel, her mouth decidedly large but so exquisite that the loss of a centimeter of its length would to a lover have been as the loss of a kingdom. For a woman, her throat was massive, her arms and hands powerful, her expression frank and almost brave, her eyes looking full at the person she addressed. As Mary gazed, a kind of admiration she had never felt before kept swelling in her throat.

But Miss Mortimer's companion impressed her very differently. Miss Yolland was not slight for her stature, but she looked small beside Hesper. Her skin was very dark, with a considerable touch of sallowness. Her large, beautifully shaped eyes were as black as eyes could be, with a touch of hardness in their core. Her eyelashes were long and black, and she seemed conscious of them whenever they rose and fell. Her true name was Septima, but Lady Margaret called her Sepia.

At first glance she seemed as unlike Hesper as possible, but Mary gradually became aware of a certain likeness between them. Sepia, a few years older and in less flourishing condition, had sharper and finer features and her complexion was darker. If one was the evening, the other was the night. Sepia was a diminished and overshadowed Hesper. Their manner too was similar, but Sepia was haughty and occasionally looked even defiant.

Sepia was the daughter of a clergyman, an uncle of Lady Margaret, whose sons had gone to the bad, and whose daughters had vanished from society. But Sepia, the youngest, had reappeared. Nobody knew with any certainty where she had been in the interim; she said she had been a governess in Russia and Austrian Poland. Lady Margaret had become reconciled to her presence, and Hesper grew attached to her.

The ladies were pleased with Mary. The simplicity of her address and manner, the pains she took to find the exact things they wanted, and the modest decision with which she answered any question made Hesper like her. When their purchases were ended, Hesper took her leave with a kind smile, which went on glowing in Mary's heart long after she had vanished.

"Home, John," said Lady Margaret, the moment the two ladies

were seated in the carriage. "I hope you have all you wanted. I fear we shall be late for luncheon. I would not for the world keep Mr. Redmain waiting. A little faster, John, please!"

Hesper's face darkened. Mr. Redmain was a bachelor of fifty, to whom Lady Margaret was endeavoring to make the family agreeable, in the hope that he might take Hesper off their hands. He was a common rich man, with cold manners which he offered like a handle. He was selfish, capable of picking up a lady's handkerchief, but hardly a wife's. He was attentive to Hesper who scarcely concealed her repugnance of him. She was afraid of him, and saw no way of escaping the fate intended for her.

"Isn't Miss Mortimer a stunner?" said George Turnbull to Mary, when the tide of customers had finally ebbed from the shop.

"I don't exactly know what you mean, George," answered Mary.

"Oh, of course, I know it isn't fair to ask any girl to admire another," said George, as he tidied his counter. "But there's no offense to you, Mary. One young lady can't carry *every* merit on her back. She'd be too lovely to live, you know. Miss Mortimer hasn't got your waist, nor your hands or hair, and you don't have her size, nor the sort of air she has about her."

He looked up from the merchandise he was folding and saw that he was alone in the shop.

3.
Thornwick
Arbor

A t last it was Sunday. It was Mary's custom to go to the Baptist chapel, and her chief pleasure in it was the company of her father. Old Mr. Duppa, the pastor, was duller than usual—he spent a mortal hour explaining the reasons all true Baptists were separated from their fellow believers. When she got out at last, sedate as she was, she could hardly help skipping along the street by her father's side. Better than chapel was their little dinner together, and greater yet was the pleasure Mary had in making her father lie down on the sofa, and playing to him on her piano or reading him to sleep. Later they had their tea, and then her father went to the evening service at the chapel.

When he was gone, Mary put on her straw bonnet and set out to visit Letty Lovel at Thornwick. Some of the church members thought this habit of taking a walk instead of going to the service was very worldly, and did not hesitate to let her know their opinion. But as long as her father was satisfied with her, Mary did not care what they thought. She was too much occupied with obedience to trouble her head about opinion, either her own or other people's.

Although it had drizzled all morning, the early evening sun was peeping out from behind the last raincloud. Mary walked quickly from the town, eager for the fields and trees, but in some dread of finding Tom Helmer at the stile. However, he had thought better of it, and soon she was crossing meadows and cornfields on the path that was the most direct route to Thornwick. Sweet odors rose about her from the wet ground. Raindrops glittered on the grass and hedgerows. A soft damp wind breathed rather than blew about the gaps and gates. The larks kept gliding aloft while the sun kept shining in the might of its peace, and Mary's heart praised her Father in heaven.

Where the narrow path ran westward for a little way, the sun was in her eyes, and in the middle of a ploughed field she would have run right into a gentleman, had he been as blinded by the sun as she. But his back was to the sun and, seeing her perfectly, he stepped out of her way into the gutter where rainwater had been collecting all day. She saw him then, and as he lifted his hat, she recognized Mr. Wardour.

"Oh, your nice boots!" she cried, in the childlike distress of discovering herself the cause for a catastrophe, for his boots were now smeared all over with yellow clay.

"It serves me right," returned Mr. Wardour, with a laugh of amusement."I shouldn't have put on such thin ones at the first smile of summer," and again he lifted his hat and walked on.

Mary turned and continued along her path, genuinely pained that he should have stepped up to his ankles in mud on her account. Except in the shop, she had never before spoken to Mr. Wardour, and although he had so simply responded to her exclamation, he did not even know who she was.

The friendship which drew Mary to Thornwick, Godfrey Wardour's home, was not an old one. For although she and Letty Lovel had known each other for years, only recently had their acquaintance ripened into friendship. Mrs. Wardour, Godfrey's mother, protested that the society of a shopgirl was far from suitable for one who, as the daughter of a professional man, might lay claim to the position of a gentlewoman; for Letty was the orphan daughter of a country surgeon, a cousin of Mrs. Wardour.

The well-meaning woman was possessed by two devils—pride and condescending benevolence. She was kind, but she must get credit for it; although Letty was the child of a loved cousin, she must not presume upon her aunt's benevolence. Mrs. Wardour counted herself a devout Christian, but her ideas of rank were absolutely opposed to the Master's teaching.

Letty was a simple, truehearted girl, who honestly tried to understand her aunt's position with regard to her friend."Shopgirls," her aunt had said,"are not fitting company for you, Letty."

"I do not know any other shopgirls, Aunt," Letty replied with hidden trembling,"but if they are not nice, then they are not like Mary. She is downright good."

"That may well be," answered Mrs. Wardour, "but it does not make a lady of her."

"I am sure," returned Letty in bewilderment,"on Sundays you could not tell the difference between her and any other young lady."

"Any other well-dressed young *woman*, my dear, you should say. I believe shopgirls do call their companions young ladies, but that cannot justify the application of the word. I am scarcely bound to speak of my cook as a lady because letters to her come addressed as Miss Tozer."

But although such was Mrs. Wardour's reasoning beforehand, her heart had so far overcome habit and prejudice that, convinced on the first visit of the high tone and good influence of Mary, she had gradually come to put herself in the way of seeing her as often as she came. On these occasions she played the grand lady, with a stateliness that seemed to say,"Because of your individual worth, I condescend and make an exception; but you must not imagine I receive your class at Thornwick."

After passing Mary, Mr. Wardour did not go very far before slackening his pace. Then he wheeled around and began to walk back toward Thornwick. Two things had produced this change of purpose—first, the state of his boots which, drying in the sun and wind as he walked, grew more and more hideous, and second, the suspicion that the girl must be Letty's shopkeeping friend, Miss Marston, on her way to visit. He decided it would be more pleasant to spend the evening with Letty and her young friend, than to spend it with his friends smoking and lounging about the stable or hearing someone's sister play polkas and mazurkas.

Upon her arrival at Thornwick, Mary narrated her small adventure, and the conversation turned to Godfrey just as he was, unknown to them, nearing the house.

"How handsome your cousin is!" said Mary, with her natural simplicity."He looks so manly, and has such a straightforward way with him."

"I have never thought about it," answered Letty.

Mary continued,"There is something in him that one could trust."

"There is something about him," returned Letty, "that makes me afraid of him. He is always giving me something to read. I wish he wouldn't—it frightens me dreadfully, and he questions me to know whether I understand what I read."

Letty ended with a little cry. Through the one narrow gap in the yew hedge near the arbor where they sat, Godfrey entered the walk and came toward them.

He was a well-made man, thirty years of age, rather tall, suntanned, and bearded, with wavy brown hair and a gentle approach. His face indicated faculty and feeling, and there was much good nature shadowed with memorial suffering in the eyes which shone so blue out of the brown.

"What treason were you talking, Letty, that you were so startled when you saw me?" he asked with a smile. "You were complaining of me as a hard master, were you not?"

"No, indeed, Cousin Godfrey!" answered Letty energetically, coloring as she spoke. "I was only saying I could not help being frightened when you asked me questions about what I had been reading. I am so stupid, you know!"

"Pardon me, Letty," returned her cousin, "I know nothing of the sort; you are very far from stupid. Nobody can understand everything at first sight. But you have not introduced me to your friend."

Letty bashfully murmured the names of the two.

"I guessed as much after seeing you on the path," said Wardour. "For the sake of your dresses, I will go and change my boots. May I come and join you later?"

"Please do, Cousin Godfrey, and bring something to read to us," said Letty, who wanted her friend to admire her cousin.

"Why you should be afraid of him, I can't imagine," said Mary when his retreating footsteps had ceased to sound on the gravel. "He is delightful—and how good of him to agree to read to us! What will it be?"

"Most likely something out of a book you never heard of before, and can't remember the name of when you have heard it; at least, that's the way with me. I wonder if he will talk to you, Mary. I should like to hear how Cousin Godfrey talks to girls."

"Why, you know how he talks to you," said Mary.

"Oh, but I am only Cousin Letty. He can talk however he pleases with me."

25

"But you were just telling me how he talks to you in the best possible way."

"Yes, but I can't help wishing sometimes he would talk a little nonsense. It would be such a relief. I am sure I should understand better if he would. I shouldn't be so frightened of him then."

"The way I generally hear gentlemen talk to girls makes me ashamed—makes me want to ask, 'Is it that you are a fool, or that you take that girl for one?' They never talk so to me."

Letty sat pulling a jonquil to pieces. She looked up. Her eyes were full of thought, but she paused a long time before she spoke, and when she did, it was only to say, "Mary, I fear I should take any man for a fool who took me for anything else."

Letty was small, with the daintiest of rounded figures, a good forehead, and fine clear brown eyes. Her mouth was not spectacular except when she smiled, but she did not smile often. When she did, it was usually with tears in her eyes, and then she looked lovely. Her charm sprang from a constitutional humility that had deteriorated into a painful and haunting sense of inferiority for which she imagined herself to blame. Hence there dwelt in her eyes an appeal which few hearts could resist. When they met another's, they seemed to say, "I am nobody. I will try to do what you want me to do, but I am not clever. I am sorry. Please be gentle with me." At least, that is what Godfrey saw in her eyes.

In ten minutes or so he reappeared at the other end of the yew walk, approaching slowly with a book in which he thoughtfully searched as he came. He sat down with the girls and said, "I am going to try your brains now, Letty," tapping the book with his finger.

"Oh, please don't!" pleaded Letty, as if he had been threatening her with the loss of a front tooth.

"Yes," he persisted, "and not your brains only, Letty, but your heart and all that is in you."

At this Mary could not help feeling a little frightened, and she was glad there was no occasion for her to speak.

With just a word of introduction, Godfrey read a passage which set forth the condition of a godless universe all at once awakened to the full knowledge of the causelessness of its own existence. Slowly, with due inflection and emphasis, he read to the end, ceased suddenly, and lifted his eyes.

"There, Letty," he said, "what do you think of that?"

Letty was looking altogether perplexed, and not a little frightened when she answered, "I don't understand a word of it."

He glanced at Mary. She was as white as death, her lips quivered, and from her eyes shot a keen light that seemed to lacerate their blue.

"It is terrible!" she said. "I never read anything like that. The author is a Unitarian, is he not?" for Mary had heard plenty of theology, if not much Christianity, in her chapel.

Godfrey looked at her, then at the book for a moment, read the passage again, and quietly laid it down when he finished. All the time a great bee kept buzzing in and out of the arbor, and Mary vaguely wondered how it could be so careless.

"I understand," said Mary.

"Do you really, Mary?" said Letty, looking at her in wondering admiration.

"I only meant," answered Mary, "—but—" she went on, interrupting herself, "I think I understand it a little. If Mr. Wardour would be kind enough to read it through again. . . ."

"With much pleasure," answered Godfrey, casting on her a glance of pleased surprise as he picked up the little volume and found the passage.

The third reading affected Mary more than the first or second, because she took in more. And this time a glimmer of meaning broke on the slower mind of Letty, and she gave a little cry of understanding.

"I can't be dead stupid after all, Cousin Godfrey," said Letty, with a broken voice, when once more he ceased, "for something kept going through and through me. But I cannot yet say I understand it. If you will lend me the book," she continued, "I will read it over again before I go to bed."

He shut the volume, handed it to her, and began to talk about something else. Mary soon rose to go.

"You will take tea with us, I hope, Miss Marston," said Godfrey.

But Mary would not. What she had heard was working in her mind with a powerful fermentation, and she longed to be alone. As she walked in the fields, she would come to an understanding with herself.

She knew almost nothing of higher literature and felt like a dreamer who, in the midst of an ordinary landscape, comes without warning upon the mighty cone of a mountain, or the breaking waters of a boundless ocean.

"If one could but get hold of such things, what a glorious life it would be!" she thought. She had looked into a world beyond the present, and already in the present all things were new.

What a place her chamber would be, if she could read such things there! How easy it would be to bear the troubles of the hour, the vulgar humor of Mr. Turnbull, and the tiresome attentions of George. Would Mr. Wardour lend her the book? Had he others like it? Were there many such books to make one's heart go as that one did? She would save every penny to buy such books, if indeed such treasures were within her reach! Under the enchantment of her first literary joy, she walked home like one intoxicated with opium—a being possessed for the time with the awesome imagination of a grander soul, and revelling in the presence of her loftier kin.

4.
Godfrey Wardour

The property of which Thornwick once formed a part had dwindled and shriveled through generations of unthrift, until at last it threatened to disappear from the family altogether. But Godfrey's father put a stop to its disintegration. He not only held the remnant together, but improved it so greatly that it once again became self-sufficient and prosperous. Doubtless, could he have used his wife's money, he would have spent it on land, but it was under trustees for herself and her children.

Considerably advanced in years before he thought of marrying, he died while Godfrey was yet a child, and his widow planned to educate the boy in law. But Godfrey had positively declined entering on the studies for a career he detested, so he took his place in the country, managing the land his father had left behind.

Godfrey was a reader; his nature was too large to allow the land and its management to occupy all of his mind. He read with a constant reference to his own views of life, and to the confirmation, change, or enlargement of his theories. But he didn't read with the highest aim of all—the enlargement of reverence, obedience, and faith. Yet by simple instincts, he was always drawn to lofty and good things, and life went calmly on, bearing Godfrey Wardour to middle age, unruffled by anxiety or ambition.

As years passed, and Godfrey revealed no tendency toward marriage, his mother's anxiety regarding the hour when she must yield the first place, both in her son's regards and in the house affairs, changed sides. She then began to fear that there would not be another heir, and that the ancient family might come to an end. As yet she had not ventured to speak to him on the subject. She had not thought of Letty as either thwarting or furthering her desires, for she felt that Letty was considerably below her Godfrey. In the last year of his college life, Godfrey had formed an attachment with a young lady. The bonds were rudely broken, and of the story nothing remained but disappointment and pain, distrust and doubt.

It would have been well if he had been left with only a wounded heart, but in that heart lay wounded pride, and he hid it carefully. Under that bronzed countenance, with its firm-set mouth and powerful jaw, below those clear blue eyes, and upright, easy carriage, lay a faithful heart haunted by a sense of wrong. But there was no hate in him. His weakness he kept concealed.

Godfrey's strong poetic nature loathed the ways of worldly women. However correct he might be in his judgment of the worldly, that judgment was less inspired by the harmonies of the universe than by the discords which jarred his being, and the poisonous shocks he had received in the encounter of the noble with the ignoble. There was still a profound need in him for redemption into the love of the truth for truth's sake.

Being an Englishman with land of his own, he could not help being fond of horses. Although he kept two for his own use, he did not feel their needs should warrant his keeping a groom. So it came about that strap and steel, as well as hide and hoof, would be partially neglected. There was no solution for it other than to do the work himself.

One night, meaning to start for a long ride early in the morning, he had gone to the stable to see how things were. It happened that Letty, attending to some duty before going to bed, had caught sight of him cleaning his stirrups, and from that moment she took upon herself the silent supervision of the harness room. When she found any part of the riding equipment neglected, she would draw on a pair of housemaid's gloves and polish away like a horseboy.

Godfrey had begun to wonder at the improvement and, going hastily one morning into the harness room, came upon Letty, who had imagined he was in the fields with the men. She was energetically polishing a stirrup. He started back in amazement, but she only looked up and smiled.

"I shall be done in a moment, Cousin Godfrey," she said, and polished away harder than before.

"But, Letty! I can't allow you to do things like that. What on earth put it in your head? Work like that is only for callused hands."

"Your hands aren't callused, Cousin Godfrey. They may be a little harder than mine, but they're no fitter by nature to clean stirrups. Is it for me to sit with mine in my lap, and yours at this? I know better."

"Why shouldn't I clean my own harness, Letty, if I like?" said Godfrey, who could not help feeling pleased as well as annoyed. In this one moment Letty had come miles nearer him.

"Hands that write poetry are not fit for work like this," Letty answered.

"How do you know I write poetry?" asked Godfrey, displeased, for here she touched a sensitive spot.

"Oh, don't be angry!" she said, letting the stirrup fall on the floor, and clasping her gloves together. "I couldn't help seeing it was poetry, for it lay on the table when I went to do your room."

"Do my room, Letty! Does my mother—"

"She doesn't want to make a fine lady of me, and I shouldn't like it if she did. I have no head, but I have pretty good hands. Of course, I didn't read a word of the poetry. I daren't do that, however much I might have wished."

A childlike simplicity looked out of the clear eyes, and sounded in the swift words of the girl, and had Godfrey's heart been as hard as the stirrup she had dropped, it could not but have been touched by her devotion. Letty picked up the stirrup, and was again hard at work with it. To take it from her and turn her out of the saddle room would scarcely be the way to thank her. Although Letty made beds and chose to clean his harness, Godfrey was enough of a gentleman not to think her less a lady.

He laid his hand on her bent head, and said, "I ought to be a knight of the old times, Letty, to have a lady serve me so," and left her at her work.

He had taken no real notice of the girl before, and felt little interest in her. Neither did he feel much now, but was there anything he could do for her—anything in her he could help?

"There must be *something* in the girl," he said to himself, and then reflected that he had never seen a book in her hand, except her prayer book. How was he to do anything for a girl like that?

Godfrey knew no way of doing people good without the intervention of books. Letty's comments about the hands that wrote poetry showed at least a respect for poetry, and Godfrey determined to find out whether she had any instincts toward that form of literature.

His projected ride was forgotten. Going up to his study, he began looking along the backs of his books. His glance fell on a beautifully bound volume of verse—a selection of English lyrics—and, taking it down, he set out to find Letty. She had finished in the saddle room, and he found her in the dairy, where he came softly to the door and peeped in. There stood Letty, warm and bright in the middle of the dusky coolness. She had changed her dress and now, in a pink rosebud print, with the sleeves tucked above her elbows, was skimming the cream in a great red-brown earthen pan. He pushed the door a little, and at its screech along the earthen floor, Letty's head turned quickly, and she saw Godfrey's brown face and kind blue eyes as she had never seen them before. In his hand glowed the book—some of the stronger light from behind him fell on it—and caught her eyes.

"Letty," he said, "I have just come upon this book in my library. Would you care to have it?"

"You don't mean to keep for my own, Cousin Godfrey?" cried Letty, in sweet, childish fashion. She let the skimmer dive to the bottom of the milkpot and hastily wiped her hands on her apron. Her face had flushed rosy with pleasure, and grew brighter still as she took the rich morocco-bound volume from Godfrey's hand.

She peeped into its leaves and cried out, "Poetry! Is it really for me, Cousin Godfrey? Do you think I shall be able to understand it?"

"You can soon settle that question for yourself," answered Godfrey with a pleased smile, and turned to leave.

"But, Cousin Godfrey—please!" she called after him. "You don't give me time to thank you."

"That you may do when you are certain you care for it," he returned.

"I care for it very much," she replied.

"How can you say that when you don't know whether you will understand it or not?" he rejoined, and closed the door.

Letty stood motionless, the book in her hand illuminating the dusk with its gold, and warming its coolness with its crimson leather and silken linings. One poem after another she read, nor knew how the time passed, until the voice of her aunt warned her to finish her skimming and carry the jug to the pantry. But already Letty had skimmed a little cream off the book also, and had taken a fresh start in spiritual growth.

The next day, Godfrey found opportunity to ask Lettie whether she had seen anything she liked in the book. To his disappointment she mentioned one of the few commonplace things the collection contained. However, that evening, he heard Letty singing over her work, and listening, discovered that she was singing verse after verse of one of the best ballads in the whole book. Godfrey then set himself in earnest to the task of developing her intellectual life, and grew more and more interested in the endeavor.

He soon discovered the main obstacle to success to be Letty's exceeding distrust of herself. With good faculties and fine instincts, Letty was always thinking she must be wrong. She got on, in spite of it, and her devotion to Godfrey grew. He was at least ten years older than Letty, and her only male relative in this world. So Cousin Godfrey grew and grew in Letty's imagination, until he was everything great and good. To her he was the heart of wisdom, the head of knowledge, and the arm of strength; but her worship was quiet.

By degrees Godfrey came to understand with what a self-refusing and impressionable nature he was dealing, and became more generous toward her, and more gentle in his ministrations. If he had seen in his new relation to Letty a possibility of the revival of feelings he had supposed forever extinguished, the mere idea of again falling in love would have sickened him with dismay. But the thought of her was making a nest for itself in his soul, and living like an elder brother with a much younger sister satisfied him. Mrs. Wardour neither saw, nor heard, nor suspected anything to rouse uneasiness.

The Sunday evening visits of Mary Marston continued to be a pleasure to all, and Letty reaped great benefits from the conversation and gentle communion of their hearts. Books were more of a pleasure to Letty now, while the mainstay of Mary's spiritual life was her father, in whom she believed absolutely. From books and sermons she had gotten little good. And now Godfrey presented to her men greater than himself, whom in a short time she would understand even better than he. Book after book he lent her, introducing her with no special intentions to much in the way of religion that was good in the way of literature as well. Only, where he delighted in the literature, she delighted in the religion.

5.
Tom Helmer

Letty knew little of Tom Helmer or of his admiration for her. When Tom's father died, his mother, who had never been able to manage him, sent him to school to get rid of him. She would lament his absence until he returned, and then fret until he was gone again. Never did those two meet without at once tumbling into an obstinate difference. While Tom was home, their sparring went on from morning to night, and sometimes almost from night to morning. At school he was a great favorite, and mostly had his own way, both with the boys and the masters. Although a fool, he was a pleasant fool—clever, fond of popularity, and complaisant with everybody except his mother. The merest word from her would at once rouse all the rebel in his blood.

Tom was handsome and vivacious, expressing far more than was in him to express. He was by no means ill-intentioned, but he never found it imperative to reach out after his own ideal of duty. He had never been worthy of the name of student, or cared much for anything beyond the amusements universities provide so liberally, except for dabbling in literature. Gifted not only with fluency of speech—that crowning glory and ruin of a fool—but with plausibility of tone and demeanor, and a confidence that imposed both on himself and others, nobody could help liking him, and it took some time to make one realize the disappointment he caused.

He was now twenty-one, at home, pretending that nothing should make him go back to Oxford, and enjoying more than ever the sport of plaguing his mother. He was altogether the true son of

35

his mother, who consoled herself for her absolute failure in his moral education with the reflection that she had reared him sound in wind and limb. Plaguing his mother, amusing himself as best as he could, riding about the country on a good mare, he was living in utter idleness, affording occasion for wonder that he had never yet disgraced himself. He talked to everybody who would talk to him, and made acquaintance with anybody on the spur of a moment's whim. He would sit on a log with a gypsy, concocting lies for his ears, then thrash him for not believing them.

He went to every party and ball to which he could get admittance in the neighborhood, and flirted with any girl who would let him. He meant no harm, and was imagined by most incapable of doing any. The strange thing to some was that he stayed in the country, and did not go to London and run up bills for his mother to pay. But what accounted for that was that upon his late return from school he had seen Letty and fallen in love with her at first sight. He had not been able to meet her alone, for Thornwick was one of the few houses of the middle class in the neighborhood where he was not encouraged to show himself; but he was constantly watching for a chance to see her, and every Sunday went to church in that same hope.

Letty knew nothing of the favor in which she stood with him. Although Tom had confessed to Mary his admiration for Letty, Mary had far too much good sense to make herself his ally in the matter.

6.
Durnmelling

In the autumn, Mr. Mortimer of Durnmelling resolved to give a harvest home to his tenants, and thought it a good opportunity to also invite a good many of his neighbors and some of the townsfolk of Testbridge, whom he could not well ask to dinner for reasons of political expediency. (For ambition opens the door to mean doings on the part of such as count themselves as gentlemen.) Not a few were invited, and not many declined. Mrs. Wardour accepted for herself and Letty; in their case, Lady Margaret had called and in person to give the invitation. Godfrey positively refused to accompany them. He would not be patronized, he said. And by an inferior, he added to himself.

Mr. Mortimer was the illiterate son of a literary father who had reaped both money and fame. The son spent the former, married an earl's daughter on the strength of the latter, and began to embody in his own behavior his ideas of how a nobleman ought to carry himself. He had never manifested any neighborliness with Godfrey Wardour; although their two houses were within a stone's throw of each other, the men scarcely nodded when they met. The Mortimer ladies had more than once remarked how well Mr. Wardour rode, and how easily he handled his horse, but not until now had so much as a greeting passed between them. It was therefore not surprising that Godfrey should not choose to accept their invitation. Finding that his mother was distressed at having to go to the gathering without him, and being far more exercised in her mind than was necessary as to what would be thought of his absence, he resolved to go to London a day or two before the event, and pay a long-promised visit to a friend.

The relative situation of the actual houses of Durnmelling and Thornwick was curious. At one time they had formed part of the same property. Durnmelling was built by an ancestor of Godfrey's who, forsaking the old nest for the new, had allowed Thornwick to sink into a mere farmhouse. In the hands of Godfrey's father, it had been restored to something like its original modest dignity. Durnmelling too had in part sunk into ruin, and had been but partially recovered from it. Still, it swelled in importance beside Thornwick. Nothing but a deep gully with a stone wall at its bottom separated the two houses, of which the older and smaller occupied the higher ground. On the Durnmelling side were trees, shrubbery, and outhouses, the chimneys of which gave great offense to Mrs. Wardour. But although the houses stood so near, there was no lawful means of communication between them except the road, and it was seldom passed by any of the unneighborly neighbors.

Although Durnmelling was new compared to Thornwick, a large portion of the original structure had for many years been nothing better than a ruin. Only a portion of one side of its huge square was occupied by the family. Lady Margaret, while she valued the old, neglected it. What money she and her husband spent on the house was devoted to addition and ornamentation, rather than to preservation or restoration. They had enlarged both the dining room and drawing room to twice their original size, when half the expense would have given them a room fit for a regal assembly. A portion of the same front in which they lived lay roofless, open to every wind that blew. It was an ancient hall, whose south wall was pierced by three lovely windows, narrow and lofty, with simple gracious tracery in their pointed heads. This hall connected the habitable portion of the house with another part, less ruinous than itself, but containing only a few rooms occasionally used for household purposes.

It was a glorious ruin, nearly a hundred feet in length, and about half that in width. The walls were broad enough to walk around on safely, and their top was accessible from a tower which formed part of the less ruinous portion, and contained the stair and some small rooms.

Once the hall had been fair with portraits and armor and arms, with fire and lights, and state and merriment. Now the sculptured chimney lay open to the weather, and the sweeping winds had made its smooth hearthstone clean as if fire had never been there. Its floor was covered with large flagstones, some a little broken; but now, in prospect of the coming entertainment, a few workmen were leveling, patching, and replacing them.

It was Miss Yolland's idea to use the hall, and to her was committed the responsibility of its preparation and adornment for the occasion, in which Hesper gave her active assistance. With colored blankets, carpets, a few pieces of old tapestry, and a quantity of old curtains, all cunningly arranged for as much harmony as could be had, they contrived to clothe the walls to the height of six or eight feet, and to give the weather-beaten skeleton an air of hospitable preparation and respectful reception.

The day and hour arrived—a hot autumnal afternoon. Borne in all sorts of vehicles, from a carriage-and-pair to a taxed cart, the guests kept coming and scattering themselves about the place. Some loitered on the lawn by the flowerbeds and fountains, some visited the stables and cow-houses, dairy and piggeries, and others the neglected greenhouses. No one belonging to the house was anywhere visible to receive them. At length the great bell summoned them to a plentiful meal spread in the ruined hall.

Then at last their host made his appearance and took the head of the table. The ladies of the house, he said, were to have the honor of joining the company afterward. They were at the time (but this he did not say) serving their tenants a less ponderous refreshment in the dining room.

By the time the eating and drinking were nearly over, the shades of evening had gathered. The merry guests were ready for dancing, and presently the company from the house joined them, and the great hall was crowded.

Much to her chagrin, Mrs. Wardour had a severe headache, and was compelled to remain at home. But she allowed Letty to go without her, for she was very anxious to have news of what she could not even lift her head to see. She sent Letty with an old servant to gather and report. The dancing had begun before they reached the hall.

Tom Helmer, among the first to arrive, had joined the tenants in their feast, and was making friends with everybody in his vicinity. When the tables were removed after the meal, and the rest of the company and the musicians began to come in, he went about searching anxiously for Letty's sweet face.

His heart had been sinking, for he could see Letty nowhere. Now had come his chance, and his chance seemed to mock him. Letty had affected him more than any girl he had ever seen, perhaps because she was so unlike his mother. Although he knew nothing of her nature, it was of little consequence to him, for he had never troubled himself to know anything of his own nature. But then, there she was! She had stolen in without his seeing her, and stood mingled with the crowd about the door. She was dressed in white muslin. Her head was bent forward, and a gentle smile was over all her face, as with loveliest eyes she watched eagerly the motions of the dance, and her ears drank in the music.

The hall was a pleasant sight to her eyes. The wide space was gaily illuminated with colored lamps in every crevice of the walls, some of them gleaming like glowworms out of mere holes. Overhead the night sky was spangled with bright pulsing stars. Outside it was dark, save where the light streamed from the great windows far into the night. The moon was not yet up, but would rise in good time to see the guests to their homes.

Tom's foolish heart gave a great bound as if it would leap to where Letty stood. He seized the first opportunity of getting nearer her. He had scarcely spoken to her before, but that did not trouble him. Mr. Mortimer had opened the dancing by leading out the wife of his principal tenant, a handsome matron whose behavior and expression were such as to give a safe, homelike feeling to the shy and doubtful of the company. But Tom knew better than injure his chance by asking Letty to dance too soon. He would wait until the dancing was more general, and the impulse to movement stronger, and then offer himself.

So he stood near Letty for some time, talking to everybody, and making himself agreeable to all, as was his manner. Then at last, as if having just caught sight of her, he walked up to her where she stood flushed and eager, and asked her to favor him with her hand in the next dance.

By this time Letty was familiar with his presence, had heard his name spoken by several who evidently liked him, and was quite pleased when he asked her to dance with him.

In the dance nothing but commonplaces passed between them, yet Tom had a certain pleasant way of saying the commonest, emptiest things in an offhand, skimming manner. But Letty was not capable of discovering the illusion. She felt no repellent atmosphere about him, and did not shrink from his advances. He pleased her, and why should she not be pleased with him?

Therefore Letty responded with smiles and pleasant words, grateful to such a fine youth for taking notice of her small self.

The sun had set in a bank of cloud which began to swell and rise, and now hung dark and thick over the still, warm night. Even the farmers were unobservant of the change—their crops were all in, they had eaten and drunk heartily, and were merry.

Suddenly there came a torrent sound in the air, heard by few and heeded by none, until a deluge of rain and half-melted hailstones rushed straight into the hall upon the happy company. Scarcely a light was left burning, except those in the holes and recesses of the walls. The merrymakers scattered like flies—into the house, into the tower, into the sheds and stables in the court behind, under the trees in front, anywhere to be out of the rain and hail.

Letty had been dancing with Tom, her hand in his. He clasped it tightly and, as quickly as the crowd and the confusion of shelter-seeking would permit, led her to the door of the tower. But many had run in the same direction, and already its lower story and stair were crowded with refugees—the elder bemoaning the sudden change, and the younger merrier than ever. To them even the soaking of their finery was but added cause of laughter.

Tom did not stay among them, but led Letty on through the crowd and up the stair to the second floor. Even here there were a few couples talking and laughing in the dark, so he passed on to the next stair.

"Let us stop here, Mr. Helmer," said Letty. "There is plenty of room here."

"I want to show you something," answered Tom. "You need not be frightened. I know every nook of the place—I used to play here as a child," and led her still higher.

At the top of the stair they entered a straight passage, in the middle of which was a faint glimmer of light from an oval aperture in the side of it. Tom led Letty to it and told her to look through. She obeyed.

Beneath lay the great gulf, wide and deep, of the hall they had just left. This was the little window, high in its gable, through which, in faraway times, the lord or the lady of the mansion could see whatever went on below.

The rain had ceased as suddenly as it had begun, and already lights were moving about in the darkness of the abyss—one, and another, and another, searching for something lost in the hurry of the scattering. It was a dismal sight. A strange fear came upon Letty, and she drew back from the window with a shudder.

"Are you cold?" asked Tom. "Of course you must be, with nothing but thin muslin! Shall I run down and get you a shawl?"

"Oh, no! Do not leave me, please! It's not that," answered Letty. "I don't mind the wind a bit—it's rather pleasant. It's only that the look of the place makes me miserable; it's as if no one had danced there for a hundred years."

"No one has, I suppose, till tonight," said Tom. "What a fine place it would be if only it had a roof. I can't think how anyone could live beside it and leave it like that!" But Tom lived a good deal closer to a worse ruin, and never spent a thought on it.

Letty shivered again, but trying to speak cheerfully said, "I'm quite ashamed of myself. I can't think why I should feel like this— as if something dreadful were watching me! I must go home, Mr. Helmer."

"It will be the safest thing to do—I fear you have indeed caught cold," replied Tom, rejoicing at the chance of accompanying her. "I shall be delighted to see you home."

"There is not the least occasion for that, thank you," answered Letty. "I have a servant of my aunt's with me, somewhere about the place. The storm is quite over now; I will go and find her."

Tom made no objection, and helped her down the dark stair, hoping in his heart that the servant would not be found.

As they went, Letty seemed to herself to be walking in some old dream of change and desertion. The tower was empty now, and the wind had risen. It rushed about like a cold wild ghost, through every cranny of the desolate place. But the wind was also blowing away the angry clouds, and by the time Tom and Letty emerged from the tower, the stars were shining down into the hall. One or two forlorn searchers were still there, a few guests were harnessing their horses to go, and some were already trudging on foot through the dark. Hesper and Miss Yolland were talking to a few friends in the drawing room, Lady Margaret was in her boudoir, and Mr. Mortimer was smoking a cigar in his study.

Nowhere could Letty find Susan, who was in the farmer's kitchen behind. Tom suspected as much, but was far from hinting the possibility. Letty found her cloak which she had left in the hall, and thought it wise to proceed home at once. She therefore accepted Tom's renewed offer of company.

They were just leaving the hall when a thought came to Letty. "Oh, I know a short way home!" Without waiting for any response from Tom, she turned and led him off in the opposite direction toward a field. There she made straight for a huge oak beside the sunken fence parting the two properties. In the slow strength of its growth, the spreading of the tree's roots had crumbled the stone wall and made a little passage which led to the top of the gully. When they reached it Letty turned to bid Tom goodnight, but he insisted on seeing her safe to the house.

"Oh, but I know the way—every inch of it. I often come down here to rest under this tree," said Letty, gazing up at the strong gnarled oak as if it were a dear friend. "That's how I know about the crack in the wall." She offered this information in perfect innocence, and Tom laid it up in his mind.

When they reached the gate of the yard behind her aunt's house, Letty would not let Tom go a step farther.

7.
The Oak

The next morning, as she narrated the events of the evening, Letty told her aunt of the acquaintance she had made. This information did not please the old lady, as Letty had expected. Mrs. Wardour knew all about Tom's mother, or thought she did, and knew little good. She also knew that, although Tom was popular, Godfrey had a very poor opinion of him. On these grounds, and without a thought of injustice to Letty, she sharply rebuked the poor girl for allowing such a fellow to pay her any attention, and declared that if she ever permitted him so much as to speak to her again, she would do something, which she left in a cloud of vague suggestion.

Letty made no reply. She was hurt, and it was no wonder that she judged this judgment of Tom by the injustice of the judgment to herself. It was of no consequence to her, she said to herself, whether she spoke to him again or not, but had anyone the right to compel another to behave rudely? Only, what did it matter since there was so little chance of ever seeing him again?

All day she felt weary and disappointed, after the merrymaking of the night before, the household was irritating. She would soon have got over both the weariness and tedium had her aunt been kind, but all day she kept driving Letty from one thing to another, unsatisfied with anything Letty did, calling her an ungrateful girl, and leaving Letty more tired and dispirited than she could ever remember.

The following day all was quiet, and a visit by a favorite sister whom Mrs. Wardour had not seen for months, set Letty at liberty such as she seldom had. In the afternoon she took the book Godfrey had given her and sought the shadow of the Durnmelling oak.

It was a lovely autumn day, the sun as glorious as ever, but there was a keenness in the air which made Letty feel a little sad without knowing why. She was trying hard to fix her attention on her reading when a yellow leaf dropped on the very line she was poring over. Thinking how soon the tree would be bare once more, she brushed the leaf aside and resumed her lesson.

But a second tree leaf floated down onto the book leaf, and again she brushed it aside.

Down on the same spot fell a third leaf, and Letty looked up. There was a man in the tree over her head! She scrambled to her feet as quickly as her startled wits would allow, just as he dropped to the ground beside her, lifting his hat as coolly as if he had met her on the road.

"I hope I haven't frightened you," said Tom. "Do forgive me," he added, becoming more aware of the perturbation he had caused her. "You were so kind to me the other night, I could not help wanting to see you again. I had no idea the sight of me would terrify you so much."

"You gave me such a start!" gasped Letty, with her hand pressed over her heart.

"I was afraid of that," answered Tom, "but what could I do? I was certain, if you saw me coming, you would run away."

"Why should you think that?" asked Letty, a faint color rising in her cheek.

"Because," answered Tom, "I was sure they would be telling you all manner of things against me. There is no harm in me— really, Miss Lovel—nothing, that is, worth mentioning."

"I am sure there isn't," said Letty, and then there came a pause.

"What are you reading, may I ask?" enquired Tom.

Letty remembered her aunt's threats, but, partly from a kind of paralysis caused by Tom's coolness, partly from its being impossible for her to be curt with anyone with whom she was not angry, partly from not knowing what to do, yet feeling she ought to run to the house, she dropped down again on the very spot where she had been so scared. Tom seated himself on the grass at her feet and looked up at her with eyes full of admiration.

Confused and troubled, she began to turn over the leaves of her book. She supposed afterward she must have asked him why he stared at her so, for the next thing she remembered was hearing him say, "I can't help it. You are so lovely!"

"Please don't talk such nonsense," she rejoined. "I am not lovely, and I know it." She spoke the last words a little angrily.

"I speak the truth," said Tom, quietly and earnestly. "Why should you think otherwise?"

"Because nobody ever said so before."

"Then it is quite time somebody should say so," returned Tom, changing his tone. "It may be a painful fact, but even ladies ought to be told the truth and learn to bear it. To say you are not lovely would be a downright lie."

"I wish you wouldn't talk to me about myself!" said Letty, feeling confused and improper, but not altogether displeased that it was possible for such a mistake to be made. Tears rose in her eyes, partly from uneasiness with the turn of the talk, and partly from the the discomfort of conscious disobedience. But still she did not move.

"I am very sorry if I have vexed you," said Tom, seeing her evident distress. "I promise not to say another word of the kind again, if I can help it. But, Letty," he went on, calling her by her name with such simplicity that she never even noticed it, "do tell me what you are reading. That will keep me from talking about you."

"There!" said Letty, almost crossly, handing him the book, and pointing to the sonnet, she rose to go.

Tom took the book and sprang to his feet. He had never read the poem, but he stood there devouring it. He was doing his best to lay hold of it quickly, for there Letty stood, with her hand out to take the book again, ready to leave. Silent and motionless he read and reread. Letty was growing quite impatient, but still Tom read, a smile slowly spreading over his face.

"It is a beautiful poem," he said at last, quite honestly, and raising his eyes, looked straight into hers.

"I am sure it must be quite beautiful," said Letty, "but I have hardly got ahold of it yet." And she stretched her hand a little farther as if to retrieve the book.

But Tom was not yet prepared to part with it. He proceeded instead, in fluent speech and language, to set forth the beauty of the phrases which particularly pleased him. Nor did he fail to remark that, according to the strict laws of English verse, there was one bad rhyme.

Letty asked him to explain, thus leading Tom to an exposition of the laws of rhyme, of which he happened to know something. Question followed question, and answer followed answer, with Letty feeling all the time she *must* go. Again and again she stretched out her hand to take the book, and although he saw the motion, Tom held onto the book as to his best anchor, hurriedly turning its leaves, searching for something more to his mind.

He found another poem and read it aloud. He had a good ear for rhythm and cadence, and prided himself on his reading of poetry.

The path to her Letty's heart through her intellect was not well-trodden, but the poem in question had wings, and something in its tone suited her heart. Her eyes filled with tears, and through those tears Tom looked large and misunderstood. "He must be a poet himself to read poetry like that!" she said to herself, and felt thoroughly assured that her aunt had wronged him greatly.

Tom closed the book and finally returned it to her, saying, "Good morning, Miss Lovel," and ran down to the crevice in the stone wall. Before Letty could gather her thoughts, she heard the soft thunder of hoofs on grass, and saw Tom on his mare at full gallop across the opposite field. She watched till she lost sight of him, then slowly turned and went back to the house and to her room. She was vaguely aware that a breeze had begun to whisper in her heart, although only the slightest sound of it had yet reached her.

8.
Confusion

Now Letty's troubles began. Up to this point, neither she nor anyone else could call her troublesome. But now she began to feel like a target which exists but to receive the piercing of arrows. Letty felt that her disobedience of her aunt's extreme orders concerning Tom was not really disobedience, because she was taken by surprise, and besides, it was next to impossible to obey them. But Letty found herself feeling very uncomfortable. On the other hand, when she recalled how unkindly, how unjustly her aunt had spoken of her new acquaintance, she truly wondered whether she must tell all that passed that afternoon.

Letty's first false step was here. She told herself she could not, and she did not. She lacked courage—a want in her case not much to be wondered at, but much to be deplored; for true courage is just as needful to the character of a woman as of a man. Already her secret had begun to work conscious woe. She contrived to quiet herself a little with the idea that, as soon as Godfrey came home, she would tell him all, confessing too that she had not had the courage to tell his mother. She was sure he would forgive her, set her at peace with herself, and be unfair neither to Mr. Helmer nor to her. In the meantime she would be careful not to go where she might meet Tom again.

And she kept to her resolve, although Tom visited the oak almost every day for the next two weeks. He waited in vain, and his disappointment only increased his longing. For the first time in his life, he followed one idea for a whole fortnight.

At length Godfrey returned, and when he saw Letty, he knew something was the matter. Every hour of his absence, he had found his thoughts with the sweet face and ministering hands of his pupil. However, it was not revealed to him that he was in love with her. He thought of her as his younger sister, loving, clinging, obedient. So dear was she to him, he thought, that he would rejoice to secure her happiness at any cost to himself. But such a crisis was far away, and there was no necessity for contemplating it. He knew he must be careful that his behavior should lead her into no error. He was not afraid that she might fall in love with him—he was not so full of himself as that; but he recoiled from the idea that she might imagine him in love with her.

Thus, even in the heart of one so far above ordinary men as Godfrey, pride had its evil place. Godfrey was firmly resolved on caution; so when Letty came knocking at the door of his study—the first time he had seen her gentle face in weeks—he perceived her shyness and hesitation, and attributed it to his own wisely guarded behavior. And thus the pride of man mingled with the love of God and polluted it. From that hour he began to lord it over her.

Letty had retained and contemplated fully the idea of making her confession to Godfrey, but the moment she saw him, she knew it would be impossible to do so. It was a sad discovery for her, for Godfrey had been the chief source of interest in her life. As soon as she realized she could not unburden the weight on her mind to Godfrey, a wall rose between them. At that moment a desire woke in her to see Tom Helmer. She could no longer bear to be shut up in herself. She must see somebody, get near to them, and talk to them before her secret choked her. Who was there besides Tom—and Mary?

She had never once gone to the oak again, but she had not altogether avoided a certain little window in the garret from which the tree was visible, and she had spotted Tom waiting for her several times. He surely must be her friend, she reasoned, or why would he care, day after day, to climb a tree to watch for her? It was so good of him! As for Mary, she treated Letty like a child. When Letty had told her that she met Tom at Durnmelling, and how kind he had been, Mary looked as grave as if it had been wicked to be civil to him, and told her in return how he and his mother were always quarreling. "That must be his mother's fault," Letty told herself. "It could not be Tom's! His mother must be something like my aunt." And after that, how could she tell Mary any more?

Letty was not blamable in desiring the company of humanity about her soul, but she was quite blamable in not being fit to walk a few steps alone, or even to sit still and expect; and now her heart was like a child left alone in a great room. She had not yet learned that she must bear her own burden, and so become able to bear the burden of someone else.

The first afternoon on which she thought her aunt could spare her, she begged leave to go and see Mary. Mrs. Wardour yielded permission, but not very graciously. She had agreed that Miss Marston was not like other shopgirls, but she did not favor the growth of the intimacy, and she liked Letty's going to her even less than Mary's coming to Thornwick.

9.
The Heath and the Hut

Letty seldom went to the shop to chat with Mary, for she knew Mr. Turnbull would not like it; but now her misery made her bold. Mary saw the trouble in her eyes, and without a moment's hesitation drew her past the counter into the house, and up to her own little room.

"Sit down, Letty, and tell me what is the matter," said Mary, placing her friend in a chintz-covered chair, and seating herself beside her. But Letty burst into tears and sat sobbing, unable to speak. Mary recognized her emotional state and said, "Then I'll tell you what. You must stay with me tonight so we may have time to talk it over. Wait here till the shop closes. I'll send up some tea for you, and maybe you'd care to rest awhile."

"Oh, but I can't!" sobbed Letty, "My aunt would never allow me to stay the night."

"We'll try her," said Mary confidently, and went to her desk to write a note to Mrs. Wardour. She took it to Beenie to have sent by special messenger to Thornwick, and asked her to take tea up to Miss Lovel in her bedroom. Mary then resumed her place in the shop under the frowns and side-glances of Turnbull, and the smile of her dear father who was pleased at her reappearance from even such a short absence.

But the return of the messenger, in an hour or so, destroyed the hope of a pleasant evening. Mrs. Wardour absolutely refused to allow Letty to spend the night away from home; she must return immediately so as to get back before dark.

51

Rare anger flushed Letty's cheeks and flashed from her eyes. In addition to the prime annoyance, her aunt's note was addressed to her and not to Mary. Mary only smiled inwardly at this, but Letty felt deeply hurt, and her displeasure with her aunt added yet a shade to the dimness of her judgment. She rose at once.

"Will you not tell me first what is troubling you, Letty?" said Mary.

"No, not now," replied Letty.

"Then I will come and see you on Sunday," said Mary, "and we shall manage to have our talk."

They kissed and parted—Letty unaware that she had given her friend a less warm kiss than usual. With glowing cheeks, tear-filled eyes, and indignant heart, she set out on her walk home.

It was a still evening, with a great cloud rising in the southwest. As the sun drew near the horizon a thin veil stretched over the sky, and a few drops came scattering. This was in harmony with Letty's mood, for her soul was clouded.

About halfway to Thornwick, the path crossed a little common. Just as Letty left the hedge-guarded edge and stepped through the gate, the wind came with a burst, and brought the rain in earnest. It was not very heavy, but with the wind at its back; and Letty, having no defense but her parasol, was thoroughly wet before she could reach any shelter. So she bent her head to the blast and walked on. She had no desire for shelter. In her pique, she would rather get wet to the skin, take a violent cold, go into a consumption, and die in a fortnight. The wind whistled about her bonnet, dashed the raindrops clinging to the drum-tight silk of her parasol, and made her skirts as fetters and chains. She could hardly get along, and was just going to take down her parasol, when suddenly, where was neither house nor hedge nor tree, came a lull. From behind, over her head and parasol, had come an umbrella, and now came a voice and an audible sigh of pleasure.

"I little thought when I left home this afternoon," said the voice, "that I should have such a happiness before night!"

At the sound of the voice Letty gave a cry of surprise, of delight. "O Tom!" she said, and clasped the arm that held the umbrella. How her foolish heart bounded! Here was help when she had sought none, and where least she had hoped for any. Her aunt would have had her run from under the umbrella at once, no doubt, but she would do as she pleased this time. Here was Tom getting as wet as a spaniel for her sake, and counting it a happiness! Oh, to have a friend like that—all to herself! She would not reject such a friend for all the aunts in creation. Besides, it was her aunt's fault; if she had let her stay with Mary, she would not have met Tom. It was not *her* doing.

But at the sound of her own voice calling him Tom, the blood rushed to her cheeks, and she felt their glow even in the chilling rain.

"What a night for you to be out, Letty!" responded Tom, taking instant advantage of the right she had given him. "How lucky it was I chose the right place to watch in at last! I was sure, if I only persevered long enough, I should be rewarded."

"Have you been waiting long?" asked Letty naively.

"A fortnight and a day," answered Tom, with a laugh. "But I would wait a year longer for another chance like this." And he pressed to his side the hand upon his arm. "Fate is indeed kind tonight."

"Hardly in the weather," said Letty, fast recovering her spirits.

"No?" said Tom with a seeming pretense of indignation. "Let anyone but yourself dare to say a word against the weather, and he will have me to reckon with. It's the sweetest weather I ever walked in. I will write a glorious song in praise of showery gusts and bare commons."

"Do," said Letty, careful not to say Tom this time, but unwilling to revert to Mr. Helmer, "and mind you bring in the umbrella."

"That I will! See if I don't!" answered Tom.

The wind blew cold, the air was dank and chill, the west was a low gleam of wet yellow, and the rain shot stinging beads in their faces. But Letty's heart was growing warm in the confidence of the friendly presence; she felt like a banished soul that had a found a whole new world; joy as of endless deliverance pervaded her being.

At the other side of the heath, almost upon the path, stood a deserted hut. The door and window were gone, but the roof remained. As they neared it the wind fell and the rain began to come down in earnest.

"Let us go in here for a moment," said Tom, "and get our breath back." Letty said nothing, but Tom felt she was reluctant.

"No one will pass by here tonight," he assured her, "and we mustn't get wet to the skin."

Letty fancied that refusal would be more unmaidenly than consent, and allowed Tom to lead her in. Once there, she told Tom the trouble their meeting at the oak was causing her, saying that now it would be worse than ever, for it was altogether impossible to confess that she had met him yet again that evening.

Now Letty's foot was truly in a snare—she had a secret with Tom. There was no room for confession now. If a secret held is a burden, a secret shared is a fetter. But Tom's heart rejoiced within him.

"Let me see—how old are you, Letty?" he asked gaily.

"Eighteen," she answered.

"Then you are fit to judge for yourself. You aren't a child, and they are not your father and mother. What right have they to know everything you do? I wouldn't let any such nonsense trouble me."

"But they give me everything, you know—food, clothes, and all."

"And what do you do for them?"

"Nothing."

"And what are you about all day?"

Letty gave a brief sketch of her day. "And you call that nothing?" exclaimed Tom. "Isn't that enough to pay for your food and clothes? Why, it's downright slavery! Of course, you are not to do anything wrong, but you surely don't owe your aunt your thoughts!"

Tom continued in this style, believing that he spoke the truth and was teaching her to show a proper spirit. His heart, as well as Godfrey's, was uplifted to think he had this lovely creature to direct and superintend. But in truth he was giving her just the instruction that goes to making a slave—the slave in heart who serves without devotion, and serves unworthily. In his words Letty seemed to hear a gospel of liberty, and she scarcely needed the following injunctions from Tom to make a firm resolve not to utter a single word concerning him.

"If you do," Tom said, "I shall never see you again. They will set everyone about the place to watch you, like so many cats after one poor little mouse, and on the least suspicion, one way or another, you will be gobbled up before you can get to me to take care of you."

Letty looked up at him gratefully. "But what could you do for me if I did?" she asked. "If my aunt were to turn me from the house, your mother would not take me in!"

"My mother won't be mistress long," answered Tom. "She will have to do as I bid her when I am twenty-one, and that will be in a few months." (Tom did not yet know the terms of his father's will.) "In the meantime we must keep quiet, you know. We don't want a row—we have plenty of that as it is. You may be sure *I* shall tell no one how I spent the happiest hour of my life! Here we are in a wretched little hut being rained upon, and I am in paradise!"

"I must go home," said Letty, recalled to a sense of her situation, yet set trembling with pleasure by his words. "See, it is getting quite dark."

"Don't be afraid, I will see you home. Who knows when we shall meet again? I'm not going to ask you to meet me anywhere. I shall just fall in with you when I have the chance. It is very hard that two people who understand each other cannot be friends without other people shoving in their ugly beaks! Where is the harm?"

"Where indeed?" murmured Letty shyly.

A tall shadow passed the opening in the wall of the hut where once had been a window, and the gloom it cast into the dusk within was awful and ominous. The moment he saw it, Tom knew it must be Godfrey, and so he threw himself flat on the clay floor in the darkest of the shadows. Godfrey stopped at the doorless entrance and stood on the threshold, bending his head to clear the lintel as he looked in. Letty's heart seemed to vanish from her body. Godfrey continued staring. He had heard of his mother's refusal to grant Letty permission to stay with Mary, and had set out in the storm in hope of meeting her and helping her home.

In the darkness he saw something white, but did not realize it was Letty's frightened face. The strange, scared, ghastly expression of it bewildered him.

Letty became aware that Godfrey did not recognize her at first, and the hope that he might not see Tom had frozen her to the spot.

"Is it really you, my child?" Godfrey asked, in an uncertain voice.

"O Cousin Godfrey!" gasped Letty, "you gave me such a start!"

"Why should you be so startled at seeing me, Letty?" he returned. "Am I such a monster of the darkness?"

"You came so suddenly," replied Letty, gathering courage from the playfulness of his tone, "and blocked up the door with your shoulders, so that not a ray of light fell on your face, and how was I to know it was you?"

Her face was now as red as fire, burning from the lie inside her. She felt all a lie now, but the gloom was friendly. With a resolution new to herself, she went up to Godfrey and said, "If you are going to town, let me walk with you, Cousin Godfrey. It is getting so dark."

She felt as if an evil necessity were driving her. It was such a relief to be assured that Godfrey had not seen Tom, that she felt as if she could forego the sight of Tom forevermore. Her better feelings rushed back, her old confidence and reverence, and she felt as if Godfrey had appeared for her deliverance.

"I am not going to town, Letty," he answered. "I came to meet you, and we will go home together. It is no use waiting for the rain to stop, or until we can put up an umbrella. We must brave the rain as best as possible."

The wind was up again, and the next moment Letty was on Godfrey's arm, struggling with the same storm she had so lately encountered leaning on Tom's, while Tom was only too glad to be left alone on the floor of the dismal hut. He did not venture to rise for some time, lest Mr. Wardour should come back. He was as mortally afraid of being discovered as any young thief in a farmer's orchard.

He had a dreary walk back to the public house where he had stabled his horse, but he trudged along cheerfully, brooding with delight on Letty's beauty and her lovely confidence in him. "Poor child," he thought to himself, "what a doleful walk home she will have with that stuck-up old bachelor!"

Nor indeed was it a very comfortable walk home she had. Godfrey talked all the way, as well as the wind and rain would permit. A few weeks ago she would have thought the walk and the talk delightful. But after Tom's airy conversation, Godfrey's sounded very wise but dull. Somewhere in her lay the suspicion that in Godfrey's talk there was a value which was missing in Tom's. Letty wanted somebody who would be kind to her. She was not lazy, but she did enjoy not having to think too much. She had no hunger for the possible results of thought.

Later, seated on the edge of her bed, weary, wet, and self-accused, she recalled, and pondered and compared the two incomparable men, until her aunt called her to make haste to change her clothes and come for tea. The old lady imagined from her delay she was angry because she had not been permitted to stay with Mary. But when she appeared, she was so ready and attentive, and so quick to help that she said to herself, "Really, the girl is very good-natured," as if she had just discovered the fact.

But Thornwick could nevermore feel like home to Letty. Not at peace with herself, she could not be at peace with her surroundings. As life resumed its regular pattern, Letty labored more than ever to lay hold of the lessons which Godfrey set before her. But success seemed further from her than ever. She was aware of a weight, an oppression, which seemed to belong to the task, but was in reality her self-dissatisfaction. She reproached herself for having given Tom cause to think unjustly of her guardians, and she tried harder than ever to please her aunt. The small personal services she had been rendering to Godfrey were now ministered with the care of a devotee. Not once should he miss a button from his shirt or find a sock insufficiently darned. But even this service of conscience did not make her happy. Duty itself could not, not where faith was wanting, or where the heart was not at one with those whom her hands were serving. She would cry herself to sleep and rise early to be sad.

She resolved at last to do all in her power to avoid Tom. Not with him, she could resist him.

Her aunt saw that something was not right and watched Letty closely. The only thing her keenness discovered was that she was eager to please Godfrey, and the conviction began to grow that Letty was indulging the impudent presumption of being in love with her cousin. Her maternal indignation misled her into the folly of dropping hints that should put Godfrey on his guard. (Men were so easily taken in by designing girls!) She did not say much with her words, but she said a good deal by her actions.

Godfrey had not failed to observe the dejection that ruled every feature and expression of Letty's countenance. Again and again he had asked himself whether she might think he was displeased with her, for he had kept stricter guard than ever over his behavior toward her.

On the next Sunday when they all went to church, Letty felt that Tom was there too, but she never raised her eyes to glance at him. He had been looking out for a sight of her—from the oak tree, from his mare's back as he haunted the roads around Thornwick, but not once had he caught a glimpse of her.

He had seated himself where he could not fail to see her if she were in the Thornwick pew. How ill she looked! His heart swelled with indignation.

"They are cruel to her," he said. "Poor girl, they will kill her! This will never do—I *must* see her somehow!"

If Letty had had a real friend to strengthen and advise her, much suffering might have been spared her, for never was there a more teachable girl. She was only too ready to accept for true whatever friendship offered itself. Mary would have been such a friend, but Letty did not yet know what she needed. It was sympathy she longed for, not strength, and therefore she was afraid of Mary.

As she had promised, Mary came to see Letty the Sunday after that disastrous visit. But the weather was uncertain and gusty, and she found both Letty and Godfrey in the parlor and did not have a chance to speak to her alone. Letty felt that Mary would insist on her making a full disclosure of the whole foolish business to Mrs. Wardour, and that required a depth of character which Letty was lacking.

10.
William
Marston

Clouds were gathering over Mary too, deep and dark, but of altogether another kind from those that enveloped Letty Few people were interested in William Marston. Of those who saw him in the shop, most turned from him to his jolly partner. But some did look for him behind the counter and were disappointed if he was absent. Most of these felt a repugnance to the overcomplaisant Turnbull. The few friends that Marston had loved him as not many are loved; they knew him, not as he seemed to the careless eye, but as he was. These friends knew that when the faraway look was on him he was all taken up with what he loved, and that was neither himself nor his business.

He was not a man of much formal education, but he read, and he was a good way on in his personal education. The main secret of his progress was that for him, action was the beginning and end of thought.

It may seem strange that such a man should have gone into business with the likes of John Turnbull, for from the first, it was an unequal yoke of believer and unbeliever. It had been a great trial, and punishment had not been spared, with the best results in his patience and purification.

Turnbull was ready to take every safe advantage from his partner's comparative carelessness about money. He drew a larger proportion of the profits than belonged to his share in the capital, justifying himself on the ground that he had a much larger family, did more of the business, and had to keep up the standing of the firm. He made Marston pay more than was reasonable for the small part of the house yielded from storage to the accommodation of him, his daughter, and their servant. He never considered that had they not lived there, someone would have to be paid to do so. Far more than this, he had for some time been risking the whole affair by private speculations. After all, Marston was the safer man of business, even from the worldly point of view. Alone, he would hardly have made money, but he would have gotten through, and would have left his daughter the means of getting through also.

One evening George went home early because of a party at the villa (as the Turnbulls called their house). Mr. Marston and Mary were left to shut the shop for themselves. When the last shutter was put up, Mr. Marston dropped his arms with a weary sigh. Mary, who had been fastening the bolts on the inside, met him at the door.

"You look so worn out, Father," she said. "Come and lie down, and I will read to you."

"I will, my dear," he answered. "I don't feel quite myself today. The seasons tell upon me now. I suppose the stuff of my tabernacle is wearing thin."

Mary cast an anxious look at him. Although never a strong man, he seldom complained. But she said nothing, and, hoping a good cup of tea would restore him, she led the way through the dark shop to the door of the house.

She hastened to make the sofa comfortable for him and covered him with a rug when he lay down. Then, as Beenie was getting the tea, Mary read to him. She chose a poem with which Mr. Wardour had made her acquainted. Her father knew next to nothing of literature, but, having pondered his New Testament for thirty years, he was more than capable of understanding her selection. When she ended, he asked her to read it again, and then again. Not until she had read it six times did he seem content. And every time she read it, Mary found herself understanding it better. Her father made no remark, but when she lifted her eyes from the sixth reading, she saw that his face shone.

"That will do now, Mary. Thank you," he said. "I have a good hold of it, I think, and shall be able to comfort myself with it when I wake in the night." He said no more. Tea was brought and he drank a cup but could not eat.

"I want a long sleep," he said, and the words went to his child's heart—she dared not question herself why. "Mary," he continued, "come here. I want to speak to you."

As she knelt beside him, he took her little hand in his two long bony ones. "Mary, my child, I love you, and I do want you to be a Christian."

"So do I, Father," answered Mary simply, the tears rushing to her eyes at the thought that perhaps she was not one. "I want to be a Christian."

"Yes, but it is not that I do not think you a Christian. It is that I want you to be a downright *real* Christian, not one who is trying to feel as a Christian ought to feel. I have lost so much precious time in that way!"

"Tell me," cried Mary, clasping her other hand over his, "tell me what you would have me do!"

"I will try. A Christian is one who does what the Lord Jesus tells him—no more and no less. It is not even understanding the Lord Jesus that makes us a Christian, although this makes us dear to the Father. But, being a Christian and doing what He tells us is what makes us understand Him. Peter says the Holy Spirit is given to those who obey Him. What else is obeying but just actually, really, doing what He says, just as if I were to tell you to go and fetch my Bible. Mary, did you ever do anything just because Jesus told you to?"

Mary did not answer immediately. She thought awhile, and then spoke. "Yes, Father," she said, "I think so. Two nights ago George was very rude to me—nothing bad, but you know he can be very crude. Well, when I was going to bed, I was still angry with him, so it was no wonder I had difficulty saying my prayers. Then I remembered how Jesus said we must forgive or we should not be forgiven. So I forgave him with all my heart, and then I found I could pray."

Her father stretched out his arms and drew her close. He stroked her hair and closed his eyes as a faint, pleased smile played at the corners of his mouth. After a little, he began to talk again.

"It is a miserable thing to hear those who believe themselves Christians talking and discussing this question and that, without a thought of the command of Christ to love one another."

"Father, I try, and I think I do love everybody who loves Him," said Mary.

"That is good, but not good enough, my child. We must be like Jesus. We must love all men, whether they are Christians or not."

"Tell me, then, what you want me to do, Father. I will do whatever you tell me."

"I want you to be just like that to the Lord Christ, Mary. I want you to look out for His will, find it, and do it. The person who does what God tells him sits at his Father's feet and looks up into His face. Look for the lovely will, my child, that you may be its servant, its priest, its queen, its slave—as Paul called himself. How that man did glory in his Master!"

"I will try, Father," returned Mary with a burst of tears. "I do want to be good. I do want to be one of His slaves, if I may."

"*May!* You are bound to be. You have no choice but to choose it. It is what we are made for—freedom, divine nature, God's life, a grand, pure, open-eyed existence! It is what Christ died for. You must not talk about *may*. It is all *must*."

Mary could not remember her father talking like this, and it frightened her. An instinctive uneasiness crept up and lay hold of her.

"Jesus is unchangeable," he continued. "What He said still holds true today, and because it may not be long before you will need to recall it, I will remind you. He said, 'Let not your heart be troubled.' "

With that William Marston rose to say good-night. He stood for a moment in front of the fire, winding his old double-cased silver watch. Mary took the little gold one he had given her and, as was her custom, handed it to him to wind for her. But it slipped from his hand into the fender.

He cried out and stooped to gather up the dying thing. The glass was broken, the case was open—it lay in his hand a mangled creature. Mary heard the rush of its departing life as the wheels went whirring and the hands circled rapidly.

"I am very sorry, Mary," he said. "It is past repair. I will get you another."

She only smiled at him.

"You don't seem to mind very much!" he remarked.

"Why should I?" she replied. "When one's father breaks one's watch, what is there to say but, 'I am glad it was you that did it'? I shall like the little thing the better for it."

He kissed her forehead and said, "My child, say that to your

Father in heaven when He breaks something for you. He will do it from love, not carelessness."

She promised, and accompanied him to his bedroom, and when she went again later he said he felt more comfortable and expected to have a good night. Relieved, she left him, but her heart was heavy. A shapeless sadness seemed to press it down.

She went to his room in the middle of the night and found him sleeping peacefully. But when she went again in the morning, he lay white and motionless, without a breath.

As if her life had rushed to overtake her departing parent and beg a last embrace, Mary stood gazing motionless. The sorrow was too huge for entrance. This could not be! Not until she stooped and kissed the pale face did the stone in her heart break and release a torrent of grief. He was gone, and she was alone. She tried to pray, but her heart seemed to lie dead, and no prayer would rise from it.

In her dull stupor she heard Beenie's knock. The old woman entered and found her on her knees, with her forehead on one of the dead hands, while the white face of her master lay looking up to heaven, as if praying for the living not yet privileged to die. Then the first peace of death was broken. Beenie gave a loud cry, and turned and ran, as if to warn the neighbors that Death was loose in the town.

Thereafter, the house was filled with noise and tumult—the sanctuary of the dead invaded by the unhallowed presence. The poor girl, hearing behind her voices she did not love, raised herself from her knees and, without lifting her eyes, crept from the room and away to her own.

Her eye fell upon her watch where it lay disfigured on her dressing table, and her father's last words came back to her. She fell again on her knees with a fresh burst of weeping with a strange mixture of agony and comfort that eventually calmed and soothed her.

She rose and wiped her eyes, and going down to Beenie, asked her to send for Mr. Turnbull. She knew her father's ideas, and must do her best to keep the funeral as simple as possible. It was a relief to have something, anything, to do in his name.

Mr. Turnbull came, and the coarse man was kind. It went against the grain with him to order what he called a pauper's funeral for the junior partner of the firm. But more desirous than ever to conciliate Mary, he promised all that she wished. He was not unaware that it would save him a great deal of money as well.

Later in her father's silent room, Mary took his old silver watch from the table—it was still measuring the time by a scale now useless to its owner. She placed it lovingly in her pocket, and sat down by the bedside. Already she found herself drawing nearer to him than she had ever been before. She was able to recall his last words, and strengthen her resolve to keep them. And sitting there, she held a vague companionship with the merely mortal presence of that which was her father. Her soul did not sink into peace, but a strange peace awoke in her spirit.

She heard the spring of the great clock that measures the years rushing rapidly down with a feverish whir, and saw the hands that measure the weeks and months careering around its face, while Death, like one of the white-robed angels in the tomb of the Lord, sat watching with a patient smile for the hour when he should be wanted to go for her.

11.
The Human
Sacrifice

The same wind that rushed about the funeral of William Marston, in the old churchyard of Testbridge, howled in the roofless hall and ruined tower of Durnmelling, and dashed against the plate-glass windows in the dining room, where the three ladies sat at lunch. Just as they finished, Lady Malice rose, saying, "Hesper, I want a word with you. Come to my room."

Hesper obeyed calmly, but without a doubt that evil awaited her there. She had never been summoned to that room for anything she could call good. When they reached the boudoir, Lady Margaret, with back as straight as the door she had just closed, led the way toward the fireplace and seated herself, motioning Hesper to a chair. Hesper again obeyed, looking as unconcerned as if she cared for nothing in this world or the next.

"Well, Hesper, what do you think?" said her mother, with a dull attempt at gaiety. "Mr. Redmain has come to the point at last, my dear child."

"What point, Mamma?"

"You tease me by pretending indifference. He had a private interview with your father this morning."

"How can a fact be pretended, Mamma? Why should I care what passes in the study? I was never welcome there. But if you wish, I will pretend. What important matter was settled in the study this morning?"

"Hesper, you provoke me!"

Hesper's eyes began to flash. Otherwise, she was still; not a feature moved. Though a mere child in the knowledge of her heart, yet she was mistress of the art of self-defense. She not only continued in silence, but looked so utterly void of interest that her mother yielded and spoke out.

"Mr. Redmain has proposed for your hand, Hesper," she said.

For one moment, and only one, the repose of Hesper's faultless upper lip gave way. Then, in a tone that emulated the indifference of her mother's she answered, "And Papa?"

"Has referred him to you, of course," replied Lady Margaret.

"Then Papa did not mean it? If Mr. Redmain is such a good match in Papa's eyes," explained Hesper, "why does Papa refer him to me?"

"That you may accept him, of course."

"How much has the man promised to pay for me?"

"*Hesper!*"

"I beg your pardon, Mamma. I thought you approved of calling things by their right names!"

"No girl can do better than follow her mother's example," said Lady Margaret, with vague sequence. "If you do, Hesper, you will accept Mr. Redmain."

"As you did Papa?"

"As I did Mr. Mortimer."

"That explains a good deal, Mamma. I don't know who to be sorrier for—you or me. Tell me, Mamma, would *you* marry Mr. Redmain?"

"That is a foolish question. It is one which, as a married woman, I could not consider without impropriety. And knowing the duty of a daughter, I did not put the question to *you*. You are the offspring of duty, and you have a duty to fulfill."

From her earliest years, it had been impressed on Lady Margaret that her first duty was to her family; that duty consisted in getting well out of its way by marrying Mr. Mortimer. She had trained her children in the bewildering conviction that it was a duty to do certain wrongs, if they be required. A wrong thing was now required of Hesper—a thing she scorned and hated, but must follow. Her turn to be sacrificed had come and she must henceforth be a living lie. But Hesper was not as ignorant as some girls.

"Duty, Mamma!" she cried, her eyes flaming, and her cheek flushed with a sense of shame. "Can a woman be born for such things? How *could* I, Mamma, how could any woman, with an atom of self-respect, consent to occupy the same . . . *room* with Mr. Redmain?"

"Hesper! I am shocked. *Where* did you learn to speak, not to say *think*, of such things? Have I taken such pains for nothing? You strike me dumb! Have I watched over my child to keep her mind as pure as her body fair, and this is the result?"

"Was it your object, then, to keep me so innocent that my first lesson in wickedness be from my husband?" asked Hesper rudely.

"Hesper, you are vulgar!" said Lady Margaret, with a cold indignation, and an expression of unfeigned disgust. She was genuinely shocked. What innocent girl would dare allude to such matters? She had no right to know an atom about them!

"You are a married woman, Mamma, you must understand," returned Hesper, in an inconsistently calm tone. "There must have been a time when you shrank from this as I do now. I appeal to you as a woman. For God's sake, save me from marrying that wretch."

"Girl! Is it possible you dare to call the man whom your father and I have chosen for you a wretch?"

"Is he not a wretch, Mamma?"

"If he is, how should I know? What has any lady got to do with a man's secrets?"

"Not if he wants to marry her daughter?"

"Certainly not. If he should not be altogether what he ought to be—and which of us is—then you will have the honor of reclaiming him. But men settle down when they marry."

"O Mother!" cried Hesper. "Is it possible that you would send me to meet things you dare not tell me, knowing they would make me sick or mad? How dare a man like that even desire in his heart to touch an innocent girl!"

"Because he is tired of the other sort," said Lady Margaret to herself. But what she said to Hesper was ten times worse. "He will settle three thousand a year on you, Hesper," she said with a sigh, "and you will find yourself mistress."

"I don't doubt it," answered Hesper, in bitter scorn. "Such a man is incapable of making any woman a wife."

"I will leave you to deal with your father, Hesper," said her mother, and rose.

"No, please, Mamma!" returned Hesper in a tone of expostulation. "Since Father has referred Mr. Redmain to me, I would rather deal with *him*. But give me a few hours first, Mamma," she begged. "Don't let him come to me just yet. For all your hardness, you feel a little for me, don't you?"

"Duty is always hard, my child," said Lady Margaret. She entirely believed it, and looked on herself as a martyr, a pattern of self-devotion and womanly virtue.

Hesper rose, and went to her own room. There, for a long hour, she sat. She neither stormed nor wept—her life went smoldering on, and she nerved herself to a brave endurance, instead of a far braver resistance.

But when she came to herself with a sigh, it was not to pray; and when she rose, it was to ring the bell. In a voice of perfect composure she asked for Miss Yolland.

Entering the room like a fast-sailing cutter over broad waves, Sepia relaxed her speed as she approached her.

"Here I am, Hesper!" she said.

"Sepia," said Hesper, "I am sold."

Miss Yolland gave a little laugh. "When is the purchase to be completed?" she asked.

"Sepia! Don't be so heartless!" cried Hesper. "Things are not quite so bad as that! The day is not fixed for the great red dragon to make a meal of me."

"Hesper," she said gravely, "you never told me there was anything of this sort going on! Who is it?"

"Mr. Redmain, of course, and I hate him!" cried Hesper, eyes blazing.

"Pooh, is that all?" returned Sepia. "If there was someone else, I could understand you being so distraught."

"Sepia!" said Hesper, almost entreatingly, "I cannot bear to be teased today. You puzzle me. Tell me, are you my friend, or are you in league with Mamma?"

"I wouldn't do that," returned Sepia, quite gravely. "That is, not so long as there was a turn of the game left."

"The game!" echoed Hesper. "Playing for love with the devil! I wish it were your *game,* as you call it!"

"Mine I'd make it, if I had it to play," returned Sepia. "But come, Hesper, I will tell you what I would do with a man I hated—that is, if I was compelled to marry him. I would give him *absolute* fair play.

"Go on," sighed Hesper, "you amuse me." Her tone expressed anything but amusement. "What would a woman of your experience do in my place?"

Sepia fixed a momentary look on Hesper. The words seemed to have stung her. She knew well enough that if Lady Malice learned anything of her real history, she would barely have time to pack up her small belongings. Sepia wanted Hesper married, so that she might go with her into the world again.

Sepia gave a ringing laugh, and threw back her head. "You want to know what I would do with a man I hated? I would send for him at once—not wait for him to come to me—and entreat him, *as he loved me,* to deliver me from the dire necessity of obeying my father. If he were a gentleman, he would manage to get me out of it somehow—that is, if I were *you.* If I were *myself* in your circumstances, and hated him as much as you do, that would not serve my turn. I would ask him all the same to set me free, but I would behave myself so he could not do it. While I begged him, I should make him feel he could not. I should make him absolutely determined to marry me, at any price to him and at whatever cost to me. He should say to himself that I did not mean what I said— as indeed, for the sake of my revenge, I should not. He should declare to me it was impossible, that he would rather die than give me up, and all that rot, you know. I would tell him I hated him, only so he would not believe me. I would say to him, 'Release me, Mr. Redmain, or I will make you repent of it. I have given you fair warning. I have told you I hated you.' He should persist and marry me, and then I *would.*"

"Would what?"

"Make him repent of it." With those words, Sepia broke into a second fit of laughter, turned from Hesper with a kind of loitering pace toward the door, glancing round more than once, each time with a fresh bubble rather than ripple in her laughter. As she reached the door, she turned quickly and, with the smile of a hearty innocent child, ran back to Hesper, threw her arms round her, and said, "There now! I've done for you what I could. I made you forget the odious man for a moment. I was curious to know whether I could make a bride forget her bridegroom. The other thing is too easy."

"What other thing?"

"To make a bridegroom forget his bride, of course! In what

shade of purity do you think of ascending the funeral pyre? Absolute white? Rose-tinged? Ivory? Or gold-suspect? Eh, happy bride?" As she ceased, she turned her head away, pulled out her handkerchief, and whimpered a little.

"Sepia!" said Hesper, annoyed. "What have *you* got to cry about? *You* do not have to marry him!"

"No, I wish I had! Then I shouldn't lose you. The moment you are married to the man, you will begin to change into a wife, a domesticated animal, a tame tabby. Must a woman consider herself only the better half of a low-bred brute with a high varnish? Then there is nothing left to do but find out the wretch's virtues— or, if he hasn't any, invent for him the least unlikely ones. When she wants for her own sake to believe in him, then she begins to repent having said hard words of him. Next she will begin to hate the person to whom she said them, and break off all communication with her. In the present instance, the obnoxious one would be Sepia Yolland, who hates Mr. Redmain with all her heart because Hesper Mortimer hates him and yet is going to love him. I wish you would hand him over to me. *I* shouldn't mind what he was—I should soon tame him! If I minded, I wouldn't marry him. Which is worse—not to mind and marry him, or to mind and marry him all the same?"

"I *can't* make you out, Sepia! I never shall."

"Then give it up. I can't always make myself out. But don't worry your poor little heart to rags about such a man as that—he's not worth a thought from a grand creature like you. Where's the use, besides? He may be underground long before the wedding— he's anything but sound. But it would be better soon after—such a rich young widow!"

"Sepia! Are you Job's comforter or a devil's advocate?"

"Not the latter, my child, for I want to see you emerge a saint from the miseries of matrimony. But whatever you do, Hesper, don't break your heart, for you will find it hard to mend. I broke mine once, and have been mad ever since."

"But I have to marry the man!"

"I never said you were not to marry him. I said you were not to break your heart. Marriage is nothing, so long as you don't make a heart-affair of it."

"Marriage is nothing, Sepia? Is it nothing to be tied to a man— *any* man—for all your life?"

"Nobody makes so much of it nowadays. The clergy themselves, who are at the bottom of the business, don't fuss about every trifle in the prayer book. They sign the articles and have done with it, meaning, of course, to break those articles if they stand in the way."

Hesper rose in anger. "How dare you—" she began.

"Good gracious!" cried Sepia. "You don't imagine I meant anything so wicked!"

"It's such a horrible business," said Hesper, more quietly. "It seems to make one capable of anything wicked only to think about it. I would rather not say another word on the subject." A shudder ran through her.

"That would be the best thing," said Sepia, "if it meant not to think any more about it. I would do anything to comfort you, Dear. I would marry him for you, but that would scarcely meet your papa's views. I would willingly hand him the purchase money, but he would not touch it, except as the proceeds of the sale of his own flesh and blood."

12.
Ungenerous Benevolence

Time went on, and Letty saw nothing more of Tom. She began to revive and feel as if she were growing safe again. The tide of temptation was ebbing away and there would be no more deceit. Even her interest in reading with Godfrey had begun to revive, and he grew kinder and kinder to her, more and more fatherly.

But Mrs. Wardour, once disquieted, lost no time in taking measures. Through friends, she was inquiring after a suitable work situation for Letty. She owed it to herself, she said, to find the right thing for the girl before sending her from the house. In the true spirit of benevolent tyranny, she said not a word to Letty of her design, and in the meantime kept her eye on the young people.

At length came news of something that seemed likely to suit Mrs. Wardour's ideas for Letty, and she thought it time to prepare the girl for the impending change. One evening, as she sat knitting one sock for Godfrey, and Letty darned another, she opened the matter.

"I am getting old, Letty," she said, "and you can't stay here at Thornwick always. Although you are a thoughtless creature, it is high time you should be thinking how you are to earn your bread. If you left it till I was gone, you would find it very awkward. So I must see you comfortably settled before I go."

"Yes, Aunt."

"There are not many things you could do."

"No, Aunt, but I do believe I should make a better housemaid than most."

"I am glad to find you willing to work, but we shall be able to do a little better for you than that. A situation as housemaid would reflect little credit on my pains for you, would hardly correspond to the education you have had."

Mrs. Wardour referred to the fact that Letty had been a day boarder at a ladies' school in Testbridge for about a year. Letty had learned far more from Godfrey in a few months than in that entire year at the school.

"It is true," her aunt went on, "you might have made a good deal more of it, if you had cared to do your best, but such as you are, I trust we will find you a tolerable situation as a governess."

Letty's heart ran halfway up her throat. A more dreadful proposal she could not have imagined. She felt, and was, utterly insufficient for such an office. She felt she knew nothing, so how was she to teach anything? Her heart seemed to grow gray within her. What she understood, she encountered willingly and bravely; but the simplest thing that seemed to involve any element of obscurity, she dreaded like a dragon in his den.

"You don't seem to relish the proposal, Letty," said Mrs. Wardour. "I hope you had not taken it in your head that I meant to leave you independent. I took you in for your father's sake. I was under no obligation to take the least trouble about you."

"It's only that I'm not suited for being a governess. I shouldn't mind being a dairymaid or a housemaid. I would go to such a place tomorrow if you liked."

"Letty, your tastes may be vulgar, but you owe it to your family to at least look like a lady."

"Oh, please! Let me stay here. Call me your dairymaid or your housemaid. It is all one—I do the work now."

"Do you mean to say that I have required menial jobs of you? I have been a mother to you, and it is up to me, not you, to choose your path in life."

Mrs. Wardour's affection for the girl had never been deep, and the moment she fancied she and her son were growing close, she drew away from Letty. But she was in some dread of what Godfrey would have to say about her plans, and so she kept silent for the present. Had she spoken then, things might have gone very differently—it might have brought Godfrey to the point of righteous resolve, or passionate utterance.

Letty believed her cousin regarded her with pity, and showed her kindness from a generous sense of duty—she was a poor dull creature for whom her cousin must do what he could. One word of genuine love from him would have caused her nature to shoot forth like a young plant, and continue to grow with a rapidity that would have astonished him. Now she felt crushed. The idea of undertaking that for which she knew herself so ill-fitted was not merely odious, but frightful to her. She must consult with Mary! She would take the first opportunity to do so; but in the meantime there was nothing to be done or said, and with a heavy heart she held her peace.

She longed to escape to her own room so she might have a cry. To her immense comfort the clock struck ten, and all that now lay between her and that refuge was the usual round of the house with her aunt, to see all safe for the night. That done, they parted, and Letty went slowly and sadly up the stairs.

13.
The Moonlight

It was a still, frosty night, with a full moon. When she reached her chamber, Letty walked mechanically to the window and stood with the candle in her hand, looking carelessly out, not taking any pleasure in the great night. The window looked over an open grassy yard, where a few large ricks of wheat shone yellow in the cold far-off moon. Between moon and earth hung a faint mist with which the thin clouds of her breath seemed to mingle. There lay her life—dank and dull, the summer faded from it, its atmosphere a growing fog. It had been six weeks since she last saw Tom. He must have ceased thinking of her by this time, and if he did think of her again, she would be far away.

Letty continued at the window for quite some time before realizing something was striking the glass with a slight ping. It was winter and there were no moths or other flying insects, so what could it be? She put her face close to the pane and looked out. There was a man in the shadow of one of the ricks. He had his hat off and was beckoning to her—it was Tom! Her heart started pounding. Clearly he wanted to speak to her, and how gladly she would again bear all the trouble of conscious deceit.

But she dared not speak to him! The very sound of her own voice in the moonlight would terrify her. And Mrs. Wardour's ears were as sharp as her eyes! She opened the lattice softly and after gently shaking her head, was closing it again, when Tom stepped into the moonlight. It was too dreadful! He might be seen! She shook her head again, but he fell on his knees and laid his hands together like one praying. Letty thought this meant that he was in trouble and that he begged her to go to him. With sudden resolve she nodded to him, left the window and crossed the room, quietly letting herself into the passageway. If she was going to be turned out of the house so soon, what did it matter?

Her room was in a little wing projecting from the back of the house over the kitchen. There was a back stair to the kitchen, and in the kitchen a door to the farmyard. She could slip out and no one need know. But Letty forgot one tiny window that overlooked the back door.

She stole down the stair and opened the door with absolute noiselessness. In a moment more she was round the corner, and creeping like a ghost among the ricks. Not even a rustle betrayed her as she came up to Tom from behind. But he was aware of her presence, and turning, took her hand and led her out of sight of the house. They were safe behind the hedge when he took her in his arms. She yielded.

"Why did you make me come down, Tom?" she whispered, half choked with fear, looking up in his face which was radiant in the moonlight.

"Because I could not bear it one day longer," he answered. "All this time I have been breaking my heart to get a word with you, and never seeing you except at church, and there you would never even look at me. It is cruel of you, Letty. Why should you try me so?"

"Do speak a little lower, Tom; sound goes so far at night. I didn't know you wanted to see me so badly," she answered, looking up in his face with a pleased smile.

"Didn't know!" repeated Tom. "I want nothing else, think of nothing else, dream of nothing else. Oh, the delight of having you here all alone to myself at last! You darling Letty!"

"I must go now, Tom. I shouldn't be out at this time of the night. If you hadn't made me think you were in some trouble, I wouldn't have come."

"And aren't I in trouble enough? To love your very shadow and not be able to get even a peep of that, except in church?"

Letty's heart leaped. He loved her! Love, real love, was what it meant! It was paradise. Anything might come that would! She would be afraid of nothing. They might say or do to her what they pleased—she did not care a straw, if he really loved her!

"I didn't know you loved me, Tom!" she said simply, with a little gasp.

"And I don't know yet whether you love me," returned Tom.

"Of course, if you love *me*," answered Letty, as if everybody must give back love for love.

Tom took her again in his arms, and Letty was in greater bliss than she had ever dreamed possible. From being looked down on by everybody, she had the whole earth under her feet. From being utterly friendless, she had the heart of Tom Helmer for her own! Yet even then the thought that she was forsaking Cousin Godfrey shot to her heart, sharp as an arrow. It probably came because of her cousin's opinion of Tom. Often she had said to herself that of course Cousin Godfrey was mistaken, and quite wrong in not liking Tom. She was sure he would like him if he knew him as she did! Yet to act against his opinion cost her a sharp pang, and many more that followed! However, seeing that they were about to send her out into the world to earn her bread, they had no more right to make such demands upon her loyalty to them as should exclude the closest and only satisfying friend she had. Tom would not turn her away—he wanted to have her forever. Not once did she suspect that Godfrey knew nothing of his mother's design.

"Now, Tom, you have seen me and spoken to me, and I must go," said Letty.

"O Letty!" cried Tom reproachfully. "Would you leave me in the very moment of my supremest bliss? That would be mockery. Do you really want to leave me all alone in the midnight, with only the moon to comfort me? Do as you like, Letty! I won't leave the place till morning. I will go back to the rickyard and lie under your window all night."

The idea of Tom out on the cold ground, while she was warm in bed, was too much for Letty's childish heart. Had she known Tom better, she would not have been afraid. She would have known that he would lie down under her window and remain there, even to the very moment when he began to feel miserable, and perhaps even a moment longer. But then he would get up, and with a last look, start home for bed.

"I will stay a little while, Tom," she offered, "if you will promise to go home as soon as I leave you."

Tom promised.

They went wandering along the farm lanes, and Tom gave full

flow to all his fine talk of love. It was characteristic of him that although he saw Letty without hat or cloak, because he was warmly clad, he never thought of her being cold until the arm he had thrown round her waist felt her shiver. Then he was kind and would have insisted that she should go in and get a shawl, had she not positively refused to go in and come out again. Then he would have had her put on his coat that she might be able to stay a little longer, but she insisted she must go. He brought her to the nearest point not within sight of any of the windows of Thornwick, and there leaving her, set out at a rapid pace for the inn where he had put up his mare.

Letty was left alone in the bare night with a diffused conscience. She felt a strange fear at her heart, like in a churchyard with the ghost-hour at hand, feeling like "a guilty thing surprised." Although she had not actively done anything wrong, she stole back to the door of the kitchen, longing for the shelter of her own room.

She had left the kitchen door an inch ajar, that she might run less risk of making noise in opening it. But as she reached it, her heart turned sick. With the moon shining full upon it, she saw plainly—and her heart turned sick when she saw—that it was closed. Between cold and terror, she shuddered from head to foot.

Recovering a little, she said to herself that some draught must have blown it to. If so, there was much danger that the noise had been heard, but in any case there was no time to lose. She glided swiftly to it. She lifted the latch softly but, horror of horrors, it was locked! She was shut out. She must lie, or confess!

The least perilous way would be to let the simple truth appear. Letty ought immediately to have knocked at the door and, should that have proved unavailing, to have broken her aunt's window to gain entrance. But that was just the kind of action of which Letty, both by constitution and training, was incapable. Human opposition, superior anger, and condemnation she dared not encounter. She sank, more than half-fainting, upon the doorstep.

The moment she came to herself, apprehension changed into active dread and rushed into uncontrollable terror. She sprang to her feet and fled like the wind after Tom. She knew where he had put up his horse, and knew he could hardly take any other way than the footpath to Testbridge. He could not be more than a few yards ahead of her, she thought. Presently she heard him whistling, she was sure, as he walked leisurely along, but she could not see him. The way was mostly between hedges until it reached the common, and there she would catch sight of him by the moonlight, in spite of the gauzy mist. On she went swiftly, still fancying at intervals she heard in front of her his whistle, and even his step on the frozen path. In her eager anxiety to overtake him, she felt neither the chilling air nor the fears or the loneliness of the night. Dismay was left behind her, and hope before her. On and on she ran. But when she reached the common and saw it lie so bare and wide in the moonlight, with the little hut standing on its edge, with gaping holes for door and window, then the terrors of the night began to crush their way into her soul. What might not be lurking in that ruin, ready to wake at the lightest rustle, and at the sight of a fleeing girl, start out in pursuit and catch her by the hair that now streamed behind her?

Miserable as was her real condition, it was rendered yet more pitiful by these terrors of the imagination. Faintly, once or twice, she tried to persuade herself that it was only a horrible dream from which she would awake in safety, but it would not do—it was all too real! More frightful than all possible dangers was the old house she had left, standing silent in the mist, holding her room inside it empty, the candle burning away in the face of the moon. Across the common she glided like a swift wraith, and again into the shadow of the hedges.

If Tom had come this way, she should have overtaken him by now. But perhaps she had stayed longer than she thought at the kitchen door, and when she started to follow him, Tom was already on his mare, headed for home!

The footpath came to an end, and she was on the high road. There was the inn where Tom generally left his mare—it was as silent as a grave! The clang of a horseshoe striking a stone came through the frosty air from far along the road. Her heart sank, and so did she, and lay insensible on the border of the same highway along which Tom, on his bay mare, went singing home.

14.
The Morning

At Thornwick, Tom had been seen in the yard by one of the young servants who herself was not altogether innocent of nightly interviews. Through the small window of her closet she had watched—and not without hope that she herself might be the object of the male presence which she recognized as Tom Helmer. But in a few minutes Letty appeared with him, and a throb of evil joy shot through her. What a thing for her to find out Miss Letty, and what a chance to now expose her naughty secret! She would have no choice but to tell Letty everything, and then what privileges would be hers! She had not thought of betraying her—there would be no fun in that, but she might encourage a little fear!

To make sure of Letty and her secret, and partly also in pure delight of mischief and enjoyment of the power to tease, she stole downstairs and locked the kitchen door—the bolt of which, for reasons of her own, she kept well-oiled. Then she sat down in an old rocking chair to wait, but soon fell fast asleep. Letty had lifted the latch almost too softly for her to have heard, had she been awake.

When the young woman awoke in the early cold grey of morning, she searched everywhere for Letty. When she discovered no trace of her, she left the door unlocked and went to bed, hoping Letty might yet find her way into the house before Mrs. Wardour was down.

When that lady awoke at the usual hour and heard no sound of stir, she put on her dressing gown and went to Letty's room. To her amazement and horror, she saw the bed had not been disturbed, and hurried to the room occupied by the girl who was the cause of the mischief. Roused so suddenly by the voice of her mistress, and assailed by a torrent of questions before she was well awake, she told all she had seen from the window but nothing of what she herself had done. Mrs. Wardour hurried to the kitchen, found the door on the latch, believed everything and much more. In a calm rage, she went to her son's room, woke him, and poured into his unwilling ears a torrent of mingled fact and fiction with Letty's name being used beside every bad adjective she could bring her lips to utter.

Godfrey's confusion was understandable. There stood his mother, dashing her cold hailstorm of contemptuous wrath on the girl he loved, whom he had gone to bed believing the sweetest creature in the world. He had been dreaming of her with the utmost tenderness when his mother woke him with the news that she had gone away in the night with Tom Helmer, the vilest creature in the neighborhood!

"For goodness' sake, Mother," he cried, "go away and let me get up!"

"What can you do, Godfrey? What is there to be done? Let her go to her ruin!" cried Mrs. Wardour, alarmed in the midst of her wrath. "You can do nothing now. She has made her bed, let her lie in it."

Her words were torture to him. He sprang from his bed and proceeded to pull on his clothes. Terrified at the wildness of his looks, his mother fled from the room. Godfrey could barely dress himself for agitation. Anger strove with unbelief, and indignation at his mother with the sense of bitter wrong from Letty. It was all incredible and shameful, yet nonetheless utterly miserable. The girl who lay in the innermost chamber of his heart like the sleeping beauty in her palace—for her to steal out at night to the embraces of a fool, a wretched, weakheaded, idle fellow who did nothing but ride the country on a horse too good for him, and quarrel with his mother from Sunday to Saturday! For such a man she had left him, Godfrey Wardour, a man who would have lifted her to the height of her nature! That fool Helmer would only sink her to the depth of his own nothingness. It was inconceivable!

He knew *now* that he loved Letty. Gnashing his teeth with rage, he caught from the wall his harvest hunting whip and rushed out of the house. Godfrey ran to the stable and to the stall of his fastest horse. As he threw the saddle over his back, he almost wept in the midst of his passion at the sight of the bright stirrups. His hands trembled so that he failed repeatedly in passing the straps through the buckles of the girths. But the moment he felt the horse under him, he was stronger, set his head straight for the village of Warrender, where Tom's mother lived, and was off. His flight led him across the back of the Durnmelling house. Hesper, who had not slept well, and found the early morning an even worse time to live than the evening, saw him from her window, going straight as an arrow. The sight arrested her. She called Sepia, who for a few nights had slept in her room.

"There now!" she said. "There is a man who looks like a man! Good heavens, how recklessly he rides. I don't believe Mr. Redmain could stay on a horse's back if he tried!"

Sepia looked, half-asleep. Her eyes grew wider and her sleepiness vanished.

"Something is wrong!" she said. "He is either mad or in love— probably both! That's a man I should like to know. I have a weakness for the kind that *could* shake the life out of me if I offended him," she added carelessly.

"Are you so anxious then to make a good submissive wife?" said Hesper.

"I should take the very first opportunity of offending him. It would be worth one's while with a man like that."

"Why? For what good?"

"Just to see his look. There is nothing on earth so scrumptious as having a grand burst of passion all to yourself." She drew in her breath like one in pain. To see it come and go! The white and the red! The tugging at the hair! The tears and oaths, and the cries and curses! To know that you have the man's heartstrings stretched on your violin, and that with one dash of your bow, one tiniest twist of a peg, you can make him shriek!"

"Sepia!" cried Hesper, "I think Darwin must be right that some of us at least are come from—"

"Tiger cats? Perhaps the Tasmanian devil?" suggested Sepia, with one of her scornful laughs.

While they talked, Godfrey became a speck in the distance. By this time, he had collected his thoughts a little, and it had grown plain to him that the last and only thing left for him to do for Letty was to compel Tom to marry her at once. But, instead of reproaching himself that he had not drawn the poor girl's heart to his own, and saved her by letting her know that he loved her, he tried to congratulate himself on the pride and self-important delay which had preserved him from yielding his love to one who counted herself of so little value.

Once he arrived at the house, he gave his horse to a boy to lead up and down, while he went through the gate and rang the bell in a porch covered with ivy. The old woman who opened the door said Master Tom was not up yet, but she would take his message. Returning presently, she asked him to come in. He declined the hospitality, and remained in front of the house.

Tom was no coward, but he was a little anxious when he heard who was below. It could mean that Letty had been found out, and here was her cousin to make a row. But what did it matter, so long as Letty was true to him? The world should know that no power on earth should keep from him the woman of his choice! As soon as he was of age he would marry her, in spite of them all. But he could not help being a little afraid of Godfrey Wardour, for he admired him.

As Godfrey waited for "the miserable mongrel," it was all he could do to keep his contempt and hate within what he would have called the bounds of reason. He kept walking up and down the little lawn, making a futile attempt to look unconcerned; yet every other moment he would strike fierce objectless blows with his whip. Catching sight of him from a window on the stair, Tom was so little assured by his demeanor that, crossing the hall, he chose from the stand a thick oak stick—poor odds against a hunting whip in the hands of one like Godfrey, with the steel of ten years of manhood in him.

Tom's long legs carried him carelessly down the two steps from the door as, with a gracious wave of the hand, and swinging his cudgel as if he were just going out for a stroll, he coolly greeted his visitor. But the other, instead of returning the salutation, stepped quickly up to him.

"Mr. Helmer, where is Miss Lovel?" he said in a low voice.

Tom turned pale, for a pang of undefined fear shot through him, and his voice betrayed genuine anxiety as he answered, "I don't know. What has happened?"

Wardour's fingers convulsively gripped his whip handle, and the word *liar* almost escaped his lips. But through the darkness of the tempest raging in him, he read truth in Tom's scared face and trembling words.

"You were with her last night," he said, grinding it out between his teeth.

"I was," answered Tom, looking more scared still.

"Where is she now?" demanded Godfrey again.

"I hope to God you know," answered Tom, "for I don't."

"Where did you leave her?" asked Wardour, in the tone of an avenger rather than a judge.

Tom, without a moment's hesitation, described the place with precision, a spot not more than a hundred yards from the house.

"What right had you to come sneaking about the place?" hissed Godfrey, in a vain attempt to master an involuntary movement of the muscles of his face at once clenching and showing his teeth. At the same moment he raised his whip unconsciously.

Tom instinctively stepped back, and raised his stick in an attitude of defense. Godfrey burst into a scornful laugh.

"You fool!" he said, "you need not be afraid. I can see you are speaking the truth. You dare not tell me a lie! I will gladly address you as a gentleman, if you will show me how it can be gentlemanly to go prowling about a neighbor's property after nightfall."

"Love acknowledges no law but itself, Mr. Wardour," answered Tom, inspired by the dignity of his honest affection for Letty. "Miss Lovel is not your property. I love her, and she loves me. I would do my best to see her, if Thornwick were the castle of Giant Blunderbore."

"Why not walk up to the house, like a man, in the daylight, and say you wanted to see her?"

"Should I have been welcome, Mr. Wardour?" said Tom significantly. "You know very well what my reception would have been. To do as you say would have been to make it next to impossible to see her."

"Well, we must find her now anyhow, and you must marry her right away."

"Must!" echoed Tom, his eyes flashing, at once with anger at the word and with pleasure at the proposal. "Must?" he repeated, "When there is nothing in the world I desire or care for *but* to marry her! Tell me what it all means, Mr. Wardour, for I am utterly in the dark."

"It means just this—the girl was last seen in your company late last night, and has been neither seen nor heard of since."

"My God!" cried Tom, now first laying hold of the fact, and then turning he began to run to the stable. But his run broke down, and with a look of scared bewilderment he came back to Godfrey.

"Mr. Wardour," he said, "what am I to do? Please advise me. If we raise a hue and cry, it will set people saying all manner of things, pleasant neither for you nor us."

"That is your business, Mr. Helmer," answered Godfrey bitterly. "You brought this shame on her."

"You are a coldhearted man," said Tom. "But there is no shame in the matter. I will soon make that clear—if only I knew where to go after her. The thing is utterly mysterious—there are neither robbers nor wild beasts about Thornwick. What can have happened to her?"

He turned his back on Godfrey for a moment, then suddenly wheeling around, broke out, "I see it all now! She found out that she had been seen, and was too terrified to go into the house again! Mr. Wardour," he continued, with a new look in his eyes, "I have more reason to be suspicious of you and your mother, than you have to suspect me. Your treatment of Letty has not been the kindest."

So Letty had been accusing him of unkindness! Ready as he was to hear anything to her disadvantage, it was yet a fresh stab to his heart. Was this the girl for whom, in all honesty and affection, he had sought to do so much? How could she say he was unkind to her? And to say it to a fellow like Tom! It was humiliating, but he would not defend himself; not to Tom, not to his mother, not to any living soul would he utter a word even resembling blame of the girl! He at least would carry himself generously! As soon as he had handed Letty over to Tom in safety, he would have done with her, and with all women forever, except his mother. Not once more would he speak to one of them in a tone of friendship.

"If I don't find Letty this very morning," said Tom, "I shall apply for a warrant to search your house."

Godfrey smiled a smile of scorn, turned from him as a wise man turns from a fool, and went out the gate.

15.
The Result

Perhaps Letty would never have come to herself in the cold of this world, under the shifting tent of the winter night, but for an outcast mongrel dog which, wandering masterless and hungry along the road, came upon her where she lay seemingly lifeless and, recognizing with pity his neighbor in misfortune, began at once to give her what help and healing might lie in a warm, honest tongue. Diligently he set himself to lick her face and hands.

By slow degrees her misery returned, and she sat up. Rejoicing at his success, the dog kept dodging about her, catching a lick here and there, wherever he saw a spot of bare flesh within his reach. Letty reached out for him, threw her arms around the dog, laid her head on his, and wept. This relieved her a little, but she was cold to the very marrow, almost too cold to feel it, and when she rose could scarcely put one foot before the other.

Not once, for all her misery, did she imagine a return to Thornwick. Without a thought of destination, she moved on, unaware even, that it was in the direction of the town. The dog, delighted to believe that he had raised up for himself a mistress, followed humbly at her heel; but always when she stopped, as she did every few paces, he ran round in front of her and looked up in her face, as if to say, "Here I am, mistress, shall I lick again?" Gladly would Letty have fondled him, but it seemed that should she stoop, she would fall flat on her face and never rise again.

Slowly the two went on, with motion scarce enough to keep the blood moving in their veins. Had she not been in fine health and strength, Letty could hardly have escaped death from the cold of that night.

When Beenie opened her kitchen door in the morning to let in the fresh air, she found seated on the step, and leaning against the wall, what she took for a young woman asleep, and then for the dead body of one, for when she gave her a little shake, she fell sideways off the doorstep. Beenie's heart smote her, for during the last hours of her morning's sleep she had been disturbed by the howling of a dog, apparently in their own yard, but had paid no further attention to it. Now here stood the offender looking up at her pitifully—ugly, disreputable, of unknown breed. When the girl fell down, he darted at her, licked her cold face for a moment, then stretching out a long gaunt neck, uttered from the depth of his hidebound frame the most melancholy appeal, not to Beenie but to the open door. Beenie stooped, and peering more closely into the face of the girl, recognized it to be Letty and drew her into the house.

Letty moved not one frozen muscle, and Beenie, growing terrified, flew up the stairs to her mistress. Mary sprung from her bed and hurried down. There on the kitchen floor, in front of the yet fireless grate, lay the body of Letty Lovel with a hideous dog sitting at her head. The moment she entered, again the animal stretched out a long bony neck, and sent forth a howl that penetrated the entire house. It sounded in Mary's ears like the cry of the whole animal creation over the absence of their Maker. They lifted Letty, and carried her to Mary's room. There they laid her in the warm bed, and proceeded to use all possible means for the restoration of heat and the renewal of circulation.

Beenie returned to the kitchen. The dog sat there motionless, with his face turned toward the door through which they had carried Letty. His sad eyes and even sadder lack of care and food raised a bit of pity in the bottom of the old woman's heart. She was not fond of dogs, but something in his eyes kept her from turning him out without some food. He ate hungrily, then Beenie drove him from her kitchen and the tiny yard, and turned back to her main concern—the almost lifeless Letty. Soon, thanks to Beenie's persistence, Letty began to breathe regularly.

But when Mary set herself at length to find out from Letty what had happened, she could get no rational response, although occasionally, and to Mary's uneasiness, Letty plainly uttered the name *Tom*. What was she to make of it? She must not betray Letty, but she must do something. Matters could not have gone wrong so far that nothing could set them at least a little straight! If only she knew what! A single false step might do no end of mischief. She must see Tom Helmer. Without betraying Letty, she might get from him some enlightenment. She knew his open nature, and had a better opinion of him than many had. A doctor must be called, but she would, if possible, see Tom first.

It was not more than a half hour's walk to Warrender, and she set out in haste. She must get back before George Turnbull came to open the shop.

Godfrey was just about to set off when he saw a young woman coming hurriedly across the road, from the direction of Testbridge. Plainly she was on business of pressing import. She came nearer, and he saw it was Mary Marston. The moment she recognized Godfrey, she began to run to him. But, as he stood with his foot in the stirrup, with no word of greeting or look of reception, and inquiry only in every feature, her haste suddenly dropped, her flushed face turned pale, and she stood panting. Not a word could she utter, but was just able to force a faint smile, with intent to reassure him.

She read in Mr. Wardour's face that he was there from the same cause as herself, but there was no good omen to be drawn from its expression. The sole acknowledgment he made of her approach was to withdraw his foot from the stirrup and stand waiting.

"You know something," he said, looking cold and hard in her face. "But I hope to goodness you are not concerned in this— business." He was about to use a bad adjective, but suppressed it.

"I *am* concerned in it," said Mary, with perfect quietness.

"You knew what was going on?" cried Wardour. "You knew that fellow there came prowling about Thornwick like a fox about a henroost? By heaven, if I had but suspected it—"

"No, Mr. Wardour," interrupted Mary, already catching a glimpse of light. "I knew nothing of that."

"Then what do you mean by saying you are concerned in the matter?"

Mary thought he was behaving so unlike himself that a shock might be of service. "Only this," she answered. "Letty is now lying in my room, whether dead or alive I am still in doubt. She must have spent the night outside—without cloak or bonnet."

"Good God!" cried Godfrey.

"Will you come and see her, Mr. Wardour?" asked Mary.

"No," answered Godfrey gruffly.

"Shall I send a note to Mrs. Wardour then?"

"I will tell her myself."

"What should I do about her?"

"I have no concern in the matter, but I suppose you had better send for a doctor. Talk to that fellow there," he added, pointing with his whip toward the Helmer house, and again putting his foot in the stirrup. "Tell him he has brought her to disgrace—"

"I don't believe it," interrupted Mary. But Godfrey went on without heeding her.

"—and get him to marry her, if you can. For, by God, he *shall* marry her or I will kill him."

He spoke looking round at her over his shoulder, a scowl on his face, his foot in the stirrup, one hand twisted in the mane of his horse, and the other stretching out the whip as if threatening the universe. Mary stood white but calm, and made no answer. He swung himself into the saddle and rode away. She turned to the gate.

From behind the shrubbery, Tom had heard the conversation, and met her as she entered the gate.

"O Miss Marston, what is to be done?" he said. "This is terrible! But I am so glad you have Letty. I heard all you said to that brute, Wardour. Thank you, thank you a thousand times, for taking her part. Indeed, you spoke the truth for her. Let me tell you all I know."

However, he had not much to tell beyond what Mary knew already.

"She keeps calling out for you, Mr. Helmer," she said, when he had ended.

"I will go with you. Come, come," he answered.

"Will you leave a message for your mother? She ought to be told."

"Never mind my mother. She's good at finding out for herself. Come along—I will soon set everything right."

"How shall we manage with the doctor?" said Mary as they went. "We cannot do without him, for I am sure she is in danger."

"Oh, no!" said Tom. "She will be all right when she sees me. But we will stop at the doctor's on the way, and prepare him."

When they came to the doctor's house, Mary went on and Tom told the doctor he had met Miss Marston on her way to him, and had come instead. Mary had wanted to let him know that Miss Lovel had come quite unexpectedly that morning, that she was delirious, and had apparently wandered from home under an attack of some sort of fever.

Letty's recovery was slow. Although rumors did go floating about the country, none of them came to the ears of Tom or Mary. Letty was safe from hearing anything, and the engagement between her and Tom soon became generally known. Mrs. Helmer was very angry, and did all she could to make Tom break it off—it was so much below him! Mrs. Wardour took care to say nothing unkind of Letty. Letty was of her own family; and besides, not only was Tom a better match than she could have expected for her, but she was more than satisfied to have Godfrey's dangerous toy thus drawn away beyond his reach.

Spring was close at hand before the bloom began to reappear in Letty's cheek. Neither her gaiety nor her usual excess of timorousness returned. A certain sad seriousness had taken the place of both, and she seemed to look out from deeper eyes. At first she behaved very sweetly to Tom, but more like a tender sister than a lover, and Mary began to doubt whether her heart was altogether Tom's. From mention of approaching marriage, she turned with a nervous, uneasy haste. Doubt filled Mary with anxiety.

But before long Mary came to the conclusion that all was right between Tom and Letty, and that the cause of her anxiety had lain merely in Letty's loss of spirit.

Now and then Mary tried to turn Tom's attention a little toward the duty of religion. Tom received the attempt with gentle amusement and a little teasing. It was all very well for girls! Indeed, he had made the observation that girls who had no religion were "strong-minded," and *that* he could not endure. Like most men, he was so well satisfied with himself that he saw no occasion to take trouble to be anything better than he was. Never suspecting what a noble creature he was meant to be, he never saw what a poor creature he was. In his own eyes he was a man any girl might be proud to marry.

In the same little sitting room, where for so many years Mary

90

had listened to the slow tender wisdom of her father, a clever young man was now courting an ignorant girl, whom he did not half understand or appreciate, while all the time feeling himself the greater and wiser and more valuable of the two. He was unaware that he did so, for he had never yet become conscious of any fact concerning himself.

The whole Turnbull family, from the beginnings of things, had appointed themselves as judges of the two Marstons, and were no less critical of the daughter now that the father had been taken from her. There was grumbling in the shop each time she ran up to see Letty, everyone regarding her and speaking of her as a servant neglecting her duty. Yet all knew well enough that she was now the co-proprietor of business and stock, and the elder Turnbull knew besides that, if the lawyer to whose care William Marston had committed his daughter were at that moment to go into the affairs of the partnership, he would find Mary had a much larger amount of money actually in the business than he. Turnbull had for some time felt no little anxiety to secure himself from investigation and possible disaster by the marriage of Mary to his son George.

Tom Helmer now learned that by his father's will (made under the influence of his mother) he was to have but a small annuity so long as she lived. Nevertheless, he determined to marry, confident in his literary faculty which, he never doubted, would soon raise it to a very sufficent income.

So in early summer Letty and Tom were married. No relative was present except Mrs. Wardour. Mrs. Helmer and Godfrey had both declined the invitation, and no friends came except Mary for bridesmaid, and a college friend of Tom's for groomsman. After the ceremony, and a breakfast provided by Mary, the young couple took the train for London.

16.
Mary in the Shop

More than a year passed and it was full summer again at Testbridge. To the careless eye, things were unchanged; and to the careless mind, they would never change. The greed and fawning did go on unchanged in the shop of Turnbull and Marston, seasoned only with the heavenly salt of Mary's good ministration.

She was very lonely. Letty was gone, and the link between Mr. Wardour and her was broken. But the shadow of her father's absence swallowed all the other shadows. The air of warmth and peace and conscious safety which had always surrounded her was gone, and in its place were cold, exposure, and annoyance. At the moment of her father's death, it became the design of John Turnbull that she should not be comfortable so long as she did not irrevocably cast her lot with his family. So long as they confined themselves to silence, neglect, and general exclusion, Mary heeded little their behavior; for no conversation with them, beyond that of shop business, could be more than indifferent to her. But when they advanced positive interference, her position became hard to endure. They would, for instance, keep watch on her serving, and as soon as a customer was gone, find open fault with something she had said or done. When they did this in the presence of the customer, she found it almost more than she could bear. She did her best, however, and for some time things went on without any symptom of approaching crisis.

But it was impossible for this quietude to continue, because

Mary was naturally quick-tempered. Although she recognized her imperative duty of controlling her temper, she was not yet perfect in it. When Turnbull would push his way past her behind the counter without other pretense of apology than something like a sneer, she felt as if evil were about to have the victory over her; and when Mrs. Turnbull came in, which happily was but seldom, she felt as if a demon sprang to meet her, for she behaved to her worst of all. The daughter of a country attorney who had not been too willing to accept a tradesman as a husband for his daughter, she bitterly cherished the feeling that she had married beneath her. She obstinately excluded the fact that she had descended to her husband's level, regarding herself much in the light of a princess whose occasional disguise takes nothing from her rank.

Mrs. Turnbull never bought a dress at the shop. She took pains to let her precious public know that she went to London to make her purchases. It was only for small occasional necessities that she ever crossed the threshold of the place whence came all the money she had to spend. When she did, she entered it with such airs as she imagined to represent her social position. (There is one show of breeding which vulgarity seldom displays—simplicity.) No sign of recognition would pass between her husband and herself—by her stern refusal to acknowledge his advances, she had from the very first taught him that in the shop they were strangers.

One day, a short time before her wedding—which had been delayed by the illness of Mr. Redmain—Miss Mortimer happened to be in the shop and was being served by Mary, when Mrs. Turnbull entered. Careless to the customer, she walked straight up to Mary as if she saw none, and in a tone that was haughty demanded that Mary bring her a reel of marking cotton. It had been a principle with Mary's father that however rude a customer might be, none must be shown to them. "If all are equal in the sight of God," he would say, "how dare I leave a poor woman to serve a rich one?" And Mary had learned it thoroughly.

"Excuse me, Ma'am," said Mary. "I am waiting on Miss Mortimer," and went on with what she was about. Mrs. Turnbull flounced away, a little abashed by finding who the customer was, and carried her commands across the shop. After a moment or two, imagining that Miss Mortimer had gone, whereas she had only moved a little farther on to look at something, she walked up to Mary in a fury.

"Miss Marston," she said, her voice half-choked with rage, "I am at a loss to understand what you mean by your impertinence."

"I am sorry you should think me impertinent," answered Mary. "You saw I was engaged with a customer and could not attend to you."

"Your tone was insufferable!" cried the grand lady, but before Mrs. Turnbull could continue, Miss Mortimer resumed her place in front of Mary. Hesper had no idea who this other customer was, and fearing the woman's accusation might do Mary wrong, felt compelled to interfere.

"Miss Marston," she said, "if you should be called to account by your employer, will you please refer him to me. You were perfectly civil both to me and to this—" she hesitated a perceptible moment, but ended with the word *'lady,'* peculiarly toned.

"Thank you, Ma'am," said Mary with a smile, "but it is of no consequence."

Mrs. Turnbull turned purple. She was so dumbfounded by Miss Mortimer's defense of Mary, which she looked on as an assault on herself, so painfully aware that all eyes were fixed on herself, and so mortified with the conviction that her husband was enjoying her discomfort that, with what haughtiness she could gather up, she made a sudden gyration and stalked out of the vile place.

George came up to Mary with an unpleasant look, intended to represent sympathy, and said confidentially, "What made my mother speak to you like that, Mary?"

"You must ask her yourself," she answered.

"There you go as usual, Mary!" he protested. "You will never let a fellow take your part."

"If you wanted to take my part, you should have done so when there would have been some good in it."

"How could I, before Miss Mortimer, you know?"

"Then why do it now?"

"Well, it's hard to bear hearing you ill-used! What did you say to Miss Mortimer that angered my mother?"

His father heard him, and taking the cue, called out in the rudest fashion, "Mary, if you think you can take such liberties with customers because you've got no one over you, the sooner you find you're mistaken, the better."

Mary made no answer.

On her way to the "villa," Mrs. Turnbull, spurred by spite, had got hold of the same idea as George, only that she invented where he had but imagined it—and when her husband came home in the evening fell out upon him for allowing Mary to be impertinent to his customers, in whom for the first time she condescended to show an interest.

"There she was, talking away to Miss Mortimer as if she was Beenie in the kitchen! Country people won't stand being treated as if one was just as good as another, I can tell you! She'll ruin the business, with her fine-lady airs. Who's *she*, I'd like to know!"

"I shall speak to her," said the husband. "But," he went on, "I fear you will no longer approve of marrying her to George, if you think she's an injury to the business!"

"You know as well as I do that that is the best way to get her out of it. Make her marry George and she will fall into my hands. If I don't make her repent her impudence then, you may call me the fool you think me."

Mary knew well enough what they wanted of her, but she had no suspicion of the real cause of their desire. She recoiled from Mr. Turnbull's business theories, but she did not doubt his honesty as the trades and professions count honesty. John Turnbull was not only proud of his reputation for honesty, but prided himself on being an honest man. Her father had always left the money affairs of the firm to Mr. Turnbull, and she did the same. Her position had become almost intolerable, and she now began to wonder if it might be possible to leave the shop.

Yet after this things went a little more quietly. Turnbull even took some pains to be polite, as if to make amends for past rudeness. This only rendered him odious in the eyes of Mary, and ripened her desire to free herself from the shop work. However, she was too much her father's daughter to do anything in haste.

Had she had any friends likeminded with herself, she might have been less inclined to leave. While former associates of her father were all kindly disposed to her, those who did not know her well did not approve of her. They generally spoke of her with a shake of the head, and an unquestioned feeling that God was not pleased with her. But she had her Bible, and when she was troubled, she had the Eternal Wisdom to cry and search for. One of the things she learned was that she could believe in the Living God in whom is no darkness, and who alone can give light to understand His own intent. All her troubles she carried to Him.

Letty was not a good correspondent; after one letter in which she declared herself perfectly happy, and another in which she said almost nothing, her communication ceased. Mrs. Wardour had been in the shop regularly, and had always sought the service of one of the Turnbulls. While Letty was in her house she had been civil; but as soon as she was gone, Mrs. Wardour seemed to show that she held Mary accountable for the scandal that had befallen Thornwick.

Once Mary met Godfrey. He was walking hurriedly as usual, with bent head and gloomy gaze fixed on nothing visible. He started when he saw her, took off his hat, and with his eyes seeing right through her, passed without a word. Mary had been a true pupil to Godfrey, for although neither of them knew it, she had learned more from him than Godfrey was capable of teaching. She had turned thought and feeling into life, into reality, into creation.

If Godfrey could have looked into Mary's soul, he would have seen what God made the earth for; but all he saw was a shopgirl to whom in happier circumstances he had shown kindness, in whom he was now no longer interested. But the sight of his troubled face called up all the mother in Mary, and a rush of tenderness born of gratitude flooded her heart. He was sad and she could do nothing to comfort him! He had been royally good to her, and no return was in her power. She could not even let him know how she had profited by his gifts. The bond between them was an eternal one, yet they were separated by a gulf of unrelation. Not a mountain range but a stayless nothingness parted them. She built many a castle with walls of gratitude and floors of service for Godfrey Wardour, but they stood on no foundation of imagined possibility.

17.
The Wedding
Dress

But Mary also had her pleasures. It was a delight to receive
the friendly greetings of those who had known her father;
and she had the pleasure of pure service, the joy of the
work that was given her to do. She gathered also the pleasure of
seeing and talking with people whose manners and speech were of
finer grain and tone than those about her.

When Hesper Mortimer entered the shop, she brought with her
delight. Her smile was light and her whole presence an enchantment to Mary. Hesper would be waited on by no other than Mary,
and always between them passed some gentle nothings, which
afforded Hesper more pleasure than she could have accounted for.

Her wedding day was now set for the third time. One morning
she entered the shop to make some purchases. Although the prospect before her was not a happy one, she was inclined to make the
best of it so far as clothes were concerned. She was now brooding
over a certain idea for her wedding dress, which she had not been
able to convey to her London dressmaker. She thought perhaps
Mary might grasp her idea and help her make it intelligible.

Mary listened, thought, and questioned, and at length begged
Hesper to allow her to ponder the thing a little—she could hardly
at once venture to say anything. Hesper laughed and said she was
taking the small matter too seriously.

"A small matter? Your wedding dress?" exclaimed Mary.

Hesper did not laugh again, but gave a little sigh instead, which
struck sadly on Mary's sympathetic heart and showed on her face.

Hesper caught the look and understood it. For one passing moment she felt as if, amidst the poor pleasure of adorning herself for a hated marriage, she had found a precious thing of which she had once or twice dreamed, but never thought as possible—a friend to love her. Then she saw the absurdity of imagining a friend in a shopgirl.

"I must make up my mind so soon!" she answered. "Madame Crepine gave me her ideas, but nothing I liked. I must write again soon—I fear she may be taking it her own way, and I am certain to hate it."

"I will talk to you about it this evening, if that will do," returned Mary. She knew nothing about dressmaking beyond what came of her simple taste, and the experience gained in cutting out and making her own garments. Hesper had been led to ask her advice mainly from observing the neat design and fit of her dresses.

"Thank you a thousand times," she drawled sweetly. "Then I shall expect you. Ask for my maid. She will take you to my room. Good-bye for the present."

As soon as she was gone, Mary's mind was on Hesper's figure and her style, as she gave herself to the important question of the dress conceived by Hesper; and during her dinner hour she cut out what she supposed to be the pattern Hesper had described.

When she was free, she set out for Durnmelling. It was a long walk, the earliest part of it full of sad reminders of the pleasure with which she had gone to pay her Sunday visits at Thornwick. But the last part, although the places were so near, was almost new to her. She had never been within the gate of Durnmelling, and was curious to see the house of which she had so often heard.

The butler opened the door. An elderly man of conscious dignity rather than pride, he received her graciously; and leaving her in the entrance hall, he went to find Miss Mortimer's maid.

The few moments Mary had to wait far more than repaid her for the trouble she had taken. Through a side door she looked into the great roofless hall, the one grand thing about the house. Its majesty laid hold upon her, and the shopkeeper's daughter felt the power of the ancient dignity and ineffaceable beauty, far more than had any of the family to which it had for centuries belonged.

She was standing lost in delight when a rude voice called to her from halfway up a stair. "You're to come this way, Miss."

With a start, she turned and went, and was led to a large room. There was no one in it, and she walked to an open window which had a wide outlook across the fields. A little to the right, over some trees, were the chimneys of Thornwick. They were so near and yet so far, like the memory of a sweet, sad story. The day had been fine and warm, and the evening was dewy and soft, and full of evasive odor. The window looked westward, and the setting sun threw long shadows toward the house. A gentle wind was moving in the treetops, and the spirit of the evening had laid hold of Mary. The day's business vanished in the rest of the coming night.

"Do you like my prospect?" asked the voice of Hesper behind her. "It is flat."

"Yes, I like it, Miss Mortimer," answered Mary, turning quickly with a bright face. "Flatness has its own beauty. I sometimes feel as if space was all I wanted, and of that there is so much here! You see over the treetops too, and that is good sometimes, don't you think?"

Miss Mortimer gave no reply other than a gentle stare which expressed no curiosity, although she had a vague feeling that Mary's words must mean something. Most girls of her class would hardly have got so far.

"This view reminds me of some beautiful poetry," sighed Mary.

"Are you fond of poetry?" drawled Hesper, not really caring.

"Yes," answered Mary, who was beginning to feel like a child questioned by a stranger in the road, "when it is good," she added hesitantly.

"What do you mean by good?" asked Hesper, not out of her knowledge, Mary thought; but it was not even out of ignorance, only out of indifference. People must say something, lest life should stop.

"That is a difficult question to answer," replied Mary. "I have often asked it of myself, but have never got a plain answer."

"I do not see why you should find any difficulty in it," returned Hesper with a shadow of interest. "You know what you mean when you say to yourself you like this or you do not like that."

"How clever she is too," thought Mary. But she answered, "I don't think I ever say anything to myself about the poetry I read— not at the time. If I like it, it drowns me, and if I don't like it, it is as the Dead Sea to me, in which I know I can't sink, if I try ever so hard." Hesper saw nothing in the words, and began to fear that

Mary was so stupid as to imagine herself clever, whereupon the fancy she had taken to her began to sink like water in sand. The two were still on their feet—Mary in her bonnet with her back to the window, and Hesper in evening attire with her face to the sunset, so that the one was like a darkling worshiper, the other like a radiant goddess. But the truth was that Hesper was a mere earthly woman, and Mary a heavenly messenger to her. Neither of them knew it, but so it was; for the angels are essentially humble, and Hesper would have been condescending to any angel out of her own class.

"I think I know good poetry by what it does to me," resumed Mary thoughtfully, just as Hesper was about to pass to the business of the visit.

"Indeed!" rejoined Hesper, no less puzzled than before. Poetry had never done anything to her.

The tone of her "Indeed" checked Mary. She hesitated a moment, but went on. "Sometimes it makes me feel as if my heart were too big for my body—as if all the grand things in heaven and earth were trying to get into me at once, or as if I had discovered something nobody else knew, and then I must go to God and pray. But I am trying to tell you what I don't know how to tell. Here, I will show you what I have been doing about your dress."

Mary took from her pocket the shape she had prepared, put it on herself, and slowly revolved before Hesper, revealing a masterpiece.

"But how clever of you!" she cried. Her own fingers had not been quite innocent of the labor of the needle, for money had long been scarce at Durnmelling, and in the paper shape she recognized the hand of an artist. "Why," she continued, "you are nothing less than an accomplished dressmaker!"

"That I dare not think myself," returned Mary, "seeing I never had a lesson."

"I wish you would make my wedding dress," said Hesper.

"I could not venture, even if I had the time," answered Mary. "The moment I began cutting, I should be terrified and lose my self-confidence. I never made a dress for anybody but myself." She was busy pinning and unpinning, shifting and pinning again the pattern, when suddenly Hesper spoke.

"I suppose you know I am going to marry money?"

"Oh, don't say that. It's too dreadful!" cried Mary, stopping her work, and looking up in Hesper's face.

"What! Did you suppose I was going to marry a man like Mr. Redmain for love?" rejoined Hesper, with a hard laugh. "It's very horrid, I know, but where's the good of mincing matters? Calling the thing by another name would not change it. You know people in our world have to do as they must—they can't pick and choose like you happy creatures. I daresay, now, you are engaged to a young man you love with all your heart, one you would rather marry than any other in the whole universe."

"Oh, dear, no!" returned Mary. "I am not engaged, nor in the least likely to be."

"So you're not in love, either?" said Hesper, with such coolness that Mary looked up in her face to know if she had really said so.

"No," she replied.

"No more am I," echoed Hesper. "That is the one good thing in the business—I shan't break my heart, as some girls do. It is bad enough to marry a man—that one can't avoid—but to die of a broken heart is to be a traitor to your sex. As if women couldn't live without men!"

Mary smiled and was silent. She had read a good deal, and thought she understood such things better than Miss Mortimer. But she caught herself smiling, and felt as if she had sinned. That a young woman should speak of love and marriage as Miss Mortimer did was too horrible to be understood! She would have been less shocked with Hesper had she known that her indifference was forced; from her heart Mary pitied her, almost as one of the lost.

"Don't look at me like that," said Hesper angrily, "or I shall cry. Look the other way, and listen. I am marrying money, I tell you, and *for* money; therefore, I ought to get the good of it. Mr. Mortimer will be father enough to see to that! So I shall be able to do what I please. I find myself taken with you, so why shouldn't I have you for my—"

She paused. She had been going to say *maid*, but something checked her. In very truth Mary Marston was already immeasurably more of a lady than Hesper Mortimer was ever likely to be in this world. What was the stateliness and pride of the one compared to the fact that the other would have died in the workhouse or the street rather than let a man she did not love embrace her? To be a martyr to a lie is but false ladyhood. She only is a lady who witnesses to the truth, come of it what may.

"—for my—my companion, or something of the sort," concluded Hesper, "and then I should be sure of being always dressed to
my mind."

"That *would* be nice!" responded Mary, thinking only of the
kindness in the speech.

"Would you really like it?" asked Hesper, in her turn pleased.

"I should like it very much," replied Mary, not imagining the
idea had any shadow of seriousness. "I wish it were possible."

"Why not then? Why shouldn't it be possible? I don't suppose
you would mind using your needle a little?"

"Not in the least," answered Mary, amused. "Only what would
they do in the shop without me?"

"They could get someone else, couldn't they?"

"Hardly to take my place. My father was Mr. Turnbull's
partner."

"Oh!" said Hesper. "I thought you only had to give notice."

The matter was dropped and Mary thought no more about it.

"You will let me keep this pattern?" said Hesper.

"It was made for you," answered Mary.

While Hesper was lazily thinking whether that meant she was to
pay for it, Mary made her a pretty curtsy and said good-night.
Hesper returned her adieu kindly, but did not ring the bell to have
her shown out. Mary found her own way, and was presently
breathing the fresh air of the twilight fields on her way home to
her piano and her books.

For some time after she was gone, Hesper was preoccupied with
her plans for her dress, but Mary kept coming to her mind. There
was nothing very striking about her, but when one had been with
her for only a short time, the charm of her individuality could not
be forgotten. The very stillness of any quiet moment was enough
to bring back the sweetness of Mary's gentle presence.

Not only had Hesper Mortimer never had a friend worthy of the
name, but no idea of pure friendship had as yet been generated in
her. Sepia was the nearest to an intimate friend—in her fits of
misery, Hesper had no one else to go to. Hesper did not think of
Mary's position as low; she did not even think about it in relation
to any life in which she was interested. She saw no difference of
level between Mary and the lawyer who came about her marriage
settlements. They were both beyond her social horizon.

Hesper's day drew on. She had many things to think about,

things very different from any that concerned Mary Marston. She was married, found life in London somewhat absorbing, and forgot Mary.

18.
Mr. and Mrs. Redmain

It is a great thing to come of decent people. Ferdinand Goldberg Redmain was the son of an intellectually gifted laborer who rose in his business to be boss. He began to take portions of contracts, and through one lucky venture after another, arrived at having his estimate accepted and the contract given to him for a rather large affair. Through his minute knowledge of details, his faculty for getting work out of his laborers, a toughness of heart, and the judicious use of inferior material, the contract paid him much too well for any good to come out of it. From that time, his life was a continuous course of what he called success, and he died one of the richest men of that time, bequeathing great wealth to his son, and leaving a reputation for substantial worth behind him. Often he had been held up by teachers as a pattern to aspiring youth of what might be achieved. Yet, he had been guilty of a thousand meannesses, oppressions, rapacities, and some quiet rogueries; and with his money he left to his son the seeds of a great unwillingness to part with money.

In spite of great wealth, the son had much against his father. His mother died while he was yet a mere child, and his father had married again. The boy was sent to a certain public school, which at the time was simply a hotbed of the lowest vices, and in devil-matters Redmain was an apt pupil.

The younger Mr. Redmain had no profession, and knew nothing of business beyond what was necessary for doing well with his money. He was approaching the end of middle age; and as

104

horrible as was the inevitability of death, it had not yet looked frightful enough to arrest his downward rush. When in tolerable health, he laughed at the notion of such a place as hell, repudiating its very existence; calling in all the arguments urged by good men against the idea of an eternity of aimless suffering, he used them against the idea of any punishment after death. Though he himself was a bad man, he reasoned that God was too good to punish sin. Though he was a proud man, he reasoned that God was too high to take heed of him. He forgot the best argument—that the punishment he had had in this life had done him no good, and he would have been glad to argue that none would, and therefore none would be tried.

There was no grace in him when he was ill, nor at any time, beyond a certain cold grace of manner, which he kept for ceremony, or where he wanted to please. Much of his character was known to his associates, for he was no hypocrite, and Hesper's father knew it perfectly, and was therefore worse than he. Had Redmain had a daughter, he would never have given her to a man like himself.

No one knew better than he that not an atom of love had mingled with Hesper's motives in marrying him; but for a time he seemed bent on showing her that she need not have been so averse to him. Whether or not this was indeed his design, he enjoyed the admiration she roused; for why shouldn't a man take pride in the possession of a fine woman as well as in that of a fine horse? At first he accompanied his wife everywhere. She was a pleasant break in the gathering monotony of his existence. As he got more accustomed to the sight of her in a crowd, however, and to her not-very-interesting company in private, and when she took not the smallest pains to please him, he gradually lapsed into his former ways, and soon came to spend his evenings in company that made him forget his wife. He had loved her in a sort of a way, and had also hated her a little; for, following her cousin's advice, she had appealed to him to save her, and when he evaded her request, had addressed him in terms too forcible to be forgotten. Hesper proved a worthy antagonist in their encounters of the polite society at their residence Billingsgate—what she lacked in experience she made up in breeding. When Redmain had been longer than usual without seeing his wife, he said the worst things to her, as if spite had grown in absence.

But Redmain did have a strong sense of justice, and if he exercised it but little in some of the relations of his life, he was nonetheless keenly alive to his own claims on its score, for chiefly he cried out for fair play on behalf of those who were wicked in similar fashion to himself. Such was the man to whom Mortimer had sold his daughter. Such was the man whom Hesper—entirely aware that none could compel her to marry against her will—had, partly from fear of her parents, partly from moral laziness, vowed to love, honor, and obey! But she did not and could not know of him what her father knew.

In the autumn the Redmains went to Durnmelling. Even though there was nothing in her heart recognizable to herself as love to her father or mother, she always behaved to them with perfect propriety.

Lady Margaret saw great improvement in her daughter. To the maternal eye, jealous for perfection, Hesper's carriage was at length satisfactory. It was cold, it was haughty, and even repellent, but by no means repulsive to the mother's eye. "Marriage has done everything for her!" said Lady Malice to herself with a dignified chuckle, and dismissed the last shadowy remnant of maternal regret for her part in the transaction of her marriage. She never saw herself in the wrong, and never gave herself the least trouble to be in the right. Of her own worth she had never had a doubt. How was she to generate doubt when, wherever she went, she was admired both for her own beauty and her husband's wealth?

To her father, Hesper was as stiff and proud as if she had been a maiden aunt bent on destroying whatever expectations he might be cherishing. He had done her all the ill he could, and by his own deed she was beyond his reach. Her husband was again out of health—certain attacks to which he was subject were coming more frequently. Hesper did not offer many prayers for his restoration; indeed, she never prayed for anything she desired. While he and she occupied separate rooms, the one solitary thing she now regarded as a privilege, how *could* she pray for his recovery?

Contrary to Mr. Redmain's unexpressed desire, Miss Yolland had been installed as Hesper's companion. Her only goal was to get from the moment the greatest possible enjoyment that would leave the way clear for more to follow. She had not been in his house a week before Mr. Redmain hated her.

Every time Mr. Redmain had an attack, the baldness on the top of his head widened, and the skin of his face tightened. His long arms looked longer, his formerly flat back rounded a little more, and his temper grew even more spiteful. From the moment he arrived ill at Durnmelling, Lady Malice, regardless of the brusqueness with which he treated her, devoted herself to him with an attention she had never shown for her husband, as if she must teach her daughter the duties of a married woman. She was the only one who showed any affection for him, and the only one of the family for whom he came to show the least consideration. At times, he almost stood in awe of her. Every night, after his man Mewkes was gone, she would visit him to see that he was comfortable, would tuck him up as a mother might have done, and satisfy herself that the night-light was shaded from his eyes. Perhaps the part in him which had never had the opportunity of behaving ill to his mother remained, in middle age and illness, capable of receiving kindness. Hesper saw the relation between them, but without the least pleasure or curiosity.

Partly out of consideration to Mr. Redmain, the Mortimers had scarcely a visitor, for he would not come out of his room when he knew there was a stranger in the house. Fond of a certain kind of company when he was well, he could not endure an unknown face when he was ill. He told Lady Malice that at such times a stranger always looked a devil to him. So the time was dull for everybody, and it was no wonder that Hesper, after a fortnight of it, should think once more of the young woman in the draper's shop at Testbridge. So one morning she ordered her broughham and drove to town.

19.
The Menial

T hings had not been going any better with Mary, though there was now more lull and less storm around her. The position was becoming less and less endurable to her, but she had as yet no glimmer of a way out. A breath of genial air never blew in the shop, except when this and that customer entered. Her father's dull old chapel had grown dear to Mary. Not that she learned anything more to her mind, or that she paid any more attention to what was said, but that the memory of her father filled the chapel, and when the Bible was read, or some favorite hymn sung, he actually seemed to be present.

When Hesper entered the shop this morning she was disappointed to see Mary so much changed. But when, at the sight of Hesper holding out her hand to her, Mary's pale face brightened, and a faint rosy flush spread from brow to chin, Mary was herself again as Hesper had known her.

"O Ma'am, I am so glad to see you!" exclaimed Mary, forgetting her manners.

"I too am glad," drawled Hesper, genuinely, though with condescension. "I hope you are well. I cannot say you look so."

"I am pretty well, thank you, Ma'am," answered Mary, flushing afresh. Not much anxiety was expressed about her health now, except by Beenie who mourned over the loss of her plumpness, and told her if she didn't eat well she would soon follow her poor father.

"Come and have a drive with me," said Hesper, moved by a

sudden impulse. "It will do you good," she went on. "You are indoors too much, and the ceiling is so low," she added, looking up.

"It is very kind of you," replied Mary, and hesitating added, "but I don't think . . . well . . . " She looked around as she spoke. "If you really wish it Ma'am, I will venture to go out for half an hour."

"Do then. I am sure you will eat a better dinner for it."

"I shall be ready in two minutes," said Mary, and ran from the shop.

She told Mr. Turnbull where she was going, and instead of answering her, he turned himself toward Mrs. Redmain, and went through a series of bows and smiles which she did not choose to see. She turned and walked from the shop, got into the broughham, and made room for Mary at her side.

Although the drive was lovely, and the view from either window delightful, Mary saw little of the country on any side, so much occupied was she with Hesper.

Mary had told her something of her miserable relations with the Turnbulls, and as they returned Hesper actually proposed that she should give up business and live with her.

Nor was this as ridiculous an idea as it may at first have appeared. It arose from what was almost the first movement in the direction of genuine friendship Hesper had ever felt. Hesper had been acquainted with a good many young ladies, but acquaintance is not friendship. Some would scorn the idea of friendship with one such as Mary. Hesper was capable of scorn, yet she felt no horror at the new motion of her heart. But she did not recognize it as friendship, and had she suspected Mary of regarding their possible relation in that light, she would have dismissed her with pride, and perhaps contempt. Mary had begun to draw out the love in her; and, being a young woman with an absolute genius for dressmaking, she would be very handy to have around. No more would Hesper have to send for the dressmaker on every small necessity!

But nothing was clear in her mind as to the position she would have Mary occupy. She had a vague feeling that one like her ought not to be expected to undertake things befitting such women as her maid Folter.

"Come and live with me, Miss Marston," said Hesper, but it was with a laugh, and that light touch of the tongue which suggests but a flying fancy spoken but for the sake of the preposterous. Mary, not forgetting she had heard the same thing once before, listened with a smile; but Hesper ventured a little more seriousness.

"I should never ask you to do anything you would not like," she said.

"I don't think you could," answered Mary. "There are more things I should like to do for you than you would think to ask. In fact," she added, looking round with a loving smile, "I don't know what I shouldn't like to do for you."

"My meaning was that I should never ask you to do anything menial," explained Hesper, venturing a little further still, and now speaking in a tone perfectly matter-of-fact.

"I don't know what you mean by *menial*," returned Mary.

"Oh, I mean things like—like—cleaning one's shoes, don't you know, or brushing one's hair."

Mary burst out laughing. "Let me come to you tomorrow morning," she said, "and I will brush your hair so that you will *want* me to come again the next day. You beautiful creature! Whose hands would not be honored to handle such lovely stuff as that?" As she spoke, she took in her fingers a little stray drift from the masses of golden twilight that crowned one of the loveliest temples in which the Holy Ghost had not yet come to dwell.

"If cleaning your shoes be menial, then brushing your hair must be royal," Mary added.

Hesper's heart was touched. "Do you really mean," she said, "you would not mind doing such things for me?" She laughed again, afraid of showing herself too much in earnest before she was sure of Mary.

"I would no more mind cleaning your boots than my own," said Mary. "I heard my father once say that to look down on those who have to do such things may be to despise them for just the one honorable thing about them. Shall I tell you what I understand by the word *menial*?"

"Do tell me," answered Hesper with careless permission.

"I did not find it out myself," said Mary. "My father taught me. He was a wise man. He said that it is menial to undertake anything you think beneath you, for the sake of money, and still more menial, having undertaken it, not to do it as well as possible.

"I've taken my father's shoes out of Beenie's hands many a

time," continued Mary, "and finished them myself, just for the pleasure of making them shine for *him*."

"Re-a-ally!" drawled Hesper, and set out for the conclusion that after all it was no great compliment the young woman had paid her in wanting to brush her hair. Evidently she had a taste for low things! But the light in Mary's eye checked her.

"Any service done without love, whatever it be," resumed Mary, "is slavery, neither more nor less. It cannot be anything else. So you see, slaves are made slaves by themselves, and that is what makes me doubtful whether I ought to go on serving in the shop. As far as the Turnbulls are concerned, I have no pleasure in it. I am only helping them make money."

"Why not give it up at once, then?" asked Hesper.

"Because I like serving my customers. They were my father's customers, and I have learned so much from having to wait on them."

"Well, now," said Hesper, with a rush for the goal, "if you will come to me, I will make you comfortable, and you shall do just as much or as little as you please."

"What will your maid think?" suggested Mary. "If I am to do what I please, she will soon find me trespassing on her domain. It might hurt her, you know, to be paid to do a thing and then not allowed to do it."

"Then she may leave. I had not thought of parting with her, but I should not be at all sorry if she went. She would be no loss to me."

"Why should you keep her, then?"

"Because she knows my ways, and I prefer not having to break in a new one. It is a bore to have to say how you like everything done." Hesper's tone was one of business, and the more she talked, the more she seemed to be playing with the proposal.

"Do you really mean you want me to come and live with you?" said Mary, waking to the fact that Hesper was serious.

"Indeed, I do," answered Hesper emphatically. "You shall have a room close to my bedroom, and there you shall do as you like all day long, and when I want you, you'll be right there for me."

"Good enough," said Mary cheerily, as if all was settled. In contrast with her present surroundings, the prospect was more than attractive. "But, would you let me have my piano?" she asked with sudden apprehension.

111

"You shall have my grand piano always when I am out, which will be every night in the season, I am sure. That will give you plenty of practice, and you will be able to have the best of lessons. And think of the concerts and oratorios you will go to!"

Before they stopped again at the shop door, the two young women were nearer being friends than Hesper had ever before been with anyone. The sleepy heart in her was not yet dead, but capable still of the pleasure of showing sweet condescension and gentle patronage to one who admired her. To herself she justified her kindness to Mary with the thought that the young woman deserved encouragement because she was so anxious to improve herself. The carriage drew up at the door of the shop, and Mary took her leave. Hesper returned her good-bye kindly.

As Mary entered the dim shop, it seemed as though everything about it had altered in its aspect to her. The very air she breathed in it seemed slavish. The whole thing was growing more sordid, for the work had become a drudgery to her. The proposal of Mrs. Redmain stood in advantageous contrast to this treadmill work. In Hesper's house Mary would be called only to the ministrations of love, and would have plenty of time for books and music. All the slavery lay in the shop, all the freedom in the personal service.

The chief attraction to her was simply Hesper herself. It was not merely that she saw Hesper as a grand creature, lovely to look upon; Mary also saw in her someone she could help, for it seemed that Hesper knew nothing of what made life worth living. She would be Hesper's servant so that she might gain Hesper.

Mary was simply a young woman who believed that the Man called Jesus Christ is a real Person, and that He is a Servant of all. Therefore, to regard any honest service as degrading would be to deny Christ, to call His life a disgrace.

The very next morning Hesper entered the shop and, to the surprise and annoyance of the master there, was taken by Mary through the counter and into the house. "What a false impression," thought the great man, "will it give of the way *we* live, to see the Marstons' shabby parlor in a warehouse!"

Before they came out, Mary had accepted a position in Mrs. Redmain's house. Mary judged Mr. Turnbull would be too glad to get rid of her to mind how brief the notice she gave him, and she would rather not undergo the remarks that were sure to be made in contempt of her scheme. She counted it only fair, however, to let him know that she intended giving up her place behind the counter, hinting that, as she meant to leave when it suited her, without further warning, it would be well to look out for one to take her place.

As to her money in the business, she scarcely thought of it, and said nothing about it, believing it as safe as in the bank. For she had not yet learned to think of Mr. Turnbull as a dishonest man, only as a greedy one, and she supposed the money was still there, as it had been ever.

Mr. Turnbull was so astonished by her announcement that, not seeing at once how the change was likely to affect him, he held his peace, with the cunning pretense that his silence arose from anger. His first feeling was of pleasure, but the man of business must take care how he shows himself pleased. After some time of reflection, he supposed it was the very best thing, for it would be easy to get George a wife more suitable to the position of the family than a canting dissenter, and her money would be in their hands all the same.

After three days of silence toward her, Mr. Turnbull, his curiosity getting the better of him, asked Mary's further intentions. In her straightforward manner, she told him she preferred not to speak of them at present, and he supposed she was looking for a place in another shop.

She asked him one day whether or not he had found a person to take her place.

"Time enough for that," he answered. "You're not gone yet."

"As you please, Mr. Turnbull," said Mary, "but I should be sorry to leave you without sufficient help in the shop."

"And I should be sorry," rejoined Turnbull, "that Miss Marston should fancy herself indispensable to the business she turned her back upon."

From that moment, the restraint he had shown for the last week or two broke, and he never spoke to her except with such rudeness that she no longer ventured to address him even on shop business. George followed the example of his father, and when, in November, a letter from Hesper heralded the hour of her deliverance, she merely told Turnbull one evening as he left the shop, that she would not be there in the morning. Mary left Testbridge before the shop opened the next day.

20.
Mrs. Redmain's Drawing Room

I t was about eleven o'clock on a November morning that felt more like March. There might be a thick fog before the evening, but now the sun was shining. Between the cold sun and the hard earth, a dust-befogged wind was sweeping the street.

Mr. and Mrs. Redmain had returned to town early because their country place in Cornwall was too far from Mr. Redmain's physician. He was now considerably better and had begun to go about again, for the weather did not yet affect him much. He was in his study where he generally had his breakfast alone. Mrs. Redmain always had hers in bed, as often as she could with a new novel; but now she was descending the staircase, straight as a Greek goddess and about as cold as the marble. She entered the drawing room with a slow, careless, yet stately step, walked to the chimney, seated herself in a low soft shiny chair almost on the hearth rug, and gazed listlessly into the fire.

Hesper's low moods were far more frequent than usual for someone of her years, health, or temperament. The fire grew hot, and thinking of her complexion, Hesper pushed back her chair, rose, and reached for the screen from the chimney piece, and was fanning herself when the door opened and a servant asked if she were home to a Mr. Helmer. She hesitated a moment—what an unearthly hour for a caller!

"Show him up," she answered. Anything was better than her own company.

Tom Helmer was much the same but a little paler and thinner.

He approached Hesper with a certain loose grace natural to him, and seated himself on the chair to which she motioned him.

Tom was well dressed, and he carried himself well. To the natural confidence of his shallow character was added the assurance born of a certain small degree of success in his profession.

"I have taken the liberty," he continued, "of bringing you the song I had the pleasure—a greater pleasure than you will readily imagine—of hearing you admire the other evening."

"I forget," said Hesper.

Tom had been brought to a small party at the Redmain house a few evenings before by a well-known leader of a literary clique who, in return for homage, frequently took aspiring young writers under his wing. Tom was ambitious of making himself acceptable to ladies of social influence. At the gathering, a certain song had been sung by a lady (not without previous maneuvers on the part of Tom) with which Mrs. Redmain had languidly expressed herself pleased. Appreciation was the hunger of Tom's life, and here was a chance! Now he was in Mrs. Redmain's drawing room with the opportunity of revealing the character of the genius who penned the verses.

"I would not have ventured," said Tom, "had it not happened that both air and words were my own."

"Indeed! I did not know you were a poet, Mr.—" She had forgotten his name. "And a musician too?" she hastily added.

"At your service, Mrs. Redmain."

"I don't happen to want a poet at present, or a musician either," she said, with just enough of a smile to turn the rudeness into what Tom accepted as a flattering familiarity.

"Nor am I in want of a place," he replied with spirit. "Will you allow me to recite the verses, and then sing this song for you?"

Mrs. Redmain was amused with the young man—he was not just like every other who came to the house.

Tom laid himself back a little in his chair, with the sheet of music in his hand, closed his eyes, and repeated his verses by heart, and a gleam as from some far-off mirror of admiration did certainly, to Tom's great satisfaction, appear on Hesper's countenance.

"Can you make a song to any pattern you please?" she asked when he had finished.

"I fancy so," answered Tom indifferently, as if it were nothing

115

to him to do whatever he chose to attempt. And, in fact, he could imitate almost anything, and well too.

"How clever you must be!" drawled Hesper, and the words were pleasant in the ears of Tom. He rose, opened the piano, and began to accompany a sweet tenor voice in the song he had just recited.

The door opened and Mr. Redmain came in. He glanced at Tom as he sang, and went up to his wife where she sat listening, with her face to the fire and her back to the piano.

"New singing master?" he said.

"No," answered his wife in the tone of one bored by question. "He used to come to Durnmelling—I forget his name."

The moment Tom struck the last chord, she called to him in a clear, cold voice. "Will you tell Mr. Redmain your name? I have forgotten it."

Tom picked up his hat, rose, came forward, and, mentioning his name, held out his hand to Mr. Redmain.

"Mr. Aylmer is an old acquaintance of our family," said his wife.

"Only you don't quite remember his name!"

"It is not my friends' names only I have an unhappy trick of forgetting. I often forget yours, Mr. Redmain!"

"My good name, you must mean."

"I never heard of that."

Neither had raised their voice, or spoken with the least apparent anger. Mr. Redmain gave a grin instead of a retort, and turning away, left the room with a quick, steady step.

The moment he disappeared, Tom's gaze sought Hesper's face. Her lips were shaping the word *brute*. Her eyes were flashing, and her face was flushed.

Tom hastened to say something foolish, imagining he had looked upon the sorrows of a lovely and unhappy wife and was almost in her confidence, when Sepia entered the room with a dark glow of dusky radiance at sight of the handsome Tom. She remembered having seen him at the merrymaking in the old hall of Durnmelling.

Hesper introduced them, and in another minute they were sitting together in a bay window, while Hesper, never heeding them, kept her place by the chimney and transferred her gaze from the fire to the novel she had sent for from her bedroom.

116

21.
Mary's
Reception

That afternoon Mary arrived in London. Cold seemed to have taken to itself a visible form in the thin gray fog that filled the huge train station from the platform to its glass roof. It was a mist, rather than a proper November fog, but every breath breathed by every porter, as he ran along by the side of the slowly halting train, was adding to its mass, which seemed to Mary to grow in bulk and density as she gazed. Her quiet, simple manner at once secured her some attention, and she was among the first who had their boxes on cabs and were driving away from the busy station.

The drive seemed interminable, and she had grown anxious and again calmed herself many times before it came to an end. The house at which the cab drew up was large, and looked as dreary as large, but scarcely drearier than any other house in London that night. The cabman rang the bell, but it was not until they had waited an unreasonably long time that the door opened and a lofty, well-built footman in livery appeared framed in it.

Mary got out and, going up the steps, said she hoped the driver had brought her to the right house—it was Mrs. Redmain's she wanted.

"Mrs. Redmain is not at 'ome, Miss," answered the man. "I didn't 'ear that she was expectin' anyone," he added, with a glance at the boxes visible on the cab through the thick darkness.

"She is expecting me, I know," returned Mary, "but, of course, she would not stay home to receive me."

"Oh!" returned the man, in a peculiar tone. Then adding, "I'll see," he went away, leaving her on the top of the steps, with the cabman behind her waiting orders to get her boxes down.

"It don't appear as you was overwelcome, Miss!" he remarked. "Leastaways, it don't seem as your sheets was quite done hairing."

"It's all right," said Mary cheerfully. She was not ready to imagine her dignity in danger; therefore, she did not provoke assault upon it by anxiety for its safety.

"I'm sorry to hear it, Miss," the man rejoined.

"Why?" she asked.

"'Cause I should ha' liked to ha' taken *you* farther. It gives a poor man with a whole family o' prowocations some'at of a chance, to 'ave a affable young lady like you, Miss, behind 'im in his cab, once a year, or thereabouts. Yet, if you're sure o' the place, I may as well be a gettin' down of your boxes."

So saying, he got on the cab, and proceeded to unfasten the chain that secured the luggage.

"Wait a bit, Cabbie," cried the footman, reappearing at the door. "Don't be in such a 'urry as if you was a 'ansom, now. I should be sorry if there was a mistake, and you wasn't man enough to put your boxes up again without assistance." Then turning to Mary, "Mrs. Perkin says—that's the 'ousekeeper, Miss—that, if as you're the young woman from the country, Mrs. Redmain did make mention of you, but didn't give any instructions. But as there you are," he continued more familiarly, gathering courage from Mary's nodded assent, "you can put your boxes in the 'all and sit down, she says, till Mrs. Redmain comes 'ome. She's seein' a new play—they call it *Doomsday*, an' there's no tellin' when parties is likely to come 'ome from that," he said with a grin of satisfaction at his own wit.

"'ere, mister! Gi' me a 'and wi' this 'ere luggage," cried the cabman, finding the box he was getting down too much for him. "Yah wouldn't see me break my back, an' my poor 'orse standin' there a lookin' on, would ye now?"

"Why don't you bring a man with you?" objected the footman as he descended the steps to give the required help. "I ain't paid as a crane—by Jupiter! What a weight this box is!"

"Only that one," said Mary apologetically. "It is full of books. The other is not half so heavy."

With that the book box came down on the pavement with a

great bump, and presently both were in the hall, the one on top of the other. Mary paid the cabman, and he departed with thanks. The facetious footman closed the door, told her to take a seat, and went away full of laughter to report to Mrs. Perkin that the young person had brought a large library with her to enliven the dullness of her new situation.

Mrs. Perkin smiled crookedly, and in a tone of pleasant reproof desired her laughing inferior not to forget his manners.

"Please, Ma'am, am I to leave the young woman sittin' up there all by 'erself in the cold?" he asked, straightening himself up. "She do look a rather superior sort of young person," he added, "and the 'all stove is out dead."

"For the present, Castle, yes," replied Mrs. Perkin. She judged it wise to let the young woman have a lesson at once in subjection and inferiority.

Mrs. Perkin was rather tall and thin, with a very dark complexion. She always threw her head back on one side, and her chin out on the other when she spoke, and had an authoritative manner which she mingled with some consideration toward her subordinates, so as to secure their obedience to *her*, while *she* cultivated antagonism to her mistress. She had had a better education than most persons of her class, but morally she was not an atom their superior in consequence. She never went into a new place without feeling that she was of more importance by far than her untried mistress, and the worthier person of the two.

She had not been taken into Hesper's confidence with regard to Mary; she had discovered that "a young person" was expected, but had learned nothing of what her position in the house was to be. She welcomed this opportunity both of teaching Mrs. Redmain the propriety of taking counsel with her housekeeper, and of letting the young person know in time that Mrs. Perkin would be her mistress.

Nothing oiled this household's wheels as well as punctuality. In a family, love, if it be strong and genuine, will make up for anything. But here there was no family and no love. The master and mistress came and went, regardless of each other and of all the household politics. Their meals were ready for them at the precise minute required, the carriage came round like one of the puppets on the Strasburg clock, the house was as quiet as a hospital, the bells were answered swiftly (except the doorbell, outside of calling hours), you could not soil your fingers anywhere, and the manners of the servants were beyond reproach. But the house was scarcely more of a home than one of the huge hotels characteristic of the age.

Mary sat in the hall for an hour, not exactly learning the lesson Mrs. Perkin had intended to teach her, but learning more than one thing Mrs. Perkin was not yet capable of knowing. While she was not comfortable—for she was both cold and hungry—she was far from miserable. This was not the reception she had pictured to herself, as the train came rushing from Testbridge to London. She had not imagined a warm one, but she had not expected to be forgotten—for so she interpreted her abandonment in the hall. She saw no means of reminding the household of her neglected presence and, indeed, would rather have remained where she was till morning than encounter the growing familiarity of the man who had admitted her.

She grew very weary, and began to long for a floor on which she might stretch herself. There was not a sound in the house but the ticking of a clock somewhere; as she was wondering whether everybody had gone to bed, she heard a step approaching, and presently Castle stood before her. With the ease of perfect self-satisfaction, and as if there was nothing in the neglect of her but the custom of the house to cool people in the hall before admitting them, he said, "Step this way, Miss." The last word was added after a pause of pretended hesitation, for the man had taken his cue from the housekeeper.

Mary rose and followed him to the basement, into a comfortable room, where sat Mrs. Perkin embroidering large sunflowers on a piece of coarse stuff.

"You may sit down," she said, and pointed to a chair near the door.

Mary, not a little amused, for all her discomfort, did as she was permitted, and awaited what should come next.

"What part of the country are you from?" asked Mrs. Perkin, with her usual diagonal upward toss of the chin, but without lifting her eyes from her work.

"From Testbridge," answered Mary.

"The servants in this house are in the habit of saying *Ma'am* to their superiors," remarked Mrs. Perkin. Although her tone was one of rebuke, she said the words lightly, as if the lesson was meant for one who could hardly have been expected to know better.

"And what place did you apply for in the house?" she went on to ask. "And what wages were you to have?" Mrs. Perkin gradually assumed a more decided drawl as she became more assured of her position with the stranger. She would gladly get some light on the affair.

"You need not object to mentioning them," she went on, for she imagined Mary hesitated, whereas she was only a little troubled to keep from laughing. "I pay the wages myself."

"There was nothing said about wages, Ma'am," answered Mary.

"Indeed! Excuse me if I say it seems rather peculiar. We must be content to wait a little then, until we learn what Mrs. Redmain expected of you, and whether or not you are capable of it. Can you use your needle?"

"Yes, Ma'am."

"Have you done any embroidery?"

"I understand it a little, but I am not particularly fond of it."

"I did not ask if you were fond of it," said Mrs. Perkin. "I asked you if you had ever done any." She smiled severely, but ludicrously, for a diagonal smile is apt to have a comic effect. "Here, take off your gloves, and let me see you do one of these loose-worked sunflowers. They are the fashion now."

"Please, Ma'am," returned Mary, "if you will excuse me, I would rather go to my room. I have had a long journey, and am very tired."

"There is no room assigned you. Nothing can be done till Mrs. Redmain gets home, and she and I have had a little talk about you. But you can go to the housemaid's room, and make yourself tidy. I believe there is a spare bed in it, which you can have for the night, only mind you don't keep the girl awake talking to her, or she will be late in the morning, and that I never put up with. I think you will do. You seem willing to learn, and that is half the battle."

Mrs. Perkin, believing she had laid in awe the foundation of a rightful authority over the young person, gave her a nod of dismissal, which she intended to be friendly.

"Please, Ma'am," said Mary, "could I have one of my boxes taken upstairs?"

"Certainly not. I cannot have two movings of them, and, I understand, your boxes are heavy. It really would *look* better in a young person not to have so much to carry about with her."

"I have but two, Ma'am," said Mary.

"Full of books, I am told!"

"Only one of them."

"You must do your best without them tonight. When I have made up my mind what is to be done with you, I shall let you have the one with your clothes. The other shall be put away in the box room. I give my people what books I think fit. For light reading, the *Fireside Herald* is quite enough. Good night!"

Mary curtsied, and left. At the door she glanced this way and that to find some indication to guide her steps. A door was opened at the end of a passage, and from the odor that met her, it seemed likely to be that of the kitchen. She approached and peeped in.

"Who is that?" cried an irate voice. It was the second cook. As Mary stepped in the cook asked, "To what am I indebted for the 'onner of this unexpected visit?" and her head jerked hither and thither upon her neck, as she seized the opportunity of turning to her own use a sentence she had just read in the *Fireside Herald* which had taken her fancy.

"Would you please tell me where to find the second housemaid?" said Mary. "Mrs. Perkin has sent me to her room."

"Why don't Mrs. Perkin show you the way, then?" returned the woman. "There ain't nobody else in the 'ouse as I knows on fit to send to the top o' them stairs with you. But I better show you the way myself. It's easier to take you than find a girl to do it. Them hussies is never where they ought to be! Follow me!"

She led the way along two passages, and up a back staircase of stone, up and up, till Mary, unused to such heights, began to be aware of her knees. At last plainly in the regions of the roof, she thought her hill surmounted, but the cook turned a sharp corner, and Mary following found herself once more at the foot of a stair, very narrow and steep, leading up to an old-fashioned roof turret.

"Are you taking me to the clouds?" she said, willing to be cheerful, and to acknowledge her obligation for laborious guidance.

"Not yet a bit, I 'ope," answered the cook. "We'll get there soon enough, anyhow, excep' you belong to them peculiars as wants to be saints afore their time. If that's your sort, don't you come 'ere, for a more wicked 'ouse, or an 'ouse as you got to work on o' Sunday's, no one won't easily find in this 'ere west end."

With these words she panted up the last few steps, immediately at the top of which was the room sought. It was a very small one, scarcely more than holding two beds. Having lighted the gas, the cook left her, and Mary, noting that one of the beds was not made up, was glad to throw herself upon it. Covering herself with her cloak, her traveling rug, and the woolen counterpane, she was soon fast asleep.

She was roused suddenly by a cry, half of terror, half of surprise. There stood the second housemaid who, having been told nothing of her roommate, stared and gasped.

"I am sorry to have startled you," said Mary, who had half risen, leaning on her elbow. "They ought to have told you there was a stranger in the house."

The poor girl seemed capable only of panting, and pressing her hand on her heart.

"I am very sorry," said Mary again. "My name is Mary Marston. I won't hurt you—I don't look dangerous, do I?"

"No, Miss," answered the girl, with a hysterical laugh. "I'm Jemima, and I've been to the play, and there was a man in it was a thief, you know, Miss!" And with that she burst out crying.

It was some time before Mary got her quieted, but when she did, the girl was quite reasonable. She deplored that the bed was not made up, and would willingly have yielded hers. She was sorry she had not a clean nightgown to offer her—"not that it would be fit for the likes of *you*, Miss!"—and showed herself full of friendly ministrations. Mary being now without her traveling cloak, Jemima judged from her dress she must be some grand visitor's maid, vastly her superior in the social scale. If she had taken her for an inferior, she would doubtless have had some airs handy.

22.
Her Position

Mary seemed to have just gotten to sleep again when she was startled awake by the violent ringing of a bell.

"Oh, you needn't trouble yet a long while, Miss!" said Jemima, who was already dressing. "I've got ever so many fires to light ere there'll be a thought of you!"

Mary lay down again and once more fell fast asleep. She was waked the third time by the girl, telling her that breakfast was ready. So Mary rose and made herself as tidy as she could.

She did feel a little shy on entering the room where all the livery and most of the women servants were already seated at breakfast. Two of the men, with a word to each other, made room for her between them, and then laughed, but she took no notice, and seated herself at the bottom of the table with Jemima. Everything was as clean and tidy as heart could wish, and Mary was glad enough to make a good meal.

For a few minutes there was loud talking—from a general impulse to show off before the stranger. Then a silence fell, as if some feeling of doubt had come amongst them. The least affected by it was the footman who had opened the door to her and had witnessed her reception by Mrs. Perkin. Addressing her boldly, he expressed a hope that she was not too much fatigued by her journey. Mary thanked him in her natural and straightforward way; the consequence was that the next time he spoke to her, it was like a gentleman, in the language of the parlor, without any mock politeness. Although the way they all talked amongst themselves made Mary feel as if she were in a strange country, she received not the smallest annoyance during the rest of the meal. But that did not last long.

For an hour or more after the rest had scattered to their respective duties, she was left alone. Then Mrs. Perkin sent for her. When Mary entered her room, she found her occupied with the cook, and was allowed to stand unnoticed.

"When shall I be able to see Mrs. Redmain, Ma'am?" she asked, when the cook at length turned to go.

"Wait," rejoined Mrs. Perkin, with a quiet dignity, well copied, "until you are addressed, young woman." Then, casting a glance at Mary, and perhaps perceiving a glimmer of amusement in Mary's eyes, she began to gather a more correct suspicion of the situation, and hastily added, "Pray, take a seat."

The idea of making a blunder was unendurable to Mrs. Perkin, and she was most unwilling to believe she had done so. But, even if she had, to show that she knew it would only be to render it the more difficult to recover her pride. An involuntary twinkle about the corners of Mary's mouth made her hasten to answer her question.

"I am sorry," she said, "that I can give you no prospect of an interview with Mrs. Redmain before three o'clock. She will very likely not be out of her room before one. I suppose you saw her at Durnmelling?"

"Yes, Ma'am," answered Mary, "and at Testbridge."

It kept growing on the housekeeper that she had made a mistake, though to what extent she sought in vain to determine. She sent for Mrs. Redmain's maid, Folter.

A cross-looking, red-faced thin woman appeared, whom Mrs. Perkin requested to let her mistress know, as soon as was proper, that there was a young person in the house who said she had come from Testbridge by appointment to see her.

"Yes, Ma'am," said Folter, with a supercilious yet familiar nod to Mary. "I'll take care she knows."

It was three o'clock when Mary was at length sumoned to Mrs. Redmain's boudoir. Folter lingered in the soft closing of the door long enough to learn that her mistress received the young person with a kiss. She hastened to report the fact to Mrs. Perkin, and succeeded in occasioning no small uneasiness in the housekeeper, who was almost as much afraid of her mistress as the other servants were of her.

But although Hesper received Mary with a kiss, she did not ask her a question about her journey, or as to how she had spent the night. Mary was there, and looking all right, and that was enough. On the other hand, she did proceed to have her at once properly settled.

The little room appointed her overlooked a small courtyard, and was dark but otherwise very comfortable. As soon as she was left to herself, Mary opened boxes, put her things away, arranged her books, and sat down to read a little, brood a little, and build a few castles in the air.

About eight o'clock, Folter summoned her to go to Mrs. Redmain. By this time Mary was tired—she was accustomed to tea in the afternoon, and since her dinner with the housekeeper, had had nothing.

She found Mrs. Redmain dressed for the evening. As soon as Mary entered, she dismissed Folter.

"I am going out to dinner," she said. "Are you quite comfortable?"

"I am rather cold and should like some tea," said Mary.

"My poor girl! Have you had no tea?" said Hesper with some concern, and more annoyance. "You are looking quite pale. When did you have anything to eat?"

"I had a good dinner at one o'clock," repled Mary, with a rather weary smile.

"This is dreadful!" said Hesper. "What can the servants be about!"

"And please, may I have a little fire?" begged Mary.

"Certainly," replied Hesper, knitting her brows with a look of slight anguish. "Is it possible you have been sitting all day without one? Why did you not ring the bell?" She took one of Mary's hands. "You are frozen!" she said.

"Oh, no!" answered Mary, "I am far from that. You see, nobody knows yet what to do with me. You hardly know yourself," she added, with a merry look. "But if you wouldn't mind telling Mrs. Perkin where you wish me to have my meals, that would put it all right, I think."

"Very well," said Hesper, in a tone that for her was sharp, and she sent for the housekeeper, who presently appeared, lank and tall, with her head on one side like a lamppost in distress.

126

"Mrs. Perkin, I wish you to arrange with Miss Marston about her meals."

"Yes, Ma'am," answered Mrs. Perkin, with sedatest utterance. But she did not even look at Mary. "Do you desire, Ma'am, that Miss Marston should have her meals in the housekeeper's room?" she asked.

"That must be as Miss Marston pleases," answered Hesper. "If she prefers them in her own, you will see they are properly sent up."

"Very well, Ma'am. Then I wait Miss Marston's orders," said Mrs. Perkin, and turned to leave the room. But when her mistress spoke again, she turned and stood, although it was Mary whom Hesper addressed.

"Mary," she said, apparently foreboding worse from the tone of the housekeeper's obedience than from her neglect, "when I am alone, you shall take your meals with me, and when I have anyone with me, Mrs. Perkin will see that they are sent to your room. We will settle it so."

"Thank you," said Mary.

"Very well, Ma'am," said Mrs. Perkin.

"Send Miss Marston some tea directly," said Hesper.

Scarcely was Mrs. Perkin gone when the brougham was announced. Mary returned to her room, and in a little while, tea, with thin bread and butter in limited quantity arrived. But it was brought by Jemima, whose face wore a cheerful smile over the tray she carried; she, at least, did not grudge Mary her superior place in the household.

"Do you think, Jemima," asked Mary, "you could manage to answer my bell when I ring?"

"I should be only too glad, Miss. It would be nothing but a pleasure. But if I was upstairs, which in this 'ouse ain't a place to hear bells, sure I am nobody would let me know you was ringin', and if you was to think as 'ow I was giving myself airs, I should be sorry and ashamed—"

"You needn't be afraid of that, Jemima," returned Mary. "If you don't answer when I ring, I shall know that either you don't hear it, or cannot come at the moment. I shall not be exacting. But, do you think you could bring me some more bread? I have had nothing since Mrs. Perkin's dinner."

"Laws, Miss, you must be nigh well clemmed!" said the girl,

and hastening away, she soon returned with a loaf, butter, and a pot of marmalade sent by the cook, who was only too glad to open a safety valve to her pleasure at the discomfiture of Mrs. Perkin.

"When would you like your breakfast, Miss?" asked Jemima, as she removed the tea things. "And you'll 'ave it in bed?"

"No, thank you, I never do."

"You'd better, Miss. It makes no more trouble. I've got to get the things together anyhow, and why shouldn't you 'ave it as well as Mrs. Perkin, or that ill-tempered cockatoo, Mrs. Folter? You're a lady, and that's more'n can be said of them!"

"You don't mean," said Mary, surprised out of her discretion, "that the housekeeper and the lady's maid have breakfast in bed?"

"Every blessed mornin', as I've got to take it up to 'em, Miss."

"Well, I certainly shall not add another to the breakfasts in bed. But I must trouble you all the same to bring it here. I will make my bed, and do out the room myself, if you will come and finish it off for me."

"Oh, no, indeed, Miss! You mustn't do that! Think what they'd say of you downstairs. They'd despise you downright!"

"I shall do it, Jemima. If they were servants of the right sort, they would think all the more of me for doing my own share. We must do our work, and not mind what people say."

"Yes, Miss, that's what my mother used to say to my father, when 'e wouldn't be reasonable. But I must go, Miss, or I shall catch it for gossiping with you—that's what *she'll* call it."

When Jemima was gone, Mary fell to thinking. It was all very well to talk about doing her work, but here she was with no idea of what her work was.

23.
Mr. and Mrs. Helmer

The next morning, Mary set out to find Letty. Mary had written about a month ago, but had had no reply. The sad fact was that Letty, for a long time and without knowing it, had been going downhill. Letty's better self seemed to have remained behind with Mary and, not even if he had been as good as she had thought him, could Tom himself have made up for the loss of such a friend.

Letty had not found marriage to be the grand thing she had expected. But with the faithfulness of a woman, she attributed her disappointment to something inherent in marriage, and not in the man whom marriage had made her husband. Tom had taken a lodging in a noisy street, unlike anything Letty had been accustomed to. Never a green thing was there to be looked on in any direction. Not a sweet sound was to be heard, and the sun was seldom seen in London at this time of the year. And the noise—a ceaseless torrent of grinding, clashing sounds, of yells and cries, of deafening and unpoetic discords! Letty had not much poetry in her and needed what could be had from the outside so much the more.

Once a week or so, Tom would take her to a play, and that was indeed a happiness, not because of the pleasure of the play, but because she had Tom beside her.

Tom was not half so dependent upon her as she was on him. Every week he spent a few evenings at houses where those who received him had not the faintest idea whether he had a wife or not, and cared as little, for it would have made no difference—they would not have invited her. Small, silly, conceited Tom, regarding himself as a somebody, was more than content to be asked to such people's houses. While Letty sat in her dreary lodging, dingily clad and lonely, Tom, dressed in the height of fashion, would be strolling about grand rooms, exchanging greetings, pausing to pay a compliment to this lady on her singing, to that on her verses, or to a third, where he dared, on her dress, for Tom was profuse in his compliments.

Like a hummingbird, all sparkle and flash, Tom flitted through the tropical delights of such society as his "uncommon good luck" had gained him admission to, forming many shallow friendships and taking many a graceful liberty.

While he was idling away time which yet could hardly be called precious, his little wife sat at home, inquired after by nobody, thought of by nobody, hardly even taken up by her own poor weary self. She would wonder when Tom would be home, try to congratulate herself on his being such a favorite, and think what an honor it was to a poor country girl like her to be the wife of a man so much courted by the best society—for she never doubted that the people to whose houses Tom went desired his company from admiration of his writings. Poor Letty thought it a grand thing to be the wife of an author; she had no idea that not one of them cared a straw about what he wrote.

Tom easily stepped into the literary profession through some of his old college friends. They were young men with money and supporters to back them, and were already in the full swing of periodical production when Tom took up with them. The best they had done for him was to bring him in contact with a weekly paper that now and then printed something of his. Now and then the editor would hand him what he called an honorarium, but what was in reality a five-pound note. When such occurred, Tom, forgetful of his mother's frugal financial assistance, would immediately invite his friends to supper—not at the lodging where Letty sat alone but at some tavern. It was at these times, and in the company of men certainly no better than himself, that Tom's hopes were brightest and his confidence greatest. Long after midnight he and his companions would sit laughing and jesting and drinking, some saying witty things, and all of them foolish things and worse, relating anecdotes which grew more and more irreverent to God and women as the night advanced. Then, sometime

between night and morning, Tom would reel gracefully home,
using all the power of his will to subdue his drunkenness that he
might face his wife with the appearance of a gentleman

When he came home happy and would drop off to sleep in the
middle of a story she could make nothing of, or when he would
burst out laughing and refuse to explain the motive, she was forced
to conclude that he had taken too much strong drink. And when
she noted that this condition reappeared at shorter and shorter
intervals, she began to be frightened, and to feel what she dared
not allow, that she was gradually being left alone—that Tom had
struck out onto a diverging path and they were slowly going their
own separate ways.

It was a sad thing for Tom that his mother, having persuaded
her dying husband to leave the money in her power could not
now have refused him money altogether. He would have been
compelled to work harder and to use what he made procuring
the necessaries of life. There might have been some for him
then. With the little money he gave Letty, which was never more
than a part of what his mother sent him, she was obliged to
make both ends meet; and while he ran in debt to tailor and
bootmaker, she never had anything new to wear.

She sometimes wished he would take her out from a little
oftener, for she was beginning to feel too lonely to to amuse
herself. But she always reflected that he could not it, and it
was a long time before she began to have any doubt uneasiness
about him. When such a thought first presented she banished it as a disgrace to herself and an insult to him it was no
wonder she found marriage dull—after such expes from her
Tom!

Her whole life now was Tom and only Tom. The day was
but the continuous and little varied hope of his ce. Most of
the time she had a book in her hands, but even book and
hands would sink into her lap, and she would sig before her
at nothing. She was not unhappy, she was only ppy. At first
it was a speechless delight to have as many no she pleased,
and she thought Tom the very prince of bo not merely
permitting her to read them, but in bringing ther, one after
the other, sometimes two at once, in spend fusion. The
first thing that made her aware she was not ppy was the
discovery that novels were losing their charm hey were not

sufficient to make her day pass, that they were only dessert and she had had no dinner. When it came to difficulty in going on with a new one long enough to get interested in it, she sighed heavily, and began to think that perhaps life was rather a dreary thing, or at least considerably diluted with the unsatisfactory.

When her landlady announced a visitor, Letty, not yet having one friend in London, could not think who it should be. When Mary entered, she sprang to her feet and stared. But when the fact of Mary's presence cleared itself to her, she rushed forward with a cry, fell into her arms and burst out weeping. Mary held her until she calmed a little; then, pushing her gently away to the length of her arm she looked at her.

Letty was not a happy sight. She was no longer the plump, fresh girl who used to go about singing, nor was she merely thin and pale; she looked unhealthy. Things could not be going well with her. Her dress been only disordered, that might have been accident but it looked neglected—not merely dingy, but plainly shabby appeared on the wrong side of clean. Presently, as Mary's got accustomed to the miserable light, she saw in the skirt of's gown an untidy darn, revealing all too evidently that to there no longer seemed occasion for being particular. The sad of it all sank to Mary's heart. Letty had not found marriage and affair. Mary's heart ached for Letty, and the ache intensely laid itself as close to Letty's ache as it could.

"You looking your best, Letty," she said, clasping her again in arms.

With choking, Letty assured her she was quite well, only rather overcome with the pleasure of seeing her so unexpectedly.

"How Helmer?" asked Mary.

"Quite and very busy," answered Letty, a little hurriedly Mary the "But," she added, in a tone of disappointment, "you always used to call him Tom!"

"Oh!" said Mary with a smile, "one must be careful about taking liberties with married people. A certain mysterious change seems to over some of them—they are not the same somehow, and you make your acquaintance with them all over again from the beginning."

"I should think such people's acquaintance worth making over again Letty.

"How tell what it may be worth," said Mary, "when

132

they are so different from what they were? Their friendship may now be one that won't change so easily."

"Don't be so hard on me, Mary. I have never ceased to love you."

"I am so glad!" answered Mary. "People don't generally take to me—at least not to come near me. But you can *be* friends without *having* friends," she added.

"I don't understand you," said Letty, sadly, "but then I never could quite, you know. Tom finds me very stupid."

These words strengthened Mary's suspicion that all was not going well between the two, but she shrank from any approach to confidences with *one* of a married pair. To have such, she felt instinctively, would be a breach of unity, unless it were already irreparably broken. To encourage in any married friend the placing of confidences that excludes the other is to encourage that friend's self-degradation. But this was not a fault to which Letty could have been tempted; she loved her Tom too much for that. With all her feebleness, there was in Letty a childlike greatness born of faith.

But although Mary would not make Letty tell anything, she was still anxious to discover if she might be able to help. She would observe, for sidelights often reveal more than direct illumination. It might be for Letty, and not for Mrs. Redmain, that she had been sent to London. He who made time, in time would show.

"Are you going to be long in London, Mary?" asked Letty.

"Oh, a long time!" answered Mary, with a loving glance.

Letty's eyes fell, and she looked troubled. "I am so sorry, Mary," she said, "that I cannot ask you to stay here. We have only these two rooms, and—and—you see—Mrs. Helmer is not very liberal to Tom, and—because they—don't get on together very well—as I suppose everybody knows—Tom won't—he won't consent to—to—"

"You little goose!" cried Mary. "You don't think I would come without even letting you know! I have got a situation in London."

"A situation!" echoed Letty. "Have you left your shop and gone into somebody else's?"

"Not exactly," replied Mary, laughing. "But I have no doubt most people would think that by far the more prudent thing to have done. I am not quite sure I have done wisely, but if I have made a mistake, it is from having listened to love more than to prudence."

"What!" cried Letty, "You're married!" Had her own marriage proved to Letty the most blessed of fates, she could not have shown more delight at the idea of Mary's. Men often find women a little incomprehensible in this matter of their friends' marriages. In their largeheartedness, women are able to hope for their friends, even when they have lost all hope for themselves.

"No," replied Mary, a little amused at having misled her. "It is neither so bad nor so good as that. But I was far from comfortable in the shop without my father, and kept thinking how to find a life more suitable for me. Then it happened—I found myself taken, not with a gentleman (don't look like that, Letty) but with a lady; and as the lady took a fancy to me at the same time, and wanted to have me about her, here I am. I am a kind of lady's maid, or a dressmaker, or a kind of humble friend. In truth, Letty, I do not know what I am, or what I am going to be, but I shall find out before long, and what's the use of knowing anything before it's wanted?"

"You take my breath away, Mary! This doesn't seem at all like you! It's not consistent! Mary Marston in a menial position! Where are you staying?"

"You remember Miss Mortimer of Durnmelling?"

"Quite well, of course."

"She is Mrs. Redmain now, and I am with her."

"You don't mean it! Why, Tom knows her very well! He has been several times to parties at her house."

"And not you too?" asked Mary.

"Oh, no!" answered Letty, laughing, superior at Mary's ignorance. "It's not the fashion in London, at least for distinguished persons like my Tom, to take their wives to parties."

"Are there no ladies at those parties, then?"

"Oh, yes," replied Letty, smiling again at Mary's ignorance of the world, "the grandest of ladies—duchesses and all. You don't know what a favorite Tom is in the highest circles!"

Now Mary could believe almost anything bearing on Tom's being a favorite, for she herself liked him a great deal more than she approved of him, but she could not see the sense of going to parties without his wife. She had old-fashioned notions of a man and his wife being one flesh, and she felt a breach of the law when they were separated. But Letty seemed much too satisfied to give her any light on the matter.

Letty continued. "Besides, Mary, how could I get a dress fit to wear at such parties? You wouldn't have me go and look like a beggar! That would be to disgrace Tom. Everybody in London judges everybody by the clothes they wear. You should hear Tom's descriptions of the ladies' dresses when he comes home!"

Mary was on the verge of crying out indignantly, "Then, if he can't take you, why doesn't he stay home with you?" but she held her peace.

"So then," reverted Letty, as if willing to turn definitively from the subject, "you are actually living with the beautiful Mrs. Redmain! What a lucky girl you are! You will see no end of grand people! You will see my Tom sometimes—when I can't!" she added, with a sigh that went to Mary's heart.

"Poor thing!" she said to herself. "It isn't anything much out of the way she wants—only a little more of a foolish husband's company!"

Mary did not stay as long with Letty as both would have liked, for she did not yet know enough of Hesper's ways. When she got home, she learned that Hesper had a headache and had not yet made her appearance.

24.
The Evening
Star

In spite of her headache, however, Mrs. Redmain was going to a small costume ball that evening. The part and costume she had chosen were the suggestion of her own name—she would represent the Evening Star clothed in early twilight. *She* was fit for the part, but the dress she had designed was altogether unsuitable to herself and to the part, and she had sufficient confidence neither in herself nor in her maid to forestall a desire for Mary's opinion. After lunch she sent for Miss Marston.

Mary found her half-dressed, Folter in attendance, and a great heap of pink lying on the bed.

"Sit down, Mary," said Hesper, pointing to a chair. "This is my dress for this evening's ball, and I want your advice," and she proceeded to explain the intent of her costume.

Folter gave a toss of her head that seemed to say, "Have I not spoken?" But what it really meant was, "How should other mortal know better than I?"

Hesper had a good deal of appreciative faculty, and knew therefore when she did or did not like a thing. But she had very little originative faculty, so little that when anything was wrong, she could do nothing to set it right. She had, with the assistance of Sepia and Folter, chosen this particular pink; and though it continued altogether delightful in the eyes of her maid, it had become doubtful in hers, and now she waited the judgment of Mary who sat silently thinking.

"Have you nothing to say?" she asked at length, impatiently.

136

"Please, Ma'am," replied Mary, "I must think if I am to be of any use. I am doing my best, but you must let me be quiet." She was in doubt whether the color—bright pink to suggest the brightest of sunset clouds—would suit Hesper's complexion. Then again, she had always associated the name *Hesper* with a later, a solemnly lovely period of twilight, having little in common with the color that so filled the room.

All was still, save for the slight noises Folter made as she went on heartlessly brushing her mistress' hair, which kept emitting little crackles as if of dissatisfaction with her handling.

"I suppose you *must* see it on!" said Hesper, and she rose, pushing Folter away.

Folter jerked herself to the bed, took the dress, arranged it on her arms, got up on a chair, dropped it over her mistress' head, got down, and having pulled it this way and that for a while, fastened it here and there, and exclaimed in a tone whose confidence was meant to forestall the critical impertinence she dreaded, "There, Ma'am! If you don't look the loveliest woman in the room, I shall never trust my eyes again."

Mary held her peace, for the commonplace style of the dress only added to her dissatisfaction with the color. It was all puffed and bubbled and blown about, here and there and everywhere, so that the form of the woman was lost in the frolic shapelessness of the cloud. The whole was a miserable attempt at combining fancy and fashion and was, in result, an ugly nothing.

"I see you don't like it!" said Hesper, with a mingling of displeasure and dismay. "I wish you had come a few days sooner! It is much too late to do anything now. I might just as well have gone without showing it to you! Here, Folter!"

With a look of disgust, she began to pull off the dress in which, a few hours later, she would yet make the attempt to enchant an assembly.

"O Ma'am!" cried Mary, "I wish you had told me yesterday. There would have been time then, and I don't know," she added, seeing disgust change to mortification on Hesper's countenance, "but something might be done yet."

"Oh, indeed!" dropped from Folter's lips, with an indescribable expression.

"What can be done?" said Hesper angrily. "There can be no time for anything."

"If only we had the fabric!" said Mary. "That shade doesn't suit your complexion. It ought to be much, much darker—in fact, a different color altogether."

Folter was furious, but restrained herself sufficiently to preserve some calmness of tone, although her face had turned almost blue with the effort, as she said, "Miss Marston is not long from the country, Ma'am, and don't know what's suitable to a London drawing room."

Her mistress was too dejected to snub her impertinence. "What color were you thinking of, Miss Marston?" Hesper asked, with a stiffness that would have been more in place had Mary volunteered the opinion she had been asked to give. She was out of temper with Mary, from feeling certain she was right and believing there was no remedy.

"I could not describe it," answered Mary. "And indeed the color I have in mind may not be available. I have seen it somewhere, but whether in cloth, or only in nature, I cannot be certain."

"Where's the good of talking like that—excuse me, Ma'am, it's more than I can bear—when the ball comes off in a few hours?" cried Folter, ending with eyes of murder on Mary.

"If you would allow me, Ma'am," said Mary, "I should like to try to find something that would suit you and your idea too. However well you might look in that, you would owe it no thanks. The worst is, I know nothing of London shops."

"I should think not!" remarked Folter with emphasis.

"I would send you in the brougham if I thought it was of any use," said Hesper. "Folter would be able to take you to the proper places."

"Folter would be of no use to me," said Mary. "If your coachman knows the best shops, that will be enough."

"But there's no time to make up anything," objected Hesper despondently, nonetheless with a glimmer of hope in her heart.

"Perhaps not like that," answered Mary, nodding at the pink catastrophe, "but let Folter have that dress ready, and if I don't succeed, you have something to wear."

"I hate it. I won't go if you don't find me another."

The brougham was ordered immediately, and in a few minutes Mary was standing at a counter in a large shop, looking at various stuffs, of which the young man waiting on her soon perceived she knew the qualities and capabilities better than he.

She had set her heart on carrying out Hesper's idea, but in better fashion; and after great pains taken, and no little trouble given, she left the shop satisfied with her success. And now for the greater difficulty!

She drove straight to Letty's lodging, and there dismissing the brougham, presented herself, with a great parcel in her arms, for the second time that day, and even more to the joy of her solitary friend.

She knew that Letty was good with her needle, and that she enjoyed such work. On several occasions when her supply of novels ran short, Letty had asked a dressmaker who lived above to let her help for an hour or two. Before Mary had finished her story, Letty was untying the parcel and preparing to receive her instructions.

They had been at work only a few minutes when Letty thought of calling in the dressmaker upstairs, so presently there were three of them busy as bees—one with genius, one with experience, and all with faculty. Mary's ideas were quickly understood and, the design of the dress being simplicity itself, Mary got all she wanted done in shorter time than she thought possible. The landlady sent for a cab and Mary was home in plenty of time for Mrs. Redmain's toilette. It was with triumph tempered with trepidation that she carried it to her room.

There Folter was in the act of persuading her mistress of the necessity of beginning to dress. Miss Marston, she said, knew nothing of what she had undertaken, and even if she arrived in time, it would be with something too ridiculous for any lady to appear in.

When Mary entered, she was received with a cry of delight from Hesper when she caught sight of the color of Mary's fabric. Mary undid the rest of the parcel, and when she lifted the dress on her arm for a first effect, Hesper was enraptured with it. The dress was aerial in texture, of the hue of a smoky rose, deep and cloudy with overlying folds, yet diaphanous, a darkness diluted with red.

Silent and grim, Folter approached to try the filmy thing, scornfully confident that the first sight of it on would prove it unwearable. But Mary judged her scarcely in a mood to be trusted with anything so delicate, and asked that, as she knew the weak points in the seams, she might be allowed the privilege of dressing Mrs.

Redmain. Hesper gladly consented, and Folter left the room. Mary found that the dress fit quite well, and having confined it round the waist with a cincture of thin gold, she advanced to her chief anxiety, the headdress.

For this she had chosen colors of the evening. In front, above the lunar forehead, among the coronal masses, darkly fair, she fixed a diamond star, and over it wound smoky green gauze, like a turbaned vapor, wind ruffled, through which the diamonds gleamed faintly. Not once did she allow Hesper to look in the mirror, but the moment Mary found she had succeeded, she led the Evening Star to the glass.

Hesper gazed for an instant; then turning she threw her arms about Mary and kissed her. "I don't believe you're a human creature at all!" she cried. "You are a fairy godmother, come to look after your poor Cinderella!"

The door opened, and Folter entered. "If you please, Ma'am, I wish to leave your service this day a month," she said quietly.

"Then," answered her mistress, with equal calmness, "go to Mrs. Perkin, and tell her that I desire her to pay you a month's wages, and you may leave tomorrow morning. You won't mind helping me to dress till I get another maid, will you, Mary?" Hesper asked, and Folter left the room, chagrined at her inability to cause annoyance.

"I do not see why you should have another maid so long as I am with you, Ma'am," said Mary. "If I have driven her away, I am bound to supply her place."

As they talked, she was giving her final touches of arrangement to the headdress. It swept round from behind in a misty cloak, the two colors mingling with and gently obscuring each other. Between them, the palest memory of light in the golden cincture helped to bring out the somber richness, the delicate darkness of the whole.

Searching Hesper's jewel case, Mary found a bracelet of oriental topaz, that clear yellow of the sunset sky. She clasped it on one arm, and when she had taken off all the rings that Hesper had just put on, except a certain glorious sapphire, she led her again to the mirror.

That night the Evening Star found herself a success, much followed by the men, and much complimented by the women. Her triumph however did not culminate until the next appearance of the *Firefly*, which published a song entitled, "To the Evening Star." Everyone knew that the Evening Star wereof it spoke ws Hesper Redmain.

To the Evening Star

From the buried sunlight springing,
Through flame-darkened rosy cloud,
Native sea-hues with thee bringing,
In the sky thou reignest proud!

Who is like thee, lordly lady,
Star-choragus of the night!
Color worships, fainting lady,
Night grows darker with delight!

Dusky-radiant, far, and somber,
In the coolness of thy state,
From thy eyelids chasing slumber,
Thou dost smile upon my fate;

Calmly shinest; not a whisper
Of my songs can reach thine ears;
What is it to thee, O Hesper,
That a heart should long or fear?

Tom had not been at the party, but had gathered enough fire from what he heard of Hesper's appearance there to write the verses. He did not show the poem to Letty—not that there was anything more in his mind than an artistic admiration of Hesper, and a desire to make himself agreeable in her eyes; but when Letty, having read it herself, betrayed no shadow of annoyance with its folly, he was a little relieved. The fact was, the simple creature took it as a pardon to herself.

"I am glad you have forgiven me, Tom," she said.

"What do you mean?" asked Tom.

"For working for Mrs. Redmain with *your* hands," she said, and breaking into a little laugh, caught his cheeks between those same hands, and reaching up gave him a kiss that made him ashamed of himself—a little, that is.

For this same dress which Tom had thus glorified in song had been the cause of bitter tears to Letty. He came home late the day of Mary's visit, and the next morning she had told him all about both the first and second surprise she had had, but not with much success in interesting the lordly youth.

"And then," she went on, "what do you think we were doing all afternoon, Tom?"

"How should I know?" said Tom, indifferently.

"We were working hard at a dress—a dress for a costume ball."

"A costume ball, Letty? What do you mean? You going to a costume ball?"

"Me!" cried Letty, with a merry laugh, "No, not me. It was for Mrs. Redmain." She clapped her hands with delight at what she thought the fun of the thing, for was not Mrs. Redmain Tom's friend? Then, stooping a little, and holding them out, she pressed them palm to palm, with the fingers toward his face.

"Letty!" said Tom. Frowning, he caught her outstretched hands and held them tightly by the wrists. The frown deepened, for he had not taken trouble to instruct her in what became the wife of Thomas Helmer, Esquire. "Letty, this won't do!"

Letty was frightened. "What won't do, Tom?" she returned, growing white. "There's no harm done."

"Yes, there is," said Tom with solemnity. "There *is* harm done when my wife goes and does a thing like that. What would people say if they knew! God forbid they should! To think that your husband was talking all evening to ladies at whose dresses his wife had been working all afternoon! What do you suppose the ladies would think if they were to hear of it?"

Poor, foolish Tom, ignorant of his folly, did not know how little those grand ladies would have cared if his wife had been a charwoman.

"But, Tom," pleaded his wife, "such a grand lady as that! One you go and read your poetry to! What harm can there be in helping make a dress for a lady like that?"

"Letty, I don't choose *my* wife to do such a thing for the greatest lady in the land! Good heavens, if it came to the ears of the staff of the *Firefly*, it would be the ruin of me! I should never hold up my head again!"

By this time Letty's head was hanging low, like a flower half-broken from its stem, and two big tears were slowly rolling down her cheeks. But there was still a gleam of satisfaction in her heart. Tom thought so much of his wife that he would not have her work for the grandest lady in the land! She did not see that it was not pride in her, but pride in himself that made him indignant at the idea. It was not "my *wife*," but "*my* wife," with Tom. She looked up timidly in his face, and said in a trembling voice—her cheeks wet, for she could not wipe away the tears because Tom still held her hands as one might those of a naughty child—"But Tom, I don't exactly see how you can make so much of it, when you don't think me—when you know I am not fit to go among such people."

To this Tom had no reply. He was not able to tell his wife that she had spoken the truth, that he did not think her fit for such company, that he would be ashamed of her, that she had no style. He did not think how little he had done to give the unassuming creature that quiet confidence which a woman ought to gather from the assurance of her husband's satisfaction in her, and the consciousness of being, in dress and everything else, pleasing in his eyes.

It was no wonder he was willing to change the subject. He let the poor imprisoned hands drop abruptly. "Well, well, Child," he said, "put on your bonnet, and we shall be in time for the first piece at the theatre."

Letty flew and was ready in five minutes. She could dress quickly because she was not delayed by the decision of selecting a gown. She scarcely had a choice. Tom, looking after his own comforts, left her to look after her necessities, and she, having a conscience and not much spirit, went even shabbier than she needed.

25.
Sepia

As naturally as if she had been born to that very duty, Mary slid into the office of lady's maid to Mrs. Redmain. She felt no more degradation in it than her mistress did, although for different reasons. If Hesper was occasionally a little rude to her, Mary was not one to accept it as rudeness. She could not help feeling some things with indignation and anger, but she made haste to send them from her and shut the doors against them. She knew herself a far more blessed creature than Hesper and felt the obligation, from the Master Himself, of so enduring as to keep every channel of service open between Hesper and her.

To Hesper, the change from the vulgar service of Folter to the ministration of Mary was like passing from a shallow purgatory to a gentle paradise. Folter handled her as if she were dressing a doll, and Mary as if she were dressing a baby—her hands were deft as an angel's, her feet as noiseless as swift.

But there was one in the house who was not pleased at the change from Folter to Mary. Sepia found herself, in consequence, less necessary to Hesper. Until Mary's service, Hesper had never been satisfied without Sepia's opinion and final approval in the matter of dress. But she found in Mary such a faculty as rendered appeal to Sepia unnecessary. Sepia was equal to dressing herself—she never blundered there, but there was little dependence to be placed upon her in dressing another. Sepia cared only for herself, and to dress another, love is needful. As far as Hesper's self was concerned, Sepia did not care whether she was well- or ill-dressed, but if the link between them of dress was severed, what other so strong would be left? And to find herself in any way a lesser object in Hesper's eyes, would be to find herself on the path to probable ruin.

Another though smaller point was that until now she had generally been able to dress Hesper as to make her more or less a foil to herself. Between Hesper and Sepia there was a physical resemblance, vaguely like that between twilight and night. It was a matter of no small consequence to Sepia that the relation of her dress to Hesper's should be such as to give herself an advantage from the relation of their looks. But this was far more difficult when she no longer had a voice in the matter of Hesper's dress, and it became obvious that the loving skill of the new maid presented her a challenge. Mary would have been glad to help Sepia as well, but Sepia drew back as from a hostile nature. This was more loss to Sepia than she knew. To dress was a far more difficult, though not more important, affair with Sepia than with Hesper, for she had no money of her own, and no fixed allowance from her cousin.

Hesper behaved generously to Sepia when she thought of it, but she did not love her enough to be watchful, and seldom thought how her money must be going or questioned whether she might not want more. Had Sepia ventured to run up bills with the tradespeople, Hesper would have taken it as a thing of course and settled them with her own money. But Sepia had a certain pride in spending only what was given her, and she also thought she had serious reason for avoiding all appearance of taking liberties.

Sepia was right in believing that Mr. Redmain disliked her, but she was wrong in imagining that he had any objection to her being present in the house. He certainly did not relish the idea of her continuing to be his wife's inseparable companion, but there would be time enough to get rid of her after he had found her out. Sepia had not long been in his house before he knew that she had to be found out, and was therefore an interesting subject for the exercise of his faculty of moral analysis. He was certain her history was composed mainly of secrets. As yet, however, he had discovered nothing.

From the first he saw through Mr. Mortimer, and all belonging to him, except Miss Yolland. She soon began to puzzle him and he did not like her. Had he been a younger man, she would have captivated him; but being considerably older than she, he had learned to recognize that she was of a bad sort. She had a history, and he believed that when he found what there was to know about her, he would hate her heartily.

For some time after his marriage, he appeared at his wife's parties oftener than he otherwise would have, just for the sake of having an eye on Sepia, and had seen nothing. But one night, by the merest chance, happening to enter his wife's drawing room, he had caught a peculiar glance between Sepia and a young man.

It seemed strange to several people that with her unquestioned powers of fascination, she had not yet married, but London is not the only place in which poverty is as repellent as beauty is attractive. There was something about her that made many men shy of her. Some found that her eyes drew them within a certain distance and then began to repel them. Others felt strangely uncomfortable in her presence from the first. Although no human eye is capable of reading more than a scattered hint of the twilight of history, the soul may yet shudder with an instinctive foreboding it cannot explain, and feel the presence of the hostile, without recognizing its nature.

Sepia's eyes were her great power. Their lightest glance was a thing not to be trifled with, and their gaze a thing hardly to be withstood. They were large, but no fool would be taken with mere size. They were grandly proportioned, neither almond-shaped nor round, neither prominent nor deep-set, but shape by itself is not much. Sepia's eyes were luminous, but not lords of the deepest light, for she was not true. Through them, concentrating her will upon their utterance, she could establish a physical contact with almost any man she chose. Their power was a selfish shadow of original, universal love. By them she could produce at once, in the man on whom she turned their play, a sense as it were of some primordial fatal affinity between her and him. Into those eyes she would call up her soul, and there make it sit, flashing light, in gleams and sparkles, shoots and coruscations, not from great black pupils alone, but from great dark irises as well. She would dart the lightnings of her present soul, invading with influence as irresistible as subtle, the soul of the man she chose to assail. She seldom exerted their full force without some further motive than mere desire to captivate. Sepia did not waste herself; her quarry must be worth the hunt. She must either need him or love him, if love were possible for her.

And now she began to amuse herself with Tom Helmer. From the first time they met that morning when he first called and they sat in the bay window of the drawing room, she brought her eyes to play upon him. Although he addressed the *Firefly* poem to Hesper in the hope of pleasing her, it was for the sake of Sepia that he desired the door of her house to be open to him. Whether he was married would have made no difference to her—her design was only to amuse herself with the youth, and possibly to make a screen of him. She went so far as to allow him to draw her to quiet corners, and even to linger when the other guests were gone, and he had had his full share of champagne. Once they remained together so long in the little conservatory, lighted only by an alabaster lamp, pale as the moon in the dawning, that she had to unbolt the front door to let him out. This did not take place without coming to the knowledge of both Mr. and Mrs. Redmain. The former was only afraid there was nothing in it, and Sepia herself was the informant of the latter. To Hesper she would make game of her foolish admirer, telling how, on this and that occasion, it was all she could do to get rid of him.

26.
Honor

Having now gained some insight into Letty's new position, Mary pondered what she could do to make life more for her. Not many knew better than she that the only true way to help a human heart is to lift it up; but she also knew that every kind of loving aid tends more or less to that uplifting, and that if we cannot do the great thing, we must be ready to do the small. The only thing Mary could think of was to secure for Letty, if possible, a share in her husband's pleasures.

Quietly, yet swiftly, a certain peaceful familiarity had established itself between Hesper and Mary. The result was the possibility of the following conversation.

"Do you like Mr. Helmer, Ma'am?" asked Mary one morning, as she was brushing Hesper's hair.

"Very well. How do you know anything of him?"

"Not many people within ten miles of Testbridge do not know Mr. Helmer," answered Mary.

"Yes, I remember," said Hesper. "He used to ride about on a long-legged horse, and talk to anybody who would listen. There was always something pleasing about him, and he is much improved. Do you know he is considered very clever?"

"I am not surprised," rejoined Mary. "He used to be rather foolish, and that is a sign of cleverness—at least many clever people are foolish, I think."

"*You* can't have had much opportunity for making that observation, Mary!"

148

"Clever people think as much of themselves in the country as they do in London, and that is what makes them foolish," returned Mary. "But I used to think Mr. Helmer had very good points, and was worth doing something for—if one only knew what."

"He does not seem to want anything done for him," said Hesper.

"I know one thing *you* could do for him, and it would be no trouble," said Mary.

"I would do anything for anybody that is no trouble," answered Hesper. "What is it?"

"The next time you invite him to a party, invite his wife also," said Mary.

"He is married then?" returned Hesper with indifference. "Is the woman presentable? Some shopkeeper's daughter, I suppose?"

Mary laughed. "You don't imagine the son of a lawyer would be likely to marry a shopkeeper's daughter!" she said.

"Why not?" returned Hesper, with a look of nonintelligence.

"Because a professional man is so far above a tradesman."

"Oh!" said Hesper. "Well, he should have told me if he wanted to bring his wife with him. I don't care who she is, so long as she dresses decently and holds her tongue. What are you laughing at, Mary?"

Hesper called it laughing, but Mary was only smiling.

"I can't help being amused," answered Mary, "that you should think it such an odd thing to be a shopkeeper's daughter, and here I am all the time feeling quite comfortable and proud of the shopkeeper whose daughter I am."

"Oh, I beg your pardon," exclaimed Hesper, blushing for the first time in her life. "How cruel of me," she went on. "But you see, I never think of you—when I am talking to you—as—as one of that class!"

Mary laughed outright this time. She was amused and thought it better to show it, for that would also show she was not hurt.

"Surely, Mrs. Redmain," said Mary, "you cannot think the class to which I belong in itself so objectionable, that it is rude to refer to it in my hearing!"

"I am very sorry," repeated Hesper, but in a tone of some offense. It was one thing to confess a fault, and another to be regarded as actually guilty of the fault. "Nothing was further from my mind. I did not intend to offend you. I have no doubt that shopkeepers are a most respectable class in their way—"

"Excuse me, Mrs. Redmain," said Mary again. "I am not in the least offended. I don't care what you think of the class. There are a great many shopkeepers who are anything but respectable, as bad indeed as any of the nobility."

"I was not thinking of morals," answered Hesper. "In that, I daresay, all classes are pretty much alike. But, of course, there are differences."

"Perhaps one of them is that, in our class, we make respectability more of a question of the individual than you do in yours."

"That may be very true," returned Hesper. "So long as a man behaves himself, we ask no questions."

"Am I right in thinking," asked Mary, "that people of your class care only that a man should wear the look of a gentleman and carry himself like one, and that whether or not his appearance is a mask, you do not care, so long as no mask is removed in your company? And as long as other people receive him, you will too, even though he may be the lowest of men?"

Hesper held her peace. By this time she had learned some facts concerning the man she had married which, in light of Mary's question, were embarrassing. She made no answer.

"The way to try a man," Mary continued, "would be to turn him the other way. For instance, make a nobleman a shopkeeper. If he showed himself just as honorable when a shopkeeper as he had seemed when a nobleman, there would be good reason for counting him an honorable man."

"What odd fancies you have, Mary!" said Hesper, yawning.

"I know my father would have been as honorable a nobleman as he was a shopkeeper," persisted Mary. "Would you mind telling me how you would define the difference between a nobleman and a shopkeeper?"

Hesper thought a little. To her the question was a stupid one. She had never had interest enough in humanity to care a straw what any shopkeeper ever thought or felt. Such people inhabited a region so far below her as to be practically out of her sight. They were not of her kind. It had never occurred to her that life must look to them much the same as it looked to her, that they had feelings, and would bleed if cut with a knife. While she was not interested, she peered about sleepily for an answer. Her thoughts

150

tumbled in a lazy fashion like waves without wind—which indeed was all the sort of thinking she knew.

At last she said with a conscious superiority, "The difference is that the nobleman is born to ease and dignity and the shopkeeper to buy and sell for his living."

"Many a nobleman," suggested Mary, "buys and sells without the necessity of making a living. Then," she questioned, "he buys and sells to make *money*, while the shopkeeper has to make a living?"

"Yes," granted Hesper lazily."*And*," she said, resuming her definition, "the nobleman deals with great things and the shopkeeper with small."

"When things are finally settled," said Mary, "and—"

"Gracious, Mary!" cried Hesper. "What do you mean? Are not things settled for good by this century? I am afraid I am harboring an awful radical! What do they call it—a communist?" She would have turned the whole matter out of doors, for she was tired of it, but Mary was not through.

"Things hardly look as if they were going to remain just as they are at this precise moment," said Mary. "How could they, when from the very making of the world, they have been changing! I do not believe there ever will be any settlement of things until the kingdom of heaven is come."

"You are leaving politics for religion now, Mary. You won't keep things in their own places! You are always mixing them up. It is so irreverent!"

"Is it irreverent to believe that God rules the world He made, and that He is bringing things to His own purpose in it?"

"You can't persuade me religion means turning things upside down."

"It means that a good deal more than people think. Did not the Lord say that many who are first shall be last, and the last first? Perhaps the shopkeeper and nobleman will one day change places."

"Oh," thought Hesper, "that is why the lower classes take so much to religion!" But what she said was, "Yes, I suppose. But everything then will be so different that it won't matter. When we are all angels, nobody will care who is first and who is last. I'm sure it won't be anything to me."

"In the kingdom of heaven," answered Mary, "things will

always look as they are. Not only will an honorable man look honorable, but a mean or less honorable man must look what he is."

"I have no doubt there will be a good deal of allowance made for some people," said Hesper. "Society makes such demands!"

27.
The Invitation

When Letty received Mrs. Redmain's card, inviting her with her husband to an evening party, it raised in her a bewildered flutter—of pleasure, of fear, of pride, of shyness, of dismay. How could she dare show her face in such a grand assembly! She would not know how to behave herself. But it was impossible, for she had no dress fit for such a function. What would Tom say if she looked dowdy? He would be so ashamed of her!

But Mary arrived soon after the postman, and a long talk followed. Letty was full of trembling delight, but Mary was not a little anxious with herself how Tom would take it.

The first matter was Letty's dress. She had no money, and seemed afraid to ask for any. At last Letty accepted Mary's proposal that a certain dress of Mary's (her best, although she did not tell Letty) which she had scarcely worn, should be made to fit Letty. It was a lovely black silk, the best her father had been able to choose for her the last time he was in London. A little pang did shoot through her heart at the thought of parting with it, but she had too much of her father in her not to know that the greatest honor that can be shown a thing is to make it serve a person. But little idea had Letty, much as she appreciated her kindness, what a sacrifice Mary was making for her that she might look her own sweet self, and worthy of her renowned Tom!

When Tom came home that night, the world and all that was in it changed speedily for Letty. He arrived in good humor—some body had been praising his verses—and the joy of the praise over-flowed on his wife. But when, pleased as any little girl with the prospect of a party and a new frock, she told him of the invitation and Mary's kindness which had rendered it possible for her to accept it, the countenance of her husband changed.

He rejected the idea of her going with him to any gathering of his grand friends, and objected most of all to her going to Mrs. Redmain's. Tom had begun to allow himself that he had married in haste, and beneath him. Wherever he went, his wife could be no credit to him, and her presence would take from him all sense of liberty! Controlling his irritation for the moment, he set forth with lordly kindness the absolute impossiblilty of accepting such an offer as Mary's. Could she for a moment imagine that he would degrade himself by taking his wife out in a dress that was not her own?

Here Letty interrupted him.

"Mary has given me the dress," she sobbed, "for my very own."

"A secondhand dress! A dress that has been worn!" cried Tom. "How could you dream of insulting me so! The thing is absolutely impossible. Why, Letty, just think! There I should be, going about as if the house were my own, and there would be my wife in the next room, or perhaps at my elbow, dressed in the finery of the lady's maid of the house! I won't bear to think of it! I declare, it makes me so ashamed!"

"It's not finery," sobbed Letty, laying hold of one fact within her reach, "it's a beautiful black silk."

"It matters not a straw what it is," persisted Tom, adding hu-miliation to cruelty. "You would be nothing but a sham! A live dishonesty! I'm sorry, Letty, your own sense of truth and upright-ness should not prevent even the passing desire to act such a lie. Your fine dress would be just a fine fib—yourself but a walking lie. I have been taking too much for granted with you. I must bring you no more novels. A volume or two of Carlyle is what you want."

This was too much. To lose her novels and her new dress together, and be threatened with nasty moral medicine was bad enough, but to be reproved by her husband was more than she could bear. However, she did not blame him. Anything was better than that. The dear simple soul had a horror of rebuke.

She wept and wailed like a sick child until at length the hard heart of selfish Tom was touched. But the truer the heart, the harder it is to console with the false. In the end, sleep, the truest of things, did for her what even the blandishments of her husband could not, and when she woke in the morning, Tom was gone.

Mary came before noon, and when she had heard as much as Letty thought proper to tell her, she was filled with indignation. The sole thing she could think of to comfort her was to ask her to spend the evening with her in her room. The proposal brightened Letty up at once. She supposed that sometime, in the course of the evening, she would at least catch a glimpse of Tom in his glory.

The evening came, and with beating heart Letty went up the back stairs to Mary's room. Mary was dressing her mistress, but did not keep Letty waiting long. Mary had provided tea beforehand, and when Mrs. Redmain had gone down, the two friends had a pleasant time together. Mary took Letty to Mrs. Redmain's room while she put away her things, and there showed her many splendors which, moving no envy in her simple heart, made her sad, thinking of Tom.

As the company kept arriving, Letty grew very restless, and kept creeping out of the room and halfway down the stairs to look over the banister to have a view of the great landing where indeed she caught many a glimpse of beauty and state, but never a glimpse of her Tom.

Worn out at last, and thoroughly disappointed, she wanted to go home. Mary accompanied her, and as they left, had they hesitated by the conservatory door, they would have seen Sepia standing there, and Tom, with flushed face, talking to her eagerly.

But it was well past midnight, and Letty only wanted the peace sleep would bring. Mary went with her, and saw her safe in bed before she left her. Letty cried herself to sleep, and dreamed that Tom had disowned her before a great company of grand ladies who mocked her.

Tom came home while she slept, and in the morning was cross and miserable, partly because he had been so abominably selfish to her. The moment she told him where she was the night before, he broke into the worst anger he had ever yet shown her. His shameful pride could not brook the idea that where he was a guest, his wife was entertained by one of the domestics!

"How dare you be guilty of such a disgraceful thing!" he cried.

"Oh, don't, Tom—dear Tom!" pleaded Letty in terror. "It was

you I wanted to see—not the great people, Tom. I don't care if I
never see one of them again."

"Why should you ever see one of them again, I should like to
know! What are they to you, or you to them?"

"But you know I was asked to go, Tom!"

"You're not such a fool as to fancy they cared about you! Everybody knows they are the most heartless set of people in the world!"

"Then why do you go, Tom?" asked Letty innocently.

"That's quite another thing! A man has to cultivate connections
his wife need not know anything about. It is one of the necessities
laid on my position."

Letty supposed it all truer than it was either intelligible or pleasant, and said no more, but let the poor, self-abused, fine fellow
scold and argue and reason away till he was tired. She was not
sullen, but bewildered and worn out. He got up and left without a
word.

Even at risk of harming his dignity—of which there was no
danger from the presence of his sweet, modest little wife—it would
have been well for Tom to allow Letty the pleasure within her
reach, for that night Sepia's artillery had played on him ruthlessly.
It may have been merely for amusement, to banish her boredom
for a short while, but Sepia had dazzled Tom, and the tinder of
Tom's heart had responded. All the way home, her eyes haunted
him. Those eyes, though not good, were beautiful. Evil, it is true,
has neither part nor lot in beauty—it is absolutely hostile to it, and
will at last destroy it utterly. Tom yielded to the haunting, and it
was partly the fault of those eyes that he used such hard words to
his wife in the morning.

About this time, from the top, lefthand corner of the last page of
the *Firefly*, it appeared that Twilight had given place to Night, for
the first of many verses began to show themselves in which
Hesper, the Evening Star, was no more mentioned. Now Tom was
infatuated with the intense darkness of Night—Sepia.

Of all who read the verses, there was not one less moved by
them than she who had inspired them. Sepia saw in them a reflex
of her own power, and that was pleasing, but it did not move her.
She took the devotion and pocketed it, as a greedy boy might an
orange. The verses in which Tom delighted were but the merest
noise in the ears of the lady to whom above all he would have had
them acceptable. One momentary revelation as to how she re-

garded them would have been enough to release him from his foolish enthrallment. Indignation, chagrin, and mortification would have soon been the death of such poor love as Tom's.

Mary and Sepia were on terms of politeness—of readiness to help, on the one side and condescension, on the other. Sepia never made an enemy if she could help it. She could not afford the luxury of hating, but she would have hated heartily could she have seen the way Mary regarded her—the look of pitiful love, of compassionate and waiting helpfulness which her soul would now and then cast upon Sepia. Above all things, she would have resented pity.

28.
A Stray Sound

Although Mary went frequently to see Letty, she scarcely
ever saw Tom. Either he was not up, or had gone—to the
office, Letty supposed. She had no idea where the office
was, or of the other localities haunted by Tom.

One day when Mary could not help remarking on Letty's pale
weary looks, Letty burst into tears and confided to her a secret of
which she was nonetheless proud, though it caused her anxiety
and fear. As soon as she began to talk about it, the joy of its hope
began to predominate. The greatness of her delight made Mary
sad for her. To any thoughtful heart it must be sad to think how
little time the joy of so many mothers lasts—not because their
babies die but because they live. Mary's mournfulness was caused
by the fear that the splendid dawn of mother-hope would soon be
swallowed in dismal clouds of father-fault.

Letty had no ideas about children—only the usual instincts of
indulgence. Mary had a few, for she recalled with delight some of
her father's ways with her. Next to God she knew him as the
source of her life, so well had he fulfilled that first duty of all
parents—the communication of true life. About such things she
tried to talk to Letty, but soon perceived that not a particle of her
thought found its way into Letty's mind. She cared nothing for any
duty concerned—only for the joy of being a mother.

Letty grew paler and yet thinner. Dark hollows came about her
eyes. She seemed to be parting with life to give it to her child. She
lost the lovely girlish gaiety Tom used to admire, and he was not

capable of seeing the something more lovely that was taking its place. He gave her less and less of his company. In her heart she grew aware that she feared him, and as she shrank from him, he withdrew even more.

When Mr. and Mrs. Redmain went again to Durnmelling, Mary asked Hesper to leave her behind. She told her the reason without mentioning the name of the friend, and Hesper only shrugged her shoulders. She did not believe that was the real cause of Mary's wish, and setting herself to find another, concluded she did not choose to show herself at Testbridge in her new position. Hesper gave permission, agreeing that Jemima would do nicely as her maid, since there would not be much occasion for dressing at Durnmelling.

All through the hottest of the late summer and early autumn weather Mary remained in London, where every pavement seemed like the floor of a baker's oven. How she longed for the common and the fields and the woods! The very streets and lanes of Testbridge seemed like paradise. But she never wished herself in the shop again, although almost every night she dreamed of the glad old times when her father was in it with her, and when, although they might not speak to each other from morning to night, their souls kept talking across the crowds and counters, and each was always aware of the other's supporting presence.

Although Mary longed for the freedom of the country, she was not miserable that she could not have it. She was at peace with her conscience, and had her heart full of loving duty. Into Letty's hot room, with the clanging street in front, and the little yard behind where, from a cord stretched across between the walls, a few pieces of ill-washed linen hung motionless in the glare, Mary would carry a tone of breeze and sailing cloud and swaying treetop. Life was so concentrated and active in her that she was capable of communicating life—the highest of human endowments.

One evening, as Letty was telling her how the dressmaker upstairs had been unwell for some time, and Mary was feeling reproachful that she might have seen what she could do for her had she been told earlier, they became aware of soft, sweet music coming faintly from somewhere. Mary went to the window, but there was nothing capable of music within sight. It came again, and intermittently came and went. For some time they would hear nothing at all, and then again the most delicate of tones would creep into their ears. Once or twice, a few consecutive sounds made a division strangely sweet, and then again, for a time, nothing would reach them but a note here and there of what had to be a wonderful melody. It lasted for about an hour, then ceased.

Letty went to bed, and all night long dreamed she heard the angels calling her. She woke weeping that her time was come so early, while as yet she had tasted so little of the pleasure of life. But the truth was, she had as yet got so little of the good of life that it was not at all time for her to go.

When her hour drew near, Tom condescended to leave word where he might be found if he should be wanted. Even this assuagement of her fears Letty had to plead for. Mary's presence was the reason for his absence—he had begun to dread Mary.

When at length he was sent for, he was in no haste. All was over before he arrived. But he was a little touched when, drawing his face down to hers, she feebly whispered, "He's as like to you, Tom, as ever a small thing was to a great!" She saw the slight emotion and fell asleep comforted.

It was night when she woke. Mary was sitting by her. "O Mary!" she cried. "The angels have been calling me. Did you hear them?"

"No," answered Mary. "It was just the same instrument we heard the other night. Who can there be in the house to play like that? It was clearer this time. I thought I could listen to it for a year!"

"Why didn't you wake me?" said Letty.

"Because the more you sleep, the better. And the doctor says I mustn't let you talk. I will get you something, and then you must go to sleep again."

Tom did not appear any more that night, and if they had wanted him now, they would not have known where to find him. He was about nothing very bad—only having supper with some friends—such friends as he did not even care to tell that he had a son. He was ashamed of being in London at this time of year, and had he had enough money to go anywhere except to his mother's he would have gone, and left Letty to shift for herself. With his child he was pleased, and would occasionally take him for a few moments. But when the baby cried, Tom got cross with him, and showed himself the unreasonable baby of the two.

160

Letty's strength grew slowly but steadily. For Mary it was a peaceful time. She was able to read a good deal, and although there were no books in Mr. Redmain's house, she generally succeeded in getting such as she wanted. She was able also to practice the piano as much as she pleased, for the grand piano was entirely at her service, and she took the opportunity of having a lesson every day.

29.
The Musician

One evening soon after the baby's arrival, the sweet tones they had heard before came creeping into Mary's ears so gently that she seemed to be aware of their presence only after they had, for some time, been coming and going. Mary stole from the room, and listening on the landing, soon determined that the sounds came from above, and so she ventured a little up the stairs.

She had already been to see the dressmaker, Ann Byron, and finding her far from well, had done what she could for her. But Ann was in no want and of more than ordinary independence—a Yorkshire woman about forty years of age, delicate but of great patience and courage. Her belief in religion rather than in God made her very strict in her observances, and she thought a great deal more of the Sabbath than of man, more of the Bible than of truth, and ten times more of her creed than of the will of God. Mary had soon discovered that there was no profit in talking with her on the subjects Mary loved most—plainly Ann knew little about them. Had Ann Byron been rich, she would have been unbearable. Women like her, when they are well-to-do, walk with a manly stride and are not infrequently Scotch.

As Mary ascended the stairs, the music ceased. Hoping Miss Byron would be able to enlighten her concerning its source, Mary continued her ascent and knocked at the door. A wooden voice invited her to enter.

Ann was sitting near the window. All Mary could see of her was

162

the reflection from the round eyes of a pair of horn spectacles.

"How do you do, Miss Byron?" she said.

"Not at all well," answered Ann, almost in a tone of offense.

"Is there nothing I can do for you?" asked Mary.

"We are to owe no man anything but love, the apostle tells us."

"You must owe a good deal of that, then," said Mary, one part vexed, and two parts amused, "for you don't seem to pay much of it."

She was just beginning to be sorry for what she said, when she was startled by a sound like a little laugh, which seemed to come from behind her. She turned quickly, but before she could see anything through the darkness, the softest of violin tones thrilled the air close beside her, and then she saw, seated on the corner of Ann's bed, the figure of a man—young or old she could not tell. His bow was wandering slowly about over the strings of his violin. But presently, having overcome his inclination to laugh, he ceased playing, and all was still.

"I came," said Mary, turning to Ann, "hoping you might be able to tell me where the sweet sounds came from, which we have heard now two or three times. I had no idea there was anyone in the room besides yourself," she added, turning towards the figure in the darkness.

"I am very sorry if I annoyed you, Miss." The musician's voice was gentle though manly, and gave an impression of utter directness and simplicity.

Mary was hastening to assure him that the fact was quite the other way when Ann prevented her. "I told you so!" she said to the man. "You make an idol of your foolish plaything, but other people take it only for the nuisance it is."

"Indeed, you never were more mistaken," said Mary. "Both Mrs. Helmer and I are charmed with the little that reaches us. It is seldom one hears tones of such purity."

The player responded with a sigh of pleasure.

"Now there you are, Miss," cried Ann, "a flattering of his folly till not a word I say will be of the smallest use!"

"If your words are not wise," said Mary, with suppressed indignation, "the less he heeds them the better."

"It ain't wise, to my judgment, Miss, to make a man think himself something when he is nothing. It's quite enough a man should deceive his own self, without another coming to help him."

"To speak the truth is not to deceive," replied Mary. "I have some knowledge of music, and I say only what is true."

"What good can it be, spending his time scraping horsehair on catgut!"

"They must fancy some good in it up in heaven," said Mary, "or they wouldn't have so much of it up there."

"There ain't no fiddles in heaven," said Ann, with indignation. "They've nothing there but harps and trumpets."

Mary turned to the man who had not said a word. "Would you mind coming down with me," she said, "and playing a little, very softly, to my friend? She has a baby, and she is not strong. It would do her good."

"She'd better read her Bible," said Ann who, finding she could no longer see, was lighting a candle.

"She does read her Bible," returned Mary, "and a little music would perhaps help her to read it to better purpose."

The woman replied with a scornful grunt, but Mary had once more turned to the musician. By the light of the candle, she saw a pair of black eyes, keen yet soft, looking out from under an over-hanging ridge of forehead. The rest of the face was in the shadow, but she could just see him smiling to himself. Mary had said what pleased him, and his eyes sought her face and seemed to rest on it with a kind of trust, as if he was ready to do whatever she might ask of him.

"You will come?" said Mary.

"Yes, Miss, with all my heart," he replied, and rising, he tucked his violin under his arm and showed himself ready to follow.

"Good night, Miss Byron," said Mary.

"Good night, Miss," returned Ann grimly. "I'm sorry for you both. But until the Spirit is poured out from on high, it's nothing but a stumbling in the dark."

Mary made no reply. She did not care to have the last word, nor did she fancy her cause lost when she did not have at hand an answer that befitted folly. She ran down the stairs and at the bottom stood waiting for her new acquaintance who descended more slowly, careful not to make a noise.

Now she could see by the gaslight that burned on the landing what the man looked like. He was powerfully built, tall, and about the age of thirty. His complexion was dark, and the hand that held the bow looked grimy. He bore himself well but a little stiffly, with a care over his violin like that of a man carrying a baby. He was decidedly handsome in a rugged way—his mouth and chin but hinted through his thick beard of darkest brown.

"Come this way," said Mary, leading him into Letty's parlor. "I will tell my friend you are here. Please, take a seat."

"Thank you, Miss," said the man, but remained standing.

"I have caught the bird, Letty," said Mary, loud enough for him to hear, "and he has some to sing for you, if you feel strong enough to listen."

"It will do me good," said Letty. "How kind of him!"

The man was already tuning his violin when Mary came from the bedroom and sat down on the sofa. He turned, and going to the farthest corner of the room, closed his eyes tight and began to play.

His music defied description, but if it is possible to imagine some music-loving sylph attempting to guide the wind among the strings of an aeolian harp—every now and then for a moment succeeding and then again for a while the wind having its own way—something like a dream-notion of the man's playing can be gained. Mary tried hard to get a hold of some clue to the combinations and sequences, but their motive evaded her understanding. Whatever their source, there was in his music not a little of the artistic, and much of disciplined wild abandon. Yet every now and then would come a passage of exquisite melody owing much to the marvelous delicacy of the player's tones, and the utterly tender expression with which he produced them.

At length came a little pause. He wiped his forehead with a blue cotton handkerchief, and seemed ready to begin again. Mary interrupted him with a question.

"Will you please tell me whose music you have been playing?"

He opened his eyes which had remained closed even while he stood motionless and, with a smile sweeter than any she had ever seen on such a strong face, answered, "it's nobody's, Miss."

"Do you mean you have been extemporizing all this time?"

"I don't know exactly what that means."

"You must have learned it from notes?"

"I couldn't read them if I had any to read," he answered.

"Then what an ear and what a memory you must have! How often have you heard it?"

"Just as often as I have played it, and no oftener. Not being able to read, and seldom hearing any music I care for, I'm forced to be content with what runs out at my fingers when I shut my eyes. It all comes of shutting my eyes. I couldn't play a thing but for shutting my eyes."

Mary was so astonished by what he said, and the simplicity with which he said it, having clearly no notion that he was uttering anything strange, that she was silent; and the man, after a moment's retuning, began to play again. Then she gathered all her listening powers and braced her attention, but with no better success, for that was not the way to understand.

Weary at last with vain effort, she ceased to try, and in a little while felt herself being molded by the music, and unconsciously received a little understanding of it. It wrought pictures in her mind, not thoughts.

Like a crowd, in slow, then rapid movement, the melody rose with cries and entreaties. Then came hurried motions, disruption, and running feet. A pause followed. Then woke a lively melody, changing to the prayer of some soul too grateful to stop for words. Next came a bar or two of what seemed calm, lovely speech, then a few slow chords, and all was still.

Mary came to herself, and then first knew that, the music had seized her unaware, and she had been understanding or at least enjoying without knowing it. The man was approaching her from his dark corner, his face shining. Plainly he did not intend any more music, for his violin was already under his arm. He made her a little awkward bow and turned to the door. He had it open before Mary could wake herself from her reverie to say anything.

From the top of the stair came the voice of Ann, screaming, "Here's your hat, Joe. I knew you'd be going when you played that." And Mary heard the hat come tumbling down the stairs.

"Thank you, Ann," returned Joe. "Yes, I'm going. The ladies don't care much for my music—nobody does but myself. But then, it's good for me."

The last two sentences were spoken in soliloquy, and Mary barely heard them, for he was closing the door behind him. He picked up his hat and went softly down the stairs.

Mary darted to the door and opened it, but the outer door had closed behind the strange musician.

30.
A Change

As soon as Letty had strength enough to attend to her baby without help, Mary—to the surprise of her mistress and the destruction of her theory concerning Mary's stay in London—presented herself at Durnmelling, and resumed her duties about Hesper.

It was with curiously mingled feelings that she gazed from her windows on the chimneys of Thornwick. How much had come to her since, in the summer seat at the end of the yew hedge, Mr. Wardour opened to her the door of literature! It was now autumn, and the woods were dying their yearly death. For the moment, she felt as if she too had begun to grow old, for her ministration had tired her a little. She regretted nothing that had come, nothing that had gone.

But she did taste some bitterness in her cup when, one day on the footpath to Testbridge—near the place where, that memorable Sunday, she met Mr. Wardour—she met him again. Looking at her, and plainly recognizing her, he passed in silence. Like a sudden wave, the blood rose to her face, and then sank to the deeps of her heart, and from somewhere came the conviction that one day the destiny of Godfrey Wardour would be in her hands. He had done more for her than anyone except her father, and when that day came, she should not fail him!

She was then on her way to the shop. She did not at all relish entering it, but, as she had a large money interest in the business, she ought at least pay the place a visit. When she went in,

Mr. Turnbull did not at first recognize her and, taking her for a customer, blossomed into his repulsive effusion. The change that came over his face when he recognized her was a shadow of such mingled and conflicting shades that she felt there was something peculiar in it which she must attempt to analyze. The expression remained hardly a moment and was almost immediately replaced with a politeness evidently false. That was the first time she began to be aware of distrusting the man.

Asking a few questions about the business, to which he gave answers most satisfactory, she kept casting her eyes about the shop, unable to account for the impression it made upon her. Something was changed, but what? Was there less in it, or was it only not so well kept as when she left it? She could not tell. Neither could she understand the profound but distant consideration with which Mr. Turnbull endeavored to behave to her, treating her like a stranger to whom he must manifest all possible respect. She bought a pair of gloves, paid for them, and left the shop without speaking to anyone else. All the time, George was standing behind the opposite counter, staring at her; much to her relief, he showed no other sign of recognition.

Before she went to see Beenie who was still at Testbridge in a cottage of her own, Mary felt she must think over her unresolved impression regarding the shop. What did it all mean? She knew they must look down on her ten times more than ever because of the menial position in which she had placed herself. But if that was what the man's behavior meant, why was he so respectful? That had not been Mr. Turnbull's way when he looked down on someone. And what did the shadow preceding this behavior mean? Was it not something more than annoyance at the sight of her? And it was with effort that he dismissed it! She had never seen that look on him before.

And the shop itself seemed to have a shabby look. Was it possible anything was wrong with the business? Her father had always spoken with great respect of Mr. Turnbull's business faculties, but she knew he had never troubled himself to look into the books or to know how they stood with the bank. She knew also that Mr. Turnbull was greedy with money, and that his wife was ambitious and hated the business. But if he wanted to be out of it, would he not naturally keep it in good shape, at least in appearance, that he might part with his share in it to the better advantage

168

Beenie greeted her warmly, and Mary was hardly seated before Beenie, who was a natural gossip, began to pour out the talk of the town, in which came certain rumors concerning Mr. Turnbull—mainly hints at speculation and loss.

After her visit, Mary immediately sought the lawyer in whose care her father had left his affairs. He was an old man and, having been ill, had no suspicion of anything being wrong, but would look into the matter at once. She went home and troubled herself no more.

She had been at Durnmelling only a few days when Mr. Redmain, wishing to see how things were on his estate in Cornwall and making up his mind to run down, asked his wife—and therefore Mary—to accompany him.

Mary was delighted at the prospect of seeing more of her country. She had traveled very little, but was capable of gathering ten times more from a journey to Cornwall than most travelers would from one through Switzerland. The place was lonely and lovely, and for the first few days, Mary enjoyed it unspeakably.

Suddenly, as was not unusual, Mr. Redmain was taken ill. Mewks had returned to London, and the only other servant they had with them besides the coachman was useless in such a need. So, of the household, Mary alone was found capable of fit attendance in the sickroom. Hesper shrunk almost with horror, and certainly with disgust, from the very idea of having anything to do with her husband as an invalid. When she had the choice of her company, she said, she would not choose his. Mewks was sent for at once, but did not arrive before the patient had had some experience of Mary's nursing; and even after Mewks did come, Mary was occasionally asked to attend to some of his needs. The attack was long and severe, delaying for many weeks their return to London, where Mr. Redmain declared he must be, at any risk, before the end of November.

It was during this time in Cornwall that Mary first ventured to discuss with her mistress her neglect of her husband. Hesper heard her patiently, and later that day paid him some small attention by handing him his medicine. The next moment one of his fits of pain came on, and he broke into a torrent of cursing that swept her in stately dignity from the room. She would not go near him again.

"Brought up as you have been, Mary," she said later, "you cannot enter into the feelings of one in my position, to whom the very tone of coarse language is unspeakably odious. It makes me sick with disgust. Coarseness is what no lady can endure. I beg you will not mention Mr. Redmain to me again."

"Mrs. Redmain," said Mary, "ugly as such language is, there are many things worse. It seems worse to me that a wife should not go near her husband when he is suffering, than that he should in pain speak bad words."

"You are scarcely in a position to lay down the law for me, Mary," said Hesper sharply. "We will drop the subject."

Mary's words were overheard, as was a good deal in the house, and reached Mr. Redmain, whom they perplexed. What could the young woman hope from taking his part? He knew nothing of her save as a nice-looking maid his wife had—perhaps rather prim, he would have said.

Mewks had been sent for, and one morning, after his arrival, Mary heard Mr. Redmain calling for him in a tone which betrayed that he had been calling for some time. The house was old, and the bells were not in good condition, nor was his in a convenient position. At first she thought to find Mewks, but pity rose in her heart. She ran to Mr. Redmain.

"Can *I* do something for you, Sir?" she said.

"Yes, you can. Go and tell that lumbering idiot to come to me instantly. No! Wait! There's a good girl. Just give me your hand and help turn me an inch or two."

The change of posture relieved him a little.

"Thank you," he said. "That is better. Wait a few minutes, will you, till the rascal comes?"

Immediately followed an agony of pain. In the compassion which she inherited long ago from Eve, Mary took his hand, the fingers of which were twisting themselves into shapes like tree roots. With a hoarse roar, he dashed her hand from his, as if it had been a serpent.

"What did you mean by that?" he said, when he came to himself. "Do you want to make a fool of me?"

Mary did not understand him, and made no reply. Another fit came. This time she kept her distance.

"Come here," he howled, "and take my head in your hands." She obeyed.

"You've got such nice hands! Much nicer than your mistress." Mary took no notice. Gently she withdrew them, for the fit was over.

"Come now," he said, "tell me how it is that a nice, well-behaved, handsome girl like you, should leave a position where, they tell me, you were your own mistress, and take a cursed place as maid to my wife."

"It was because I liked Mrs. Redmain so much," answered Mary, "and I wasn't very comfortable where I was."

"What the devil did you see to like in her? I never saw anything."

"She is so beautiful!" said Mary.

"Is she! Ho! Ho!" he laughed. "What is that to another woman! You are new to the trade, my girl, if you think *that!* One woman taking to another because "she's so beautiful'! Ha! Ha! Ha!" He repeated Mary's words with an indescribable contempt, and his laugh was insulting, but it went off in a cry of suffering.

"Come, give me a better reason for waiting on my wife?"

"She was kind to me," said Mary.

"It's more than ever she was to me! What wages does she give you?"

"We have not spoken about that yet, Sir."

"You haven't had any? Then what the deuce made you come to this house?"

"I hoped to be of some service to Mrs. Redmain," said Mary, growing troubled.

"And you aren't of any? Is that why you don't want wages? Look, never mind—you needn't bother telling me—give me that pocketbook on the table."

Mary brought it to him.

"If your mistress won't pay you your wages, I will." He opened it, and taking from it some notes, held them out to her. "There! Take that!"

Mary made no move. "I don't take wages from Mrs. Redmain," she answered, "and I certainly shall not from anyone else. Besides, it would be dishonest."

"Where would be the dishonesty," said Mr. Redmain, "when the money is mine to do with as I please?"

"Where the dishonesty, Sir!" exclaimed Mary, astounded. "To take wages from you, and pretend to Mrs. Redmain I was going without!"

"Go along," cried Mr. Redmain, losing—or pretending to lose—

his patience with her. "You are too unscrupulous a liar for me to deal with."

Mary turned and left the room. As she went, his keen glance caught the expression of her countenance, and noted the indignant red that flushed her cheeks, and the lightning of wronged innocence in her eyes. "I ought not to have said it," he remarked to himself. He did not for a moment fancy that she had spoken the truth, but her look went to a deeper place in him than he knew existed.

"Stop!" he cried as she was disappearing. "Come back!"

"I will find Mr. Mewks," she answered, and went.

After this, Mary naturally dreaded any talk with Mr. Redmain, and he, thinking she must have time to get over the offense he had given her, made no fresh attempt to understand her character and scheme of life. His curiosity, however, had not been assuaged, and he meditated how best to renew the attempt in London.

31.
Godfrey and
Sepia

When the Redmains went to Cornwall, Sepia stayed at Durnmelling, in the expectation of joining them in London within a fortnight. Her stay was prolonged because of Mr. Redmain's illness in Cornwall, and boredom set in. She found herself capable of doing almost anything to relieve it—even going for a solitary walk. She thought she had the poor possibility of a distraction coming her way, and the hope was not altogether a vague one, for was there not a man somewhere underneath those chimneys she saw over the roof of the laundry? She had never spoken to him, but Hesper and she had often talked about him and watched him ride. In her wanderings she had come upon the breach in the gully wall and, clambering up, had found herself on the forbidden ground of a neighbor whom the family did not visit.

On one of her rambles on the grounds of Thornwick, she had her desire and met Godfrey Wardour. He lifted off his hat, and she stopped and addressed him by way of apology.

"I am afraid you think me very rude, Mr. Wardour," she said. "I know I am trespassing, but this field of yours is higher than the ground about Durnmelling, and seems to take pounds off the weight of the atmosphere."

For all he had gone through, Godfrey was no less than courteous to ladies. He assured Miss Yolland that Thornwick was as much at her service as if it were a part of Durnmelling.

"Though, indeed," he added with a smile, "it would be more correct to say, 'as if Durnmelling were a part of Thornwick'; for

173

that was the real state of the case once upon a time."

The statement seemed to interest Miss Yolland, giving rise to many questions, and a long conversation ensued. Suddenly she woke, or seemed to wake, to the consciousness that she had forgotten herself and the proprieties together, and hastily wished him a good-morning. But she was not too much confused to thank him for the permission he had given her to walk on his ground.

It was not by any intention on the part of Godfrey that they met several times after this, but they always had a little conversation before they parted. Sepia did not find any difficulty in getting him sufficiently within the range of her powerful eyes; but she was too prudent to bring to bear upon any man all at once the full play of her mesmeric battery, and things had gotten no further when she left for London, about two weeks before the return of the Redmains. She made it appear that her early presence in London was to prepare things for Hesper, but that this may have been a pretense appears possible from the fact that Mary arrived from Cornwall on the same mission a few days later.

An acquaintance of Sepia was in London at this time. He spoke both English and French with a foreign accent, and gave himself out as a Georgian—Count Galofta, he called himself. During the few days that Sepia was alone, he came to see her several times, calling early in the morning first, the next day in the evening when they went together to the opera, and once came and stayed late.

Mary, arriving unexpectedly at the house, met him in the hall as she entered—he had just taken leave of Sepia who was going up the stairs. Mary had never seen him before, but something about him caused her to look at him as he passed.

Somehow, Tom also had discovered Sepia's return, and had gone to see her more than once.

When Mr. and Mrs. Redmain arrived, there was so much to be done for Hesper's wardrobe that for some days Mary found it impossible to go and see Letty. Hesper seemed harder to please than usual.

The morning after her arrival, Hesper, happening to find herself in want of Mary's immediate help, instead of calling her as she generally did, opened the door between their rooms and saw Mary on her knees by her bedside. Hesper had heard of saying prayers and, when she was a child, had been expected to say her prayers. But to be found on one's knees in the middle of the day looked to her a thing exceedingly odd. Mary was not much in the way of kneeling at such a time—she had to pray much too often to kneel always, and God was too near her, wherever she happened to be, for her to think she must seek Him in a particular place; but so it happened now. Startled rather than troubled, she rose and followed her mistress into her room.

"I am sorry to have disturbed you, Mary," said Hesper, herself a little annoyed, "but people do not generally say their prayers in the middle of the day."

"I say mine when I need to say them," answered Mary, a little cross that Hesper should take any notice. She would rather the thing had not occurred, and it was worse to have to talk about it.

"For my part, I don't see any good in being too religious," said Hesper. "How is one with such claims on her as I have to attend to these things? Society has claims—no one denies that."

"And God has none?" asked Mary.

"Many people now think there is no God at all," returned Hesper, with an almost petulant expression.

"If there is no God, that settles the question," answered Mary. "But if there should be one—"

"Then I am sure He would never be hard on one like me. I do just like other people. One must do as people do. If there is one thing that must be avoided more than another, it is peculiarity. How ridiculous it would be of anyone to set herself against society!"

"Then you think the Judge will be satisfied if you say, 'Lord, I had so many names in my visiting book, and so many invitations I could not refuse, that it was impossible for me to attend to these things'?"

"I don't see that I'm at all worse than other people," persisted Hesper. "I don't see what I've got to repent of."

"Then, of course, you can't repent," said Mary.

Hesper recovered herself a little. "I am glad you see the thing as I do," she said.

"I don't see it at all as you do, Ma'am," answered Mary, gently.

"Why!" exclaimed Hesper, taken by surprise, "what have I got to repent of?"

"Do you really want me to say what I think?" asked Mary.

"Of course, I do," returned Hesper, getting angry, and at the

175

THE SHOPKEEPER'S DAUGHTER

same time uneasy. She knew Mary's freedom of speech upon occasion, but felt that to draw back would be to yield the point. "What have I done to be ashamed of?"

"If I had married a man I did not love," answered Mary, "I should be more ashamed of myself than I could tell."

"That is the way of looking at such things in the class you belong to," rejoined Hesper. "With *us* it is quite different. There is no necessity laid upon *you*. Our *position* obliges us."

"But what if God should not see it as you do? When you married, you promised many things, not one of which have you ever done."

"Really, Mary, this is intolerable!" cried Hesper. She wished heartily she had never challenged Mary's judgment. "But," she resumed more quietly, "how could you, how could anyone, how could God Himself, ask me to fulfill the part of a loving wife to a man like Mr. Redmain? There is no use mincing matters with *you*, Mary."

"But you promised," persisted Mary. "It belongs to the very idea of marriage."

"There are a thousand promises made every day which nobody is expected to keep. It is the custom, the way of the world! How many of the clergy, now, believe the things they put their names to?"

"They must answer for themselves. We are not clergymen, but women who ought never to say a thing except we mean it, and when we have said it, to stick to it."

"But just look around you and see how many there are in precisely the same position! Will you dare to say they are all going to be lost because they do not behave like angels to their brutes of husbands?"

"I say they have got to repent of behaving to their husbands as their husbands behave to them."

"You can never, in your sober senses, Mary," she said, "mean that God requires me to do things for Mr. Redmain that the servants can do a great deal better! That would be ridiculous, not to mention that I oughtn't and couldn't and wouldn't do them for any man!"

"Many a woman," said Mary, with a solemnity in her tone which she did not intend to appear there, "has done many more trying things for persons of whom she knew nothing."

176

"I daresay! But such women go in for being saints, and that is not my line. I was not made for that, and I do not know how they find it possible."

"I can tell you how. They love every human being because he is human. Your husband might be a demon from the way you behave to him."

"I suppose *you* find it agreeable to wait upon him—he is civil to you, I daresay!"

"Not very," replied Mary, with a smile, "but the person who cannot bear with a sick man or baby is not fit to be a woman."

"You may go to your room," said Hesper.

For the first time, a feeling of dislike to Mary awoke in Hesper. The next few days she scarcely spoke to her, sending directions for her work through Sepia who discharged the office with dignity.

32.
Lydgate Street

Letty's whole life was now gathered about her boy, and she thought comparatively little about Tom. And Tom thought so little about her that he did not perceive the difference. When he came home, he was always in a hurry to be gone again. He always had something important to do, but it never showed itself to Letty in the shape of money. He gave her a little now and then, and she made it go incredibly far, but it was always with a grudge that he gave it.

She found that he had not paid the lodging for two months, and that bills for various things he had told her to order had been neglected. When she reminded him, he treated it at one time as a matter of no consequence which he would speedily set right, and at another as if the behavior of the creditor were hugely impertinent and Tom would punish him by making him wait. Letty's heart sank within her and she felt as if she lay already in the depths of a debtors' prison. Therefore, as sparing as she had been from the first, she was now more sparing than ever. She would buy nothing for which she could not pay immediately, and in consequence, she often had to go without proper food. Even when she had a little money in hand, she would save it rather than spend it. She grew very thin, and indeed, if she had not been of the healthiest, she could not have stood her own treatment many weeks.

Her baby soon began to show suffering, but this did not make her alter her way or appeal to Tom. She was ignorant of the simplest things a mother needs to know, and never imagined her abstinence from nourishing food could hurt her baby. So long as she went on nursing him, it was all the same, she thought. He cried so much that Tom sometimes would not come home at night—the child would not let him sleep, and how was he to do his work if he had not his night's rest?

The baby went on crying, and the mother's heart was torn. The woman of the house said he must be cutting his teeth and recommended some devilish syrup. Letty bought a bottle with the next money she got, and thought it did him good—because, lessening his appetite, it lessened his crying, and also made him sleep more than he ought.

One night Tom came home having drunk too much and, in maudlin affection, insisted on taking the baby from its cradle. The baby shrieked. Tom was angry with the weakling, rated him soundly for ingratitude to "the author of his being," and shook him roughly to teach him the good manners of the world he had come to.

In Letty sprang up the mother, erect and fierce. She darted to Tom, snatched the child from his arms, and turned to carry him to the inner room. But, as the mother arose in Letty, the devil arose in Tom. With one stride he overtook his wife, and mother and child lay together on the floor. Although he did not strike his wife as he would have struck a man, for days she carried the record of it on her cheek in five red fingermarks.

When he saw her on the floor, Tom came to himself, knew what he had done, and was sobered. He took the baby, and laying him on the rug, lifted the weeping Letty. Placing her on the sofa, he knelt beside her—not humbly to entreat her pardon, but rather to justify himself by proving that all the blame was hers, and that she had wronged him greatly in driving him to do such a thing. Letty, never having had from him fuller acknowledgment of wrong, accepted the "apology." She turned on the sofa, threw her arms about his neck, kissed him, and clung to him with an utter forgiveness. But all this did for Tom was to restore him his good opinion of himself and enable him to go on feeling as much of a gentleman as before.

Reconciled, they turned to the baby. He was pale, his eyes were closed, and they could not tell whether he breathed. In a horrible fright, Tom ran for the doctor. Before he returned with him, the child had come to, and the doctor could discover no injury from

179

the fall they told him he had had. But he did say he was not properly nourished, and must have better food.

This was a fresh difficulty for Letty, for it meant more money. Their landlady, who had been very kind and patient, was in trouble about her own rent, and began to press for at least part of theirs. Letty's heart seemed to labor under a stone. She forgot that there was a thing called joy. So sad she looked that the good woman, full of pity, assured her that come what might, she should not be turned out, but at the worst would only have to go a story higher to inferior rooms. The rent could wait, she said, until better days. But this kindness relieved Letty only a little, for the rent past and the rent to come hung on her like a cloak of lead.

But the rent wasn't the worst that now oppressed her. Possibly from the fall, but more from the prolonged want of suitable nourishment and wise treatment, after that terrible night the baby grew worse. Many were the tears the sleepless mother shed over the sallow face and wasted limbs of her slumbering treasure, her one antidote to countless sorrows, and many were the foolish means she tried to restore his sinking vitality.

While at Testbridge Mary had written to Letty, and she had written back, but without saying anything of the straits to which she was reduced—*that* would bring blame upon Tom. Mary, with her fine human instinct, felt things must be going worse than before, and when she found that her return was indefinitely postponed by Mr. Redmain's illness, she ventured upon a daring measure. She wrote to Mr. Wardour, telling him she had reason to fear things were not going well with Letty Helmer and suggesting, in the gentlest way, whether it might not now be time to let bygones be bygones and make some inquiry about her.

Godfrey returned no answer to the letter. For all her denial, he had never ceased to believe that Mary had been Letty's accomplice throughout that miserable affair, and the very name of Letty Helmer stung him to the quick. He took it as a piece of utter presumption that Mary would write to him about Letty. But while he was indignant with Mary, he was also vexed with Letty that she would not herself have written to him if she was in any need, forgetting that he had never hinted at any open door of communication between them. His heart quivered at the thought that she might be in distress—he had known for certain that fool Tom would bring her to misery! For himself, the thought of Letty was an ever-open wound, with an ever-present pain, now dull and aching, now keen and stinging. But while thus he brooded, a fierce and evil joy awoke in him at the thought that now at last the expected hour had come when he would heap coals of fire on her head. He was still fool enough to think of her as having forsaken him, although he had never given her grounds for believing that he cared for her. If he could but let her have a glimmer of what she had lost in losing him! She knew what she had gained in Tom Helmer!

Godfrey passed a troubled night, dreamed painfully, and started awake to renewed pain. By morning he had made up his mind to take the first train to London. But he thought far more of being her deliverer than of bringing her deliverance.

33.
Godfrey and Letty

====================

It was a sad, gloomy, night when Godfrey arrived in London. The wind was cold, and the very dust that blew in his face was cold. He was chilled to the heart when he walked up to the door and rang the bell.

It was not a house of ceremonies. He was shown up into the room where Letty sat, without a word carried before to prepare her for his visit. It was so dark that he could see nothing but a figure at work by a table on which stood a single candle. There was but a spark of fire in the dreary grate, and Letty was colder than she could ever remember. At the moment she was cutting down the last woolly garment she had, in the vain hope of warming her baby.

She looked up. She had thought it was the landlady, and waited for her to speak. Now she gazed for a moment in bewilderment, saw who it was and jumped up, half-frightened, half-ready to go wild with joy. All the memories of Godfrey rushed in and overwhelmed her. She ran to him, and the same moment was in his arms, with her head on his shoulder, weeping tears of such gladness as she had not known since the first week of her marriage.

Neither spoke for some time. Letty could not because she was crying, and Godfrey would not because he did not want to cry. Those few moments were pure, simple happiness to both of them—to Letty, because she had loved him from childhood, and hoped that all was to be as of old between them, and to Godfrey, because for the moment he had forgotten himself, and had thought neither of injury nor of hope, remembering only the old days and the Letty that used to be. It may seem strange that, having never once embraced her in all the time they lived in the same house, he should do so now. But Letty's love would have responded to the least show of affection, and when at the sight of his face she rushed into his arms, how could he help kissing her?

The embrace could not be a long one. Godfrey was the first to relax its hold, and Letty responded with an instant collapse, afraid that she feared she had done it all and disgusted Godfrey. But he led her gently to the sofa and sat down beside her on the hard old slippery horsehair. Then he saw how she had changed. She was pale and thin and sad, and with such big eyes.

"My poor girl!" said Godfrey, in a voice which, if he had not kept it lower than usual, would have broken. "You are suffering."

"Oh, no, I'm not," replied Letty, with a pitiful effort at being cheerful. "I'm only so glad to see you again!"

She sat on the edge of the sofa, and put her open hands, palm to palm, between her knees, in a childish way. For a moment Godfrey sat gazing at her, with troubled heart and troubled looks, then between his teeth muttered, "Damn the rascal!"

Letty sat straight up, and turned upon him eyes of appeal, scared, yet ready to defend. Her hands were now clenched, one on each side of her.

"Cousin Godfrey!" she cried. "I will go away if you speak a word against Tom, I will—I *must*, you know!"

Godfrey made no reply—neither apologized nor sought to cover up.

"Why child!" he said at last, "you are half-starved!"

The pity and tenderness of both word and tone were too much for her. Such an utterance from the man she loved like an elder brother caused her to break into a cry. She tried to suppress it, fought it, and in her agony she would have rushed from the room, had not Godfrey caught her, drawn her down beside him, and kept her there.

"You shall not leave me!" he said in that voice Letty had always been used to obey. "Come, you must tell me all about it."

"I have nothing to tell, Cousin Godfrey," she replied with some calmness, for Godfrey's decision had enabled her to conquer herself, "except that my baby is ill and looks as if he would never get better, and it is like to break my heart. Oh, he is such a darling!"

"Let me see him," said Godfrey, in his heart detesting the child—the visible sign that another was nearer to Letty than he.

She jumped up, almost ran into the next room, and coming back with her little one, laid him in Godfrey's arms. The moment he felt the weight of the sad-looking, sleeping baby, he grew human toward him, and saw in him Letty, not Tom.

"Good God! The child is starving too," he exclaimed.

"Oh, no, Cousin Godfrey!" cried Letty. "He had a fresh-laid egg for breakfast this morning, and some arrowroot for dinner, and some bread and milk for tea—"

"London milk!" said Godfrey.

"Well, it is not like the milk in the dairy at Thornwick," admitted Letty. "If he had milk like that he would soon be well!"

But Godfrey dared not say, "Bring him to Thornwick." He knew his mother too well for that!

"When were you last out in the country?" he asked, still holding the baby.

"Not since we were married," she answered sadly. "Poor Tom can't afford it. He gets some money from his mother, but it can't be much."

But Godfrey happened to have heard "from the best authority" that Tom's mother was very liberal with him. His suspicions against Tom increased every moment. He must learn the truth. He sat silent a moment, then said, with assumed cheerfulness, "Well, Letty, I suppose, for the sake of old times, you will give me some dinner?"

Then her courage gave way. She turned from him, laid her head on the end of the sofa, and sobbed so that the room seemed to shake with the convulsions of her grief.

"Letty," said Godfrey, laying the baby down and placing his hand on her head, "it is no use trying to hide the truth. I don't want any dinner; in fact, I dined long ago. But you would not be open with me, and I was forced to find out for myself. You have not had enough to eat, and you know it. I will not say a word about who is to blame—for anything I know, it may be no one. I am sure it is not you. But this must not go on! I have brought you a little pocketbook." He reached into his coat and withdrew the small purse. "I will call again tomorrow, and you will tell me then how you like it."

He laid it on the table. There was ten times as much money in it as Letty had ever had at once, but she never knew how much. She rose with instant resolve as all the woman in her waked at once. She felt that a moment was come when she must be resolute, or lose her hold on life.

"Cousin Godfrey," she said, in a tone he scarcely recognized as hers, "if you do not take that purse away, I will throw it in the fire without opening it. If my husband cannot give me enough to eat, I can starve as well as another. If you loved Tom, it would be different, but you hate him, and I will have nothing from you. Take it away!"

Mortified, hurt, miserable, Godfrey took the purse, and without a word walked from the room. Somewhere down in his secret heart was dawning an idea of Letty beyond anything he used to think of her, but in the meantime he was only blindly aware that his heart had been shot through and through. Nor was this the time for him to reflect that under his training, Letty, even if he had married her, would never have grown to such dignity.

Indeed it was only in that moment she had become capable of the action. She had been growing under the heavy snows of affliction, and this was her first blossom. Had it been her pride refusing the help of an old friend, that should not be counted a blossom. But the dignity of her refusal was that she would accept nothing in which her husband had no spiritual share. She married Tom because she loved him, and she would hold by him, wherever that might lead her. She would not knowingly allow Godfrey's kindness to come between her and Tom. To accept Godfrey's help in place of the provision of her husband would be to let him, however innocently, step into his place! There was no reasoning in her resolve; it was simply that Letty felt that taking the money would be the opening of a gulf to divide her from her Tom forever.

The moment Godfrey was out of the room, she cast herself on the floor and sobbed as if her heart must break. But her sobs were tearless. Unsought came the conviction that Tom would have had her take the money! More than once or twice, in the ill-humors that follow a forced hilarity, he had forgotten his claims to being a gentleman so far as to remind her that if she was poor, she was no poorer than she had been when dependent upon the charity of a distant relation!

The baby began to cry. She rose and gathered him into her arms and held him fast to her bosom, as if by laying their two aching lives together they might both be healed. And rocking him to and fro, she said to herself, for the first time, that her trouble was greater than she could bear. "O Baby, Baby, Baby!" she cried, and her tears streamed on the wan little face. But as she sat with him in her arms, the blessed sleep came to them both, and the storm sank to a calm.

It was dark, when she awoke. For a minute she could not remember where she was. The candle had burned out—it must be late. The baby was on her lap, very still. One faint gleam of satisfaction crossed her at the thought that he slept so peacefully, hidden from the gloom which somehow appeared to be all the same gloom outside and inside of her. In that gloom she sat alone.

But suddenly she started to her feet in an agony—a horrible fear had taken possession of her. With one arm she held her child fast to her bosom, with the other hand searched in vain to find a match. And still as she searched, the baby seemed to grow heavier upon her arm, and the fear sickened more and more at her heart.

At last she had light, and the face of the child came out of the darkness. But the child himself had gone away into it. The unspeakable had come while she slept—had come and gone, and taken her child with him. What was left of him was no more good to kiss than the last doll of her childhood.

34.
Relief

That same night, Tom went to see Sepia. But she had planned to go to a play with a cousin of the Redmains. Before the hour arrived, Count Galofta called, and Sepia went out with him, telling the doorman to ask her escort to wait. The doorman was rather deaf and did not catch the name she gave.

Tom, in jealous disapproval, had left the house and spent the greater part of his evening in a tavern in gloomy solitude, drinking brandy and building castles of the most foolish type. Through all their rooms glided Sepia, his evil genius. He rose at last, paid his bill, and stalked into the street. Almost unconsciously, he turned and walked westward. It was getting late, and before long the theatres would be emptying, he might have a glimpse of Sepia as she came out. But then, growing more daring, Tom thought he would just go to the house and see her after her escort had left her at the door.

He went to the house and rang the bell. The doorman came and said that Miss Yolland was out, but desired that Mr. Helmer wait. Tom walked in and up the stairs to the drawing room, then into a second and a third room, and at last into the conservatory. After pacing for many minutes, he grew tired and threw himself on a couch and fell fast asleep.

He woke in the middle of the night in pitch darkness—it was some time before he could remember where he was. When he did, he recognized that he was in an awkward predicament. But he

187

knew the house well and would make the attempt to get out undiscovered. It was foolish, but Tom was foolish. Feeling his way, he knocked down a small table with a great crash of china, and losing his head, rushed for the stair. Happily, the hall lamp was still burning, and he had no trouble with the bolts or locks.

The first breath of the cold night air brought with it such a gush of joy as he had rarely experienced, and he trod the silent streets with something of the pleasure of an escaped criminal, until the wind reminded him he had left his hat behind! He felt as if he had committed a murder and left his cardcase with the body, and vague terror grew upon him as he hurried along. Justice seemed following on his track.

He hurried up the stair of his home, his long legs taking three steps at a time. Never before when going home to his wife had he felt as if he were fleeing to a refuge.

When Tom opened the door, there on the floor lay Letty as if dead, and a little way from her the child, dead indeed and cold with death. He lifted Letty and carried her to the bed, amazed to find how light she was—it was a long time since he had carried her thus in his arms. Then he laid her dead baby by her side and ran to rouse the doctor, who came and pronounced the child quite dead—from lack of nutrition, he said. To see Tom, no one could have helped contrasting his dress and appearance with the look and surroundings of his wife, but no one would lay blame on him. As for himself, he was not in the least aware of his guilt.

The doctor gave the landlady, who had responded at once to Tom's call, full directions for the care of the bereaved mother. Tom handed her the little money he had in his pocket, and she promised to do her best. And she did, for she was one of those who, knowing little of religion toward God, yet are full of religion toward others. As soon as it was light, Tom had to see about burying his baby.

He went first to the editor of the *Firefly*, and told him his baby was dead and he needed money. The man was kind, and told him it was forthcoming at once, for literary men, like all other artists, are in general as ready to help each other as the very poor themselves.

"But," said the editor, who had noted the dry, burning palm, and saw the glazed, fiery eye of Tom, "my dear fellow, you ought to be in bed yourself. It's no use worrying about the poor child—

you couldn't help it. Go home to your wife, and tell her she's got you to nurse, and if she needs anything, tell her to come to me."

Tom went home, but did not give his wife the message. She lay all but insensible, never asking for anything or refusing anything that was offered her, and never said a word about her baby. Her baby was buried, and she knew nothing of it. Not until nine days later did she begin to revive.

For the first few days, Tom, moved with undefined remorse, tried to take part in nursing her. She took things from him as she did from the landlady, without heed or recognition. Just once, suddenly opening her eyes wide upon him, she uttered a feeble wail of "Baby!" and turning her head, did not look at him again. Then for the first time, Tom's conscience gave him a sharp sting.

He was far from well. The careless and, in many respects, dissolute life he had been leading had begun to tell on him, but he had never become aware of his weakness, nor had ever felt really ill until now.

But that sting, although the first sharp one, was not his first warning of a waking conscience. Ever since he took his place at his wife's bedside, he had been fighting off the conviction that he was a brute. He could not believe it! What? Tom Helmer—the fine, indubitable fellow? With that pitiful cry of his wife after her lost child, disbelief in himself got within the lines of his defense.

Conscience reacts on the body, and the moment it spoke plainly to Tom, the little that was left of his physical endurance gave way, and his illness got the upper hand. He took to his bed—all he could have for a bed, that is—the sofa in the sitting room, widened out with chairs, and a mattress over all. There he lay, and their landlady had enough to do. Not that either patient was exacting— they were both too ill and miserable for self-pity or coddling.

Tom groaned and tossed and cursed himself, and soon passed into delirium. His visions, animate with shame and confusion of soul, were more distressing than even his ready tongue could have told. Dead babies and ghastly women pursued him everywhere. His fever increased. The cries of terror and dismay he uttered reached the ears of his wife, and were the first thing that roused her from her lethargy. She rose from her bed and, just able to crawl, began to do what she could for him. If she could but get near enough to him, the husband would yet be dearer than any child. She helped him to the bed, and took to the sofa herself. To and fro between bed and sofa she crept, let the landlady say what she might, giving him all the food he would take, cooling his burning hands and head, and crying over him because she could not take him on her lap like her baby that was gone. Once or twice he looked at her pitifully, and seemed about to speak, but the fever carried far away the word of love for which she listened so eagerly.

The doctor came daily, but Tom grew worse, and Letty could not get well.

35.
The Helper

One morning, when she believed Mrs. Redmain would not rise before noon, Mary felt she must go and see Letty. She did not find her in the quarters where she had left her, but a story higher in a mean room, sitting with her hands in her lap. Letty did not lift her eyes when Mary entered; where hope is dead, curiosity dies. Not until Mary had come quite near did she raise her head, and then she seemed to know nothing of her. When she did recognize her, she held out her hand in a mechanical way, as if they were two specters met in a miserable dream in which they were nothing to each other.

"My poor Letty!" cried Mary, greatly shocked, "what has happened? Has anything happened to Tom?"

Letty broke into a low, childish wail, and for a time that was all Mary heard. Presently she became aware of a feeble moaning in the adjoining chamber, the sound of a human sea in trouble mixed with a wandering babble, which to Letty was the voice of her own despair, and to Mary a cry of help. She abandoned the attempt to draw anything from Letty and went into the next room. There lay Tom, but so changed that Mary took a moment to be certain it was he. Going softly to him, she laid her hand on his burning head. He opened his eyes, but she saw their sense was gone. She went back to Letty, and sitting down beside her, put her arm about her and asked, "Why didn't you send for me, Letty? I would have come at once. I will come now, tonight, and help you nurse him. Where is the baby?"

Letty gave a shriek, and starting from her chair she walked wildly about the room, wringing her hands. Mary went after her, and taking her in her arms, said, "Letty, has God taken your baby?"

Letty gave her a lackluster look.

"Then," said Mary, "he is not far away, for we are all in God's arms."

Mary saw that for Letty, God was nowhere. It went to her very heart. Death and desolation and the enemy were in possession. She turned to go, that she might return able to begin her contest with ruin. Letty saw that she was going, and imagined her offended, and abandoning her to her misery. She flew to her, stretching out her arms like a child, but was so feeble that she tripped and fell. Mary lifted her, and laid her on her couch.

"Letty," said Mary, "you didn't think I was going to leave you! But I must go for an hour, perhaps two, to make arrangements for staying with you until Tom is over the worst."

Then Letty clasped her hands in her old beseeching way, and looked up with a faint show of comfort.

Mary drove straight home, and heard that Mrs. Redmain was annoyed that she had gone out.

"I offered to dress her," said Jemima, "and she knows I can do quite well, but she would not get up till you came, and made me fetch her a book. So there she is, waiting for you!"

"I am sorry," said Mary, "but I had to go, and she was fast asleep."

When she entered her room, Hesper gave her a cold glance over the top of her novel, and went on with her reading. Mary proceeded to get her things ready for dressing, but by this time Hesper had got interested in the story.

"I shall not get up yet," she said.

"Then, please, Ma'am," replied Mary, "would you mind letting Jemima dress you? I want to go out again, and should be glad if you could do without me for some days. My friend's baby is dead, and both she and her husband are very ill."

Hesper threw down her book, and her eyes flamed. "What do you mean by using me so, Miss Marston? I have nothing to do with their problems. When you made it necessary for me to part with my maid, you undertook to perform her duties. I did not engage you as a sick nurse for other people."

"No, Ma'am," replied Mary, "but this is an extreme case, and I cannot believe you will object to my going."

"I do object. How is the world to go on, if this kind of thing be permitted! I may be going out to dinner, or to the opera tonight, for anything you know, and who is there to dress me? No, on principle, and for the sake of example, I will not let you go!"

"I thought," said Mary, not a little disappointed in Hesper, "I did not stand to you quite in the relation of an ordinary servant."

"Certainly you do not! I look for a little more devotion from you than from a common, ungrateful creature who thinks only of herself. But you are all alike."

More and more distressed to find one she had loved so long show herself so selfish, Mary's indignation had almost got the better of her. But a little heightening of her color was all that showed.

"Indeed, it is quite necessary, Ma'am," she persisted, "that I should go."

"The law has fortunately made provision against such behavior," said Hesper. "You cannot leave without giving me a month's notice."

"The understanding on which I came to you was very different," said Mary sadly.

"It was, but since then, you consented to become my maid. I have to protect myself, and the world in general, from the consequences that must follow, if such lawless behavior is allowed to pass."

Hesper spoke with calm severity and Mary, making up her mind, answered now with almost equal calmness.

"The law was made for both sides, Ma'am, and as you bring the law to me, I will take refuge in the law. It is, I believe, a month's warning or a month's wages, and as I have never had any wages, I imagine I am at liberty to go. Good-bye, Ma'am."

Hesper made no answer, and Mary left the room. She went to her own, stuffed her immediate necessities into a bag, including some of her savings, let herself out of the house, called a cab, and with a great lump in her throat, drove to the help of Letty.

First she had a talk with the landlady and learned all she could tell. Then she went up, and began to make things as comfortable as she could—all was in sad disorder and neglect.

With the mere inauguration of cleanliness, and the first dawn of coming order, Letty's courage began to revive a little. The impossibility of doing all that ought to be done had, in her miserable weakness, so depressed her that she had not done even as much as she could—except where Tom was immediately concerned. There she had not failed!

Mary next went to the doctor to get instructions, and then to buy what things were most wanted. Under her skillful nursing (skillful not from experience, but simply from her faith), the crisis of Tom's fever at length passed, but the result remained doubtful. By late hours and strong drink, he had weakened his constitution.

While he was yet delirious, and grief and shame and consternation operated at will on his poetic nature, the things he kept saying over and over were very pitiful. But they would have sounded more miserable by much in the ears of one who did not look so far ahead as Mary. She was glad to find him loathing his former self, and beyond the present suffering saw the gladness at hand for the sorrowful man, the repenting sinner. Had she been mother or sister to him, she could hardly have waited on him with more devotion.

One day, as his wife was doing some little thing for him, he took her hand in his feeble grasp, and pressing it to his face, said, "We might have been happy together, Letty, if I had but known how much you were worth, and how little I was worth myself!" And he burst into an uncontrollable wail that tortured Letty with its likeness to the crying of her baby.

"Tom!" she cried. "When you speak as if I belonged to you, it makes me as happy as a queen. When you are better, you will be happy too, Dear. Mary says you will."

"O Letty!" he sobbed. "The baby!"

"The baby's all right, Mary says, and someday, she says, he will run into your arms, and know you for his father."

"And I shall be ashamed to look at him!" said Tom.

Both Mary and Letty were in his room when an hour or so later he woke from a short sleep, and his eyes sought Letty's watching face. "I have seen Baby," he said, "and he has forgiven me. I daresay it was only a dream," he added, "but somehow it makes me happier." He paused, for talking exhausted him. But shortly he resumed. "You and Mary have saved me from what I dare not think of! I could die happy now—if it weren't for one thing."

"What is that?" asked Mary.

"I am ashamed to say," he replied, "but it is horrid to think that even when I am in my grave, people will still have a hold of me and a right over me still, because of debts I shall never be able to pay."

"Don't be too sure of that, Tom," said Mary cheerfully. "I think you will pay them yet."

"I always did mean to pay them. I don't think they would come to more than a hundred pounds."

"Your mother would not hesitate to pay that for you?" asked Mary.

"I know she wouldn't, but I'm thinking of Letty."

He paused, and Mary waited. "You know when I am gone, there will be nothing for her but to go to my mother, and it breaks my heart to think of it. Every sin of mine will be laid to her charge."

"I will pay your debts, Tom, and gladly," said Mary, "if they don't come to much more than you say they are."

"But don't you see, Mary, that would only be a shifting of my debt to you? Except for Letty, it would not make things any better."

"Well, I will tell you what will be better; let your mother pay your debts, and I will look after Letty. I will care for her like my own sister, Tom."

"Then I shall die happy," said Tom, and from that day he began to recover.

Tom would not hear of his mother being written to. "I have done Letty wrong enough already," he said, "without subjecting her to the cruel tongue of my mother. I have enough conscience left to not have anybody else abuse her."

"But, Tom," expostulated Mary, "if you want to be good, one of your first duties is to be reconciled to your mother."

"I am very sorry things are wrong between us, Mary," said Tom. "But if you want her to come here, you don't know what you are talking about. She must have everything her own way, or storm from morning till night. I would gladly make it up with her; but live with her or die with her, I could *not*. To make either possible, you must convert her too. When you have done that, I will invite her at once."

"Never mind me, Tom," said Letty. "So long as you love me, I don't care what your mother thinks of me. I will do all I can to make her comfortable."

"Wait till I am better, Letty; for if she comes, I haven't a chance of recovery. For the present, I will dictate a letter, if you will write it, bidding her good-bye, and asking her pardon for everything I have done wrong. If I die, you can send the letter for me. I cannot and will not promise more."

He was excited and exhausted, and Mary dared not say another word. Nor did she see what more could be done. Where all relation has been perverted, things cannot be set right by force. Perhaps all that can be done is to be willing to wait.

The letter was dictated and written; a lovely one, Mary thought, and it made her weep as she wrote it. Tom signed it with his own hand. Mary folded, sealed, and addressed it, and laid it away in her desk.

36.
The Leper

The faint, luminous strain of bow and string came hovering—none could have said whether it was in the soul only, or in the outer world too.

"Mary!" Letty called into the other room. "There is our friend with the violin again! Don't you think Tom would like to hear him? Would you mind asking him to come and play a little for us?"

Mary went up the stairs and found the musician with his half sister.

"I *thought* we should have you in on us!" said Ann. "Joe thinks he can play so as nobody can hear him, and I was fool enough to let him try! I am sorry."

"I am glad," rejoined Mary, "and I came to ask him downstairs. We think it would be good for Mr. Helmer to hear him. He is very fond of music."

"Much help music will be to him, poor young man!" said Ann scornfully.

"Wouldn't you give a sick man a flower, even if it only made him a little happier for a moment?" asked Mary.

"No, I wouldn't. It would only be to help the deceitful heart be more desperately wicked."

"I read my Bible a good deal," said Mary, "but I have never found anything that says the beauty of creation can lead to wickedness."

"That's because you were never taught to look for it," said Ann.

197

"Very likely," returned Mary. "In the meantime I prefer the violin—that is, with one like your brother to play it."

She turned to the door, and Joseph Jasper, who had not spoken a word, rose and followed her. As soon as they were outside, Mary turned to him and begged him to play the same piece with which he had ended on the previous occasion.

"I thought you did not care for it!" he said.

"I care for it very much," replied Mary, "and have often thought of it since. But you left in such haste, before I could find the words to thank you!"

"You mean the ten lepers, don't you?" he said. "But of course you do. I always end off with that one."

"Is that what you call it?" returned Mary. "Then you have given me the key to understanding it much better, I hope."

"That is what I call it—to myself, I mean, not to Ann. She would count it blasphemy. God has made so many things that she thinks must not be mentioned in His hearing!"

When they entered the room, Joseph cast a quick look around and made at once for the darkest corner. Three swift strides took him there, and without more preamble than if he had come upon a public platform to play, he closed his eyes and began to play.

Now that Mary understood at least this one specimen of his strange music, she was able to fill up the blanks in the impression it formerly made upon her.

The violin brought before her mind's eye the Man who knew all about everything. She saw Him walking in the hot day between Galilee and Samaria. Sounds arose which she interpreted as the stir of village life, the crying and calling of domestic animals, and of busy housewives at their duties. The instrument then began to tell the gathering of a crowd with beelike hum, and the crossing of voice with voice, but at a distance, the sounds confused and obscure. Swiftly then they seemed to rush together, to blend and lose themselves in the unity of an imploring melody, in which she heard the words, uttered afar, with uplifted hands and voices, drawing nearer and nearer as often repeated, "Jesus, Master, have mercy on us." A brief pause, and then what, to her seemed the voice of the Master saying, "Go, show yourselves to the priests." Then followed the slow, half-willing march of timeless feet! A clang as of something broken, a silence as of sunrise, and then air and liberty—long drawn notes divided with quick hurried ones, the tramping of many feet going farther and farther, merrily with dance and song, once more a sudden pause, and a melody in which she read the awestruck joyous return of one man. Steadily yet eagerly the feet drew near, the melody growing at once in awe and jubilation, as the man came nearer and nearer to Him whose word had made him clean, until at last she saw him fall on his face before Him, and heard his soul rushing forth in a strain of adoring thanks, which seemed to end only because it was choked in tears.

The violin ceased and, as if its soul had passed from the instrument into his, the musician himself took up the strain, and in a mellow tenor voice, with a mingling of air and recitative, and an expression which to Mary was entrancing, sang the words, "And he was a Samaritan."

At the sound of his own voice, he seemed to wake up, hung his head for a moment, as if ashamed of having shown his emotion, tucked his instrument under his arm and walked from the room, without a word spoken on either side.

37.
Mary and Mr. Redmain

A few rudiments of righteousness lurked in the being of Mr. Redmain. The soul of his mother carried a strain of generosity which had left a mark on him, and it was the best thing about him. But in action these rudiments took an evil shape.

He preferred inferior company, and because he did not seek the good, never yet in all his life had he come near enough to a righteous man to recognize that one as different from himself. As for women, there was his wife—of whom he was willing to think as well as she would let him—and beside Sepia, she was an angel! He believed he understood Sepia, although he did not yet know her history. Ever since his marriage he had been scheming how to get rid of her; through finding her out, he must unmask her. There would be no satisfaction in getting rid of her without his wife's convinced acquiescence. So he was always on the watch to uncover the wickedness he felt sure lay at no great depth beneath her surface. Between Sepia and Mr. Redmain continued a distance too great for either difference or misunderstanding. Their few words were polite, and their demeanor was civil but his attentions were seldom wasted at home. Although he lived on good terms with her, she had no idea how thin was the crust between her and the lava.

In Cornwall he had begun to puzzle himself about Mary. Of course, she was just like the rest, but he did not succeed in fitting what he saw of her to what he entirely believed of her. She remained, like Sepia, a riddle to be solved. He was not so ignorant as his wife concerning the relations of the different classes, and he felt certain there must be some discreditable reason for her leaving her former position. The attack he had in Cornwall afforded him unexpected opportunity of observing her.

He was very annoyed to discover a few days after their return that she was no longer in the house. He questioned his wife, and told her she was utterly heartless in refusing Mary leave to go and nurse her friend. Hesper, neither from desire to do right nor from regard to her husband's opinion, but because she saw that as Mary no longer dressed her, she no longer caused the same sensation on entering a room, resolved to write to her, as if taking for granted she had meant to return as soon as she was able. And to prick the sides of this intent came another spur.

Dear Mary,
    Can you tell me what has become of my large sapphire ring? I have not seen it since you brought my case up with you from Cornwall. I have been looking for it all morning— you must have it. I shall be lost without it, for it has no equal for color and brilliance. I do not believe you intended for a moment to keep it, but only to punish me for thinking I could do without you. If so, you have your revenge, for I find I cannot do without either—you or the ring. If you cannot come at once, write and tell me it is safe, and I shall love you more than ever. I am dying to see you again.

Yours faithfully,

H.R.

By this time Letty was much better, and Tom no longer required such continuous attention, so Mary took herself at once to Mr. Redmain's. Hesper was out shopping, and Mary went to her own room to wait for her, where she was glad of the opportunity of getting at some of the things she had left behind her.

While she was looking for what she wanted, Sepia entered, and was—or pretended to be—astonished to see her. "Ah!" she said. "I hope you will find it."

"If you mean the ring, that is not likely, Miss Yolland."

"A pity if there should be trouble about this ring."

"The ring will be found."

"In any case the blame will come to you; it was in your charge."

"The ring was in the case when I left. I remember quite well."

"You will have to prove that."

Mary grew so angry that she dared not speak.

"Don't imagine I mean you have taken it," Sepia continued. "I am only warning you how the matter will look. Mr. Redmain is one to believe the worst things of the best people. And you should know that some suspicion is attached to a friend of yours as well, a young woman who used to visit you. She was here, I remember, one night when there was a party—I saw you together in my cousin's bedroom."

"That was Mrs. Helmer," said Mary.

"A few days before you left, one of the servants heard someone in the house in the middle of the night, and went down only in time to hear the front door open and shut. In the morning a hat was found in the drawing room, with the name *Thomas Helmer* in it. Is that not your friend's husband?"

What Sepia told was true enough, but she did not know the whole truth.

"Why have I heard nothing of this before?" asked Mary.

"I am not aware of any right you have to know what happens in this house."

"Not from you, of course, Miss Yolland, and perhaps not from Mrs. Redmain. But the servants talk of most things, and I have not heard a word—"

"How could you," interrupted Sepia, "when you were not in the house? And so long as nothing was missed, the thing was of no consequence," she added. "Now it is different."

This confused Mary a little. She stopped to consider. One thing was clear—that, if the ring was not lost till after she left—and of so much she was sure—it could not be Tom who had taken the ring, for he was ill in bed. She managed to say something to this effect.

"I told you already," returned Sepia, "I had no suspicion of him, but you may be required to prove all you say, and it is as well to let you understand—though there is no reason why *I* should take the trouble—that your going to those very people at the time, and their proving to be friends of yours, adds to the difficulty."

"How is that?" asked Mary. "For myself I am astonished you seem so indifferent, if the character of a gentleman with whom you have been so intimate is as seriously threatened as you would imply. I know he has been to see you more than once while Mr. and Mrs. Redmain were not here."

Sepia's countenance changed—an evil fire glowed in her eyes, and she looked at Mary as if she would search her to the bone. "The foolish fellow," she said, with a smile of contempt, "chose to fall in love with me. And a married man too!"

"If you understood that, why did he come here so often?" asked Mary, looking her in the face.

"Have I not just told you," she said in a haughty tone, "that the man was in love with me?"

"And have you not just told me he was a married man? Could he have come to the house so often without at least your permission? You do not seem to have thought of his wife!"

"Certainly not! She never gave me offense. Why should I think of her?"

"Because she was your neighbor, and you were doing her a great wrong."

"That's enough, Marston!" cried Sepia, overcome at last. "This kind of thing will not do with me. I may not be a saint, but I have honesty enough to know the genuine thing from humbug. You have thrown dust in a good many eyes in this house, but none in mine."

By this time Mary had her temper quite in hand. She hardly knew what fear was, for she had in her something a little stronger than what generally goes by the name of faith. She was able to see that she ought, if possible, to learn Sepia's object in talking thus to her.

"Why do you say all this to me?" she asked quietly. "I cannot flatter myself it is from friendship."

"Certainly not. But you are not the only one involved. This man's wife is your friend, and the man is my friend, in a sense."

A strange shiver went through Mary, and seemed to make her angry.

Sepia went on. "I confess I allowed the poor boy—he is little more—to talk foolishly to me. I was amused at first, but perhaps I have not quite escaped unhurt." Here her voice faltered, and she did not finish her thought, but began afresh. "What I want of you is, through his wife, or any way you think best, to let the poor fellow know he better slip away, to France, say, and stop there till

203

this thing blows over."

"But why should you imagine he has had anything to do with the matter? The ring will be found, and then the matter of the hat will mean nothing."

"Well," replied Sepia, putting on an air of openness and familiarity, "I see I must tell you the whole truth. I never did believe Mr. Helmer had anything to do with the business, but there is sure to be trouble, for Hesper is miserable about her sapphire. If it is not found, the affair will be put to the police, and then what will become of poor Mr. Helmer, be he as innocent as we believe him! They will put you in the witness box, and make you confess the man an old friend of yours from the same part of the country, and the counsel for the prosecution will not fail to hint that you ought to be standing beside the accused. Believe me, Mary, if Mr. Helmer is taken up for this, you will not come out of it clean."

"You see now why I came to you. You must go to his wife, or better still, to Mr. Helmer himself, and tell him what I said. He will at once see the necessity of disappearing for a while."

Mary had listened attentively. She could not help fearing that something worse than unpleasant might be at hand, but she did not believe in Sepia, and in no case could she consent that Tom should compromise himself. Danger of this kind must be met, not avoided. Still, whatever could be done ought to be done to protect him, especially in his present critical state. A breath of suspicion of this reaching him might be the death of him, and of Letty too.

"I will think over what you have said," she answered, "but I cannot give him the advice you wish me."

"You have no choice that I see," said Sepia. "It is either what I propose or ruin. I give you fair warning that I will stop at nothing where my reputation is concerned. You and yours shall be trod in the dirt before I allow a spot on my character."

To Mary's relief they were interrupted by the hurried entrance of Mrs. Redmain. She almost ran up to Mary, and took her by both hands.

"You dear creature! You have brought me my ring!" she cried.

Mary shook her head with a little sigh. "No," she said, "I'm afraid not. But I will do all I can to help you find it."

"Oh, you *must* find it! My jewel case was in your charge."

"But there has been time to lose everything in it since I gave it up. The sapphire ring was there when I left."

"That cannot be. You gave me the box, and I put it away myself, and the next time I looked in it, it was not there."

"I wish I had asked you to open it when I gave it you," said Mary.

"I wish you had," said Hesper. "But the ring must be found, or I shall send for the police. I must have my ring. I have searched everywhere I can think of."

"Would you like me to help you look? I feel certain it will be found."

"No, thank you. I am sick of looking."

"Shall I go then, or is there something you would like me to do?"

"Go to your room and wait till I send for you."

"I must not be away too long from my invalids," said Mary, as cheerfully as she could.

"Oh, indeed! I thought you had come back to your work!"

"I did not understand from your letter you wished that, Ma'am, though, indeed, I could not have come just now."

"Then you mean to go and leave things just as they are?"

"I am afraid I must. But I will call again tomorrow, and every day till the ring is found, if you like."

"Thank you," said Hesper, dryly. "I don't think that would be of much use."

"I will call anyhow," returned Mary, "and inquire whether you would like to see me. I will go to my room now, and while I wait, will get some things I want."

"As you please," said Hesper.

Scarcely was Mary in her room, however, when she heard the door closed and locked behind her, and she knew she was a prisoner. For one moment a frenzy of anger came over her, but the next, she remembered where her life was hid, knew that nothing could touch her, and she was calm. While she took her things from the drawers and put them in her bag, she heard the door being unlocked, but as no one entered, she sat down to await what would happen next.

The moment Mary was out of the room, Hesper had risen and had said, "I should be a fool to let her leave the house."

"Hesper," cried Sepia, "you do nothing but mischief."

Hesper had paid no attention, but going after Mary, had locked the door of her room, and running to her husband's room, had told him of the matter.

Unlike his usual self, Mr. Redmain showed interest in the affair. She attributed this to the value of the jewel, rather than the fact that he had chosen it himself as a gift for her. He was quite knowledgeable about stones, and the sapphire was a most rare one. But it was for quite different reasons that he was interested in the situation. He hoped it would cast light all round it.

No sooner was Hesper in her husband's room than Sepia hastened to unlock Mary's door. But hearing someone on the stairs, she only had time to unlock it, and did not venture into the chamber.

Mary heard a knock at her door, and then Mewks entered. He brought a request from his master that she would go to his room. She rose and went with him.

"You may go now, Mrs. Redmain," said her husband when Mary entered. "Get out, Mewks," he added, and both lady and valet disappeared.

"So!" he said with a grin of pleasure. "Here's a pretty business. You haven't got the ring in that bag there?"

"Nor anywhere else, Sir," answered Mary. "Shall I shake it out on the floor?"

"No! You don't imagine me such a fool as to suppose, if you had it, you would carry it about in your bag!"

"You don't believe I have it, Sir, do you?" she returned, in a tone of appeal.

"How am I to know what to believe? There is something dubious about you. How am I to know that robbery mayn't be your little dodge? All that rubbish you talked at Cornwall about honesty and taking no wages and loving your mistress, and all that rot, looks devilishly like something off the square! That ring, now, the stone of it alone, is worth seven hundred pounds. One might let pretty good wages go for a chance like that!"

Mary looked him in the face, and made no answer. He spied a danger. If he irritated her, he would get nothing out of her. "My girl," he said, changing his tone, "I believe you know nothing about the ring. I was only testing you."

Mary could not help a sigh of relief, and her eyes fell, for she felt them beginning to fill. She could not have believed that the judgment of such a man would ever be of consequence to her.

Although Mr. Redmain was by no means so sure of her innocence as he had pretended, he did at least wish and hope to find her innocent—from no regard for her, but only because there was another he would be more glad to find concerned in the ugly affair.

"Mrs. Redmain," he went on, "would have me hand you over to the police, but I won't. You may go home when you please, and need fear nothing."

He already had the house where the Helmers lodged being watched, and knew this much, that someone there was ill, and that the doctor came almost every day.

"I certainly shall fear nothing," said Mary, not quite trusting him. "My fate is in God's hands."

"We know all about that," said Mr. Redmain. "But look here, my girl, if you just tell me what you are up to, I will make it better for you."

Mary had been trying to get at what *he* was up to, but found herself quite bewildered.

"I am sorry, Sir," she faltered, "but I haven't the slightest idea what you mean."

"Then go home!" he roared. "I will send for you when I want you."

The moment she was out of the room he rang his bell violently and Mewks appeared.

"Go after that young woman, do you hear? If she goes straight home, come back as soon as she's inside. Go, or you'll lose sight of her!"

"Yes, Sir." And he left the room.

Mary was too much absorbed in her own thoughts to note that she was followed by a man with the collar of his greatcoat up to his eyes, and a woolen muffler round his face. She walked steadily on for home, scarcely seeing the people who passed her. Mewks saw her to her door and went back to his master, but carrying another fact to Mr. Redmain—that as Mary came near the door of the house, she was met by a "rough-looking man" who came walking slowly along, as if he had been going up and down waiting for her.

Mewks gave his master an accurate description of the man and Mr. Redmain grinned, for he suspected him to be a thief disguised as a workman.

38.
Joseph Jasper

The man who stopped Mary was Joseph Jasper, the blacksmith. That he was rough in appearance no one could deny. His hands were very rough and ingrained with black. His fingers were long, but chopped off square at the points, and had no resemblance to the long tapering fingers of an artist or pickpocket. His clothes were of corduroy, but not very grimy because of the huge leather apron he wore at his work, and all topped with his tall Sunday hat. His complexion was a mixture of brown and browner, with black eyebrows hanging far over the blackest of eyes, the brightest flashing of which was never seen, because all the time he played he kept them closed tight. His face wore its natural clothing, a moustache thick and well shaped, and a beard the color of which looked like black burned brown. His hair was black and curled all over his head. His whole appearance was that of a workman; a careless glance could never have suspected him a poet-musician. He spoke very fair old-fashioned English, with the Yorkshire tone and turn. His walk was rather plodding, and his movements slow and stiff; but in communion with his violin they were free enough, and at the anvil they were as supple as powerful.

Mary held out her hand to Jasper, and it disappeared in his. He held it for a moment with a gentle grasp, and as he let it go, said, "I took the liberty of watching for you, Miss. I wanted to ask a favor of you. It seemed to me you would take no offense."

"You might be sure of that," answered Mary. "You have a right to anything I can do for you."

He fixed his gaze on her for a moment, as if he did not understand her. "That's where it is," he said. "I've done nothing for your people. It's all very well to go playing and playing, but that's not doing anything, and if *He* had done nothing, there would ha' been no fiddling. You understand me, Miss, I know; work comes before music, and makes the soul of it. It's not the music that makes the doing. I'm a poor hand at saying without my fiddle, Miss, you'll excuse me."

Mary's heart was throbbing. She had not heard words like this since her father died. She felt as if the spirit of her father had descended upon the strange workman and had sent him to her. She looked at him with shining eyes but did not speak. He resumed, as if fearing he had not conveyed his thought.

"The poor gentleman in there must want all the help you can give him, and more. There must be something left, surely, for a man to do. He must want lifting at times, for instance, and that's not fit for either of you ladies."

"Thank you," said Mary heartily. "I will mention it to Mrs. Helmer, and I am sure she will be very glad of your help sometimes."

"Couldn't you ask her now, Miss? I should like to know when I might call. Perhaps I should walk about here in the evening, after my day's work is over, and then you could run down any time and look out. That would be enough that I should be here. Saturday nights I could just as well be there all night."

To Tom and Letty it seemed peculiar that a man who was so much a stranger should be ready to walk about the street in order to be at hand with help for them, but Mary was only delighted, not surprised, for what the man had said to her made the thing not merely intelligible, but absolutely reasonable.

However, Joseph was not allowed to wander the street. The arrangement made was that as soon as his work was over, he should come and see whether there was anything he could do for them. And he never came but that there was plenty to do. He took lodging close by that he might be with them earlier and stay later. When nothing else was wanted of him, he was always ready to discourse on his violin. Sometimes Tom enjoyed the music and at other times he preferred having Mary read to him.

On one of these latter occasions, Mary, occupied in some cooking, asked Joseph to read for Tom. He consented, but read very badly—as if he had no understanding of the words, but, on the other hand, stopping every few lines, apparently to think, and master what he had read. This was not good reading, anyway, least of all for an invalid who required the soothing monotonous sound, and it was long before Mary asked him again.

Many things showed that he had had little education and, therefore, probably the more might be made of him. His father, a blacksmith before him and a local preacher, had married a second time, and Joseph was the only child of the marriage. His father had brought him up to his own trade and after his death Joseph came to work in London. He was now thirty, and had from the first been saving what he could of his wages in the hope of one day having a smithy of his own.

Mary saw that on his violin he possessed a grand fundamental but undeveloped education; he was like a man going about the world with a 10,000-pound note in his pocket and not many sixpences to pay his way with. But there was another education working in him far deeper and already more developed than that which divine music was giving him. Mary thoroughly recognized this as that which chiefly attracted her, and the man himself knew it as underlying all his consciousness.

Though he struggled in reading aloud, he read well for his own inward nourishment. He could write tolerably well, and if he could not spell, that mattered a straw and no more. He had never read a play of Shakespeare, had never even seen a play, and knew nothing of grammar or geography or history. He knew nothing of science, but he could shoe a horse as well as any other blacksmith, and make his violin talk about things far beyond the ken of most men of science.

So much of a change had passed upon Tom in his illness that Mary saw it as not unreasonable to try on him now and then some of her favorite poems. Occasionally, of course, the feeling was altogether beyond him, but even then he would sometimes enter into the literary merit of the utterance.

Tom's insight had always been ahead of his character, and of late he had been growing. People do grow very fast in a sickbed sometimes. Also, he had in him plenty of material to which a childlike desire now began to give shapes and sequences.

Mary had taken for herself rooms below, formerly occupied by the Helmers, with the hope of seeing them reinstated in them before long. She had a piano, the best she could afford to hire, and with its aid she hoped to do something toward the breaking of the invisible bonds that tied the wings of Joseph's genius.

His great fault lay in his timing. He contented himself with measuring it to his inner ear, and let his fingers, like horses which he knew he had safe in hand, play what pranks they pleased. But Mary was too wise to hurry anything.

One evening when he came as usual, and she knew he was not at the moment wanted, she asked him to take a seat while she played something to him. But she was disappointed in the reception he gave her offering—a delicate morsel from Beethoven. She tried something else, but with no greater result. He was not capable of showing a response when he felt none. His dominant thoughts were in musical form and easily found their expression in music, but the forms in which others gave themselves utterance could not find a way to the sympathetic place in him. Pride or repulsion had no share in this defect, for the man was as open and inspired as a child.

The next time she made the attempt to open this channel between them, something Mary played did find him, and for a few minutes he seemed lost in listening.

"How nice it would be," she said, "if we could play together sometimes."

"Do you mean both at once, Miss?"

"Yes, you on your violin, and I on the piano."

"That could hardly be, I'm afraid, Miss," he answered, "for you see, I don't know always—not exactly—what I'm going to play. And if I don't know, and you don't know, how are we to keep together?"

"Nobody can play your own things but you yourself, of course—that is, until you are able to write them down. But if you will learn that, we could play together. Will you let me teach you to read music?" said Mary, desiring to contribute to his growth—the one great service of the universe.

"If you would, Miss, perhaps I might be able to learn. You see I was never like other people. My mother used to talk big things about me, and the rest used to laugh at her. She gave me her large Testament when she was dying, but if it hadn't been for Ann, I should never have been able to read it well enough to understand because I don't go to chapel with her—it does seem such a waste of time. I'll go to church though, Miss, if you tell me it's the right thing to do, only it's hard to work all the week and be weary all the Sunday. I should only be longing for my fiddle all the time. You don't think, Miss, that a great Person like God cares whether we pray to Him in a room or in a church?"

"No, I don't," answered Mary. "For my own part, I find I can pray best at home."

"So can I," said Joseph, with solemn fervor. "Indeed, Miss, I can't pray at all sometimes till I get my fiddle under my chin, and then it says the prayers for me till I grow able to pray."

Mary thought of the "groanings that cannot be uttered." Perhaps that is just what music is meant for—to say the things that have no shape and, therefore, can have no words, yet are intensely alive. Certainly the musician can groan better with the aid of his violin. Surely this man's instrument was the gift of God to him. All God's gifts are a giving of Himself. The Spirit can better dwell in a violin than in an ark, or in the mightiest of temples. But there was another side to the thing, and Mary felt bound to present it.

"But you know, Mr. Jasper," she said, "when many violins play together, each taking a different part, a much grander music is the result than any single instrument could produce."

"I've heard of such things, Miss, but I've never heard them." He had never been to a concert or oratorio, any more than the play.

"Then you shall hear them," said Mary, her heart filling with delight at the thought. "But what if there should be some way in which the prayers of all souls may blend like the many violins? Imagine one mighty prayer made up of all the desires of all the hearts God ever made, breaking like a huge wave against the foot of His throne!"

"There would be some force in a wave like that, Miss!" said Joseph. "But answer me one question. Ain't it Christ that teaches men to pray? Let me tell you why it seems that churches can't be the places to tune the fiddles for that kind of concert. I never heard a sermon that didn't seem to be taking my Christ from me and burying Him where I should never find Him any more. For the Somebody the clergy talk about is not only nowise like my Christ, but nowise like a man at all. It always seemed to me more like a guy they had dressed up and called by His name, than the Man I read about in my mother's Testament."

"How my father would have delighted in this man!" said Mary to herself.

"You see, Miss," Jasper resumed, "I can't help knowing something about these matters, because I was brought up in it all, my father being a local preacher, and a very good one. Perhaps if I had been as clever as Ann, I might be thinking now just as she does; but it seems to me a man that is born stupid has much to be thankful for—he can't take in things before his heart's ready for believing them, and so they don't get spoiled, like a child's book before he's able to read it.

"All I heard when I went with my father to his preachings was no more than one of the chapters full of names in the Book of Chronicles. I wasn't even frightened at the awful things my father said about hell, and the certainty of our going there if we didn't lay hold of the Saviour. All he ever showed was a ghost or cloud of a Man that he called the Saviour—it wasn't possible to lay hold of Him. But after my father and mother were gone, and I was at work away from all my old friends, I started to read my mother's Testament in earnest, and then my conscience began to speak. Here was a Man that said He was God's Son, sent to look after us, and that we must do what He told us or we should never be able to see our Father in heaven!

"That's what I made out of it, Miss. So I set about getting ahold of anything He did say, and trying to do it. And then it was that I first began to play the fiddle, though I had been muddling away at it for a long time before. I knew I could play then, because I understood what it said to me, and got help out of it. And that's how I came to meet you, Miss.

"I used to be so frightened of Ann that after I came to London, I wouldn't have gone near her. But I thought Jesus Christ would have me go; and if I hadn't gone to see her, I should never have seen you. When I went to see her, I took my fiddle with me to take care of me, and when she would be going on at me, I would just give my fiddle a squeeze under my arm, and that gave me patience."

"But we heard you playing to her, you know."

"That was because I always forgot myself while she was talking. The first time, I remember, it was from misery; what she was saying sounded so wicked, making God out not fit for any honest man to believe in. I began to play without knowing it, and it couldn't have been very loud, for she went on about the devil picking up the good seed sown in the heart. Off I went into that, and there I saw no end of birds with long necks and short legs gobbling up the corn. But a little way off, there was the long beautiful stalks of corn growing strong and high, waving in God's wind, and the birds did not go near them."

Mary drew a breath, and said to herself, "The man is a poet." But out loud, "You're not afraid of your sister now?"

"Not a bit," he answered. "Since I know you, I feel as if we have in a sort of way changed places, and she is a little girl that must be humored. When she scolds, I laugh and try to make a bit of fun with her. But she's always so sure she's right, that you wonder how the world got made before she was up."

They parted with the understanding that when he came next, she should give him his first lesson in reading music. Within herself, Mary made merry at the idea of teaching the man of genius his letters.

39.
The Sapphire

O ne morning as Mary sat at her little rented piano, Mewks was shown into her room. He brought a request from his master that she go to him; he wanted particularly to see her. Although she did not like it, she did not hesitate to go.

She was shown into the room Mr. Redmain called his study, which communicated by a dressing room with his bedroom. He was seated waiting for her.

"Ah, Miss Marston! I have good news for you," he said, holding out what she saw at once was the lost ring.

"I am so glad!" she said, and took it in her hand. "Where was it found?"

"There's the point!" he returned. "That is why I sent for you! Can you suggest any explanation of the fact that it was found after all, in a corner of my wife's jewel box? Who searched the box last? Did you?"

"No, Sir. I offered to help Mrs. Redmain look for the ring, but she said it was no use."

"Mrs. Redmain swears it was not there when she looked for it. There is something mysterious about it." He looked hard at Mary.

Mary had very much admired the ring, as anyone must who had an eye for stones, and had often looked into the heart of it, almost loving it, and while they were talking now, she kept gazing at it, standing silent. In her silence her attention concentrated itself upon the sapphire. She stood looking closely at it, moving it about a little, and changing the direction of the light. While her gaze was on the ring, Mr. Redmain's was on her, watching her with equal attention. At last, with a sigh as if she waked from a reverie, she laid the ring on the table. But Mr. Redmain still stared in her face.

"Now what is it you've got in your head?" he said at last. "I have been watching you think for three full minutes. Come, out with it!"

"Hardly *thinking*, Sir," answered Mary. "I was only plaguing myself between my recollection of the stone and the actual look of it. It is so annoying to have what seemed a clear recollection prove a deceitful one. It may appear a presumptuous thing to say, but my recollection is of a finer color."

While she spoke, she had again taken the ring, and was looking at it. Mr. Redmain snatched it from her hand. "Are you hinting that the stone has been changed?" he cried.

"Such a thing never entered my head," said Mary, laughing, "but now that you mention it, I could almost believe it."

He cast her a strange look which she could not understand, and pulled the bell hard. That done, he began to examine the ring intently, as Mary had been doing, and did not speak a word. Mewks came.

"Show Miss Marston out," said his master, "and tell my coachman to bring the hansom round directly."

Mr. Redmain set about making certain inquiries. He was acquainted with many people of different sorts, and had been to jewelers and pawnbrokers, gamblers and lodging-house keepers, and had learned some things to his purpose.

Once more Mary received from him a summons, and once more, considerably against her liking, obeyed. She was less disinclined to go to the Redmains' this time, for she was curious about the ring.

"I want you to move back to the house," he said abruptly, the moment she entered his room.

For such a request Mary was not prepared. Even since the ring was found, so long a time had passed that she never expected to hear from the house again. But Tom was now much better and Letty so much like her former self that, if Mrs. Redmain had asked her, she might perhaps have consented.

"Mr. Redmain," she answered, "you must see that I cannot do so at your desire."

"Oh, rubbish!" he returned, with annoyance. "Don't fancy I am

216

asking you to go fiddle-faddling about my wife again. I don't see how you can do that, after the way she used you. I have reasons for wanting to have you within call. Go to Mrs. Perkin. I won't take a refusal."

"I cannot do it, Mr. Redmain," said Mary, and she turned to leave the room.

"Stop, stop!" cried Mr. Redmain, and jumped from his chair to prevent her.

He would not have succeeded had not Mewks met her in the doorway. She had to draw back to avoid him, and the man, perceiving at once how things were, closed the door the moment he entered, and stood with his back against it.

"He's in the drawing room, Sir," said Mewks.

A scarcely perceptible sign of question was made by the master, and answered in kind by the man.

"Show him here directly," said Mr. Redmain. Then turning to Mary, "Go out that way, Miss Marston, if you will," he said, and pointed to the dressing room.

Without any suspicion, Mary obeyed. But, just as she discovered that the door into the bedroom beyond was locked, she heard the door behind her close and the key turn in the lock.

"Stay where you are," said Mr. Redmain, in a low, but imperative voice from the other side of the door. "I cannot let you out till this gentleman is gone. You must hear what passes. I want you for a witness."

Bewildered and annoyed, Mary stood motionless in the middle of the room; presently she heard a man whose voice seemed familiar to her greet Mr. Redmain like an old friend. The two exchanged some small talk and Mary realized what a false position she was in. She withdrew to the farthest corner, sat down, closed her ears with the palms of her hands, and waited.

While Mary sat deaf, Mr. Redmain asked his visitor what he would have to drink, and a good deal of conversation followed about a disputed point in a late game of cards at one of the clubs. Then the talk veered in another direction, that of personal adventure, so guided by Mr. Redmain. He told extravagant stories about himself and his doings, in particular various ruses by which he had contrived to lay his hands on some money. And whatever he told, his guest capped, narrating trick upon trick to which on different occasions he had had recourse. At all of them Mr. Redmain

217

laughed heartily, and applauded their cleverness extravagantly, though some of them were downright swindling.

At last Mr. Redmain told how he had once got money out of a lady. Though there was not of word of truth in it, it was capped by the other with a narrative that seemed specially pleasing to the listener. In the midst of a burst of laughter, he rose and rang the bell. Count Galofta thought it was to order something more in the way of "refreshment" and was not a little surprised when he heard his host ask Mewks to request the favor of Miss Yolland's presence. The count had not studied nonexpression in vain, and had brought it to a degree of perfection not easily disturbed. Casting a glance at him as he gave the message, Mr. Redmain could read nothing. This was in itself suspicious to him—and justly, for the man ought to have been surprised at such a close to the conversation they had been having.

Sepia had been told that Galofta was in the study and therefore, received the summons thither—which had never happened before—with the greater alarm. She made what preparation she could against surprise, but her anxiety was sufficient to deprive her of any power over her complexion, and she entered the room with the pallor peculiar to the dark-skinned. Having greeted the count with the greatest composure, she turned to Mr. Redmain with question in her eyes.

"Count Galofta," said Mr. Redmain in reply, "has just been telling me a curious story of how a certain rascal got possession of a valuable jewel from a lady with whom he pretended to be in love, and I thought the opportunity a good one for showing you a strange discovery I have made with regard to the sapphire Mrs. Redmain missed for so long. Very odd tricks are played with gems—such gems, that is, as are of value enough to make it worth a rogue's while."

So saying, he took the ring from one drawer and from another a bottle, from which he poured something into a crystal cup. Then he took a file and, looking at Galofta in whose well-drilled features he believed he read something that was not mere curiosity, said, "I am going to show you something very curious," and began to file asunder that part of the ring which held the sapphire, the setting of which was open.

"You are destroying the ring!" cried Sepia. "What will Cousin Hesper say!"

Mr. Redmain filed away, then with the help of a pair of pincers freed the stone, and held it up in his hand.

"You see this?" he said.

"A splendid sapphire!" answered Count Galofta, taking it in his fingers, but, as Mr. Redmain saw, not looking at it closely.

"When I bought that ring," said Mr. Redmain, "the stone was a star-sapphire worth seven hundred pounds. Now, the whole affair is worth about ten."

As he spoke he threw the stone into the crystal cup, let it lie a few moments, and took it out again. With almost a touch, he easily divided it in two, one of which was a mere slice.

"There!" he said, holding out the the thin slice on the tip of his finger. "That is a slice of sapphire, and there," holding the rest of the seeming stone, "that is glass."

"What a shame!" cried Sepia.

"Of course," said the count, "you will prosecute the jeweler."

"I will not!" answered Mr. Redmain. "But I have taken the trouble to find out who changed the stones."

With that he threw both the bits of blue into a drawer, and the contents of the cup into the fire. A great flame flew up the chimney, and he stood gazing at it for a moment after it had vanished.

When he turned, the count was gone, as he had expected, and Sepia stood with eyes full of anger and fear. Her face was set and colorless.

"Very odd, isn't it?" said Mr. Redmain, who rose, and opening the door of his dressing room, called out, "Miss Marston!"

When he turned, Sepia too was gone.

When Mary did not appear, Mr. Redmain went into the dressing room calling. When Mary heard her name, she raised her head and saw the white face of Mr. Redmain looking down on her, grinning.

"I fancy you've had a dose of it!" he said.

As he spoke, she rose to her feet, her countenance illumined both with righteous anger and the tender shine of prayer. Her look went to what he had of a heart, and the slightest possible color rose to his face.

"I see that it's been a trifle too much for you, and I don't wonder. You needn't believe a word I said about myself."

"I have not heard a word, Mr. Redmain," she said with indignation.

"Oh, you needn't trouble yourself," he returned. "I meant you to hear it all. What did I put you there for, but to get your oath to what I drew from the fellow? A fine thing if your pretended squeamishness should ruin my plot. What do you think of yourself, hey? But I don't believe it."

He looked at her keenly, expecting a response, but Mary made him none. For some moments he regarded her curiously, then turned away into the study saying, "Come along. By Jove, I'm ashamed to say it, but I half begin to believe you. I did think I was past being taken in, but it seems possible for once. Of course you will return to Mrs. Redmain now that all is cleared up."

"It is impossible," said Mary. "I cannot live in a house where the lady mistrusts me, and the gentleman insults me."

She left the room, and Mr. Redmain did not try to prevent her. As she left the house she burst into tears, the fact of which Mewks carried to his master.

Mewks was careful to report everything about Mary, but there was one in the house of whom he never reported anything, but to whom, on the contrary, he told everything he thought she would care to know. Till Sepia came, he had been conventionally faithful to Mr. Redmain, but she had found no difficulty in making him spy on his master.

Mr. Redmain was sitting in the study, deep in thought when Mewks brought to him the information of Mary's emotion. But his mind was far too occupied with Sepia to be concerned with Mary.

Mr. Redmain did not believe Sepia was an accomplice in the robbery—she was too prudent for that. But his idea was that she had been wearing the ring—Hesper often allowed Sepia access to her jewel case as well as to her wardrobe—and that the fellow had got ahold of it and carried it away, returning it days later, treating the matter as a joke, and she was only too glad to return it to the jewel case, hoping its loss would pass as an oversight on the part of Hesper. If he was right, then the count certainly had hold upon her, and she dared not, or would not, expose him!

He had discovered, that about the time the ring disappeared, the count had had losses and was supposed unable to meet them, but had suddenly shown himself again "flush of money" and from that time had had a run of luck.

When the count left Mr. Redmain's study, he vanished from the house and from London. Turning the first corner he came to, and the next and the next, he stepped into a court which seemed empty, and slipped behind the gate. He was wearing a new hat, and was clean shaven except for his upper lip. Presently a man came out of the court in a Scotch cap and a full beard. What became of him Mr. Redmain did not care. He had no desire to punish him—it was enough that he had found him out, proved his suspicion, and obtained evidence against Sepia. He had not made up his mind how to act regarding Sepia. While he lived it did not matter much, and besides, he had a certain pleasure in watching his victim.

For the present, therefore, the thing seemed to blow over. Mr. Redmain bought his wife the best sapphire he could find and for once really pleased her.

As he said nothing, Sepia was the more certain he meant something. She lived in constant dread of his sudden vengeance, against which she could take no precaution. From that hour she was never at peace in his presence. She avoided every possible encounter with him, as if fleeing from judgment.

Nor was it a small addition to her misery that she imagined Mary cognizant of Mr. Redmain's opinion and intention with regard to her. Whatever had passed first between the count and Mr. Redmain, she did not doubt Mary had heard and was prepared to bring against her. How much the count might or might not have said, she could not tell. But seeing their common enemy had permitted him escape, she more than dreaded he had sold her secret for his own impunity, and had laid upon her a burden of lies as well.

40.
Reparation

With all Mr. Redmain's faults, there was a certain love of justice in the man, but he made a far greater demand for justice upon other people than upon himself, and was highly indignant at any shortcoming of theirs which crossed a desire or purpose of his. As badly as he himself had behaved to Mary, he was now furious with his wife for having treated her so heartlessly that she could not return to her service. He began to think Mary might be one to depend upon—he desired her alliance in the matter of ousting Sepia from the confidence of his wife.

Within a few minutes of Mary's departure, he walked into his wife's boudoir and shut the door behind him. His presence there was enough to make her angry, but she took no notice of it.

"I understand, Mrs. Redmain," he began, "that you wish to bring the fate of Sodom upon this house."

"I do not know what you mean," she answered, scarcely raising her eyes from her novel. She spoke the truth, for she knew next to nothing of the Bible, while the Old Testament was all the literature Mr. Redmain was "up" on.

"You have turned out the only just person in it, and we shall all be in hell soon."

"How dare you come to my room with such horrid language!"

"You'll hear worse before long, if you keep on at this rate. My language is not so bad as your actions. If you don't have that girl back, and in double-quick too, I shall know how to make you. You shall find me capable of doing a good deal. Do you imagine I have

222

found you a hair worse than I expected? I need not ask you whether I married you to please you, or to please myself?"

"You need not. You can best answer that question yourself."

"Then we understand each other."

"We do not, Mr. Redmain, and if this occurs again, I shall go to Durnmelling." She spoke with a vague idea that he also stood in the same awe of her parents as she did. But he burst into a loud and almost merry laugh.

"Happy they will be to see you, Madam! Why, you goose, if I send them a telegram before you, they won't so much as open the door to you! *They* know on which side their bread is buttered!"

Hesper started up in a rage. This was too much. "Mr. Redmain, if you do not leave the room, I will."

"Oh, don't!" he cried, in a tone of pretended alarm. His pleasure was great, for he had succeeded in stinging the impenetrable. "You really ought to consider before you utter such an awful threat! I will go myself a thousand times rather. But will you not feel the want of pocket money when you come to pay a rough cabman? The check I gave you yesterday will not last you long."

"I suppose you have a meaning, Mr. Redmain, but I am not in the habit of using cabs."

"Then you had better get into the habit, for I swear to you, if you don't fetch that girl home within the week, I will discharge your coachman next Monday, and send every horse in the stable to Tattersall's. Good morning."

She had no doubt he would do as he said—she knew he would enjoy selling her horses. But she could not at once give in. She had a week to think about it!

During the interval, he took care not once to refer to his threat, for that would but weaken the impression of it.

On Sunday after service, she knocked at his door, and being admitted, bade him good-morning, but with no very gracious air.

"We have had a sermon on the forgiveness of injuries, Mr. Redmain," she said.

"By Jove!" interrupted her husband. "It would have been more to the purpose if I or poor Mary Marston had had it, for I swear you put our souls in peril!"

"The ring was no common one, Mr. Redmain, and the young woman had, by leaving this house, placed herself in a false position. Everyone suspected her as much as I did. Besides, she lost her temper and talked about forgiving *me,* when I was in despair about my ring!"

"And what was your foolish ring compared to the girl's character?"

"A foolish ring indeed! Yes, it was foolish to let you ever have the right to give it to me! But as to her character, that of persons in her position is in constant peril. How was I to know? We cannot read each other's hearts."

"Not where there is no heart in the reader."

Hesper's face flushed, but she did her best not to lose her temper. Not that it would have been any great loss if she had, for there is as much difference in the values of tempers as in those who lose them. She said nothing, and her husband resumed.

"So you came to forgive me?" he said. "Well, I will accept the condescension—that is, if the terms are to my mind."

"I will make no terms. Marston may return when she pleases."

"You must write and ask her, and you must write so as to make it possible to accept your offer."

"I am not deceitful, Mr. Redmain."

"You are not. A man must be fair, even with his wife."

"I will show you the letter I write."

She had to show him half a score of letters ere he was satisfied, declaring he would do it himself if she could not make a better job of it.

At length one was dispatched, received, and answered. Mary would not return. She had lost all hope of being of any true service to Mrs. Redmain, and she knew that with Tom and Letty she was really of use for the present.

With ill-concealed triumph Mrs. Redmain carried the letter to her husband. He did not conceal his annoyance.

"You must have behaved very cruelly to her," he said. "But you have done your best now—short of a Christian apology. I fear we have seen the last of her."

But Mary lay awake at night and thought of many things she might have said and done better when she was with Hesper, and would gladly have given herself another chance.

41.
Another Change

For some time Tom made progress toward health, and was
able to read a good part of the day. Most evenings he asked
Joseph to play for a while. After their music, Mary was
always ready to give Joseph a lesson, and even had he been a less
gifted man than he was, he could not have failed to make progress
with such a teacher.

The largehearted, delicate-souled woman felt nothing strange in
the presence of the working man, but on the contrary was comfortably aware of a being much like herself, less privileged but more
gifted. And no teacher could have failed to be pleased at the
thorough painstaking with which he followed the slightest of her
hints, and the delight his flushed face would reveal when she
praised the success he had achieved. It was not long before he
began to write some of the melodies that came to his mind.

Mary's delight was great when first he brought her one of his
compositions; one followed another with a rapidity that astonished
her, and they enabled her to understand him better and better.

To the first one he brought her, she contrived to put a little
accompaniment, and when she played his air to him so accompanied, his delight was touching, and not a little amusing. Plainly he
thought the accompaniment a triumph of human faculty and beyond anything he could ever develop. Never was a pupil more
humble or more obedient; thinking nothing of himself or anything
he had done or could do, his path was open to the swiftest and
highest growth.

There soon came a change, and the lessons ceased altogether. For Tom and Letty had moved down to their old quarters, and in the arrogance of convalescence, Tom presumed on his imagined strength and caught cold. An alarming relapse was the result, and there was no more playing, for now his condition began to deteriorate. The cold settled in his lungs and he sank rapidly.

Joseph's violin was useless now, but he was nonetheless in attendance. Every evening when his work was done, he came knocking gently at the door of the parlor, and never left until Tom was settled for the night. Joseph was the most silently helpful, undemonstrative being that a doctor could desire to wait upon a patient. When it was his turn to watch, he never closed an eye, and at daybreak would rouse Mary, and go off to work without even any breakfast.

Tom speedily became aware that his days were numbered. He was sorry for his past life and thoroughly ashamed of much of it, saying in all honesty he would rather die than fall for one solitary week into the old ways—not that he wished to die, for with the confidence of youth, he did not believe he could fall into the old ways again.

But he did die. Letty enshrined him in her heart as the best of husbands—as her own Tom, who had never said a hard word to her, as the cleverest as well as the kindest of men, who had written poetry that would never die while the English language was spoken. Nor did the *Firefly* spare its dole of homage to the memory of one of its liveliest writers. Indeed, all in its office had loved him, each after his faculty. A certain little verse flowed no more through the pages of the *Firefly*, and in a month there was not even the shadow of Tom upon its page. But the print of him was deep in the heart of Letty. Happy was he to have left behind him any love, especially such a love as Letty bore him!

His mother's memory was mostly in her temper. She had never understood her wayward child, just because she had given him her waywardness and yet not parted with it herself, so that between them the two made havoc of love. When she heard of his death, she howled and cursed her fate, and cursed too the woman who had parted her and her Tom, swearing she would never set eyes upon Letty, and never let her touch a farthing of Tom's money. She would not hear of paying his debts until Mary told her *she* then would, upon which the fear of public disapprobation wrought for right if not righteousness.

What was Mary to do now with Letty? She was little more than a baby yet, not silly from youth, but young from silliness. But Mary was relieved from some perplexity for the present by the arrival of a letter from Mrs. Wardour to Letty, written in a tone of stiffly condescendent compassion that was not so unpleasant to Letty, because from childhood she had been used to the nature that produced it.

Mrs. Wardour's letter was in substance kind, and perhaps even a little repentant. It contained a poverty-stricken expression of sympathy, and an invitation to spend the summer months with them at her old home. It might, the letter said, prove but a dull place to her after the gaiety to which she had of late been accustomed, but it might nonetheless suit her present sad situation.

Letty's heart felt one little throb of gladness at the thought of being again at Thornwick, and in peace. With all the probable unpleasant accompaniments of the visit, nowhere else, she thought, could she feel the same sense of shelter as where her childhood had passed. Mary also was pleased, for although Letty might not be comfortable, by the end of the summer she might know what could be devised best for her comfort and well-being.

42.
Dissolution

Now it was Mary's turn to feel that she was, for the first time in her life, about to be cut adrift. For ten days or so, she could form no idea of what she would like to do next. Joseph called once or twice, but for Letty's sake they had no music. As they met so seldom now, Mary, anxious to serve him as she could, offered him the loan of some of her favorite books. He accepted with a gladness that suprised her, for she did not know how much he had been reading lately.

One day she received an unexpected visit from Mr. Brett, her lawyer. He had been searching into the affairs of the shop, and had discovered enough to make him uneasy. He was filled with self-reproach that he had not done more immediately upon her father's death.

Mr. Brett had found the affairs of Mr. Turnbull in havoc. He had been speculating in several companies, making haste to be rich, and had periled and lost what he had saved of the profits of the business, and all of Mary's as well that had not been elsewhere secured. He had even used the original capital of the firm, by postponing the payment of monies due, and allowing the stock to run down and deteriorate, and things out of fashion to accumulate, so that business had perceptibly fallen off. But what displeased Mary more than anything was that he had used money of her father's to speculate with in more than one public house. She knew that if in her father's lifetime Mr. Turnbull had so used even his own money, it would have been enough to make her father insist on dissolving the partnership.

It was impossible to allow her money to remain any longer in the power of such a man, and she gave authority to Mr. Brett to make necessary arrangements for putting an end to business relations between them.

It was a somewhat complicated and tedious business—things looked worse the further they proceeded. Unable to varnish the facts, Mr. Turnbull wrote Mary a letter almost cringing in its tone, begging her to remember the years her father and he had been as brothers, how she had grown up in the shop and had been, until misunderstanding arose, in the place of a daughter. He entreated her to leave things as they were, to trust him to see after the interests of the daughter of his old friend, and not insist upon measures which must end in a forced sale, in the shutting up of the shop of Turnbull and Marston, and the disgracing of her father's name along with his.

Mary replied that she was acting by the advice of her father's lawyer, and with the regard she owed her father's memory was severing all connection with a man in whom she no longer had confidence. She insisted that the business must be wound up as soon as possible.

At the same time, she instructed Mr. Brett that, if it could be managed, she would prefer getting the shop into her own hands, even at considerable loss, with what stock might be in it, so she could conduct the business on principles her father would have approved. But it would be necessary to keep her desire a secret, else Mr. Turnbull would be certain to frustrate it.

Mr. Brett approved of her plan, for he knew she was well-respected in Testbridge. Mr. Turnbull said he would be glad to give up the whole to escape prosecution; at least that was how Mary interpreted his somewhat technical statement of affairs between them.

She made up her mind not to go near Testbridge till everything was settled, and the keys of the shop were in Mr. Brett's hands. Therefore she stayed with Letty who, to keep her company, delayed her departure as long as she could without giving offense at Thornwick.

A few days before Letty was at last compelled to leave, Jasper called and heard about as much as they knew themselves of their plans. When Mary told him how much she would miss her pupil, he smiled in a sort of abstract way, as if not quite apprehending what she said. This seemed a little odd to Mary, since his manners were always those of a gentleman.

So Mary was left alone, more alone than she had ever been in her life. But she did not feel lonely and for the best of reasons—she never fancied herself alone. She had books at her command, and there were picture galleries to go to, and music lessons to be had. Of these last, she crowded in as many as her master could be persuaded to give her, for she knew it would be a long time before she was able to have them again.

Joseph Jasper never came near her. She could not imagine why, and was disappointed and puzzled. To know that Ann Byron was in the house was not a great comfort to her; Ann regarded so much that Mary loved as of earth and not of heaven. But Mary did go up and see her now and then. She seemed very different from the time when they first were at work together over Hesper's twilight dress! Ever since Mary had made the acquaintance of her brother, Ann seemed to have changed toward her. Perhaps she was jealous, or believed Mary was confirming him in his bad ways.

It was the middle of summer before the affairs of the firm were wound up, and the shop in the hands of the London man whom Mr. Brett had employed in the purchase.

However, Mr. Brett had not been sharp enough for Turnbull. The very next day, a shop in the same street, that had been to let for some time, displayed above its now open door the sign, *John Turnbull,* then a very small *of Turnbull and Marston,* whereupon Mr. Brett saw the oversight of which he had been guilty. There was nothing in the shop when it was opened, but even that Turnbull utilized for advertisement. He arranged that within the hour the goods should begin to arrive, and they kept arriving by every train for days and days after, while all the time he made public show of himself, fussing about, the most triumphant man in the town. It made people talk, and if not always as he would have liked to hear, yet it was talk; and, in the matter of advertisement, that is the main thing.

When Mary was told, she felt no uneasiness; she only saw this as what had almost happened several times in her father's lifetime. She would not have moved a finger to prevent it. Let the two principles meet, with whatever result God pleased!

Things appeared to go on with the Turnbulls just as before.

They still inhabited the villa, the wife scornful of her surroundings, and the husband driving a good horse to his shop every morning. How he managed it all, nobody knew but himself; and whether he succeeded or not was a matter of small interest to any except his own family and his creditors. To those who alluded to the change, he represented it as entirely his own doing, to be rid of the interference of Miss Marston in matters of which she knew nothing. The country people were flattered by the confidence he seemed to put in them by this explanation, and those who liked him before sought the new shop as they had frequented the old one.

43.
Thornwick

It was almost with bewilderment that Letty revisited Thornwick. She had never been accustomed to reflect on her own feelings—things came and went, were welcome or unwelcome, proved better or worse than anticipated, passed away and were mostly forgotten. Letty lived as one in a dream, where mingle sounds and glimmers from the waking world.

On the threshold of her old home, Letty found her old self awaiting her. She crossed it and was once more just Letty, a Letty wrapped in the garments of sorrow and with a heavy heart, but far from such a miserable Letty as during the last of her former life there. Little joy had been hers since the terrible night when she fled from its closed doors, and now that she returned, she could take up everything where she had left it, except the gladness. But peace is better than gladness, and she was on the way to find that.

Mrs. Wardour was touched with compassion at the sight of Letty's worn and sad look and, granting to herself that the poor thing had been punished enough, broke down a little and took Letty in her arms. Letty, loving and forgiving always, nestled there for a moment, and in her own room quietly wept a long time. When she came out, Mrs. Wardour pleased herself with the fancy that her eyes were red with tears of repentance, but Letty never dreamed of repenting, for that would have been to deny Tom.

She slid into all her old ways, took charge again of the dairy as if she had never left it, attended to the linen, and darned the stockings. In everything but her pale, thin face and heavy, ex-

232

hausted heart, she lived as the young Letty. She even went to the
harness room to look after Cousin Godfrey's stirrups, but she
found for a whole week that not once had they been neglected, and
so dismissed the care.

Mrs. Wardour continued to be kind, but every now and then
would allow a tone of remembered naughtiness to be heard in
speech or request. Yet Letty never resented it. She had been so
used to it in the old days that it seemed only natural. And then her
aunt considered her health in the kindest way. Now that Letty had
known some of the troubles of marriage, Mrs. Wardour felt more
sympathy with her, did not look down upon her from quite such a
height; and to Letty this was strangely delightful.

Godfrey saw her moving about the house like one of the ghosts
of his saddest dreams, and a new love began to rise out of the
buried seed of the old. The image of Letty, with her trusting eyes
fixed on him with solemn sadness, haunted him and was too much
for him.

Gladly would Godfrey have taken Letty to his arms. He had to
recall every restraining fact of their positions to prevent him from
now precipitating that which he had before too long delayed. But
the gulf of the grave and the jealousy of a mother were between
them. If he were to rouse Mrs. Wardour's suspicions, she would
certainly get rid of Letty, as she had intended before. So he kept
out of Letty's way as much as he could, went more about the farm,
and took long rides.

Nothing was further from Letty than any suspicion of the sort of
regard Godfrey cherished for her. There was in her nothing of the
self-sentimental. Her poet was gone from her, and to her, Tom was
the one poet of the age. He had been hers, and was hers still. She
dreamed of her Tom in heaven waiting for her carrying her little
boy in his arms, and telling him of the mother who was coming to
them by and by.

Godfrey could not fail to see how much of a woman she had
become, but he made one great and serious mistake in reference to
her. Love and marriage are two of the Father's most powerful
means for the making of His foolish little ones into sons and
daughters. Godfrey assumed that Letty had come to think of Tom
as he did, and that she had dismissed from her heart every remnant of love for him. But he did not know that in a woman's love
there is more of the specially divine element than in a man's.

God's love is not founded upon any merit—it rests only upon being and need.

The Redmains came again to Durnmelling for a visit of some weeks, and Sepia took care that she and Godfrey should meet on the footpath to Testbridge, or anywhere else suitable for a little detention and talk that should seem accidental, and be out of sight. A man less vulnerable might perhaps have realized these meetings were not all so accidental as they appeared; but no glimmer of such a thought passed through the mind of Godfrey.

Had it not been for the return of Letty, Sepia would by this time have had him for her slave—nothing but slavery could it ever be to a woman like her, who gave no love in return and only exercised power. Although he was always glad to meet her, and his heart had begun to beat a little faster at sight of her approach, the glamour of her presence was nearly destroyed for him by the arrival of Letty; and Sepia was more than sharp enough to perceive the difference in the expression of his eyes the next time she met him. At very first glance she suspected some hostile influence at work—intentionally hostile—for persons like Sepia are always imagining enemies. And as the two worst enemies she could have were the truth and a woman, she was alternately terrified and jealous.

She soon found there was a young woman at Thornwick, and learned who she was—one who already had a shadowy existence in her life. Was it possible the shadow should now be taking solidity and threatening to foil her? She had heard of Tom's death through the *Firefly*, which had a kind, extravagant article about him, but she not once had thought of his widow, and there she was now, a hedge across the path where she wanted to go! If only the house of Durnmelling had been but one story higher, so that she might see all round Thornwick!

For some time now, Sepia had been fashioning a man to her thrall—Mewks, Mr. Redmain's man. It was a very gradual process she adopted, and it had been successful. She had got so far with him that whatever Sepia showed the least wish to understand, Mewks would take endless trouble to learn for her. The rest of the servants, both at Durnmelling and in London, were not very friendly with her—least of all Jemima, who was now with her mistress as lady's maid.

The more Sepia realized, or thought she realized, the position she was in, the more desirous she was to get out of it, and the only feasible and safe way, in her eyes, was marriage. She saw nothing between that and a return to what she considered slavery. If she could secure Godfrey for a husband, then she might hold up her head with the best.

From all she could learn, there was nothing that amounted even to ordinary friendship between Mr. Wardour and the young widow. She was in the family only as a distant poor relation, "Much as I am myself," said Sepia, with a bitter laugh. But the fact remained that Godfrey was a little altered toward her. Letty must have been telling him something against her, something she heard from that detestable little hypocrite who was turned away on suspicion of theft! That was how Sepia thought of Mary.

One morning Letty found she had an hour's leisure, and wandered out to the hedge by the gully, so memorable with its shadowy presence of her Tom. She had not been seated under it very long before Godfrey caught sight of her from horseback. Knowing his mother was gone to Testbridge, he yielded to an urgent longing, took his horse to the stable, and crossed the grass to where she sat.

Letty was thinking of Tom—what else was there of her own to do?—and gazing up into the cloud-flecked sky. All the enchantment of the first days of her love had come back upon her, all the ill that had crept in between had failed from her memory. She was sitting with her back toward the tree and her face to Thornwick, but did not see Godfrey till he was within a few yards of her. She smiled, expecting his kind greeting, but was startled to hear from behind her instead the voice of a lady greeting him. She turned and saw the head of Sepia rising above the breach in the gully. Godfrey turned aside, and ran to give her his hand.

"Thank you," said Sepia, holding fast by Godfrey's hand, and coming up with a little pant. "What a lovely day it is for your haymaking! How can you afford the time to play knight to a distressed damsel?"

"The hay is nearly independent of my presence," replied Godfrey. "Sun and wind have done their part too well for my being of much use."

"Take me with you to see how they are getting on," she said. "I enjoy the scent so much."

"I will, with pleasure," said Godfrey, perhaps a little consoled in the midst of his disappointment, and they walked away.

In a short while they came back together, nothing of any importance having passed between them, and Sepia saw Letty under the great bough of the Durnmelling oak. Godfrey handed Sepia down the gully. She ran home, and up to a certain window with her opera glass. But the branches and foliage of the huge oak would have concealed pairs and pairs of lovers.

Godfrey turned toward Letty who had not stirred.

"What a beautiful creature Miss Yolland is!" she said, looking up with a smile of welcome, and a calmness that prevented the slightest suspicion of a flattering jealousy.

"I was coming to see you," returned Godfrey. "I never saw her till her head came up over the edge of the gully. Yes, she is beautiful; at least, she has lovely eyes."

"They are splendid! What a wife she would make for you, Cousin Godfrey!"

Letty was beyond the faintest suggestion of coquetry, but her words stung the heart of Godfrey. He turned pale. But not a word would he have spoken then, had not Letty in her innocence gone on to torture him. She sprang from the ground.

"Are you ill, Cousin Godfrey?" she cried in alarm, with that sweet tremor of the voice that shows the heart is near. "You are quite white! Oh, dear, I've said something I oughtn't to have said! Do forgive me."

In her childlike anxiety she would have thrown her arms around his neck, but her hands only reached his shoulders. He drew back, mastered himself and, alarmed at the idea of having possibly hurt her, caught her hands in his. As they stood regarding each other with troubled eyes, the embankment of his prudence gave way, and the stored passion broke out.

"You don't mean you would like to see me married, Letty?" he groaned.

"Yes, indeed I do! I care for you more than anybody in the world—except perhaps Mary," said Letty. Truthfulness was a part of her.

"And I care for you more than all the world! Letty! Your eyes haunt me night and day! I love you with my whole soul."

"How kind of you," faltered Letty, trembling, and not knowing what she said. She was very frightened, but hardly knew why, for the idea of Godfrey in love with her was all but inconceivable. Nevertheless, its approach was terrible. Like a fascinated bird she

236

could not take her eyes off his face. Her knees began to tremble—it was all she could do to stand. But Godfrey was full of himself, and had not the most shadowy suspicion of how she felt. He took her emotion as a favorable sign, and stupidly went on.

"Letty, I can't help it! I know I oughtn't speak to you like this, so soon, but I can't keep quiet any longer. I love you more than the universe and its Maker. I would rather cease to live, than live without you to love me. I have loved you for years and years, longer than I know."

"Cousin Godfrey!" shrieked Letty. "Don't you know I belong to Tom?" And she dropped like one lifeless on the grass at his feet.

Godfrey felt as if suddenly damned. He stood gazing on the white face. The world, heaven, God, and nature were dead, and there was the soul of it all, dead before him! Mechanically he stooped and lifted Letty in his arms, and carried her to the house. He felt no thrill as he held the treasure to his heart—it was the merest material contact. He bore her to the room where the housekeeper sat doing handwork, laid her on the sofa, said he found her under the oak tree, and went away to his study.

On a chair in the middle of the floor he sat, like a man bereft of all. All that came between him and suicide was an infinite scorn. A slow rage devoured his heart. Here he was, a man who knew his own worth, his faithfulness, his unchangeableness, cast over the wall of the universe, into the waste places among the broken shards of ruin! If there was a God, why did He make him? To make him for such a misery was pure injustice, was willful cruelty! Henceforward, he would live above what God or woman could do to him! He rose and went to the hayfield, and did not return till after midnight.

He did not sleep, but he came to a resolution. In the morning he told his mother that he wanted a change. Now that the hay was safe he would take a journey, possibly on the continent. She must not be uneasy if she did not hear from him for a week or two. The old lady was filled with dismay, but scarcely had she begun to expostulate, when she saw in his eyes that something was seriously amiss and held her peace.

Godfrey went and courted distraction. Ten years earlier he would have brooded, but now the thing was not worth it! He entrenched himself in his pride.

Mary had by now got her affairs settled, and was again in the old hallowed place that held many holy memories. In that shop God had been worshiped with holiest worship—obedience—and would be again. Mary wrote to Letty at once saying the room which had been Mary's was at her service as soon as she pleased to occupy it—she would take her father's. Letty breathed a deep breath of redemption and prepared to accept the offer. But to let Mrs. Wardour know of her resolve was a severe strain on her courage.

Her aunt met Letty's announcement with scorn and indignation. Ingratitude, laziness, love of low company, all the old words of offense she threw afresh in her face. But Letty could not help being pleased to find that her aunt's storm no longer swamped her boat. When Mrs. Wardour began, however, to abuse Mary, calling her a low creature who actually gave up an independent position to put herself at the beck and call of a fine lady, Letty grew angry.

"I will not hear you call Mary names, Aunt," she said. "When you cast me out, she stood by me. You do not understand her. She is the only friend I ever had—except Tom."

"You dare, you thankless hussy, to say such a thing in the house where you've been clothed and fed and sheltered for so many years! You're the child of your father with a vengeance! Get out of my sight!"

"Aunt," said Letty, rising.

"No aunt of yours!" interrupted the wrathful woman.

"Mrs. Wardour," said Letty with dignity, "you have been my benefactor, but hardly my friend. Mary has taught me the difference. I owe you more than you will ever give me the chance of repaying you. What friendship could have stood for an hour the hard words you have been giving me, as far back as I can remember! Hard words take all the sweetness from shelter. Mary is the only Christian *I* have ever known."

"So we are all pagans except your lowlived lady's maid! Upon my word!"

"She often makes me feel," said Letty, bursting into tears, "as if I were with Jesus Himself, as if He must be in the room somewhere."

So saying, she went to pack up her things. Mrs. Wardour locked the door of the sitting room where she sat, and refused to see or speak to Letty again. Letty left and walked to Testbridge.

"Godfrey will do something to make her understand," she said to herself, weeping as she walked.

Whether Godfrey ever did, Letty could never tell. He was away a month, and came back in good health and high spirits. But it was no small relief to him to find on his arrival at Thornwick that Letty was no longer there.

When he went into his study the day after his return, he found a letter addressed to him in Letty's childish writing. His heart leaped at the sight of the ill-shaped letters, but his first thought was, "She shall find it too late!" It was a lovely letter—the utterance of a simple, childlike spirit—with much in it that was prettily childish. She poured out on Godfrey the affection of a woman-child. She told him what a reverence and love he had been to her always, and that it would change her love into fear if he tried to make her forget Tom. She told him he was much too grand for her to dare love him in that way, but that she could look up to him like an angel, only he must not come between her and Tom. Nothing could be plainer, simpler, or stronger, than the way the little woman wrote her mind to the great man. Had he been worthy of her, he might even yet, with her help, have gotten above his passion in a grand way and been a great man indeed.

When he read it, however, it was with a curling lip of scorn at the childishness of the creature to whom he had offered the heart of Godfrey Wardour. Instead of admiring the lovely devotion of the girl-widow to her boy-husband, he scorned himself for having dreamed of a creature who not only could love a fool like Tom Helmer, but could go on loving him after he was dead, and even when Godfrey Wardour had condescended to let her know he loved her.

Godfrey rose from the reading of that letter cured, as he called it. But it was a cure that left the wound open as a door to the entrance of evil things. He tore the letter into a thousand pieces and threw it in the empty grate, not even showing it the respect of burning it with fire.

44.
Despair

T he day Turnbull opened his new shop, a man was seen on a ladder painting out the sign above the old shop. But the paint took time to dry.

That same day, Mary had returned to Testbridge. She spent that night alone in the house but could not sleep, so she got up and went down to the shop. It was a bright, moonlit night, and all the house, even where the moon could not enter, was full of glimmer and gleam, except for the shop. There she lit a candle, sat down on a pile of goods, and gave herself up to memories of the past. Back and back went her thoughts as far as she could send them, and God was everywhere in all the story.

The dead hours of the night came, that valley of the shadow of death, where faith seems to grow weary and sleep, and all the things of the shadow wake up and come out. But to Mary, her father seemed near all the time. Wherever she turned she saw the signs of him, and she pleased herself to think that perhaps he was there to welcome her. In spite of time and space, she knew that she was and must be near him so long as she loved and did the truth. She knew there is no bond so strong, so close, or so lasting as the truth. In God alone, who is the truth, can creatures meet.

The place had been left in sad confusion and dirt, and she did much that night to restore some order. But at length she was tired and went up to her room. On the landing, where there was a window to the street, she stopped and looked out, but drew back with a start. On the opposite side of the street a man stood looking up at the house! She hurried to her room and to bed. If God was not watching, waking was of no use; and if He was watching, she could sleep in peace. But she had the strange feeling that the man was vaguely familiar. She finally slept and woke refreshed.

Her first care the next morning was to write to Letty with the invitation to stay with her. The next thing she did was to go and ask Beenie to give her some breakfast. The old woman was delighted to see her, and was ready to lock her door at once to come back to her old quarters and responsibilities. They returned together, while Testbridge was yet half-awake.

Many things had to be done before the shop could be opened. Beenie went after charwomen, and soon a great bustle of cleaning arose. But the door and front windows were kept shut.

In the afternoon Letty came fresh from misery into more than counterbalancing joy. She barely took off her bonnet and shawl before she was at work helping Mary, cheerful as hope and a good conscience could make her.

Mary was in no hurry to open the shop. There was stock to be taken, many things to be rearranged and not a few to be added before she could begin with comfort. She must see to it all herself, for she was determined to engage no assistant until she could give orders without hesitation.

She was soon satisfied that she could not do better than make a proposal to Letty that she should take up her permanent abode with her and help in the shop. Letty was charmed, never thinking of the annoyance it would be to her aunt. Mary had thought of it; but she saw that for Letty to allow the prejudices of her aunt to influence her would be to order her life not by the law of God whose Son was a workingman, but after the whim and folly of an ill-educated old woman. A new spring of life seemed to bubble up in Letty the moment Mary mentioned the matter, and in serving she soon proved herself one after Mary's own heart. Many customers were as pleased with her as Mary was. Before long Mary gave her a small share in the business.

The new shop sign read *Mary Marston*. She would have liked to make it *William and Mary Marston*, but people were too dull to understand and, therefore, she set the sign so in her heart only. Her old friends soon began to come about her again, and it was not many weeks before she saw fit to go to London to add to her stock.

The evening of her return, as she and Letty sat over a late tea, a silence fell during which Letty began to brood. "I wonder how Cousin Godfrey is getting on," she said at last, and smiled sadly.

"What do you mean by getting on?" asked Mary.

"I was wondering whether Miss Yolland and he—"

Mary started from her seat, white as the tablecloth. "Letty!" she said, in a voice of utter dismay. "You don't mean that woman is—is making friends with him?"

"I saw them together more than once, and they seemed, well, on very good terms."

"O Letty!" cried Mary, in despair. "What is to be done? Why didn't you tell me before?"

"But what's the harm, Mary? She's a very handsome lady, and of a good family."

"We're all of good enough family," said Mary, a little petuantly. "But that Miss Yolland—Letty, that Miss Yolland—she's a bad woman."

"How can you be so sure?"

Mary was silent. She could not say anything regarding the situation without mentioning Tom, and she could not bring herself to do that.

"I cannot tell you, Letty," she said. "You know the two bonds of friendship are the right of silence and the duty of speech. I daresay you have some things which, truly as I know you love me, you neither wish nor feel at liberty to tell me."

Mary was pacing about the room, her hands clasped behind her, the fingers interlaced and twisted with a strain almost fierce.

"There's no time! There's no time!" she cried at length. "How are we to find out? And if we knew all about it, what could we do? O Letty! What am I to do?"

"Mary, you can't be to blame! One would think you fancied yourself accountable for Cousin Godfrey!"

"I *am* accountable for him. He has done more for me than any man but my father, and I know what could be his ruin. I know that one of the best men in the world is in danger of being married to one of the worst women, and I can't bear it! I can't!"

"But what can you do, Mary? If he's in love with her, he wouldn't believe a word anyone—even you—told him against her."

"That is true, I suppose, but it won't clear me. I must do

something." She threw herself down on the couch with a groan. "It's horrid!" she cried, and buried her face in the pillow.

All this time Letty had been so bewildered by Mary's agitation, the cause of which was so vague to her, that apprehension for her cousin did not wake. But when Mary was silent, then came the thought that if she had not been so repulsed by him . . . but she could not help it, and would not think in that direction.

Mary started from the couch, and began pacing the room, wringing her hands, and walking up and down like a wild beast in its cage. It was so unlike her to be so seriously discomposed that Letty began to be frightened. She sat silent and looked at her. Then spoke the spirit of truth in the scholar, for the teacher was too troubled to hear. She rose, and going up to Mary from behind, put her arm round her, and whispered in her ear, "Mary, why don't you ask Jesus?"

Mary stopped short and looked at Letty. But she was not thinking about her. She was questioning herself. Why had she not done as Letty said? She threw herself again on the couch, and Letty saw her body heaving with sobs. Then Letty was more frightened and feared she had done wrong. Was it her part to remind Mary of what she knew so much better than she?

After a few minutes Mary rose. Her face was wet and white, but perplexity had vanished from it, and resolution had taken its place. She threw her arms round Letty, and kissed her, and held her face against hers. Letty had never received such an expression of emotion and tenderness.

"Thank you, thank you, Letty. You are a true sister. I have found out why I did not go at once to ask Him what I ought to do. It was just because I was afraid of what He would tell me to do."

And with that the tears ran down her cheeks afresh.

"Then you know now what to do?" asked Letty.

"Yes," answered Mary, and she sat down.

45.
A Hard Task

The next morning, leaving the shop to Letty, Mary set out for Thornwick. But the duty she had there to perform was so distasteful that her very limbs trembled so under her that she could scarcely walk; so she sent to the neighboring inn for a fly. As she rode she was hoping she might be spared an encounter with Mrs. Wardour; but the old lady heard the fly, saw her get out, and imagining she had brought trouble, hastened to prevent either of them from entering the house. As Mary approached the door, it opened and Mrs. Wardour met her on the step.

"Good morning, Mrs. Wardour," said Mary, trying to speak without betraying emotion. Is Mr. Wardour at home?"

"What is your business with *him?*" rejoined the mother. "Is it about that hussy?"

"I do not know whom you call by that name," replied Mary, who would have been glad indeed to find a fellow protector of Godfrey in his mother.

"You know well enough who I mean. Who should it be but Letty Lovel!"

"My business has nothing to do with Letty Helmer," answered Mary. "It has to do with Mr. Wardour."

"You can't see Mr. Wardour. He's not one to be at the beck and call of every silly woman who wants him."

"Then I will write to tell him I called, and that you would not allow me to see him."

"I will give him a message, if you like."

"Then tell him what I have just said. I am going home to write to him. Good morning."

She was just getting into the fly again when Mrs. Wardour, reflecting that it must be something of consequence that brought her there so early in a fly, and made her show such a determined front to so great a personage as herself, called after her. "I will tell him you are here, but you mustn't blame me if he does not choose to see you. We don't feel you have behaved well about that girl."

Mary turned back toward the house saying, "Letty is my friend. I have behaved to her as if she were my own sister."

"You had no business to behave to her in such a way. You had no right to tempt her down to your level. She would have done very well if you had but left her alone."

"Excuse me, Ma'am, but I have *some* right in Letty. But I will not talk with you about it—you do not know the circumstances to which I refer. I request to see Mr. Wardour. I have no time to waste in useless altercation."

Mary was angry and it did her good—it made her fitter for the hard task before her.

At that moment they heard the step of Godfrey approaching through a long passage in the rear. His mother went into the parlor, leaving the door ajar. Reaching the hall, Godfrey saw Mary and came up to her with a formal bow and a face flushed with displeasure.

"May I speak to you alone, Mr. Wardour?" said Mary.

"Can you not say here what you came to say?"

"It is impossible."

With a sigh of impatience, he turned and led the way to the drawing room, which was at the other end of the hall. Mary turned and shut the door he left open.

"Why all this mystery, Miss Marston?" he said. "I am not aware of anything between you and me that can require secrecy. "He spoke with unconcealed scorn.

"Mr. Wardour," returned Mary, "I am here for your sake, not my own. I beg you will not render a painful duty yet more difficult."

"May *I* beg then that you will be as brief as possible? I am more than doubtful whether what you have to say will seem to me of so much consequence as you suppose. I cannot give you more than ten minutes."

Mary looked at her watch and began. "You have lately become acquainted with Miss Yolland, I am told. I have been compelled to know a good deal of that lady."

"As lady's maid in that family, I believe."

"Yes," said Mary. Then changing her tone after a slight pause, she went on. "Mr. Wardour, I owe you more than I can ever thank you for. I strongly desire to fulfill the obligation your goodness has laid upon me, though I can never discharge it. For the sake of that obligation, for your sake I am risking much—namely, your opinion of me."

He made a gesture of impatience. Mary hesitated, then flung herself into the purpose of her visit. "I know Miss Yolland to be a woman without principle. I know it by the testimony of my own eyes, and from her own confession. She is capable of playing a coldhearted, cruel game for her own ends. Be persuaded to consult Mr. Redmain before you commit yourself. Ask him if Miss Yolland is fit to be the wife of an honest man."

There was nothing in Godfrey's countenance but growing rage. Turning to the door, Mary would have gone without another word.

"Stay!" cried Godfrey, in a voice of suppressed fury. "Do not dare to go until I have told you that you are a vile slanderer. You would never have entered this room had I known how far your effrontery could carry you. Listen to me! If anything more than the character of your statement had been necessary to satisfy me of the falsehood of every word of it, you have given it me in your reference to Mr. Redmain—a man whose life has rendered him unfit for the acquaintance, not to say the confidence of any decent woman. This is a plot—for what final object, God only knows—between you and him! I should be doing my duty were I to expose you both to the public scorn you deserve."

Standing tall with face and eyes glowing with indignation, Mary said, "Then why not do your duty. Mr. Wardour? I should be glad of anything that would open your eyes. But Miss Yolland will never give Mr. Redmain such an opportunity. Nor does he desire it, for he might have had it long ago, by the criminal prosecution of a friend of hers. For my part, I should be sorry to see her brought to public shame."

"Leave the house," said Godfrey through his teeth, and almost under his breath.

"I am sorry it is so hard to distinguish between truth and false-hood," said Mary, as she went to the door. She walked out, got into the fly, and drove home. She served in the shop the rest of that morning, but was obliged to lie down that afternoon.

The reception she had met with did not surprise her. Plainly Sepia had been there before her. Pretending to make Godfrey her confidant, she had invented, dressed, and poured out injuries to him, and so blocked up the way to all testimony unfavorable to her. Was there ever a man in a more pitiable position?

What added to Godfrey's rage was that he had not a doubt that Mary knew what had passed between Letty and him. That, he reasoned, was at the root of it all. She wanted to bring them together yet; it would be a fine thing for her to have her close friend the mistress of Thornwick! What a cursed thing that he should ever have been civil to her! And what a cursed fool he was ever to have cared a straw for such a low-minded creature as that Letty! Thank heaven, he was cured of that!

Cured? He had fallen away from love, but was that a cure? His rage against Letty, just because of her faithfulness, had cast him an easy prey into the arms of clinging Sepia.

And now what more could Mary do? Just one thing was left—to commit the burden on her heart to her Heavenly Father, and leave the matter in the hands of the One who loved Godfrey Wardour as He loves all His children and seeks only their good.

The thing that ought to be done had been done, but not to the purpose Mary desired. She could think of nothing else. Sepia, like a moral hyena, must range her night. Mary went to bed and dreamed she was pursued by a crowd, hooting after her and call-ing her all the terrible names of those who spread evil reports. She woke in misery, and slept no more that night.

46.
The Summons

One hot Saturday afternoon, in the sleepiest time of the day, nobody was in the shop except a poor boy who had come begging for string to help him fly his kite. Jemima came in from Durnmelling, greeted Mary with the warmth of the friendship that had always been true between them, and gave her a letter.

"Mr. Mewks gave it to me," said Jemima. "He didn't say who it was from."

Mary hastened to open it—she had an instinctive distrust of everything that passed through Mewk's hands; she greatly feared that, much as his master trusted him, he was not true to him. It was from Mr. Redmain.

Dear Miss Marston,
  Come and see me as soon as you can. I have something to talk to you about. Send word by the bearer when I may look for you. I am not well.

Yours truly,

F.G. Redmain

Mary went to her desk and wrote a reply, saying she would be with him the next morning at eleven o'clock. "Put it into Mr. Redmain's own hand, if you can, Jemima," she said, giving Jemi-

248

ma the sealed envelope. "Between ourselves, I do not trust that man Mewks."

"Nobody does, Miss, except the master and Miss Yolland. I'll do what I can, Miss," she went on. "But he's so sharp! Mr. Mewks, I mean."

After she was gone, Mary wished she had given her a verbal message, that she mght have insisted on delivering in person.

Jemima managed to reach Mr. Redmain's room, but just as she knocked at the door, Mewks came behind her from somewhere, and snatching the letter out of her hand (for she carried it ready to justify her entrance to the first glance of her irritable master), pushed her rudely away and went in. But as he did so, he put the letter in his pocket.

"Is the messenger back yet?" asked Mr. Redmain.

"No, Sir, not yet. She'll be here in a minute, though. I saw her coming up the avenue."

"Go and bring her here."

"Yes, Sir."

Mewks went, and in two minutes returned with the letter.

"Confounded rascal! I told you to bring the messenger here."

"She ran the whole way, Sir, and not being very strong, was so tired that the moment she got in, she dropped in a dead faint. They ain't got her to yet."

His master gave him one look straight in the eye, then opened the letter and read it."Miss Marston will call here tomorrow morning," he said. "See that she is shown up here directly here, to my sitting room. I hope I am explicit."

When the man was gone, Mr. Redmain nodded his head and grinned. "There isn't a damn soul of them to be trusted!" he said to himself, and sat silently thoughtful.

In the evening he was worse. By midnight he was in agony, and Lady Margaret was up with him all night. In the morning came a lull, and Lady Margaret went to bed. His wife had not come near him. But Sepia might have been seen more than once or twice, hovering about his door. Both she and Mewks thought, after such a terrible night, he must have forgotten his appointment with Mary.

Finally he fell into a doze, but his sleep was far from profound. Often he woke and again dozed off.

The clock in the dressing room struck eleven. "Show Miss Marston up the minute she arrives," he said—his voice almost like that of a man in good health.

"Yes, Sir," replied the startled Mewks, and felt he must obey.

So Mary was shown to the chamber of the sick man, and she was surprised. Mewks had given her no warning he was in bed looking so ill. He made the slightest of signs to her to come nearer, and again nearer. She went close to the bed. Mewks sat down at the foot of it, out of sight. It was a great four-poster bed with curtains.

"I'm glad you've come," he said, with a feeble grin, all he had for a smile. "I want to have a talk with you. But not with that brute sitting there. I have been suffering horribly. Look at me, and tell me if you think I'm going to die—not that I think your opinion worth anything. That's not what I wanted you for, though. I want to talk to you now. You have a bit of heart, even for people who don't deserve it—at least I'm going to believe you have. If I am wrong, I almost think I would rather not know till I'm dead and gone! Good God! Where shall I be then?"

"Mewks!" he called suddenly, and his tone was loud and angry.

Mewks was by his bed instantly.

"Get out. If I find you in this room again without having been called, I will kill you—I *am* strong enough for that. They won't hang a dying man."

Mewks vanished.

"You need not mind, my girl," he went on to Mary. "Everybody knows I am ill—very ill. Sit down there on the foot of the bed, only take care you don't shake it, and let me talk to you. People are saying nowadays there ain't any hell—or perhaps none to speak of. Do you believe there is?"

"How can I imagine there is no hell when *He* said there is?"

"Who's *He?*"

"The Man who knows all about it."

"Oh, yes, I see. Hmm! But I don't for the life of me see what a fellow is to make of it all. Those parsons! They say there's no way out of it but theirs, and I never could see a handle anywhere to that door!"

"I don't see what the parsons have to do with it. If a thing is true, you have as much to do with it as any parson in England. If it is not true, neither you nor they have anything to do with it."

"But if it *is* true—that we are all sinners—I don't know what to do! And it's been ages since *that* Man was here, if ever He was at all, and there hasn't been a sign of Him since!"

Mary smiled. "There you may be quite wrong. I think I could find some who believe Him just as near now as ever He was, and believe that He hears them when they speak to Him, and heeds what they say."

"That's bosh. You would have me believe against the evidence of my senses!"

"You must have strange senses, Mr. Redmain, that give you evidence where they can't possibly know anything! If He spoke the truth when He was in the world, He is near us now."

"The nearer He is, the worse for me!" sighed Mr. Redmain.

"The nearer He is, the better for the worst man that ever breathed."

"That's queer doctrine! It does seem cowardly to go asking Him to save you, after you've been all your life doing what ought to damn you—if there *be* a hell, mind you. I can't see it anything better than sneaking, to do a world of mischief and then slink away into heaven, leaving all the poor wretches after themselves."

"I don't think Jesus Christ is worse pleased with you for feeling like that," said Mary.

"What? What's that you say? Jesus Christ worse pleased with me? That's a good one! As if He ever thought about a fellow like me!"

"If He did not, I suspect you would not be thinking about Him now. There's no sense in it, if He does not think about you. He said He didn't come to call the righteous, but sinners, to repentance."

"I wish I could repent, but I can't make myself sorry for what's gone and done with."

"But you *can* turn from your old ways, and ask Him to take you for a pupil. Are you willing to learn, if He be willing to teach you?"

"I don't know. It's all so dull and stupid! I never could bear going to church."

"It's not one bit like that! It's like going to your mother and saying you're going to try to be good, and not vex her any more."

"I see. It's all right, I suppose. But I've had as much of this kind of talk as I can stand, and you see I'm not used to such things," he said, trying to ease his pain by shifting in the bed. "Go away and send Mewks. Don't be far off though, and mind you don't go home without letting me know. There! Go along."

Mary went and sat on the lowest step of the stair just outside Mr. Redmain's room. In about an hour, Mewks came and said his master wanted her.

He was very ill, and could not talk, but he would not let her go. He made her sit where he could see her, and now and then he stretched out his hand to her. Even in his pain he showed a quieter spirit.

It was late afternoon when at length he sought further conversation. "I have been thinking, Mary," he said, "that if I do wake up in hell when I die, no matter how much I deserve it, nobody will be better for it, and I shall be all the worse."

He spoke with coolness, but it was by a powerful effort. He had waked from a frightful dream, drenched fom head to foot.

"Whereas," rejoined Mary, taking up his clue, "everybody will be the better if you keep out of it, everybody," she repeated, "God, and all His people."

"How do you make that out?" he asked. "God has more to do than look after such as me."

"Why should He not care for the souls He created? Isn't He making them into His own children to understand Him, and be happy with His happiness?"

"I can't say I care for His happiness. I want my own. And yet I don't know any that's worth the worry of it. No, I would rather be put out like a candle."

"That's because you have been a disobedient child, taking your own way, and turning God's good things to evil. You don't know what a splendid thing life is. You actually and truly don't know. You have never experienced in your being the very thing you were made for."

"My father had no business leaving me so much money. I didn't quite know what I was doing."

"You do now."

Then a pause.

"You think God hears prayer, do you?" he asked.

"I do."

"Then I wish you would ask Him to let me off—I mean, to let me die right out when I die. What's the good of making a body miserable?"

"It would be of no use to pray for that. He certainly will not throw away a thing He has made, and besides, I would leave you in God's hands rather than inside the gate of heaven."

"You wouldn't say so if you cared for me! Only why should you care for me? I wouldn't care about other people."

"You are not His disciple. I would give my life for you."

"Come now, I don't believe that!"

"I couldn't be a Christian if I wouldn't. How could I be His disciple, if I wouldn't do as He did?"

"And you are His disciple?"

"Yes, for many years. Besides, I cannot help thinking there is one for whom you would die."

"If you mean my wife, you never were more mistaken. I would do nothing of the sort."

"I did not mean your wife. I mean Jesus Christ."

"Oh, well, perhaps, if I knew Him as you do, and if I were quite sure He wanted it done for Him."

"He does want it done for Him, always and every day—not for His own sake, though it does make Him very glad. To give up your way for His is to die for Him. That's how my father used to teach me, and now I see it for myself to be true."

"It's all very grand, no doubt, but you can't positively believe all that!"

"So much so, that I live in the strength and hope it gives me, and order my ways according to it."

"Why didn't you teach my wife so?"

"I tried, but she didn't care to think about it. I could not get any further with her. She has had no trouble yet to make her listen."

"I should have thought marrying a fellow like me might have been trouble enough to make a saint of her."

A pause followed.

"I don't love God," he said.

"How could you," replied Mary, "when you don't know Him?"

"Then what's to be done? I can't very well show myself where I hate the Master of the house!"

"If you knew Jesus Christ, you would love Him."

"You wear me out! Will you ever come to the point? *Know Jesus Christ!* How am I to go back 2,000 years?"

"What He was then, He is now," answered Mary. "And you

may know Him even better than those who actually saw Him. It was not until they understood Him better by His being taken from them, that they wrote down His life."

"I suppose you mean I must read the New Testament?" said Mr. Redmain pettishly.

"Of course!" answered Mary, a little surprised, for she was unaware of how few have a notion what the New Testament is, or is meant for.

"Then why didn't you say so at first? I can't read. I should only make myself twice as ill. I won't try."

"I will read to you, if you will let me."

"How did you come to be such a theologian? A woman is not expected to know about that sort of thing."

"I am no theologian. I had a father who was child enough to understand what the Master said, and I was child enough to believe him, and so grew able to understand it for myself. The whole secret is to do what the Master tells you; then you will understand what He tells you."

"Well, you shall be my chaplain. Tomorrow, if I'm able to listen, you shall see what you can make of this old sinner."

Mary did not waste words—what would have been the use? Many good people are such sticklers for propriety! Mary took joyous refuge with the grand simple everyday humanity of the Man she found in the story—not the man who has been obscured by church worldliness for hundreds of years.

Later that day, when she had just rendered him one of the many attentions he required, and which there was no one but herself to render, for he would scarcely allow Mewks to enter the room, he said to her, "Thank you. You are very good to me and I shall remember you. I want to show that I have turned over a new leaf. Don't you think God will give me one more chance, now that I really mean it? I never did before."

"God can tell whether you mean it or not," she answered. "But you said you would remember me, Mr. Redmain. I hope you don't mean in your will."

"I certainly did," he answered, but in a tone of displeasure. "I must say, however, I should have preferred you had not *shown* quite such an anxiety about it. I shan't be in my coffin tomorrow, and I'm not in the way of forgetting things."

"Please, Mr. Redmain," returned Mary, "do nothing of the sort.

I have plenty of money, and don't care about more."

"Think how much good you might do with it!" said Mr. Redmain satirically. "It was come by honestly, so far as I know."

"Money can't do half the good people think. It is stubborn stuff to turn to any good. And in this case, it would be directly against good."

"Nobody has a right to refuse what comes honestly in his way. There's no end of good to be done with money—to judge, at least, by the harm I've done with mine," said Mr. Redmain, this time with seriousness.

"If money had been of importance, our Lord would have used it, and He never did."

"Oh, but He was an exception!"

"On the contrary, He is the only Man who is no exception. We are the exceptions. Don't you see? He is the very One we must all come to be like, or perish! No, Mr. Redmain, don't leave me any money, or I shall be altogether bewildered what to do with it."

"Well, well! I'll think about it," said Mr. Redmain, who had now got so far on the way of life, as to be capable of believing that when Mary said a thing she meant it. "I can't think where on earth you got such a sackful of extravagant notions!" he added.

"I told you before, Sir, I had a father who set me thinking!" answered Mary.

"I wish I had had a father like yours," he rejoined. "I fear mine wasn't just what he ought to have been, though he can't have been such a rascal as his son. He hadn't time for me—he had his money to make."

Mary was with Mr. Redmain the rest of the day, mostly by his bedside, sitting in silent watchfulness when he was unable to talk with her. Nobody entered the room except Mewks, who seemed to watch everything, and try to hear everything.

On into the gloom of the evening Mary sat. No one brought her anything to eat or drink, and Mr. Redmain was too much taken up with himself, soul and body, to think of her. She was now past hunger and growing faint when, through the settled darkness, words came to her from the bed.

"I should like to have you near me when I am dying, Mary."

The voice was softer than she had ever heard from Mr. Redmain, and its tone went to her heart.

"I will, if God please," she answered.

"There's no fear of God," returned Mr. Redmain. "It's the devil will try to keep you away. But never you heed what anyone may do or say to prevent you. Do your very best to be with me. By that time I may not be having my own way anymore. Don't place confidence in a single soul of this house. I don't say my wife would play me false so long as I am able to swear at her, but I wouldn't trust her one moment longer. You come and be with me, in spite of the whole posse of them."

"I will try, Mr. Redmain," she answered faintly. "But, indeed, you must let me go now. It is getting late, and I feel rather faint."

"They've given you nothing to eat!" cried Mr. Redmain, but in a tone that seemed rather of satisfaction than displeasure. "Ring— no, don't."

"Indeed, I would rather not have anything now till I get home," said Mary. "I don't feel inclined to eat where I am not welcome."

"Right! Right!" said Mr. Redmain. "Stick to that. Never eat where you are not welcome. Go home directly. You will come tomorrow?"

"I can't during the day," answered Mary.

"I would much rather have you in the evening. The first of the night is worst of all. It's then the devils are out. Look here," he added, after a short pause, "being in business, you've got a lawyer, I suppose?"

"Yes," she answered.

"Then go to him tonight, the first thing, and tell him to come here tomorrow, about noon. Tell him I am ill, and in bed, and particularly want to see him. He mustn't let anything they say keep him from me, not even if they tell him I am dead."

"I will," said Mary and, stroking the thin hand that lay outside the counterpane, she turned and left him.

"Don't tell anyone you are gone," he called after her, with a voice far from feeble. "I don't want any of them in here."

Mary let herself out into the night.

47.
A Friend in Need

The night was very dark. There was no moon showing, and the stars were hidden by thick clouds. Mary had to walk all the way to Testbridge. She felt weak, but the fresh air was reviving.

She had not gone far when the moon rose from behind the clouds, and the darkness diminished a little. The first part of her journey lay along a narrow lane, with a small ditch, a rising bank, and a hedge on each side. Up a lane was a farmyard, and a little way farther a cottage. Soon after passing the gate of the farmyard, she thought she heard steps behind her, soft and swift, and she naturally felt a little apprehensive. But her thoughts flew to the one hiding place for thoughts and hearts and lives, and she felt no terror. At the same time something moved her to quicken her pace. As she drew near the common, she heard the steps more plainly, and almost wished she had sought refuge in the cottage she had just passed.

The clouds were thinning about the moon, and a pale light came filtering through upon the common in front of her. She cast one look over her shoulder, saw something turn a corner behind her, and sped on again. She would have run, but there was no place of refuge to flee to. How lonely and shelterless the common looked! The swift steps came nearer and nearer.

Was that music she heard? She dared not stop to listen. But it poured forth on the dim air such a stream of pearly sounds as if all the necklaces of some heavenly choir of woman-angels were broken, and the beads came pelting down in a cataract of hurtless hail. They could be from no source other than the bow and violin of Joseph Jasper! Where could he be? She rejoiced to know he must be somewhere near.

She was now near the ruined hut on the common. In the meantime the moon had been growing out of the clouds, clearer and clearer. The hut came in sight, but the look of it was different. Leaning against the side of the door stood a figure she could not mistake for another than Joseph. Absorbed in his music, he did not see her.

"Joseph, Joseph!" she called out, and ran toward him.

He started, threw his bow from him, tucked his violin under his arm, and bounded to meet her. She tried to stop and at the same moment look behind her. The consequence was that she fell—but safely into the blacksmith's arms. That instant appeared a man running. He half-stopped, and turning from the path took to the common. Jasper handed his violin to Mary and darted after him. The chase did not last a minute—the man was nearly spent. Joseph seized him by one wrist, saw something glitter in the other hand, and turned sick as the fellow stabbed him. With indignation, as if it were a snake that had bit him, the blacksmith flung from him the hand he held. The man gave a cry, staggered, recovered himself, and ran. Joseph would have followed again, but he fell, and for a minute or two lost consciousness. When he came to, Mary was binding up his arm.

"What a fool I am!" he said, trying to get up, but yielding at once to Mary's prevention. "Ain't it ridic'lous now, Miss, that a man of my size, and ready to work a sledge with any smith in Yorkshire, should turn sick for a little bit of a job with a knife? But my father was just the same, and he was a stronger man than I'm like to be."

"It's no wonder," said Mary. "You have lost a good deal of blood." Her voice faltered. She had been greatly alarmed—and more so that she had not light enough to get the wound properly dressed. "I think I've stopped the bleeding."

"Then I'll be after the fellow."

"No, no! You must not. Lie still for a while. But tell me—I don't understand. That cottage used to be a mere hovel, without door or window! It can't be that you live in it?"

"Ay, that I do! And it's not a bad place either," answered

Joseph. "That's what I went to Yorkshire to get my money for. It's mine, bought and paid for."

"But what made you think of coming here?"

"Let's go into the smithy—*house* I won't presume to call it," said Joseph. "But it does have a lean-to for the smith, and I'll tell you everything about it. But really, Miss, you oughtn't to be out like this after dark. There's too many vagabonds about."

With a little help from Mary, Joseph got up and led the way to what was now a respectable little smithy, with forge and bellows, anvil and bucket. Opening a door where none had been, he brought a chair and made her sit down. Then closing the door, he lit a candle, and Mary looking about her could scarcely believe the change that had come upon the miserable place. Joseph sat down on his anvil, and begged to know where she had just been, and how far she had run from the rascal. When he learned something of the peculiar relations in which Mary stood to the family at Durnmelling, he began to think there might have been something more in the pursuit than a chance assault, and the greater were his regrets that he had not secured the fellow. Mary also told him of the man she had seen lurking in the shadows by the shop that first night following her return to Testbridge, and it now occurred to her that she had been watched for some time. She shuddered at the thought of it.

"Anyhow, Miss," he said, "you'll never come alone from there in the dark again."

"I know you would not have me stop doing what I can for the poor man up there, because of a little danger in the way."

"No, that I wouldn't, Miss. That would be as much as to say you would do the will of God when the devil would let you. What I mean is, since I am here, you must call me to help you home."

"I must not take you from your work, Joseph."

"Work's not everything, Miss," he answered, "and it's seldom so pressing—except I be shoeing a horse—that I can't leave it when I choose. Anytime you want to go anywhere, don't forget as you've got enemies about, and just send for me. You won't have long to wait till I come."

As soon as Joseph seemed all right, Mary, who had forgotten hunger and faintness, insisted on setting out at once. In her turn, she questioned Joseph and learned that as soon as he knew she was going to settle at Testbridge, he started off to find a place in the neighborhood humble enough to be within his reach, and near enough for the hope of seeing her sometimes, and having what help she might please to give him. The explanation afforded Mary more pleasure than she cared to show. She had a real friend near her, one ready to help her on her own ground, one who understood her because he understood the thing she loved! He told her he already had enough work to keep him going, that the horses he once shod were always brought to him again, and that he had plenty of time for both his violin and his books.

When they reached the edge of town, she sent him home, and went straight to Mr. Brett with Mr. Redmain's message. He promised to be at Durnmelling at the appointed time, and to let nothing prevent him from seeing his new client.

(Sometime later, it came out that a man speaking with a foreign accent went to one of the surgeons in Testbridge to have his shoulder set, which he said had been dislocated by a fall. When Joseph heard it, he smiled, and thought he knew what it meant.)

48.
Night Shadows

Mr. Redmain had given Mewks instructions he dared not disobey—his master had often ailed and had recovered again, and he must not venture too far! As soon as he had shown Mr. Brett into the room, he was dismissed, but not before learning he was a lawyer. He carried the news at once to Sepia, and it wrought no little anxiety in the house. A will was already in existence, and there was no ground for thinking a change in it boded anything good. Mr. Mortimer never shared his thoughts, anxieties, or hopes with any of his people, but the ladies met in deep consultation, though, of course, there was nothing to be done. Mr. Redmain's utter silence had long convinced Sepia he was but biding his time. She was certain he would not depart this life without leaving his opinion of her and the proofs of its justice behind him, carrying weight as the affidavit of a dying man. Sepia's one thought was whether something could be done to prevent the making of another will, or the leaving of any fresh document behind him. What he had already done she could not alter, but what he might yet do could perhaps be prevented. Once more she impressed upon Mewks the absolute necessity of learning as much as possible of what might pass between his master and the lawyer.

Mewks was driven to the end of his wits to find excuses for going into the room, and for delaying to go out again, while with all his ears he listened. But both client and lawyer were almost too careful for him, and he had learned positively nothing when the latter rose to depart. He instantly left the room, with the door a trifle ajar and, listening intently, he heard his master say that Mr. Brett must come again the next morning, that he felt better, and would think over the suggestions he had made, and that he must leave the memoranda within his reach on the table by his bedside. Before the lawyer reached his carriage, Mewks was on his way to Sepia with all this. She concluded there had been some difference of opinion between Mr. Redmain and his adviser, and hoped that nothing had been settled. Was there any way to prevent the lawyer from seeing him again? Could she by any means get a peep at the memoranda mentioned? But she dared not show herself in Mr. Redmain's room. Was Mewks to be trusted to the point of such danger as grew in her thought?

Toward evening Mr. Redmain had a dreadful attack. Any other man would have sent before now for what medical assistance the town could afford him, but he hated having a stranger about him, and as he knew how to treat himself, it was only when very ill that he would send for his own doctor in London. But Lady Margaret took it upon herself to send a telegram to summon the doctor.

An hour before her usual closing time, Mary set out for Durnmelling, and at the appointed spot on the way, found her squire of low degree waiting. She did not recognize him at first sight. Out of respect to one who would honor him with her company, Joseph had dressed in a new suit of gray, with a very wideawake hat. He took off his hat as she approached, if not with ease yet with the clumsy grace peculiar to him; for, unlike many whose manners are unobjectionable, he had in his something that might be called his own. But the best was that he knew nothing about his manners, beyond the desire to give honor where honor was due.

He walked with her to the door of the house, for they agreed that it would be wise to show that she was attended. They had also arranged at what hour, and at what spot close at hand, he was to be waiting to accompany her home. Even though he said nothing about it, Joseph was determined not to leave the place until she rejoined him.

It was nearly dark when he left her, and when he had wandered up and down the avenue awhile, it seemed dark enough to return to the house to wait.

Mary resolved not to give any notice of her arrival if she could get in without it. She found the hall door on the latch, entered quietly, and walked straight to Mr. Redmain's bedroom. When she opened the door, Mewks came hurriedly to meet her, as if he would have made her go out again. But she scarcely looked at him, and advanced to the bed. Mr. Redmain was just waking from the sleep into which he had fallen after a severe paroxysm.

"Ah, there you are!" he said, smiling her a feeble welcome. "I am glad you are come. I have been looking out for you. I am very ill. If it comes tonight, I think it will make an end of me."

She sat down by his bedside. He lay quite still for some time, breathing like one very weary. Then he seemed to grow easier and said with great gentleness, "Can't you talk to me?"

"Would you like me to read to you?" she asked.

"No," he answered, "I can't bear the light—it makes my head pound."

"Shall I talk about my father?" she asked.

"I don't believe in fathers," he replied. "They're always after some notion of their own. It's not their children they care about."

"That may be true of some fathers," answered Mary, "but it is not the least true of mine."

"Where is he? Why don't you bring him to see me, if he is such a good man? He might be able to do something for me."

"None but your Heavenly Father can do anything for you," said Mary. "My father has gone home to Him, but if he were here, he would only tell you about Him."

The annoyance was great when Mewks brought the news that Mary was in the master's bedroom again—and how she ever got into the house he was sure *he* didn't know.

"All the same thing over again," he told Sepia. "She's hard at tryin' to convert 'im! And where's the use, you know, Miss? If a man like my master's to be converted and get off, I don't for my part see where's the good o'keepin' up a devil."

"I am quite of your opinion, Mewks," said Sepia, but in her heart she was ill at ease.

All day long she had been haunted with an ever-returning temptation which, instead of dismissing it, she kept like a dog on a leash. Varying kinds of evil affect people differently. A man will feel grandly honest against the dishonesties of another trade than his, and be eager to justify those of his own. Here was Sepia—who did not care the dust of a butterfly's wing for causing any amount of family misery, who would without a pang have sacrificed the genuine reputation of an innocent man to save her own false one—shuddering at an idea as yet bodiless in her brain, an idea which she did not dismiss, and so grew able to endure!

It seemed to her that her very existence was at stake. If by his dying Mr. Redmain should drive her from under Hesper's roof, what was to become of her? She would be compelled to take a situation and teach music, which she hated, and French and German, which gave her no pleasure apart from certain of their literature, to insolent girls whom she would be constantly wishing to strangle, or stupid boys who would bore her to death. Her very soul sickened at the thought, as well it might, for to have to do such service with a heart such as hers must indeed be torment. All hope of marrying Godfrey Wardour would be gone, of course.

Since Mr. Redmain's last attack she had scarcely slept, and what Mewks now reported only fueled the fires of torment in her heart. For several weeks she had been awake half the night, and last night she had been wandering here and there about the house, frequently couched where she could hear every motion in Mr. Redmain's room. Haunted by fear, she in turn haunted her fear. She could not keep from staring down the throat of the pit. She was a slave of the morrow, the undefined awful morrow, ever about to bring forth no one knew what. Could she but forestall that morrow!

Sepia had grown very thin during these trying days. Her great eyes were larger yet and filled with a troubled anxiety, and a dull pallor possessed her cheeks. If one had met her as she roamed the house that night, he might well have taken her for some naughty ancestor whose troubled conscience, not yet able to shake off the madness of an evil deed, made her wander still about the place where she had committed it.

She had heard a good deal about euthanasia, and had taken her share in advocating it; and since she did not believe in God, it could not be counted against her. But the notion of euthanasia might well work for evil in a mind that had not any more thought for the ease than for the betterment of humanity, or indeed for anything but its own consciousness of pleasure or comfort. Opinions work differently on different constitutions. She was used to asking the question, "What's the good?" but always in respect of something she wanted out of her way.

"What's the good of an hour or two more if you're not enjoying it?" she said to herself again and again that Monday. "What's the good of living when life is pain?" But the question had no reference to her own life. She was judging for another.

All day she wandered about the house, with such thoughts as these in her heart, and in her pocket a bottle of concentrate which Mr. Redmain was taking much diluted for medicine. But she hoped she would not have to use it. If only Mr. Redmain would yield the conflict and depart this life without another interview with the lawyer!

Two drops from the said bottle, taken not by herself but by another, would save her from endless anxiety and grinding care, from weariness and disgust and, indeed, from want.

She had not learned to fear temptation. She feared poverty, dependence, humiliation and labor. The thought of the life that must follow, in the case of the dreaded disclosure, was unendurable.

All afternoon Sepia hovered about Mr. Redmain's door, down upon Mewks every time he appeared. Her head ached, she could hardly breathe, and she could not rest! Once when Mewks, coming from the room, told her his master was asleep, she crept in, and softly approaching the head of the bed, looked at him and stole out again.

"He seems dying, Mewks," she said.

"Oh, no, Miss! I've often seen him as bad. He's better."

"Who's that whispering?" murmured the patient angrily.

Mewks went in and answered, "Only me and Jemima, Sir."

"Where's Miss Marston?"

"She's not come yet, Sir."

"I want to sleep again. You must wake me the moment she comes."

"Yes, Sir," and Mewks returned to Sepia.

"His voice is different," she said.

"He always speaks like that, now, Miss. He'd always swear bad when he woke, but Miss Marston do seem t' 'ave got a good deal of that out of him. Anyhow, during these last two days, he's scarce swore enough to make it feel homelike."

"It's death has got it out of him," said Sepia. "I don't think he can last through the night. Fetch me at once if . . . and don't let that Marston into the room again, whatever you do."

She spoke with the utmost emphasis, then went slowly up the

stairs to her own room. Surely he would die tonight, and she would not be led into temptation! She would then have but to get a hold of the paper! What a hateful and unjust thing it was that her life should be in the power of that miserable creature hanging between life and death! That such as he should be able to determine her fate, and say whether she was to be comfortable or miserable all the rest of her life!

She stole again down the stairs. Her cousin was in her own room safe with a novel, and there was Mewks fast asleep in an easy chair in the study, with the doors of the dressing room and chamber ajar. She crept into the sickroom. There was the tumbler with the medicine, and her fingers were on the vial in her pocket. The dying man slept.

She drew near the table by the bed. He stirred as if about to wake. Her limbs and her brain seemed to rebel against her will. But what folly it was! The man was not for this world a day longer. What could it matter whether he left it a few hours earlier or later? The drops on his brow rose from the pit of his agony, and every breath was torture. It would be a mercy to help him across the verge—if to more life, he would owe her thanks; if to endless rest, he would never accuse her.

She took the vial from her pocket, but a hand was on the lock of the door! She turned and fled through the dressing room and study, waking Mewks as she passed. He hurried into the chamber and saw Mary enter.

When Sepia learned who it was that had scared her, she felt she could kill her with less compunction than Mr. Redmain. She hated her far worse.

"You *must* get that viper out of the house, Mewks," she said. "It is all your fault she got into the room."

"I'm sure I'm willing enough," he answered. "But what am I to do? She's so brazen you wouldn't believe, Miss! It wouldn't be becomin' to tell you what I think that woman fit to do."

"I don't doubt it," responded Sepia. "But surely," she went on, "the next time he has an attack, and he's certain to have one soon, you will be able to get her hustled out!"

"No, Miss, least of all just then. She'll make that a pretense for not going a yard from the bed, as if me that's been about him so many years didn't know what ought to be done with him in his pain better than the likes of her! Of all things I do loathe a row,

Miss, and the talk of it after. The only way is to be quiet and seem to trust her, and watch for the chance of her going out and then shut her out, and keep her out."

"I believe you are right," returned Sepia, almost with a hope that no such opportunity might arrive, but at the same time growing more determined to take advantage of it if it should.

So it came that Mary met with no interruption to her watching and ministering. Mewks kept coming and going, watching her and waiting his opportunity. Mr. Redmain scarcely heeded him, only once and again saying in sudden anger, "What can that idiot be about? He might know by this time I'm not likely to want *him* so long as you are in the room!"

Patiently Mary sat and waited, full of help that would have flowed in a torrent, but which she felt to be only like a stream that is lost on the face of the rock down which it flows.

All at once she thought of Joseph and looked at her watch. He had been waiting for her more than an hour, and would not, she knew, go away without her! She could not forsake the poor man her presence seemed to comfort, but he was sleeping now, and she could slip out, send Joseph away, and be back before the patient or anyone else should miss her.

She went softly from the room and glided down the stairs and out of the house, seeing no one, but not unseen. Hardly was she from the room, when the door of it was closed and locked behind her, and hardly from the house, when the house door also was closed and locked behind her. But she heard nothing and ran, without the least foreboding of mishap, to the corner where Joseph was to meet her. There he was, waiting as patiently as if the hour had not yet come.

"I can't leave him, Joseph," she said. "I cannot leave before morning. I will look in on you as I pass."

Without giving him time to answer, she bade him good-night and ran back to the house, hoping to get in as before without being seen. But to her dismay she found the door locked and concluded the hour had arrived when the house was shut up for the night. She rang the bell, but there was no answer, for there was Mewks himself standing close behind the door, grinning an evil grin. As she knocked and rang in vain, the fact flashed upon her that she was intentionally shut out, and she was overwhelmed with despair.

49.
Discovery

Mary turned and saw Joseph behind her, and hastily explained the situation.

"It makes me miserable," she went on, "to think of the poor man calling, and me nowhere to answer. The worst of it is that I seem the only person he has any faith in, and what I have been telling him about the Father whose love never changes will seem only the idler tale, when he finds I am gone and nowhere to be found—as they're sure to tell him. Rather than go, I will sit on the doorstep all night, just to be able to tell him in the morning that I never went home."

"Why have they done it, do you think?" asked Joseph.

"None of them like me but Jemima—not even Mrs. Redmain now, I am afraid. I shouldn't wonder if they fancy I have a design on his money—as if anybody fit to call herself a woman would condescend to such a thing! But when a woman would marry for money, she may well think as bad of another woman."

"This is serious," said Joseph. "To have a dying man believe you false to him would be dreadful! We must find some way in! Let us go to the kitchen door."

"If Jemima happens to be near, then perhaps!" rejoined Mary. "But if they want to keep me out, you may be sure Mewks has taken care of one door as well as another. He knows I'm not so easy to keep out."

"If you did get in," said Joseph, speaking in a whisper as they went, "would you feel quite safe after this?"

"I have no fear. They might lock me up somewhere if they

268

could, before I got to Mr. Redmain's room, but they wouldn't dare touch me."

"I shall not go out of hearing so long as you are in this house," said Joseph with decision. "Not until I have you out again will I leave the premises. If anything should make you feel uncomfortable, you cry out, and I'll make a noise that everybody at Thornwick over there shall hear."

As he spoke, they reached the kitchen door, the most likely of all to be still open, but it was locked and dark as if it had been bolted for years. One or two more entrances they tried, but with no better success.

"I believe I know a way," said Mary, "through the hall." She led him to a place used for a woodshed.

At the top of a great heap of sticks and faggots was an opening in the wall that had once been a window, or perhaps a door. "That is the wall of the tower," she said, "and there can be no difficulty in getting through there. Once in, it will be easy to reach the hall—that is, if the door of the tower is not locked."

In an instant Joseph was at the top of the heap, and through the opening, hanging on, and feeling with his feet. He found footing, and presently Mary was beside him. They descended softly and found the door into the hall wide open.

"Can you tell me what window that is?" whispered Joseph, "Just above the top of the wall, with the flickering fire—could it be Mr. Redmain's room?"

"I cannot tell—I don't think so. It has no window in this direction, so far as I know. But—"

Mary was silent as in her mind she followed the turns she had made once inside the house to get to Mr. Redmain's room, and then thought how the windows lay when she entered it. Her conclusion was that one side of the room must be against the hall, but she could remember no window in it.

"But," she added, "I never was in that room when I was here before, and both times I have been in it these past days, I have been too occupied to take notice of things about me. Two windows look down into a quiet little corner of the courtyard where there is an old pump covered with ivy. But I remember no other."

"Is there any way of getting to the top of that wall from this tower?" asked Joseph.

"Certainly. People often walk round the top of these walls, and I have been round them more than once. But I don't like the idea of looking in at a window."

"Nor do I, Miss. But you must remember, if it is his room, it will only be your eyes going where the whole of you has a right to be."

"You may be right," answered Mary, and led the way up the stair of the tower, and through a gap in the wall out upon the top of the great walls.

It was a sultry night. The moon was not up yet, and it was so dark that they had to feel their way along the wall, glad for the protection of a fence of thick ivy on the outer side. Looking down into the court on the one hand, and across the hall to the lawn on the other, they saw no living thing in the light from various windows, and there was little danger of them being discovered. Mary went first as better knowing the path, also as having the better right to look in. Through the window, as she went, she could see the flicker, but not the fire. All at once came a great blaze. It lasted but a moment—long enough, however to let them see plainly into a small closet, the door of which was partly open.

"Yes, that is the room," whispered Mary. "The window is in the closet, but I was never in it."

"If only the window be not bolted!" returned Joseph.

The same instant Mary heard the voice of Mr. Redmain call in a tone of annoyance, "Mary! Mary Marston! I want you. Who is that in the room?"

"Let me pass you," said Joseph, and, making her hold to the ivy, he got between Mary and the window. It was not bolted, and he easily lifted the sash. They entered.

Mary crept softly to the door of the closet, and peeped into the room. She saw Hesper, as she thought, standing by a chest of drawers, invisible from the bed. Her back was to Mary. A candle stood on the farther side of her, and she held in one hand the tumbler from which, repeatedly that evening, Mary had given the patient his medicine. Into this she was pouring, with an appearance of care, something from a small dark bottle.

With a sudden suspicion of foul play, Mary glided swiftly into the room. The woman started with a smothered shriek, turned white, and almost dropped the bottle. It was Sepia! Then, seeing it was Mary, she recovered herself. But such a look as she cast on Mary! Such fire of hate throbbed out of those great black eyes!

Mary thought for a moment Sepia would dart at her, But she
turned away and walked swiftly to the door. Joseph, peeping in
behind Mary, had caught a glimpse of the bottle and tumbler, and
also of Sepia's face. Seeing her now retiring with the bottle in her
hand, he sprang after her and, thanks to the fact that she had
locked the door, was in time to snatch it from her. She turned like
a wild beast, and a terrible oath came hissing as from a feline
throat. But when she saw the unknown figure was that of a powerful man, she turned again to the door and fled. Joseph shut and
locked it, and went back to the closet. Mary drew near the bed.

"Where have you been all this time?" asked the patient queru-
lously. "And who just left the room? What's all the hurry about?"

Anxious he should be neither frightened nor annoyed, Mary
replied to the first part of his question only.

"I had to go and tell a friend who was waiting for me that I
shouldn't be home tonight. But I am here now, and will not leave
you again."

"How did the door come to be locked? And who was that who
went out of the room?" While he was thus questioning, Joseph
crept softly out of the window, and all the rest of the night lay on
the top of the wall under it.

"It was Miss Yolland," answered Mary, "but she shall not enter
again while I am here."

"Don't let Mewks in either," he rejoined. "I heard the door
unlock and lock again. What did it mean?"

"Wait till tomorrow. Perhaps we shall find out then."

He was silent for a while. Then, "I must get out of this house,
Mary," he sighed at length.

"When the doctor comes, we shall see," said Mary.

"What! Is the doctor coming? I am glad of that. But your
lawyer, Mary, what's his name? He will be here first. We'll talk
the thing over with him, and take his advice. I feel better, and
shall go to sleep again."

All night long Mary sat by him and watched. Not a step, so far
as she knew, came near the door; certainly not a hand was laid
upon the lock. Mr. Redmain slept soundly, and in the morning
was beyond a doubt better.

But Mary could not think of leaving him until Mr. Brett came.
At Mr. Redmain's request she rang the bell. Mewks made his
appearance with the face of a ghost. His master told him to bring

his breakfast.

"And, Mewks," he added, in a tone of gentleness that terrified the man, so unaccustomed was he to such from the mouth of his master, "see there is enough for Miss Marston as well. She has had nothing all night. Wait!" he cried, as Mewks was going. "I won't have you touch it, either. I am fastidious this morning. Tell Jemima to come here to Miss Marston."

Mewks slunk away. Jemima came, and Mr. Redmain ordered her to get breakfast for himself and Mary. It was done speedily, and Mary remained in the sickroom until the lawyer arrived.

50.
Disappearance

I am afraid I must ask you to leave us now, Miss Marston," said Mr. Brett, seated with pen, ink, and paper, ready to receive his new client's instructions.

"No," said Mr. Redmain, "she must stay where she is. I fancy something happened last night which she has to tell us about."

"Oh? What was that?" asked Mr. Brett, facing round on her.

Mary began her story with the incident of her having been pursued by someone and rescued by the blacksmith, whom she told her listeners she had known in London. Then she told all the details of the night before.

"Just let me see the memoranda," said Mr. Brett to Mr. Redmain, rising and looking for the paper where he had left it the day before.

"It is not here!" said Mr. Brett.

"I thought as much!" said Mr. Redmain. "The fool! There was a thousand pounds for her! I didn't want to drive her to despair— a dying man must mind what he is about. Ring the bell and see what Mewks has to say about it."

Mewks came, in evident anxiety.

Mr. Brett took it for granted he had deliberately and intentionally shut Mary out, and Mewks did not attempt to deny it, protesting he believed she was boring his master. The grin on that master's face at hearing this was not very pleasant to behold. When examined as to the missing paper, he swore by all that was holy he knew nothing about it.

Mr. Brett next requested the presence of Miss Yolland. She was nowhere to be found. The place was searched throughout, but there was no trace of her.

When the doctor arrived, the bottle Joseph had taken from her was examined, and its contents discovered.

Lady Malice was grievously hurt at the examination she found had been going on. "Have I not nursed you like my own brother, Mr. Redmain?" she said.

"You may be glad you have escaped a coroner's inquest in your house, Lady Margaret!" said Mr. Brett.

Hesper sought Mary, and kissed her with some appearance of gratitude. She saw what a horrible suspicion, perhaps even accusation, Mary had saved her from. The behavior and disappearance of Sepia seemed to give her little trouble.

Mr. Brett got enough out of Mewks to show the necessity of his dismissal, and the doctor sent for a man from London to take his place.

Almost every evening, until he left Durnmelling, Mary went to see Mr. Redmain. She read to him and tried to teach him, as one might an unchildlike child. And something did seem to be getting into him, waking him up. The man had never before in the least submitted, but now it looked as if the watching Spirit of life were feeling through the dustheap of his evil judgments, low thoughts, and bad life, to find the thing that Spirit had made, lying buried somewhere in the frightened mass of confusion. Sometimes he would utter the strangest things, as if all the old evil modes of thinking and feeling were in full operation again; and sometimes for days Mary would not have an idea what was going on with him. Occasionally he would break into fierce and evil language when suffering, and then suddenly be silent. God and Satan were striving for the man, and victory would be to the one with whom the man should side.

For some time it remained doubtful whether this attack was the last one. The doctor, having no reason to think his death would be a great grief in the house, did not hesitate to express his doubt. And, indeed, it caused no gloom. For there was little love in the attentions the Mortimers paid him, and in what other hope could Hesper have married, than that one day she would be free with a freedom informed with power—the power of money!

Strange rumors came to them about Sepia. Godfrey Wardour

heard something of them, and laughed them to scorn. There was a conspiracy in that house to ruin the character of the loveliest woman in creation! But when week after week passed, and he heard nothing of or from her, he became anxious, and at last lowered his pride so far as to call on Mary, under the pretense of buying something in the shop.

His troubled look filled her with sympathy, but she could not help being glad and relieved that he had escaped the snares laid for him. He looked at her searchingly, and at last murmured a request that she would allow him to have a little conversation with her.

She led the way to her parlor, closed the door, and asked him to take a seat. But Godfrey was too proud, or too agitated to sit.

"You will be surprised to see me on such an errand, Miss Marston!" he said.

"I do not yet know your errand," rejoined Mary, "but I may not be as surprised as you think."

"Do not imagine," said Godfrey stiffly, "that I believe a word of the contemptible reports in circulation. I come only to ask you to tell me the real nature of the accusations brought against Miss Yolland. Your name is, of course, coupled with them."

"Mr. Wardour," said Mary, "if I thought you would believe what I told you, I would willingly do as you ask me. As it is, allow me to refer you to Mr. Brett, the lawyer."

The character of Mr. Brett was well known in Testbridge, and from him Godfrey Wardour learned the truth about Sepia. What became of her, none of her family ever learned.

No sooner was Hesper back in London than she wrote to Mary, inviting her to visit her. But Mary answered she could not leave home, and must content herself with the hope of seeing Mrs. Redmain when she came to Durnmelling.

But when Mary went to London on business, she always called on her, and generally saw Mr. Redmain. But they never had any more talk about the things Mary loved most. That he continued to think of those things, she had grounds of hoping, namely because of the kindness with which he invariably received her, and the altogether gentler manner he wore as often and as long as she saw him. Whether the change was caused by something better than physical decay, who knows save Him who can use even decay for redemption? He lived two years more, and then died rather suddenly.

After his death, and that of her father soon after, Hesper went again to live at Durnmelling, and behaved better to her mother than before. Mary sometimes saw her, and a flicker of genuine friendship began to appear on Hesper's part.

Mr. Turnbull was soon driving what he called a roaring trade. He bought and sold a great deal more than Mary, but she had business sufficient to employ her days and leave her nights free, and bring her and Letty enough to live on as comfortably as they desired, with a little left over, and something to lay by for the time of lengthening shadows.

Turnbull seemed to have taken a lesson from his late narrow escape, for he gave up the worst of his speculations and confined himself to genuine business principles. He grew quite rich and died happy, or so his friends said. Mrs. Turnbull left Testbridge and went to live in a small country town where she was unknown. There she was regarded as the widow of an officer in Her Majesty's service, and as there was no one within a couple of hundred miles to support an assertion to the contrary, she did not think it worth her while to explain the actual ticket of ill luck attached to her—widow of a linen draper.

George carried on the Turnbull business, and when Mary and he happened to pass in the street, they nodded to each other.

Letty was diligent in business, but it never got into her heart. She continued to be much liked, and in the shop was delightful. If she ever had another offer of marriage, the fact remained unknown. She lived to be a sweet gracious little old lady, and often forgot that she was a widow, but never that she was a wife. All the days of her appointed time she waited till her change should come and she should find her Tom on the other side, looking out for her, as he said he would.

Her mother-in-law never forgave her—for what, nobody knew. But after a year or so, Mrs. Wardour began to take a little notice of her again, though she never asked her to Thornwick until she found herself dying. Perhaps then she remembered a certain petition in the Lord's Prayer.

Once more Joseph Jasper became Mary's pupil. She was now no more content with her little cottage piano, but obtained an instrument of quite another capacity on which to accompany the violin of the blacksmith.

To him trade came in steadily, and before long he had to build a larger shoeing shed. From a wide neighborhood horses were brought to him to be shod, cartwheels to be tied, axles to be mended, plowshares to be sharpened, and all sorts of odd jobs to be done. He soon found it necessary to make arrangements with a carpenter and wheelwright to work on his premises. Before two years were over, he was what people call a flourishing man, and laying by a little money.

"But," he said to Mary, "I can't go on like this, you know, Miss. I don't want money. It must be meant to do something with, and I must find out what that something is."

51.
A New Treasure

One winter evening, as soon as his work was over for the day, Joseph locked the door of his smithy, washed himself well, put on clean clothes, took his violin, and set out for Testbridge—Mary was expecting him for tea. It was the afternoon of a holiday, and she had closed early.

Was there ever a happier man than Joseph that night, as he strode along the footpath—a day of invigorating and manly toil folded up in the sense of work accomplished, a clear sky overhead beginning to breed stars, the pale amber hope of tomorrow's sunrise low in the west, and a frosty air around him. His heart and brain were at rest with his Father in heaven, his precious violin under his arm, before him the welcoming parlor where two sweet women waited for him—one of them the brightest angel in or out of heaven—and the prospect of a long evening of music between them. He pressed his violin case to his heart, as if it were a living thing that could know he loved it.

Before he reached the town the stars were out, and the last of the sunset had faded away. Earth was gone, and heaven was all. When he reached the suburbs, the light of home was shining through curtains of all colors. "Every nest has its own birds," said Joseph, "and every heart its own joys!" Just then he was in no mood to think of the sorrows, for they are sickly things that die, while the joys are strong divine children that shall live forevermore. He was in the mood for music.

Beenie let him in and took him up to the parlor. Mary came

278

halfway to meet him and the pressure of heaven's atmosphere fell around him, calming and elevating. He stepped across the floor, laid down his violin, and sat where Mary told him—in her father's armchair by the fire. Gentle nothings with a down of rainbows were talked until tea was over, and then without a word they set to their music—Mary and Joseph, with their own hearts, and Letty for their audience.

They had not gone far on the way to fairyland when Beenie called Letty from the room, to speak to a friend and customer who had come from the country on a sudden necessity for something from the shop. Letty, finding herself not quite equal to the emergency, came to call Mary. The music was broken, and Joseph left alone with the dumb instruments.

But in his hands solitude and a violin were sure to marry in music. He began to play, forgot himself utterly, and when the customer had gone away satisfied, and the ladies returned to the parlor, there he stood with his back to them, his eyes closed, playing on, obviously unaware of their presence. They sat down, and listened in silence.

Mary had not listened long before she found herself strangely moved. Her heart seemed to swell up into the throat, and it was all she could do to keep from weeping. A little longer and the silent tears flowed freely. Letty too was overcome. She was not so open to the influences of music as Mary, but her eyes were full, and she sat thinking of her Tom, far in the regions that are nonetheless true that we cannot see them.

In a garment of mood whose color and texture was music, the soul of Joseph Jasper came knocking at the door of Mary Marston's. It was the very being of the man, praying for admittance. And there Mary saw Joseph stand, thinking himself alone with his violin. The instrument was his mediator with her, and was pleading for the admittance of its master. It prayed, it wept, it implored. It cried aloud that eternity was very long, and like a great palace without a quiet room.

All the time Joseph knew nothing of where his soul was—he thought Mary was in the shop, and beyond the hearing of his pleader. A prayer grew in his heart, and burst out through the open fountain of the violin—"I love thee! I love thee!" cried the violin. On and on it went, ever beginning ere it ended, as if it could never come to a close, and the two sat listening as if they would listen forever, listening as if when the sound ceased all would be at an end, and chaos would come again.

Then, gently, almost with a sigh, the music ended, and the musician suddenly knew his heart and its desire. Softly, almost too softly for even himself to hear, Joseph murmured, "I *do* love thee, Mary, I *do!*"

A sob, like a bird newborn, burst from Mary's bosom. It broke the enchantment in which Joseph was bound. He started—to conscious confusion only, neither knowing where he was and barely what he had just said. His limbs for the moment were hardly his own. How it happened he never could tell, but he brought down his violin with a crash against the piano, then somehow stumbled and all but fell. In the act of recovering himself, he heard the neck of his instrument part from the body with a tearing discordant cry, like the sound of the ruin of a living world. He stood up, holding in his hand his dead music, and regarding it with a smile sad as a winter sunset gleaming over a grave. But Mary darted to him, threw her arms around him, laid her head on his shoulder and burst into tears.

Tenderly he laid his broken violin aside and, like one receiving a gift straight from the hand of God, folded his arms around the woman. His violin was broken, but his being was made whole! His treasure taken, and a woman given him instead!

"It's just like Him," he murmured.

He was thinking of Him who, when a man was brought to be delivered from a poor palsy, forgave him his sins.

52.
The End of the
Beginning

Joseph Jasper and Mary Marston were married the next summer. Mary did not leave her shop nor Joseph his forge. Mary was proud of her husband, not merely because he was a musician, but because he was a blacksmith. For with the true taste of a right woman, she honored the manhood that could do hard work.

There came a lovely morning in summer, two years after their marriage—time long enough to have made common people as common to each other as the weed by the roadside. Mary and Joseph were up early, and taking their walk together before the day's work should begin. The foolish larks were up, of course, for they fancied—come what might of winter and rough weather—that the universe was founded in eternal joy. In all the trees, in all the flowers, in every grass blade and every weed, the sun was warming and coaxing and soothing life into higher life. And in those two on the path through the fields from Testbridge, the same sun, light from the Father of lights, was nourishing the highest life of all—that for which the Lord came, that He might root it in growing hearts.

The joy of the sunrise would linger about Mary all the day long in the gloomy shop, and for Joseph, he had but to lift his head to see the sun hastening on to the softer and yet more hopeful splendors of the evening. The wife, who had not to begin so early, was walking with her husband, as was her custom, even when the weather was not of the best to see him started on his day's work. It was with pride that she would watch the quick blows of his brawny arm, as he beat the cold iron on the anvil till it was all aglow like the sun that lighted the world, then stuck it into the middle of his coals, and blew softly with his bellows till the flame on the altar of his work-offering was awake and keen. The sun might shine or forbear, the wind might blow or be still, the path might be crisp with frost or soft with mire, but the lighting of her husband's forge-fire was a ceremony Mary never omitted to grace with her presence. It was to her the "Come let us worship and bow down" of the daily service of God-given labor. That done, she would kiss him, and leave—she had her own work to do. Filled with prayer, she would walk the well-known way to the shop, where all day long she would minister to the wants of her people.

That morning, as they went, they talked. "O Mary!" said Joseph, "Hear the larks! They are all saying, 'Jo-seph, Jo-seph! Hearkentome, Jo-seph! WhatwouldyouhavebeenbutforMary, Joseph?' That's what they keep on singing, singing in the ears of my heart, Mary!"

"You would have been a true man, Joseph, whatever the larks may say. And what should I have been, Joseph? An inarticulate harmony—sweetly mumbling, with never a thread of soaring song!"

A pause followed.

"I shall be rather shy of your father, Mary," said Joseph. "Perhaps he won't be content with me."

"Even if you weren't what you are, my father would love you because I love you. But I know my father, and I know you are just the man it must make him happy—even in heaven, to think of his Mary marrying."

"That was a curious speech of Letty's yesterday. You heard her say, did you not, that, if everybody was to be so very good in heaven, she was afraid it would be rather dull?"

"We mustn't make too much of what Letty says, either when she's merry or when she's miserable."

"I wasn't meaning to find any fault with her—I was only wishing to hear what you would say. Nobody can make a story without somebody wicked to set things wrong in it, and then all the work lies in setting them right again, and as soon as they are set right, then the story stops."

"There's nothing of that sort in music, Joseph."

"Yes, there is Mary. There's strife and difference and compensation and atonement and reconciliation."

"But there's nothing wicked."

"No, that there is not."

"Well," said Mary. "Perhaps it may only be because we know so little about good that it seems to us not enough. We know only the beginnings and the fightings, and so we write and talk only about them. For my part, I don't feel that strife of any sort is necessary to make me enjoy life; of all things, it is what makes me miserable. I grant you that effort and struggle add immeasurably to the enjoyment of life, but I look upon those as labor, not strife. There may be whole worlds for us to help bring to order and obedience. And I suspect there must be no end of work in which is strife enough—and that of a kind hard to bear. There must be millions of spirits in prison that want preaching to, and whoever goes among them will have that which is behind in the afflictions of Christ to fill up. Anyhow, there will be plenty to do, and that's the main thing. Seeing we are made in the image of God, and He is always working, we could not be happy without work."

"You don't want to die, do you, Mary?" asked Joseph.

"No, I want to live. And I've got such a blessed plenty of life, while waiting for more, that I am quite content to wait. But I do wonder that some people should cling as they do to what they call life. It is not that they are comfortable, for they are constantly complaining of their sufferings. They profess to believe the Gospel, and say that it is their only consolation. Yet they speak of death as the one paramount evil. In the utmost weariness, they yet seem incapable of understanding the apostle's desire to depart and be with Christ."

"Don't you think, though," said Joseph, "that some people have a trick of putting on their clothes wrong side out, and so making themselves appear less respectable than they are? There was Ann—she used to go on scolding people for not believing, all the time saying they could not until God made them believe. And yet Ann once went for months without more to eat than what just kept her body and soul together, that she might feed the children of a neighbor, of whom she knew next to nothing, when their father lay ill of a fever and could not provide for them. And she didn't look for any thanks, either, except it was from the same God she would have to be a tyrant from the beginning—one who would calmly

behold the unspeakable misery of creatures whom He had com-
pelled to exist, whom He would not permit to cease, and for whom
He would do a good deal, but not all that He could. Such people,
I think, are nearly as unfair to themselves as they are to God."

"You're right, Joseph," said Mary. "If we won't take the testimony of such against God, neither must we take it against themselves. Only why is it they are always so certain they are in the
right?"

"For the perfecting of the saints," suggested Joseph, with a
curious smile.

"Perhaps," answered Mary. "Anyhow, we may get that good
out of them, whether they be here for the purpose or not. I
remember Mr. Turnbull once accusing my father of irreverence
because he spoke about God in the shop. Father said, 'Our Lord
called the old temple His Father's house and a den of thieves in
the same breath.' Mr. Turnbull saw nothing but nonsense in the
answer. Then Father said, 'You will allow that God is everywhere?' 'Of course,' replied Mr. Turnbull. 'Except in this shop, I
suppose you mean?' said my father. 'No, I don't. That's just why I
wouldn't have you do it.' 'Then you wouldn't have me think about
Him either?' 'Well, there's a time for everything.' Then said my
father very solemnly, 'I came from God, and I'm going back to
God, and I won't have any gaps of death in the middle of my life.'
And that was nothing to Mr. Turnbull either."

Just as they came in sight of the smithy, they saw a lady and
gentleman on horseback flying across the common.

"There go Mrs. Redmain and Mr. Wardour!" said Joseph.
"They're to be married next month. Well, they're a handsome
couple, and the two properties together'll make a fine estate!"

"I hope she'll learn to like the books he does," said Mary. "I
never could get her to listen to anything for more than three
minutes."

Though Joseph generally dropped work long before Mary shut
the shop, she managed to meet him on his way home. That very
evening they were gradually nearing each other—the one from the
smithy, the other from the shop—with another pair between them,
however, going towards Testbridge—Godfrey Wardour and
Hesper Redmain.

"How strange," said Hesper, "that after all its chances and
breakings, old Thornwick should be joined up again at last!"

Partly by a death in the family, partly through the securities her husband had taken on the property, partly by the will of her father, the whole of Durnmelling now belonged to Hesper.

"It is strange," answered Godfrey with an involuntary sigh.

Hesper turned and looked at him. It was not merely sadness she saw on his face. There was something there almost like humility, though Hesper was not able to read it as such. He lifted his head and did not avoid her gaze.

"You are wondering, Hesper," he said, "that I do not respond with more pleasure. To tell you the truth, I have come through so much that I am almost afraid to expect any good. Please do not imagine, you beautiful creature, I am thinking of the property. In your presence that would be impossible. I shall one day come to care for it, but I keep looking for the next slip that is to come between my lip and this full cup of happiness. I have told you all, Hesper, and I thank you that you do not despise me. But it may well make me solemn and fearful to think that, after all the waves and billows that have gone over me, such a splendor should be mine! But do you really love me, Hesper—or am I walking in my sleep?"

"I am a poor creature beside you, Godfrey, but I am so glad to think whatever I know for love you have taught me. It is only I who have to be ashamed!"

"That is all your goodness!" interrupted Godfrey. "Yet at this moment I cannot quite be sorry for some things I ought to be sorry for—but for them I should not be at your side right now and happier than I dare allow myself to feel."

"There are things I am compelled to know of myself, Godfrey, which I shall never speak to you about, for even to think of them by your side would blast all my joy. How plainly Mary used to tell me what I was! I scorned her words! It seemed then too late to repent, and now I am repenting. One thing I am sure of—if I had known you, not all the terrors of my father would have made me marry Mr. Redmain."

Was this all the feeling she had for her father and dead husband? Although Godfrey could hardly feel regret she had not loved him, her words made him shiver. In the perfected grandeur of her external womanhood, she seemed to him the very ideal of his imagination, and he felt at moments the proudest man in the world. But at night he would lie in torture, brooding over the horror a woman such as she must have encountered. There had been a time in Godfrey's own life when, had she stood before him in all her splendor, he would have turned from her with sad disgust because of her history. Was he less pure now?

They had talked of Mary more than once, and Godfrey came to see that he had been unjust to her. He had not come to know the depth and extent of his injustices—that would imply a full understanding of Mary herself, which was yet far beyond him. A thousand things had to grow, to shift and shake themselves together in Godfrey's mind before he could begin to understand one who cared for the highest.

Godfrey and Hesper made a glorious pair to look at—but would theirs be a happy union? If they had both been born again before they began, so to start fresh, then like two children hand-in-hand they might have run through the gates into the city. But what is love and loss and even defilement, what are pains and hopes and disappointments, what sorrow and death and all the ills that our flesh is heir to, but means to this very end, to this waking of the soul to seek the home of our being—the life eternal?

Turning a clump of bushes on the common, they met Mary who stepped from the path. Mr. Wardour took off his hat. Then Mary knew that his wrath was past, and she was glad.

"Well, Mary," said Hesper, stopping and holding out her hand, and speaking in a tone from which both haughtiness and condescension had vanished, "where are you going?"

"To meet my husband," answered Mary. "I see him coming." With a deep loving look at Hesper, and a bow and a smile to Godfrey, she left them and hastened on.

Behind Godfrey Wardour and Hesper Redmain walked Joseph Jasper and Mary Marston, a procession of love toward a far-off eternal goal. But which of them was to be first in the kingdom of heaven is not to be told. They had yet a long way to walk, and many are first that shall be last, and last that shall be first.

MORE FICTION FROM VICTOR BOOKS

THE PASTORS' BARRACKS *by Robert L. Wise*

From 1933 to 1945 nearly 200,000 people were imprisoned in Dachau Concentration Camp. Pastors and other church leaders who spoke out against Hitler were among those sent there. Christian Reger was one such German pastor. This story is based on his experiences in the Nazi death camp. (6-2157)

THE WHEATHEART CHRONICLES

RITES OF AUTUMN *by Cliff Schimmels*
Fall means football in Wheatheart and Abe Ericson wants his son, Jimmy Charles, to play. Sense the struggle within Jimmy Charles as he meets his father's expectations on the outside and tries to meet his own on the inside. What will happen to Abe's priorities when he's faced with a loss that can never be replaced? (6-2334)

WINTER HUNGER *by Cliff Schimmels*
In 1957 Vince Benalli was a first year teacher and coach at the high school in Wheatheart. Now it's 1980 and Vince, the principal of Wheatheart High, is faced with the dreams he never fulfilled. What will he discover as he reaches out for ways of life he has never tried before? (6-2333)

RIVALS OF SPRING *by Cliff Schimmels*
Delbert Goforth and Chuck Murphy are friends, bound together by a common loneliness. Through that bond, they discover what true friendship really means. This is the story of their maturing, as Delbert and Chuck learn what it means to grow up, throw off the frivolity of youth, and carry on their shoulders the dreams of the community of Wheatheart. (6-2335)

SUMMER WINDS *by Cliff Schimmels*
When K.D. Garrett comes to Wheatheart as an interim pastor, he is already a confident young preacher. He's sure there isn't much left for him to learn. But that's before he meets the Wheatheart people and discovers the heartwarming lessons of life in a rural community. Follow K.D. Garrett in his summer at Wheatheart—and learn with him what it means to be God's servant. (6-2262)

VICTOR BOOKS BY GEORGE MACDONALD

A Quiet Neighborhood

The Seaboard Parish

The Vicar's Daughter

The Last Castle

The Shopkeeper's Daughter

The Prodigal Apprentice